Killer With A Heart

Thanks to Athina Paris, Editor for your dedication and tireless effort.

Published By

RockHill Publishing LLC
PO Box 62241
Virginia Beach, VA 23466-2241
www.rockhillpublishing.com

Killer With A Heart

J L Hill

Dedication

To my beautiful wife, Yvonne, who has been there for me during the good times, the bad, and especially during the crazy times. I knew the day I met you, that you were someone special. Someone I would always love and never be able to forget. You are my light through dark twisted nights, keeping my demons at bay.

CONTENTS

CHAPTER 1
A Hundred Friends

The sun is rising in the cloudless pale blue sky when I stop for a moment in front of my house and think about climbing through the bathroom window over the back porch; but I really don't want Mom seeing me like this, and I definitely do not want to explain how I escaped a mob hit squad, or why. Instead, I decide to keep going and hang out at the Raven until I have a good story to tell her. Besides, the way my sides throb I don't think I can climb onto the back porch. I probe my left side gently; it hurts like hell but I don't think the ribs are broken. I run my tongue around my teeth and find the hole at the back on the right where my tooth used to be. Those guys tossed me a pretty good beat-down.

The Raven Social Club is locked up tight. Even the back door on the first-floor hallway of the three-family house is padlocked. I slide down the cement wall of the Old Lady's house on the corner across the street from the Raven. It's our usual hangout opposite the deli, when we are not in The Raven shooting pool and drinking.

Sitting on the sidewalk with my back against the wall feels good. I slowly begin picking morsels from the French roll I took from the bread bag as I walked past the deli. I hadn't realized until I pop that first piece of bread into my mouth how hungry I am; haven't eaten since yesterday afternoon. I get like this in the summer, especially when it's hot. And even though it is only the first week of June, the temperature is already in the nineties and that is unusually hot for New York. I close my eyes and let the sunshine melt the pain away and clear my head of any thoughts. There is nothing but the red glow of the inside of my eyelids.

Blackness interrupts the crimson haze in my head momentarily. My eyes dart open, I instinctively spring to my feet, and reach around my back for the 007 switchblade.

"You're one jumpy jungle bunny," says Nicky Rocci. "But I guess you would be from the looks of you. Black eye, swollen jaw, some nasty black and blues... Well, blues on your sides," he continues while holding my leather jacket open.

"You look like you had a rough night too, you whop cocksucker," I reply, sliding back down to the sidewalk. "Who worked over your face, Nails?" I call him Nails partly because his family is in the construction business and he likes to tell everyone that he can chew nails and spit bullets. He is sporting a black eye, busted lip, and his nose looks like it was moved around his face a bit.

"My Dad wasn't too happy about the job we pulled on the Deli Man. Let me get a piece of that bread."

"Get your own," I say. "And while you're over there, grab a couple of quarts. I know the Deli Man won't mind."

Nicky Nails disappears into the alley that leads to the back of the deli and comes out with two quarts of Budweiser then reaches into the big brown bread bag and pulls out an Italian loaf. As he crosses the street, I notice a slight limp, probably got stomped on too.

"So, why did you tell him about the Deli Man? I thought we all agreed to keep our mouths shut. No matter what!" I ask as I shade my eyes and gaze up at him.

"I didn't tell him anything. It seems the Deli Man is more connected than we thought."

"Not, we thought," I correct, "You thought. You said he was a small-time numbers guy. Easy pickings."

"Well, MoJo," Nicky sits down beside me.

He calls me MoJo, which is short for Morris Johnson, and after the lyrics in the Doors song, 'L. A. Woman'. I love that song, play it all the time.

"Not only is he more mobbed up than I thought; he was paying my family to keep his bank here. Naturally, when we hit him, he complained to my father about not protecting his money. My dad asked me what I knew."

"And you bitched up!"

"Does it look like I talked?"

I take a long deep swig of cold beer.

Nicky continues, "We saw Deli Man's guys grab you. I guess you kept quiet too."

"Of course I did; we wouldn't be here if I didn't. He was going to keep on beating me until I gave him the answer he wanted. That's when he found out about Elizabeth and me and went fucking ape shit."

Nicky shakes his head, "I told you fucking his daughter was a bad, bad idea. She talked, didn't she?"

"No." I pause for a moment, as my mind jumps back to Deli Man's kitchen, "Elizabeth was in the hall crying. Deli Man looked at her, and said something in Italian, which I didn't understand. Her mother dragged her off down the hall. I thought he told her to get Elizabeth out of there. But a few minutes later her mother yelled 'mignotta', which I did understand, 'whore'. She must have given her the old Virgin Finger Test. Deli Man forgot all about his money and told his men to kill me."

"Yeah, well, I told you, if you fucked his daughter, he would kill you."

"But at least he stopped beating on me."

"Wait a second," Nicky has a surprised look on his face. "If he told his guys to kill you, how are you here?"

I am about to answer when a black Ford Fury jumps the curb and screeched to a stop, its bumper inches from our faces. Detects. We know who they are, Fitzpatrick and Mancotti, or Batman and Robin as we call them. They grab us by the shirt, well, me by my leather jacket since I'm not wearing a shirt and shove us into the back of the car. No one says a word, not the two cops, not Nicky, and definitely not me. They drive a couple of blocks up to East Tremont and then down a little side street that dead-ends at the train tracks. It's a secluded place where junkies come to shoot up or do other deeds that one won't do in public. They get out of the car and walk back up the street a bit, leaving Nicky and I locked in the back.

Nicky and I look at each other; knowing we are both thinking the same thing. Either this is an open mike trick, or we are being setup for a hit. I am leaning more towards the former. It's an old cop ploy. Leave a couple of suspects in a room with a hidden microphone or tape recorder and wait for them to turn on each other. It works just as well in the back of a police car, but Nicky and I are not about to fall for that. We sit in absolute silence. And if they are going to turn us over to the mob it will be just as easy to do, as it is really early in the morning and no one saw us get picked up. But then they would have been here waiting for us already. In my mind, there is no doubt this is the open mike bullshit, so all we have to do is sit here and be quiet. They will eventually get bored and cut us loose.

Fifteen- or twenty-minutes pass and the two detectives get back in the car. We smile at them. We are not some scared little schoolboys afraid they are going to tell our mommies on us.

Nicky says, "If you are finished playing games, you can drop us off back on the corner, our beers are going flat."

"Shut the fuck up!" yells Mancotti. "You boys will be lucky if you see the light of day again."

The car rips up the street in reverse and spins around at the intersection. They flip on the siren and speed down East Tremont Avenue again, catching the attention of the few people waiting at the bus stop. Thankfully, there are some people on their way to work this early Saturday morning already. We race through the street until we get to the police station, where we are summarily marched upstairs, not in handcuffs mind you, and into individual cells. They push us in and slam the doors shut behind us. It's dark and stinks of urine and shit but there is also a long and narrow metal bench opposite the door. I sit on it then lie on my back; I am finally going to get some sleep.

Almost complete darkness greets me when I open my eyes again and I lie there staring at the ceiling. 'This has been one long fucked up day,' I think. Hell, it has been one long fucked up month, as it has been just about that long since Nicky told us of his plan for robbing the Deli Man. May, second, to be exact.

It is the first really nice day in spring; so naturally, we all ditched school and are going to hang out at my house.

Maria, Bonnie, and Betty walk in and come straight up to my room.

"Your mom's gone to work, right?" asks Maria.

I grab her by the waist and pull her down on me, "Of course. And she thinks I left for school already." I kiss her as her long black hair drapes over my face. "Get in," I command.

"Oh no," objects Bonnie, "you get up and come downstairs. We want to have some fun. And we have to call everybody's school and report them absent for the day." She grabs Maria's arm and hauls her from the bed.

Maria pulls away and gives me another kiss, her blue eyes darting wildly over my body.

"No, no, no, there will be none of that." Bonnie drags her from my bedroom.

I come down to the living room about five minutes later, as Maria is ending her call with Fr. Robinson, my Dean of Discipline, "OK Father, you have a good day. Yes, I will. I have to go now or I'll be late for work. Good Bye." She smiles at me standing in nothing but cut off shorts. "Nice legs."

"Your man is a track star, baby." I strike a running pose.

"Fr. Robinson sounded a bit annoyed. I don't think he believes you're sick," she says, scolding me. "How many days have you missed young man?"

"I don't miss any of them," I laugh. "Give me the phone, and I'll call Aquinas for you."

"Betty will call Aquinas for her and St. Catharine's for me, thank you very much. You can go finish getting dressed. You need to cover up that stick figure you call a body."

"I'm agile, lean, and a real power pumping sex machine. Go ahead, you can tell them, baby."

"I don't know anything about that," Maria wraps her arms around my waist and I try to slide one knee between hers.

"Quiet fools," Betty orders, "it's ringing!"

"Ah, yes, is this Sister Thomas... This is Maria Marino's mother. She is having a bad day this morning. No, it's nothing serious, just the start of her time."

"That's a croc," I blurt out loudly then dash to the kitchen and grab the other phone. "That's what's wrong with you women today. You cry about God's natural ways, with your pills and feminist products..."

"Shut the hell up, you, old fool," Betty yells into the phone. "I'm so sorry Sister, that's her senile drunkard idiot grandfather on the other phone."

The girls get the message and rush to the kitchen. I'm not only fighting off laughter, but also Bonnie, and Maria, with the phone held above my head.

"Who's gonna make me breakfast? Forget that, get my vino!" I yell just before Bonnie slaps down the receiver and cuts off the line.

"So sorry Sister, but I got to go." Betty hangs up abruptly and joins the other two girls in the kitchen punching and slapping me. "You are such an idiot! Maria, take him upstairs and keep him out of trouble. Bonnie, you go with them and keep her out of trouble. I'll get you when it's your turn to call."

Dino, the Greek, Sweet Jesus–pronounced just as when you're excited–and Frank, walk in to see the girls piled on top of Morris. From the way the girls cover him they think he's naked.

"All right, it's going to be one of those parties," Sweet Jesus shouts as he quickly pulls his shirt above his head.

Betty turns to see Jesus with his shirt half off, "Great, the other morons are here. Can we just get through making the calls first?"

Nicky busts into the kitchen, "good youse guys are here. I got a plan that you got to hear, let's go downstairs. Sorry girls, it's boys only."

"Good, get out of here," Betty tells him, "We also got real business here."

Nicky likes to talk business in my basement because of the foot-thick stone walls and shuttered windows. No way for the cops to ever eavesdrop on us.

I think he's overly paranoid, as he says the cops are always listening.

"OK guys. I was hanging out on the corner the other day and for two hours I saw a couple of guys go into the deli and leave after a minute or two. I recognized two of them; numbers guys for the Bananas." The Bananas is what Nicky calls the Banoas, a mob family, whose territory is north of Tremont Avenue. "Deli Man is running a drop in my neighborhood! Can you believe that?" He's watching us across the pool table, expecting us to be as outraged as he is. We aren't. After a couple of seconds, he continues, "I watched the comings and goings for the next couple of days..."

"You haven't been to school at all this week?" I ask and immediately know that it was a stupid question.

"Yeah, it's been really nice this week. Besides, what do I need school for? I'm going to work at my father's construction business."

"It might be good if you know how to add and subtract, or the difference between area and perimeter, or anything useful for the business." I point out.

"That's for youse guys. My job will be making sure I get my cut, or I bust somebody's head. Now, let's get back to the business at hand. Deli Man leaves around three, when Elizabeth gets there. The bagmen make their drops and then Deli Man returns about five. For about a half-hour or so Elizabeth is there all by herself with the money. Guys, we are going to rob the deli before the Deli Man gets back."

Sweet Jesus is the first to object, "You want us to rob Elizabeth? You do realize that she knows all of us."

"I'm not talking about pulling a gun on her or anything like that. That's for amateurs, I'm a professional. First of all, the five bagmen go straight to the back stockroom, so she probably doesn't even know what they are doing there. We are going to sneak in, find the hiding place, and take it without her even knowing we are there."

"And how do you plan to do that?" asks Frank, who is six- one and redheaded, not quite the sneaky type.

"Well, I'm guessing Deli Man leaves his daughter there because he figures the cops won't bust it when she's there. His first mistake, Elizabeth has the hots for our friend here, MoJo. And she has it bad."

"Jungle fever is easy to catch, and incurable," I say. "That's why I excluded the girls, we need you to work your black magic on that dizzy little blonde and keep her busy while Sweet Jesus steals the cash."

"That's HEY-ZEUS, you blasphemous bastard. And what are you gonna be doing while me and Morris are taking chances stealing mob money?"

Nicky lays out the rest of the plan. "I'll be covering you, so you can get into the back room without being seen.

Dino and Frank will be lookouts and warn us if Deli Man comes back."

I think about a saying we have, 'You have a hundred friends who can get you into prison, but not one who has a plan to get you out.' Then, there is Nicky; his plans could get you killed, and I'll bet this is one of those plans.

As Nicky sees it, Elizabeth is the insurance that no one will suspect us of the robbery. She will be able to swear that I was nowhere near the back room, and Nicky, while boosting beers, will also be cleared. It is risky, but it seems like an easy in and out job. Just like when we go shoplifting, all the store detects follow Betty and me around the aisles, while the others clean up. And if we really want a big score, we go to the jewelry counter. While Betty tries on cheap items, Maria and Bonnie try on expensive things and pocket them. The more upscale the stores, the easier it is to work them. While Betty is black, well, more like a cinnamon chocolate, with beautiful long lustrous obsidian hair down her back from her Indian heritage, she is still black.

We agree that it is a good plan, but also point out that stealing from the mob is asking for a bullet in the head. According to Nicky, Deli Man is small potatoes, probably not even connected to the Banana family. Nicky is also almost sure it's a rogue operation; that they are possibly skimming money from the Bananas. If that's the case, the job is most likely good for a couple of thousand and they won't be able to tell anyone about the loss. We plan to make a go of it next Friday, because that is the heaviest gambling day.

We join the girls in the living room again. Frank had brought along five quarts of Budweiser, so now we crack the caps.

I take mine to the window and pour a bit out, "To the brothers down below."

"Why do you always do that?" asks Frank.

"Respect," I walk back to the couch and Sweet Jesus pulls out a baggie full of weed. I go to work rolling joints and tossing them to the guys. In about two minutes, I rolled five fatties, and Maria, who has been sitting on my right leg the whole time, sticks the last one in my mouth and lights it up. I take a big deep toke and hold it in.

"Let it out," Maria tells me. When I finally exhale a thick cloud of smoke straight up, she says, "Give me a shotgun." I oblige, flipping the joint backwards in my mouth so only the tip is visible. I inhale deeply through my nose and blow a steady long stream of thick white smoke up her nose. As she starts to exhale, I pinch her nose shut and cup her mouth. After a couple more seconds, she shakes her head and I release her.

She lets out a huge cloud and a little cough. "Stupid, you're choking me."

"Now that's how you smoke reefer... like a man." I take a swig and another toke, but before I can exhale, she locks her lips to mine. After a few seconds, I manage to break away coughing out smoke. We break out in laughter, hugging and kissing, our eyes red and tearing. It's such a rush.

'Brown Sugar' blares out of the speakers, as one of the girls puts on my new Sticky Fingers album. The party is just getting under way.

Nicky walks around the room holding up a little red capsule for either an open mouth or a beer bottle. I offer the beer bottle and he drops in the barbiturate. Maria and I sip on the downer-laced beer as we stretch out on the couch, entwined in each other's arms and legs. By the time 'Can't You Hear Me Knocking' pumps through the air, time is slowing down, and I can feel Maria's heartbeat through her breast as I fondle her nipple under the blouse.

Her breath is wet and hot in my ear, "People can see us."

My body completely covers her petite five-two frame, "Nobody can see a thing." I say as I turn my head to scan the room. Only Betty and Dino are left, but they are too involved with each other on the other sofa to know what else is going on. "We're alone," I whisper softly as I unbutton the blouse. I feel her hand slip into my pants and wrap around my dick. Either the combination of marijuana, barbies, and beer, or her wanton emotions have completely erased any concerns. I study her plump white breasts and flush pink nipples rising to my mouth and dropping away from my flickering tongue as her hand works my hard-on in time to the music. I run a hand over her pussy, petting her kitty, as she likes to say, my fingers gently spreading her lips and my index finger probing her vagina. I hear her moan with resistance then sigh in acceptance as I slide just the tip of my finger into her.

"It's OK," I comfort her, running my free hand through her silky black hair. "I'm not going to finger you all the way." I slide my finger, wet from her juices, up her slit until I reach her tiny clit and work it around in little circles as she grinds and grips my dick tighter. I can feel how wet I am as her hand glides up and down; not as hard as I could be, thanks to the drugs, but Maria doesn't mind, or notices, her body heating up as she writhes rhythmically to my stroking.

We are oblivious to everything, no other sounds other than our moaning and groaning intrude, and the only sight is the shimmer of our sweating half-nude bodies. Suddenly, her grip seizes up like a chokehold on my dick. Her other fingers dig into my back and rip down, setting me ablaze. Her legs clamp on my hand and I fight to slide my fingers down and into her tightening hole. I force my index and middle fingers in seeking her heat and hear her gasp and squeal as she continues to come. I'm so intent on pumping her throbbing pussy I don't realize I am cumming in her hand too. Finally, our bodies come to a halt, our hands wet and sticky inside each other's pants.

Maria let's out an, "Ooh yuck."

"Yeah, I know what you mean," I tell her, pull my hand out of her pants, and slide it under her buttocks. Then in a single movement, I roll over, sit up, and pick her up into my arms. "I'll take you upstairs to the bathroom. Hang on."

Maria pulls her hand from my pants and makes a motion towards my face.

"Don't you dare!"

"What. What's the matter?" She's laughing and rocking in my arms.

"Do it and I'll drop you on your head," I warn. We are so stoned she doesn't realize I almost dropped her while standing up.

I steady myself and carry her up to the bathroom. Our clothes loosely draped over our bodies, we peel them off and drop them to the floor, stand for a few seconds admiring each other's body, then hug for even longer. This is the first time we have been completely naked, and even in my hazy state I am taken with her beauty. Her black wavy hair frames her tanned face and those blue eyes sparkle like crystal opal. Two marble white breasts dotted with dirty pink nipples are just big enough to fill my hands and perfectly proportion her body. Bikini tan lines accentuate them as well as her black-haired kitten reaching down towards her shapely legs. At just eighteen, she already possesses a well-developed woman's body. I reach over and turn on the shower, we climb in and I pull her close.

"Don't you even think of it," Maria sternly warns me, as my dick is hard again.

"What?"

"Let's just get washed up," she says with a little trepidation.

"Don't worry, I'll never hurt you. You know that." I begin to gently rub the warm water on her belly, and she does the same to me. Within seconds, the warmth of the water combined with the effect of the downers gets us woozy. I wash her off quickly then myself then wrap a towel around her and another about my waist.

We cross the hall to my bedroom. Maria reaches for the doorknob but I take her hand, "Let's check first." I knock and Frank answers. We wait while Frank and Bonnie get dressed then open the door.

Bonnie gives Maria a look and she shakes her head "No."

Frank also gives me an enquiring gaze and I confirm Maria's denial.

As the door closes on us, she spreads the towel open behind her and begins shaking and gyrating to the music in her head.

"You are really pushing your luck, young Lady," I tell her, feeling myself get turned on again.

She takes one arm and pulls the towel across her body to her shoulder. "What's the matter? Don't like what you see?" She flashes me a quick glimpse then covers up again.

"You little cock teaser," I call her with mock anger.

She drops onto my bed, towel wide open, and her legs spread apart, showing her pink pussy, "don't be mad, baby. You want this, don't you? You want it bad." She snaps her legs shut as I take a step toward her. "No. No. No."

I can't tell if she is just playing or if she is really that stoned.

She springs up as I reach the bed and sticks her face against my throbbing dick beneath the towel wrapped around my waist. "Ooh that feels so good." Maria looks up at me, pulls the towel down, and rolls her face in my crotch. Without another word, she opens her mouth and placing both hands on my ass, pulls my dick all the way in. Slowly, she draws my dick in and out, sucking as hard as she can. With each motion, my dick gets harder and when it's rock hard I run my hands down her back. She stops moving but continues sucking harder still and I feel as if I am sobering up; Jesus, she is sucking the high right out of me. She goes on and on for what seems like an hour then unexpectedly pulls back. My dick is big, red, and pulsing painfully. "That's enough," she announces and slips past me with cat-like agility.

I stand there, unable to move, struggling to even bring one coherent thought to mind. I finally turn around, as I hear her shutting my dresser's drawer. She's standing in my Sly Stone tee shirt, which on her drops all the way down to her thighs like a mini dress. She bounces back onto the bed and pulls me down to sit beside her.

Maria falls over on her side and curls up into a ball, "stay with me. Forever."

I brush the hair away from her face tenderly. Her eyes closed already; she is long gone. I pull the covers from behind her and fold them over her. This has been a fantastic day and it's only 11:30. I look down at my lap, "God damn it, she left me with a raging hard-on."

We spend the weekend as usual, hanging out at the Raven drinking beer, doing shots of vodka, and shooting pool during the day, then, at the stash house at night getting high. We could do jellybeans in the Raven without a hassle, but they frown on us lighting up in the place.

Thankfully, we don't need to stand on the corner smoking joints like the other yokels in the neighborhood, not when we have a house of our own. We don't actually own the stash house, it belonged to an old lady who Bonnie and Maria befriended. They used to help her out, taking her to the store, to go cash her social security check, anything the old lady needed, they did for her. They even used to call her Momma.

Bonnie and Maria spent many nights there, especially when their mothers picked up new boyfriends they didn't particularly care for. They had grown up together; Bonnie was like Maria's big sister, and both had seen some bad times, so Momma and the stash house saved them for some real ugly situations. I never met her; regrettably, she had died before I moved to the neighborhood.

Maria never spoke of Momma but became deeply melancholic when the others started talking about her with great fondness. Bonnie told me one night after everyone had passed out that Momma had collapsed in the street while they were at school and because she had no ID, no one knew who she was. It was days before Bonnie and Maria found out what had happened to her, and then only by chance. Bonnie overheard a woman at the Laundromat talking about an old lady she thought lived around the corner with her two granddaughters, who had died of a heart attack. She wasn't clear on the older girl but described Maria to a tee.

The girls had figured out long ago that Momma had outlived everyone in her own family. Her husband died in an accident and both sons during the Korean War. Momma was all alone, except for Bonnie and Maria.

It was also at the stash house that they met Nicky, Frank, and Dino. Dino lived next door to Momma and struck up a friendship with the girls. It wasn't long before the five of them were hanging out at the house regularly, and Nicky started stashing his pharms in her basement.

That is also when they began calling it the stash house. After Momma died, the girls continued cashing her checks and paying the gas and electricity. The house was paid for and they felt that Momma wouldn't mind them keeping the place for her.

I get an eerie feeling every time I am in the place, like being in somebody's crypt. They have retained everything the old lady possessed, pictures of people nobody knows, furniture that is decades out of date, and we keep the drapes closed at all times so no one realizes the old lady is gone. In fact, we enter the house from Dino's backyard through the cellar door so nobody can see us come and go. Only Bonnie and Maria ever use the front door, as it is natural to them. The whole thing creeps me out, but it is no different from the hideouts I stayed in back in Fort Apache.

Back in my gang days with the Original Sinners, I never let anyone see me coming or going from those spots either. If someone accidentally did, I never went back there again anyway. It was a matter of survival and so is this. While the old lady was alive, the girls had been strict and only let Nicky stash a few bottles of pills, but now we stash everything there; pills by the case, a brick or two of marijuana, guns and knives for the arms business, and fake IDs. It is a safe haven because none of us is tied directly to the house, so the cops will have to bust us carrying stuff in or out of the house to make an actual case. A fact we were forced to drive home to the girls one day.

It happened a couple of months ago when I returned from making a pick up from a solid weed connection in Harlem. I had my book-bag loaded with a high potent weed called blonde, and some even better Thai Stick for our personal pleasure. Nicky arrived at the house at the same time with a shipment of uppers and downers.

We walked into the basement and Betty, Bonnie, and Maria were in there playing Cops and Robbers with the .22's and .38's. I thought Nicky would lose his mind.

"What the fuck are you bitches doing?"

"Hey," Betty yelled back, "You better watch who you are calling a bitch."

"Are you bitches out of your fucking minds?" he yelled even louder.

"What's your fucking problem?" asked Bonnie.

"Yeah," Maria jumped in, "The guns aren't loaded, you, stupid prick!"

"Morris! Morris, talk to them," Nicky told me as he threw down his book bag of pills, and grabbed his slick black hair.

"First of all," I said as calmly and politely as possible, "Put the fucking guns down. I don't give a shit if they are loaded or not. If you are stupid enough to shoot yourselves that is your problem." I paused for a moment, waiting for them to put the damn things down. Finally, they complied, placing the guns on the table. I shook my head in disgust, "I guess you're not worried about getting pinched for murder?"

"What murder?" Maria asked. "I told you the guns aren't loaded."

"They are not loaded now, but one day they will be, and someone will probably kill somebody with them. And when the police get them and dust for prints... wouldn't it be a bitch if yours are the fingerprints they come up with!"

All three girls let out a simultaneous, "Oh."

"Oh," Nicky returned with three hand towels, "Oh well, you'd better start cleaning. Unless you want to do a twenty-five to life bid for something you know nothing about. And girls, please clean all the guns, I can't sell any of them thinking they may be traced back to me. These ain't fucking toys! This isn't a fucking game! Jesus Christ. Stunod!"

But what we mostly do at the stash house is get high and chill out.

The rest of the week goes by in the usual manner; we go to school, hang out at the Raven, move merchandise, and now are casing the deli for the job. Frank is logging the Deli Man and his bagmen's comings and goings, as we need a precise timetable to work with on Friday. I go into the deli with Nicky and start rapping to Elizabeth. Nicky boosts a couple of beers, a practice run for Friday.

"You look sexy sweet, Liz," I half whisper to her, leaning forward on the counter.

"Oh come on now," she says, "I'm just wearing my school uniform. It's nothing special."

It's a white short-sleeved blouse, blue skirt, and vest.

"It's not what you're wearing," I emphasise; "It's what's inside what you're wearing." I reach out and with my index finger playfully flip her button loose.

She quickly grabs my hand and holds it down on the counter, "Stop it," she says sternly, "don't think I don't know about you, Mr. Morris Johnson."

"What do you mean? What do you think you know about me?"

"Some of the girls in school know you from your old neighborhood," she continues, a blush growing on her face. "They said you had a lot of girlfriends and that you, umm, took advantage of them... for lack of a better word. And I know you have a girlfriend now."

I notice she hasn't buttoned her blouse and her cleavage and top of her lace bra are still showing. I make believe I am distracted by her breasts. "Huh... What girlfriend? And who are these girls spreading these lies and slandering my good name? Are any of them a supposedly ex-girlfriend?"

"Oh, come on. Everyone knows you are going out with that little Italian girl, Mary. And I have heard her talking about you to her friends at school." Elizabeth studies my face, looking for me to lie about Maria.

Instead, I slyly change the subject, "You girls spend way too much time talking about boys, don't you? And that's why your math homework is wrong." I point to the third answer on the open page in her book on the counter. "That should be x square plus xy minus y square. The next one is x over y plus ten."

Nicky taps me on the shoulder, "Let's go, genius. Nice tits, babe."

Elizabeth clutches her blouse and buttons it all the way to the top. "Hey, are you going to pay for those beers?"

"No," Nicky yells back as he walks out of the store.

"Just put it on his dad's tab," I tell her and start to walk out. Elizabeth grabs my arm. "What about your girlfriend, Mary?" "I'm not looking for a girlfriend," I tell her, then, turning back, I take her by the hand. "I need a woman. Are you a woman, Liz? Are you ready to be my woman?"

"No," she blurts out. "I mean; I'm not going to be your girlfriend. You are so full of it."

"Woman," I correct her and leave.

I catch up with Nicky, grab one of the beers, crack the cap, and pour a splash out, "to the brothers down below. We've got a problem; Liz goes to Aquinas."

"I know. What's the problem?"

"She goes to school with Maria," I take a drink, "Girls talk. They talk a lot, and mostly, about their boyfriends."

"So, you shoot her the breeze another day or two, and come Friday, we pull the job," he slaps me on the back. "Then you are done. No problems."

By Friday, we have our window of opportunity pinpointed from 4:30 to 5 o'clock. That is ten minutes after the last drop is made and fifteen before Deli Man returns. I go in first and draw Elizabeth away from the door. The door has a bell, so Nicky needs to come in and hold it ajar for a second to let Sweet Jesus sneak in behind him. They will go up the aisle and across the back of where they will wait until I give a signal. After I have Elizabeth's undivided attention, Sweet Jesus will disappear into the stockroom and locate the cash. Nicky in turn will cover his exit by unlocking the back door. Elizabeth will never know Sweet Jesus was in the store.

At 4:30 I enter the deli, "Hey, Sweet Thing, how are they shaking?"

"Uh... Ok. No, wait, what did you say?"

I walk over to the end of the counter, "Never mind. How's the algebra coming along?"

"Not too good," Elizabeth immediately bends down to pull out he r textbook.

Nicky opens the door, Sweet Jesus slips in, and makes his way to the back of the third aisle. "You kids do what you do I'm just going to pick up a couple of beers." He crosses the front of the store and down the last aisle to the cooler.

"Come on, Nicky, you are going to get me in trouble," Elizabeth objects.

"Don't sweat it, Liz," I comfort her, "Just put it on his dad's tab. He already knows what a drunk he is. Let me see what you got."

Elizabeth flips the pages of the textbook, "I have these word problems to do."

"Yeah, but that's not what I was talking about." I run one finger along the opening of her blouse.

"Come on, Morris, stop it. Help me with this one," she pleads. "Train A leaves the station at 7 a.m. travelling 45 mph. Train B leaves 2 hours later travelling 60 mph. At what time will train B catch up with train A?"

"Pittsburgh," I tell her confidently. "Now let's see those sugar cones."

"No. And that's not the right answer," Elizabeth replies in disgust. "Come on now, be serious."

I look back at Nails and flash him a 'what's up' expression.

Nicky shrugs.

"I am serious. I want to have a peek at your little sugar cones."

"No, I'm not doing that," Elizabeth defies me. "And you know the answer can't be Pittsburgh."

"Well, they have to be travelling west. Because if they were heading east they would be in the ocean in an hour." I hear the tin bell ring.

"Let's go genius, these beers ain't gonna drink themselves."

"Ok," I tell Nicky, knowing Sweet Jesus has scored. "3 p.m." I turn to leave.

"3 p.m. Is that really the answer?" asks Elizabeth.

"Yep. 3 p.m. Pittsburgh," I look at the clock on the wall near the refrigerators, it's 4:45.

"Wait. How did you come up with the answer?" Elizabeth demands desperately. "I have to show the equation."

"You need the equation," I smile at her, as I walk back to the counter. "And I need a peek. I may be a genius, but I'm a horny genius."

Elizabeth glances up at the clock, knowing her father will be back soon then looks around and notices Nicky has left the store already. "OK," she quickly pulls up her blouse and bra, showing me her breasts. Her nipples stiffen instantly with subconscious excitement.

A smile spreads across my face as she re-adjusts her bra and tucks her blouse into her skirt. "Lucky guess," I say, having more fun with her but see the look of frustration on her. "OK, it's 45 times X equals 60 times X minus 2. X is the number of hours the trains travel. Only when X is eight is the equation equal, 360 miles is about the distance from New York to Pittsburgh. You add 8 hours to 7 a.m. and you get 3 p.m. for train A; you add 6 hours to 9 a.m. and you get 3 p.m. for train B."

She writes down the equation, $45X = 60X - 2$. I take her pen and put parenthesis around the X - 2. "Thank you," she slips a kiss on my cheek.

"Au contraire," I tell her, "My pleasure, truly."

I cross the street to the guys and notice they all have disappointed looks on their faces. "What's the matter, didn't you find it?" I ask Sweet Jesus.

"The Deli Man has a safe," he informs me.

"Not here," Nicky warns us, "Let's go to the stash house. Fuck!"

As we head down the block, I look back and see Elizabeth watching me. A smile creeps back onto my face.

Nicky asks, "What are you so happy about?"

"Elizabeth has nice tits."

"She showed you her tits?" Sweet Jesus asks in disbelief. "Next time, I work on the girl and you can do the sneaky work."

"It won't work. You don't have the magic."

"Oh yeah? Spanish men got machismo," he shoots back, "We're born with that shit. I can go all night."

"Remember who you're talking to," I tell him as we cut through Dino's backyard, "I got you your first lay and you couldn't go five minutes."

Everyone bursts into laughter.

"Hey, no mention of Elizabeth's tits," I caution as we make our way to the living room of the stash house.

"Meow… Whittist… Meow… Whittist…" They mock and make whipping motions.

I flop down into a chair that is hard from years of wear and pull a beer from one of the six packs Nicky took from the deli. Music playing upstairs informs us that the girls are already here.

"Let's get down to it;" Nicky turns to Sweet Jesus, "What kind of safe does the Deli Man have?"

"A safe safe. It's about this high and this wide," Sweet Jesus holds his hand to his waist, then apart about three feet. "It has a combination dial and everything."

"Fuck. Fuck. Fuck Me," shouts Nicky.

"Oh yeah, it also has a slit cut into the top," Sweet Jesus continues. "About a foot long and two or three inches wide. I guess it's for dropping the money in."

"Did you look in? Could you tell how much was in there?" asks Nicky, still pissed.

The girls walk in, grab a beer, and take their seats in ourlap s. Betty looks us over, knowing something is up, "Tough day at the office, boys?"

"You could say that," Dino clues her in. "Our little robbery at the deli hit a snag."

"The corner deli?" she questions. "That's just stupid. You don't shit where you eat. Everyone knows that."

"Thank you for that ageless insight," Nicky snaps. "Maybe you can embroider it on a couple of throw pillows. Let's get back to business; did you see any money in the safe?"

"No, it was too dark. But it has to have some because it is hidden behind cases of toilet paper. I had to move them out of the way to get a good look at the safe."

"Did you put them back the way they were?" I ask.

"Of course," Sweet Jesus assures me, "Exactly as they were. This is not my first time."

"Why are you robbing a rinky dink place like the corner deli?" Maria asks.

"Because that rinky dink little deli is a numbers money drop," answers Nicky. Frustration rising, he begins pacing around the room.

"Oh," Maria jumps up and looks down at me accusingly, "That is the stupidest plan you guys have come up with yet. Nicky, I know this had to be your idea, and you are going to get yourselves killed. Everyone knows you don't rob the mob and live."

The girls stand up and in unison shake their heads.

Dino takes hold of Betty's hand, "You don't have to worry about that. The money is locked up in a safe, so that's that."

"Not so fast guys," Nicky grabs another beer, "MoJo, you're the fucking genius, always making explosives in your backyard. How about you make a little boom-boom juice and we blow the safe?"

I got a chemistry set for Christmas when I was eight. Two years ago, I did an experiment that produced sulphur dioxide, a pretty nasty smelling gas. My mother demanded I get the set out of the house immediately, and I moved it to the tool shed behind the garage. Of course, this was my plan anyway, so I could have fun making nitroglycerin, boom-

boom juice. It was a dangerous process and I didn't want to blow up my mom by mistake, or the house.

The gang knows about the lab and won't go near it, but Nails, naturally, wants to know if my mom can smell weed if he lights up in there. I forbid any smoking around the lab as carelessness will most likely blow the place up.

He was in the lab one day when I was making bombs for some Puerto Rican radical group, who wanted to blow up banks. They wanted the United States out of Puerto Rico, or to stop bombing Puerto Rico, or who knows what. All I know is that they paid $5000 for five ready-to-blow pipe bombs and promised that nobody would be killed.

Nails couldn't understand not robbing the banks, just destroying some office furniture. I told him I didn't care about the banks or those guys' politics; I just didn't need the F.B.I. coming after me for murder. And also told him that I had warned them, "If anyone dies, I don't care if it's the bank's president or the cleaning lady, I'm making a sixth bomb for you." Over the next two weeks, there were five midnight bank bombings in Manhattan.

The F.B.I. is investigating.

"Two things wrong with that idea, Nails. First, I don't know how much nitro it will take to blow open a safe, but I'm pretty sure it would blow up the entire building too. You know, because it is old and wooden. Second, how am I supposed to keep Elizabeth busy while you are blowing up a safe in the backroom? Not to mention that the rest of the neighborhood is going to hear it and see it. What happened to this being a secret affair?"

"Excuse me," interjects Maria, now very upset. "What do you mean, 'Keep Elizabeth busy'?"

"Yeah, it seems Elizabeth has a bit of a crush on our boy here," Sweet Jesus offers the explanation gladly.

"Don't worry," I say as calmly as I can, "I'm just shooting her some BS while he sneaks into the stockroom."

"I'll keep that little mignotta busy. I'll scratch her fucking eyes out so she won't be able to see a God Damn thing when I get through with her!"

"This is supposed to be a clandestine affair, so the Deli Man won't know we robbed him. You fucking up his daughter is as bad as Nails blowing up his shop." Dino offers.

"How about we steal the whole fucking safe?" Nicky quickly proposes. "Then again, it is the size of a washing machine and probably weighs several hundred pounds. How do we sneak it past Elizabeth and the rest of the neighborhood?"

"I can scratch her eyes out and rip her ears off," Maria vents, "that fucking little whore."

"Why don't you guys crack the safe?" Betty suggests. "You must have someone in your family who specializes in that sort of thing."

"Not really," Nicky replies, "most safes have electronic locks nowadays, timers, and what have you. Safe cracking is a dying art. Besides, if I did know someone, they would want a hefty cut."

"Wait a second," I wrap my arms around Maria. Mainly to make sure she doesn't try to hit me with a beer bottle or something. "It probably is a pretty old safe, so we get a stethoscope and crack it ourselves. The tumblers should sound like bowling pins when they fall." I'm really careful not to mention Elizabeth's name again.

"Yes! Hell yes," Nicky gets amped up, "That'll work. We can go to that old folk's home on the other side of Parkchester and steal a stethoscope."

"Give me forty dollars," Bonnie demands with her hand in Nicky's face, "I know this goes against your religion and all, but there is a medical supplies store in Parkchester too, we will just go buy one." She snatches the money from his hand and the girls head out the front door.

Bonnie looks back at us in the living room, "try not to commit any felonies until we get back."

"Good thing no one mentioned Elizabeth's tits," Sweet Jesus jokes after we hear the door close.

For the next week and a half, the guys take turns trying to crack the safe. I keep helping Elizabeth with her algebra and helping myself to a peek-a-boo feast. Each time, I push the limits a little farther. It's also coming up to finals so she is desperate for my help, and she really wants me, whether I have a girlfriend or not. She hasn't asked me about Maria since she showed me her tits the first time and although she keeps telling me that I'm a nasty boy, she does whatever I tell her to do.

"What color is your hair?" I ask her. "What's the matter, you blind? It's blonde."

"I'm not talking about that hair. It's very pretty by the way, like waves of wheat in those commercials about America," I smile at her.

"Thank you," Elizabeth responds. "But I'm not going to do that."

"Do what, Liz?" I play innocent.

"Come on," she says with mock anger. "You want me to show you my downstairs. It's the same as the hair on my head, so there."

"Now, we both know that's not true," I tell her. "The hair on your head has been bleached by the sun for eighteen years."

"Seventeen," she corrects me, "I'll be eighteen next month. June 4th."

"Really? You seem much older, and mature. Anyway, the hair on your pussy has only been there for what, three, four years now?"

"Four years. Go on."

"You are more mature. But... your pussy has never seen the sun, so the hair must be darker. I say a light brown," I try to sound professional, "It's science, you know."

"Ha, you're wrong, mister smarty pants," like lightening, she pulls up her skirt with her left hand and pushes down her panties with her right, exposing a full and very light blonde bush. A second later, she realizes what she has done and her face reddens with embarrassment.

I double over laughing and she slaps me hard on the back of the head.

"You are the devil, Mr. Morris Johnson, but think you are so smart. If I told my father about what you've done, he'd cut your balls off."

"Why do you girls always want to blame us guys?" I say accusingly. "You know you wanted to show what you've got. By the way, very nice, I'm impressed. And I'm going to have to re- think my whole sunlight theory. Unless," I stop for a moment, pretending to think. "You have been taking her out for a sunning on a regular basis."

"That's disgusting and you better get out of here before my father gets back. But thanks for helping me with my homework," she leans across the counter and gives me a kiss on the lips.

"Thanks for giving me something to dream about," I say, running one hand across her ass.

"Get out of here, you pig, before my father catches you and does cut your balls off."

I meet up with the guys at the stash house. Today, it was Nicky's and Dino's turn at the safe. Dino was the listener, so every time he thought he heard a click he nodded and Nicky wrote down the number. When they got a group of three numbers, they tried them in various combinations, but always without luck. When time ran out, they left by the back door in the stockroom, which leads to the alley. It was easier for them since they only had to sneak into the store.

Wednesday afternoon went the same as all the days before. "I'd just like to say, for the record, that you four guys suck. I don't know how much longer I can do this." I tell them.

"Mi Dios me ayuda," exclaims Sweet Jesus, "We're in the cramped, dark, dirty stockroom risking our lives if we get caught, while you're playing show and tell with— what was that you called her today, you're lovely, Lizzie."

"First of all, it was vivacious Lizzie, and second, you can never get caught back there. If you hear the deli door open, you get out, fast. If y'all don't crack that safe soon, I'm going to have to fuck that girl and let Nails blow the safe, before her father finds me there with her."

"Don't you fuck that girl," warns Nicky, "because if Deli Man catches you with his daughter, he will cut your balls off. If you fuck her, he will kill you."

At that moment, the girls storm into the smoke-filled room and all hell breaks loose. Maria is on me like a flash, slapping me in the face as hard as she can; the sound hangs in the air only to be replaced by the guys', "Oh Shit."

She starts punching me in the gut and I try uselessly to catch her failing hands. I finally get a bear hug on her, not a good move, as she knees me in the groin.

"You no good fucking Nigger," she yells.

I'm in shock, from the pain and her calling me nigger. It's the first time I've ever heard her said the word. "I'm BS-ing her, just shooting the breeze, helping with her homework to keep her from noticing the guys."

"What part of helping with her homework is this?" Maria pulls her top over her head, exposing herself to the whole room. The guys start to cheer and she flashes them a look Medusa would be proud of. She pulls her tee shirt back down, "oh, I know, it's the part where she shows her gratitude. Or is that your normal fee for helping girls with their homework? You no good bastard!" Maria runs out of the room and storms upstairs crying.

"You're in trouble now."

"Shut the fuck up, Nicky! In fact, you guys get the fuck out of my house," commands Bonnie.

"You guys leave," I say quietly, "Catch up with y'all at the Raven."

"Oh no, you're getting the fuck out too! Now!" Bonnie points to the front door.

"I'm not leaving. I'm not leaving her like this."

"Go," Betty says. "We'll take care of her."

"The girls are right," Frank takes hold of my arm, "If you stay, you'll only make matters worse."

"Get your hands off me or I'll cut your mother-fucking throat."

"Whoa... Whoa... Whoa..." Nicky steps in, "MoJo, you got to give her time to cool down. But from that look on her face, it may be a day or two."

"Maybe never," Bonnie rips into me, "You fucking asshole."

"Just go," Betty says in a kinder, gentler voice.

CHAPTER 2
A Long Hot Day

It's 2 p.m. Saturday, three days since the incident at the stash house, the girls have not been around, and we have not made another attempt to crack the Deli Man's safe. The guys are shooting pool at the Raven Social Club when I walk in and give them a quick nod, I haven't been around much lately. I go to the bar and get a straight shot of vodka, throw it down and get another. I drop a five on the bar, "I'm gonna need a couple more of these."

"Oh, so you're the one with the girl troubles," Benny tells me.

He's a greying old Italian but still in pretty good shape, so I assume he works out and is mobbed up. And as the Raven is Nicolas Rocci's club, it is a safe assumption.

"I figured it was you, as I haven't seen you or the girls around in nearly a week. Little Nick and the others been here every day looking like somebody's been kicking their dog. Can I give you a little advice?"

"If I say no are you going to give it to me anyway?"

"Of course," he laughs, "Italian women are like firecrackers and have a short fuse. They make a lot of noise, but man they are fun to play with. The trick is to wait for the smoke to clear and then light the fuse again."

"Huh, thanks," I crack a smile, "That was really a lot of no help." Benny is an all right guy to talk to. He lines up three more drinks and slides my five back to me, telling me some crap about being bad business to kick a man when he's down.

I join the guys at the pool table, just as the five shots are starting to kick in. "I know what the problem is, you're too rushed. A half hour is not enough time to work on the box. I've got a new plan."

"We throw a tarp over the washing machine, wheel it out the back, and take it to someone's garage where we can fix it," Nicky suggests.

"No, still a stupid idea," I flip him off. After a minute, as the effects of the vodka have slowed me down somewhat, I say, "Let me tell you why." And I proceed to tell them a story that took place a couple of years ago in my old neighborhood.

One night, two guys cut three parking meters off their poles and took them into a basement to break them open for the dimes. It had taken them about an hour to cut the meters off the poles. In the basement, they took a sledgehammer and tried busting them open. They couldn't even dent them a little. Then, they tried a sledgehammer and chisel, one of the guys almost took his partner's hand off, missing it by an inch. Again, they barely scratched the surface. Finally, they took one of the meters up to the roof and dropped it five stories onto the other ones. It cracked the cement sidewalk but nothing happened to the meters. "So I asked the guys to let me have one to see if I could open it."

I have their full attention now, and even Benny is listening from behind the bar. "I had watched the meter man come by to collect the money. Seen him stick a long sliver key into the hole in the middle of the cash box and turn it again, and again, and again. He kept turning that key until the cash box slid forward a little; he pulled it out and dumped the dimes into a canvas bag. Then, he placed the box back into its housing and turned the key a dozen or so times in the other direction to lock it. Now I knew that the locking mechanism was a screw position deep inside the body of the meter."

"So what did you do?" asks Benny.

"I made an acid drip of sulphuric acid and in two days it dissolved the screw. When I opened the cash box there was $3.20 inside. Hardly worth the trouble to get it out. The other two meters had a little more. Altogether, the guys got about

$11.00. The moral of the story, don't steal something unless you know what it's worth."

"Amen to that," Benny chimes in. "What did the two fellars do when they realized there was no money in the meters?"

"They did the next stupid thing," I tell him. "They robbed the meter man after he emptied all the meters on his route. They got a couple of bags of dimes, a lot more money, but got busted trying to convert them into dollars."

"So what is your plan?" whispers Nicky.

"When you are in the back today," I whisper back. This was not a conversation for Benny's ears. "You are going to work on the lock. Don't break it, just pull out the screws that hold the cylinder in place. Then we can go in at night and work on the washing machine without any pressure."

They all like the new plan and start forcing me to drink water to sober up, so I can get them into the backroom one more time. It doesn't work.

We all go into the store together and while Elizabeth is distracted, Sweet Jesus slips into the back and fixes the lock. Deli Man locks up a little after midnight, getting the last beer buyers for the weekend, as the deli closes on Sundays. The guys wait until 2 a.m. before entering the store again, as most people are asleep by then; they have flashlights, stethoscope, and adhesive tape to hold the stethoscope to the safe. They take turns coming up with three number combinations and trying them out.

As for me, I have another job to do. I finally wake up from my afternoon binge around midnight and head to Maria's apartment to wait for her. I can hear her arguing with Carl, her mother's boyfriend. She storms into her room and violently slams the door shut. I'm sitting on her windowsill three stories up thinking this could be a big mistake. She flicks the light switch on and lets out an ear-splitting shriek.

"What's the matter now?" her mother yells.

Carl says, "I'm coming in there, missy..." Then he adds, "You know she's high on something."

"Don't you dare, you perv," Maria stares at me with ice-cold blue eyes and I am sure her command is directed at me, not Carl. "How the hell did you get in here?" She asks in a lower but not softer tone.

"You won't answer my calls, and your Gestapo bodyguard won't let me get near you," I explain, "I just had to see you."

"OK, you've seen me," she is seething, "Now get the fuck out of here."

I remember what Benny told me, I don't think the smoke cleared yet but I'm about to light the fuse again. I turn facing out the window and prepare to jump. "I don't know what you heard or who told you what, but what I did in the deli was just part of the job. That's why I didn't tell you, because I know you can't handle it."

"Wait a minute," she walks over to me, I hope not to push me off the ledge. "What do you mean it's just part of the job? Are you telling me, you don't like her? There is nothing going on between you and her?"

"I have to make sure she doesn't know the guys are back there, and at the same time see she doesn't tell her father I was around either. She ain't the smartest girl, but she can't tell her father she was showing me her tits, can she?" Now I strike a big match and light her fuse, "besides, you know your tits are much better than hers."

"Of course they are, but that is as far as you better go for this job. If you put a hand on that bitch, if that little whore..."

"I know," I swing my legs into the room. Obviously, she doesn't know I already fingered Liz the day after she showed me her pussy. So I am definitely not going to let slip how far I got already.

Maria grabs my shirt with both fists and gives me a little shove, "Just so we are clear. I will give you... what do you call it, a Bronx flying lesson."

"Yeah, that's what it's called," I confirm, "But it's best done from the roof, a fall from the third floor might not kill a person. And I'm tired of that nonsense, so I changed the plan; we are now working on the safe at night so I only have to work on her a couple more days before we actually rob the place."

"You are such a criminal," Maria draws me into the room. "How did you get in here?"

"I'm a criminal, it's my job. Anyway, I'll hang out here and leave when your mom and Carl fall asleep."

Maria pulls a little pink baby-doll nightgown from her drawer and holding in front of her then waves it like a matador's cape.

I put my fingers up to my temples like bull's horns and charge towards her. She pulls it away and I land on the bed.

She stuffs the nightie back into the drawer, takes out a flannel top, and bottoms, "Not on your life, mister, I'm still mad at you. And don't think you're getting in my bed either, you are sleeping on the floor."

"Wouldn't dream of it," I lie. Those blue eyes have warmed up a little, but they still have an intensity that relays her less than loving emotions. Maria is one hot firecracker and her fuse is always lit. I watch her change; the white flannel pajamas have little wrapped gifts of green, red, and blue, two red ones hang from her breasts and her stiff nipples poke tartly through the bows. I am trying to force myself not to get a hard-on, but losing, as I can't help thinking that winter pajamas in this heat are not going to stay on long. Make up sex for our first time would be great, but with her mom and Carl out there, it's not going to happen.

I sit cross-legged on the floor as she gets into bed, knowing that I have to get my mind off of doing her. Eventually, I ask, "What were y'all arguing about?"

"It was nothing," she says, "He's always trying to tell me to do things."

"What things! I'll cut his fucking throat."

"SHH, Sophia will hear you," Maria cautions, "And get your mind out of the gutter. The lazy bastard wanted me to get him a beer from the fridge."

"Take it from a pervert, I see the way that pervert looks at you," I warn her. "But if he ever tries anything, says something, gets out of line..."

"Don't worry about Carl, I can handle myself. Had to learn fast with some of Sophia's other boyfriends." Maria pats the bed beside her, "Come on up. Besides, Carl won't be around much longer. My mother goes through guys pretty quick, and he's starting to get cheap."

"Just the same, I'll bury his ass if he even thinks about you." I sit on the bed and start taking my clothes off.

"Hold it," she grabs my hand. "You can take those cruddy sneakers off, and that's it. And you, are lying above the covers, so don't get comfortable, and are out of here as soon as the coast is clear. Now, hold me and no funny stuff."

It's almost dawn and time for me to go. I take one last long look, burning her image into my brain, and then pull the sheet over her naked body. 'Wish I fucked her', I think, as I slowly and silently close her bedroom door, make my way through the apartment to the kitchen, out the window, and finally down the fire escape.

Everyone is at the stash house by the time I arrive with Maria in the middle of the afternoon. The guys start cheering like we won a football game or something. I smile and throw up both hands, going around the room giving them high fives in a mock victory lap.

Maria just holds up her middle finger and tells them, "vaffanculo!"

"OK guys, OK," I say, taking a seat on the sofa and putting my arm around Maria's neck.

She smiles at Bonnie, who is sitting in Frank's lap across the room and gets a hard cold look back.

I whisper in her ear, "Not everyone is glad we are back together."

Bonnie starts forward and Frank holds onto her tighter. "So, how did you make out last night? Did you get the safe open?" I'm not asking anyone in particular but Frank, feeling the tension, answers.

"We were at it all night, but none of the combinations worked."

"Really," I am surprised. I thought if they had enough time they would get it open. "Let me see the numbers you were working with."

Nicky hands me a sheet of paper with sets of numbers listed and separated by horizontal lines. There are seven groups in all, each has come up with the sets and the sets have some of the same numbers.

"These are them, 23, 7, 41, 18, 19, 54, 8, 21, and 42. I see that 7, 18, 54 show up in multiple sets."

"Yes, those have to be the right numbers," Nicky confirms, "But no matter what order we tried them in, the safe wouldn't open."

"Here's a thought for you masterminds," I offer, "Maybe it's not a three-digit combination. Maybe it's a four or five-digit combination. Or more."

"What?" A collective question rises.

"Don't tell me you guys have been at this for weeks and don't even know how many digits are in the combination." I look around the room and receive blank clueless stares. "The first thing you have to figure out when trying to pick a lock is how many tumblers or in this case wheels there are." More puzzled looks. "You turn the dial in one direction and count the number of clicks. That tells you how many digits are in the combination. Then you work the dial left and right, trying to find where the slots are. I would think the other two digits around the 20 and 40 would be close."

"Damn, my man is a master thief," boasts Maria and kisses my cheek. "Tomorrow night, you go in there and show them how it's done, Baby."

"That's fine," Nicky agrees, "But I think we need to celebrate you two love birds getting back together. Is everyone down for a little shopping? You girls can do the 'Sorority Bride' thing and MoJo and I will pull the 'Don't call me nigger' act."

"I'm down, but this time I win the fight," I insist.

"MoJo, I would love to let you win," Nicky says in a southern drawl, "But when you do, the store dicks are going to arrest you for hitting a white boy like myself. Then they'll discover the jewelry robbery and you will be pulling hard time. We can't have that happen, can we? Nope. Girls, get your things; we got to get upstate quick, this being Sunday, the malls will close early."

"Oh, one last thing," I add, "I talked to a guy I know about blowing the safe."

"You told someone? Not cool," objects Nicky.

"Relax," I assure him, "I only told him what he needed to know. Remember, people who make explosives know people who use explosives. He told me there are two ways to blow the safe without an excessive amount of noise. One is to fill an air hose from an aquarium with nitro, tape it around the doorframe, and cover it with a mattress or two to smother the blast. That should bend the door and separate it from the frame. The other and the Deli Man helped us with this plan already, is to fill the safe with water, put about eight ounces of nitro in a bottle in the safe, then seal the slit and blow it from the inside. The water will keep the money from burning and somewhat silence the explosion. It will be messy though."

"How could filling the safe with water help crack it open?" asks Dino.

"It's the same principle behind depth charges and torpedoes," I explain. "Water can't be compressed, and that's why when you push water from a larger pipe through a smaller one the pressure goes up. That's how you get water in your house. So when the nitro goes off the pressure is increased thousands of times per square inch, it has to go somewhere and the safe door is forced open. The same thing happens with depth charges and torpedoes, when they go off under a boat or sub the water is forced up through the vessel. You'll notice in war movies that when the depth charges go off above the sub, it gets shaken up but not destroyed. The force can't travel down as well because of the water, but once a charge goes off beneath the sub, it's done for."

"That's great," Nicky says, "If we don't crack the safe soon, we'll blow it. Let's get going now, time's a-wasting."

Bonnie and Maria enter Kohl's dressed as sorority sisters wearing short white dresses, mini pink cashmere sweaters with a delta symbol over the left breast, and three-inch pink satin heels. They stroll over to the jewelry department in short blonde wigs and designer shades.

Maria looks over the selection of wedding rings on display with disappointment. "Becky, these will never do. Not only can Josh afford better than this, but you deserve so much better. And imagine what your sisters will say if you show up with something like this on your finger, especially that little..." she points.

The saleslady interrupts, "Oh, we have a much better selection. Please have a seat and let me show you."

"I don't know." Maria looks at her exasperated. "But I guess it's too late to head to the city, so OK, dazzle us."

The girls sit down, aware of the camera over the saleslady's shoulder.

The woman unlocks the cabinet and pulls out a black velvet tray of engagement rings and wedding sets. "Here is a nice 18 karat white gold with a half karat solitaire surrounded by begets. Total weight is one and a half for the wedding ring and one for the engagement. What do you think, Becky?"

"You're joking, right?" Maria answers.

The plan is, only one person speaks, and the saleslady will have only one face to identify. Just like when they covered their fingertips with glue to mask their prints on a drive to Yonkers.

Maria is giving it her best spoil rich bitch act, "that set is, what, 3000 dollars, tops. Both of Josh's parents are surgeons, Becky, who gave him a Porsche for getting a C, so you can't show them that. They'll never respect you if you accept something as trivial as any of these. They won't think you are worthy of their precious son."

"I see where you are going with this," the saleslady nods and pulls another black velvet tray from the cabinet.

Bonnie picks up a ring and holds it up to the light.

There is a loud crash across the store. Nicky dropped an armful of tools.

"Watch where the fuck you're walking," he shouts, "Niggers think they own the fucking world."

"Better watch your mouth, white boy," I retort just as loud, "As you are in for an ass-kicking." I step over to Nails. We are inches apart, slowly circling, about to go at it, but waiting for the store detectives to move in.

Nicky notices that we've caught the saleslady's attention and gives me a shove.

I stumble into a rack of clothes and take them to the floor. Security is running in our direction from all over.

"I'm gonna fuck you up!" I charge into him and we wrestle around knocking down more racks. Finally, as security guards and undercover detects surround us, I reach back and throw a wide looping punch. To my horror, it lands squarely on Nail's jaw and he drops to the floor. One of the security guards grabs my arm with one hand and pulls out his handcuffs with the other.

"What are you doing?" Frank demands, as he steps from the crowd and gets between me and the guard with the cuffs. "This guy is obviously not at fault. I saw the whole thing," he says, while steadily pushing me towards the door.

"Yeah, well, he's the one who threw the punch," the burly white guard says as he advances.

"Do you want to press assault charges?" another security guard asks Nicky.

"I'll tell you what I'm going to press," Nicky yells at me, "I'm going to press that coon's face into the ground under my boot."

"Yeah? Come on," I make a motion towards him.

"Kid, just get the hell out of here," says the burly guard with a shrug and an apologetic tone.

The guard helping Nicky ushers him out the other door.

As the crowd disperses, the saleslady turns back to her two customers. They are gone. Dropping her gaze to the counter, she realizes the trays are also gone. Ah good, she returned them to the cabinet amidst the commotion. She peers inside, relived to see them there, but when she bends over to lock the cabinet, she sees they are empty, four of them. She paces back and forth behind the counter, wanting to yell out, "we've been robbed!" but she can't find the strength. Finally, after ten long minutes, she breaks down and cries.

Flashing the diamond was the signal and it didn't take much to capture the saleslady's attention. When she went to the other end of the counter for a better view of the fight, Bonnie and Maria got to work. Maria swept all the rings from the two trays on the counter into her white clutch handbag, and Bonnie's tall 5-11 frame made it easy for her to reach over the counter and pull out two more trays she had noticed in the mirrored wall behind the counter. It was a big risk, as the wall was probably a two-way mirror for monitoring the jewelry by security officers. But when two plain-clothes security guys shot past them, she knew it was time to clean house. They swept those rings into the bag and Bonnie placed the trays back into the cabinet, knowing it would confuse the saleslady and give them a few precious minutes to escape.

The two girls calmly walked around the corner to the Misses department, where Betty was waiting next to a counter piled high with colourful tops. As the girls passed her, Maria dropped the clutch into a larger shoulder bag. Betty abandoned the empty handbag she was carrying on the floor, walked towards the other, picked it up, and headed for the exit.

Bonnie, holding up a long dress shielded Maria. Maria bent down, pulled off the wig and sweater and slipped on a blue- green kerchief. In one smooth move, she glided out of her dress, revealing a blue halter-top and slacks. She rolled down her pants' legs, stepped out of the heels, and put on flats that she had brought along, the costume now tucked in the handbag. Bonnie followed suit, changing into an orange tank top, red shorts and white cap. When done, they headed towards different exits, away from the jewelry department.

The transformation took less than a minute, and they were out the store in two. The whole robbery, including the fight was through in five, and Bonnie, is now also in charge of the large handbag.

Dino sees Betty exit the store, starts the car, and drives down the block. She places the handbag in the trunk and climbs into the back seat. Maria comes out another door and Dino quickly picks her up. I leave with Frank and turn right; Dino is waiting for me at the corner. Bonnie catches up to Frank and entwines her arm with his. Nicky is the first to be picked up by Sweet Jesus, then Bonnie and Frank. They drive north, we go west, towards the highway.

The light ahead of us turns yellow and I tell Dino to try make it. "We need to hit the highway and get to the Bronx before they can set up roadblocks," I say.

I'm in the backseat with Betty, Dino and Maria are up front. We are three exits from the Bronx on the Major Deegan Expressway when I see a state trooper pull onto the highway and speed ahead of us. "Get off at the next exit and we'll take the streets the rest of the way." It's always better to be safe. As we exit the highway, another state trooper is entering.

"Do you think they know about the heist?" Dino asks.

"Heist, listen to you getting all big time," I joke. "But by now, I'm sure they do, and probably about to step up a roadblock before the next exit."

We get back to the stash house without incident, although, we do notice a lot of police activity on the way.

Betty places the shoulder bag on the table, and we light up and wait for the others to arrive. It is our practice to view the loot together, and not because we don't trust one another, just the opposite, we celebrate a score as a team. We start making out, but it doesn't go on for long, as our minds are focused on the others. Minutes pass, then an hour, and another, night falls and they are still not back.

"What if they've been caught?" asks Dino.

"Nothing," I answer. "They have nothing on them." Of course I am lying, Bonnie has the disguises. If they get caught with them, they're done for, especially Bonnie. It's nearly four hours later when the others get back.

"What the fuck?"

Maria rushes to Bonnie, "Were you stopped?"

"No, but we did stop. And we stopped. And stopped."

"It's like I told you," Nicky defends himself; "We had to ditch the clothes."

"And it took you four hours?" I ask in disbelief.

"Hell yeah. We drove three miles north of Kohl's and threw the wigs in a dumpster behind a pizza shop," Sweet Jesus says. "Then we drove another three miles east and buried the pink sweaters in somebody's trash can."

"You guys threw away my delta sweater?" Maria complains.

"Is that what you call it?" Nicky questions her. "I call it, Exhibit A for the prosecution. We threw the dresses in another trashcan a couple of miles from there. The cops will never find those."

"What about my pink satin pumps?"

Bonnie pulls out the shoes from the shoulder bag, shakes them in front of her then hands them over. "I told him I was not parting with my shoes either."

"Yesss! What? She looks damn good in those heels. But even with spreading the stuff all over town, it still shouldn't have taken four hours," I tell them.

"Oh, we also stopped to eat. What can I say? Grand larceny makes me hungry. OK, let's see how you girls did."

Bonnie pulls the little white purse out of the other handbag and dumps its contents on the table. She spreads the forty or so rings around, clearly looking for one in particular. The smallest diamonds in the group are about a half karat. She finds what she's looking for; a wedding ring with a 2.5 karat round cut blue diamond. "I don't care what you do with the rest, but this will be the ring I'm wearing on my honeymoon."

"I guess you plan to honeymoon on beautiful Riker's Island," quips Nicky. "How many times do I have to tell you? We don't keep the loot, we fence it and you buy whatever you want."

"I don't care, don't care, don't care," she says stamping her feet. "This ring spoke to me. It said 'take me, I'm yours'."

"OK, you'll probably be wearing it in Bellevue. But seriously, this is an amazing haul, you girls did a great job. I say there is two or three large here." Nicky examines the rings, as we all do.

"You can thank Maria," Bonnie says grabbing and throwing an arm around her neck. "You played that saleslady like a fiddle, getting her to pull out the good stuff. It was a work of art."

"Thank you. Thank you," Maria curtsies, "But we couldn't have scored this big if not for my friend and partner in crime. This crazy woman reaches over the counter and pulls out two more trays. I thought my heart was going to stop dead."

Frank takes the ring from Bonnie's hand with some difficulty and places it back on the table. "I had a different plan for this night, but I guess it is all working out for the good. I have something I want to say to you."

We stop looking over the rings and pay attention to what Frank is about to say.

He continues, "Bonnie, as you know my draft notice arrived last week. My dad told me that if I enlisted, I would sign up for a shorter time, and I could pick my job. So I did."

"What the hell," Nicky blurts out. "You should have talked to my dad; he could have got you out of it."

"I enlisted, I don't want to get out of it. Our guys are fighting and dying in Nam for democracy and freedom, so I'm going to do what's right."

"Bullshit," I tell him. "People are fighting and dying for Coca- Cola and GM."

"You don't think we need to stop the Red Chinese and the spread of communism across Asia?"

"First of all, I don't live in Asia. The Red Chinese or the Viet Cong never did anything to me, but when they start coming down Commonwealth, that's when I'll start shooting. Until then, if I want to get shot at I'll go back to hanging out in Fort Apache."

"You got that right." Nicky gives me a high five. "Anyway, that is not what I wanted to say," Frank says looking at us with disgust. "What I wanted to say to Bonnie," he emphasizes her name as he goes down on one knee, "I have this summer before I go to basic training, and I want to spend it with you as husband and wife. Will you marry me?"

"What? Yes. Of course yes I will. But I still want that ring for my wedding ring."

Frank pulls out a little box, opens it and puts an engagement ring on her finger, its diamond much smaller than even the smallest one on the table. The girls pull her away and start acting like... well, girls. I'm still pretty mad at him for enlisting, but happy for them.

I pick up the blue diamond ring and with my dagger tip pop it out of its setting. "Here, tell the jeweler that it was your grandmother's. Tell him you buried her with the ring, not the stone. He won't question it."

Bonnie runs over and hugs me so hard and violently I think she is going to break my back.

Nicky takes Frank's hand with the diamond and drops the one-karat blue diamond from the engagement ring in it too. "No sense in breaking up a set. Now get her a something that will do them justice and you can put that one back in the Cracker Jack box you got it out of."

"No way," Bonnie objects. "I love it. I'm keeping it. But thank you guys, I love all of you."

"Yeah, well, I hope they will at least give you two communal cells," jokes Nicky.

I go to the basement and return with an armload of shot glasses and a bottle of Stoli. I pour a shot for everyone.

Frank says, "I have champagne in the car. We just have to chill it."

"Champagne is for you two later. Vodka is what your gang uses to seal your happiness."

Nicky raises his glass and we all join him, "may you two always be as thick as thieves."

"Salut," adds Dino and we down the shot.

The girls go back to their group and girl talk, and we grill Frank about joining the army. He tells us he will be a forward observer, a high tech job targeting the enemy with lasers and radioing their position. It's better than ending up as a grunt in the infantry; he's trying really hard to convince us that enlisting was the right thing to do.

"That's what they told you, isn't it?" I give him the truth about the job, "Those guys are the first killed. While you are calling in the enemy's position, they are getting a lock on yours, and then boom."

"What? No," Bonnie tells him from across the room, "You are going to be a cook, nice and safe, no going trampling through some jungle, no getting shot or blown up."

"I don't know how she heard us, but I think she's right," I agree. "I don't know of too many cooks who are killed in action."

"Hey," Maria says, "No talk of war, this is a happy party. Besides, I have a question for you. When can I expect one of these on my finger?" She dangles her left hand in my face, sporting one of the larger rocks.

"Not until you graduate," I tell her, "No wife of mine is going to be a high school drop-out."

"He called me his wife," she bubbles.

"How about you, Betty, are you wondering when I'll slip one of those on your finger?" Dino asks.

"Oh, my sweetie," Betty consoles him; "You know my dad will shoot you dead before you get the second foot in the door. Hell, I can barely keep him from popping a cap in Morris' ass."

"That's because he is a degenerate sex fiend criminal. No offense, MoJo."

"No apology necessary, Dino. I work very hard to keep my rep up," I laugh.

We continue to drink and party the rest of the evening then before we call it a night, we stash the rings in the safe place. Nicky says he will take them to the fence before school. We have to unload them quickly so we can get the best price. Once the heist becomes public knowledge, as it will be in a couple of days, the pay-off will drop.

I grab the stethoscope as we leave, "Nails, let's go take a crack at that safe, we still have a couple of hours before the Deli Man opens."

We set up in the back room and I go to work turning the dial; each click and added resistance is another wheel. "Five digits," I announce softly, remembering that there are still families who live above the store. "2 times to the right 42," I whisper as I put pressure on the handle and work the dial, "once around to the left to 7. Right to 24, back around to 18, and then 54. Voila," I yell out, momentarily forgetting where we are. Then return to hush tones, "Piece of cake."

"Oh sure," responds Nicky, "After we loosened it up for you." "What the hell is this? A jar of Ragu, you fucking dumbass, Dago. Don't hate, appreciate the skills."

With the safe open, we plan making a move this coming Friday. Until then, we work on how to get the money from the store to the stash house without being observed, because in the middle of any afternoon, there are plenty of people in the streets, so we cannot be seen carrying anything away from the deli. In the past weeks, we noticed Deli Man leave Friday nights with the large bread bag, yet, not a lot of bread. We decide on a dry run Monday, to see how much money is in the safe, not for the value, but to figure out the size of the take.

Nicky and I go to the deli as usual; Sweet Jesus comes in through the back door, no need to sneak in anymore. Elizabeth is working on her homework and does not hear us right away.

I flip her book closed, startling her. "Whatcha doing?"

"Studying for finals," she says.

I notice she is avoiding eye contact.

"Shouldn't you be home studying too?"

I chuckle. "I never study. You know what you know, and don't know what you don't know. Besides, I'll probably be exempt."

"From all your classes," she seems surprised. "Then what are you going to do for the next two weeks while everyone else is at school?"

"Probably stay stoned," I give her a wink. "It's the burden of being a genius. Anyway, what's up with you?"

"What do you mean?" she asks sheepishly.

"For starters, you can't look at me. What's the matter?" I press.

She glances at me then over to Nicky, who is behind me munching chips.

I give Nicky a nod and he walks away to get a beer.

She whispers, "Saturday, you were really messed up. I know it was my fault that you and Maria broke up. But I swear I didn't say anything to her, and I don't know who did. I mean, I only told some of my girlfriends about you helping me." She turns red, "And some of the things we did. I know none of them would tell her."

I think she is either a lying ass bitch, or really stupid if she thinks other girls will not blab or talk about her behind her back. Females are jealous back-stabbers, and it seems that it starts at birth and never stops. But it doesn't matter to me; I flip her book open, tell her it's OK, slip my hand behind her head, and tongue her.

Elizabeth makes us sandwiches, as requested by Nicky. We're eating and drinking beers at the counter, and I'm helping her with her history. Nicky and I forget all about Sweet Jesus in the back of the store until Deli Man walks in.

"Hello, Deli Man," Nicky damn near shouts.

"My name is not Deliman, I tell you," he sneers at Nicky, his dislike obvious then walks behind the counter and over to Elizabeth. "And what are you doing?"

He gives me the same look as he gave Nicky and I am sure he is talking to me, but Elizabeth quickly answers, "Morris is helping me with my homework."

"She no needs no help," he slams her book shut.

"Yes she does," I counter, "If you want her to get good grades."

"You, you get good grades? But you are black," he states with disbelief. "Anyway, she no need good grade. She no need school. When she graduates, I find her a nice Italian boy. She gets married and make him home and babies."

"Welcome to the seventeenth century, Liz." "I'm a nice Italian boy," Nicky taunts him.

"No!" Deli Man shouts, his face turning red with anger, "You no good. You're a brutto figlio di puttana bastardo."

"I'm half Italian," I joke, "On my mother's and father's side."

"No! Get out! You go now," he snatches the sandwiches from us and throws them in the trash.

"But papa," pleads Elizabeth, "My finals start next week, I need his help."

Deli Man goes off in Italian, speaking so fast and frantically I don't think even Nicky knows what he's saying. He grabs my arm and tells me it's time to go.

We rendezvous in my basement; Sweet Jesus, Dino and Frank had been waiting a good while for us to show up.

They also raided the fridge while they waited impatiently and are wolfing down sandwiches.

Sweet Jesus informs us that the bills in the safe are in stacks of ones, tens, and twenties an inch thick, and there are multiple stacks of each denomination. We realize this job is going to have a big payload to carry.

"We can stash the money in the trash can and come back for it later," suggests Dino, "You know, like in the movie 'Ocean's Eleven'."

"Everybody's seen that movie, you stupid faggot," retorts Nicky.

"Ante gamisou paliopoustav," replies Dino with a smile.

"Nails is right," I agree, "they will toss every trash can in the alley, and I'd also wager they will be waiting for anyone who returns. No, we have to get the money out of there right away."

"How about if I put it in a garbage bag and take it down the
alley to the other end of the block? Then I can take it out to the street," Sweet Jesus says, "Nobody will know where I'm coming from."

"You would have to climb a bunch of fences separating the yards," Frank tells him, "With a bag of money on your back. What are you going to say if someone catches you? That you're Ghetto Santa?"

"There is a sewer cap in the alley behind the store," Nicky says.

"Oh hell, no! I'm not going down no sewer; there are alligators in the sewers."

"You stupid fucking Spic."

Laughter fills the basement.

I console him, "there are rats probably the size of dogs, and water bugs for sure, but an alligator, I don't think so."

"My uncle told me that people buy them as pets and when they get too big, they flush them down the toilet. It's true!"

"Even if someone did flush an alligator down the toilet," I concede, "It's a fucking reptile, it will die come winter."

"But it's not winter now."

"If it's small enough to fit down the toilet, the rats will eat it."

"Shut the fuck up you morons," Nicky explodes. "We drop the money down the sewer, with a brick or two in the bag to keep it from getting washed away, and come back for it when the heat is off."

"I don't like the idea of leaving money anywhere," I protest. "But I do like using the sewer to move it. We run a line from that sewer to one a block away, drop the money in and pull it out the other end. Then we stuff the bag in a book bag and no one will be the wiser."

"That will work," Frank agrees, "But how do we know which way the sewer runs? And we are going to need a lot of rope."

"Not rope, fishing line," I tell him, "It's thinner, stronger, and comes a couple of hundred yards to the spool. We'll need two spools, a Spalding, pen lights, and a drop net, unless, you want to climb down into the sewer and get the other end of the line."

Next day, we put the plan into action. We each find a sewer cap in the neighboring alleys. Nicky opens the fire hydrant on the corner and kids start splashing around in the water fountain. Within seconds, the flow races past the sewer cap behind the store. Minutes later, it moves past the sewer cap to the east at the end of the block and two blocks away to the north. Nicky joins Sweet Jesus behind the store, the penlights and fishing line are already taped to the ball. They feed the line into the sewer and watch the ball wash away. Nicky lights up a joint.

"What if someone asks us what we are doing?"

"Tell them you're fishing for sewer gators," Nicky tells him.

"Look, we are coming to the end of the line," Sweet Jesus says excitedly.

"That was quick," Nicky says, "Don't let it run off the spool. Two hundred and fifty yards of line, do you think they missed the ball?"

"I don't know," Sweet Jesus says, "But as dark as it is in the sewer, they should see the light coming long before the ball gets there."

Half of the second spool unwinds before it slows down and stops. Moments later, there is a tug on the line.

"We caught us a sewer gator," announces Sweet Jesus. He ties the line to the top rung of the ladder, and then together they quietly replace the sewer cap.

We are back at the corner a few minutes before the Deli Man returns. He comes over to complain about the hydrant and we ignore him, spraying water at his store. Within minutes, cops arrive and shut off the pump. When we meet Frank, he tells us the sewer runs north to the cap two blocks down, just far enough away not to raise suspicion.

Wednesday, at 4:30, Nicky and I are hanging out at the deli, planning to make this the last time we go there before the robbery.

When we enter, Elizabeth gets real excited, walks away from us to the other end of the counter, and looks out the door nervously.

"You can't be here. My father says he doesn't want you in his store."

"He can't be serious," Nicky jokes, "We are his best customers. Granted, we don't actually pay for anything, but we do keep his stock from getting stale."

"Please," I can hear she is on the verge of tears, "Just go. I don't want to get in trouble."

I walk over to her and sweep her long blonde hair from her face, revealing a reddened cheek.

"I got hit in the face playing basketball in gym today. It's nothing."

The mark is dark red, at least a day old, and more or less a handprint.

Nicky walks out the door saying, "I'll keep a look out."

"Your father did this because I was talking to you," I can't disguise my anger.

"It's not you," she excuses his behaviour, "He doesn't want me talking to any boys."

"But especially not to the black ones. I caught his drift the other day when Nails told him I was helping you. He couldn't believe a black person had the smarts. He thinks we're dumb Niggers," I end hard on niggers.

"No, he's not like that," she is trying hard to defend him, "He liked Martin Luther King Jr. and felt really bad when he was killed. He made us all go to church that day."

"Well, God bless us, Miss Lizzie," I mock in a southern accent. "Col. Delitanni is gonna free us'in poor black folk. Com'on, he doesn't like me and not just because I'm a guy and after his daughter."

"OK," she relents, "he thinks you are a hoodlum. But it's because of the way you dress, not because you're black. And admit it, you have that big afro, and are always wearing that black leather jacket. He thinks you are a Black Panther or something."

"You're not helping his case," I tell her. "He still should not have slapped you. He's not looking to marry you off; he wants you to replace Mrs. Delitanni."

"You are disgusting," she huffs. "I shouldn't have talked back to him. Can I tell you something? He absolutely hates Nicky." She giggles.

"Yeah? But if he hits you again, I'll give him a reason to absolutely hate me too." I pull out my dagger from the sheath in the back of my jacket and turn it very slowly in her face. "And here's the reason I always wear my black leather. Can I also tell you something, Liz?"

"What?"

"I am going to make love to you," I say with certainty. "You want me to and I am burning with desire for your soft, tender, and beautiful body."

Her whole face lights up and blushes, "Not going to happen. I'm going to be a virgin when I get married."

"Why do you think I've been coming here these weeks, only to help you with your school work?"

Nicky opens the door, "Let's book."

We walk down the block away from the store as the Deli Man pulls up. "I'm going to fuck that girl, Friday, Nails."

"Are you crazy? Why? The Deli Man will cut your balls off."

"Two reasons," I announce. "First, the Deli Man disrespected me, thinking I'm not good enough for his daughter."

"You're not, you fucking nigger."

"Fuck you, you lousy guinea, he doesn't know me. What, her cunt is lined with gold?" I ask, and without waiting for a response I continue my reasoning, "Second, he's going to grill her when he discovers he's been robbed. After what he did to her for just talking to me, she will never tell him I was in there Friday."

"How do you know she's gonna fuck you?" he asks in disbelief.

"Do you know what the strongest emotion is?"

"Enlighten me, o wise one."

"Desire," I tell him. "You will do crazy things when you're in love. Strange things when you hate someone. But to fulfil your desires, you will do the impossible. That girl's pussy is dripping with desire. She'll fuck me and swear to her father I was nowhere near the store, no matter what he does to her. It's our guarantee that we will get away with this."

"You are gonna get your fucking balls cut off," he repeats. "If not by Deli Man, then by a little donna pazza named, Maria. If she finds out, I wouldn't want to be you."

Friday afternoon, we watch from the Raven as the last bagman drive off, "Time to go to work." I say and cross the street quickly.

Elizabeth is waiting for me at the door. "Expecting someone?" I ask.

"Just you," she replies, "Where is Nicky?"

"It's just me today," I take her by the hand and lead her back inside. I run my hands up the back of her legs, stopping just short of her butt. I begin tonguing her passionately, she wraps her arms around my neck, and I lift her off the floor by her ass.

After a few minutes, she pushes away, "I need your help with my biology."

"That's what I'm doing," I say and start pulling her panties down.

"No. No. Come on," she objects, "Let's do school work, please."

"Come on, Lizzie," I lift her up and sit her on the counter. "School is out, time to graduate." I start to unbutton her blouse and notice a corsage of bubble gum and tootsie rolls pinned to it. "That's right, today is your birthday." I continue opening her blouse.

"What did you get me?" she sighs as I fondle and lick her nipples.

"I got a big present for you." I spin her around on her back on the counter and hop on top of her.

"Are you crazy? Everybody will see us through the window," she pulls her blouse together.

I climb off the counter, go lock the door then take my jacket off and lay it on the floor behind the counter. I hold out my hand and she takes hold of it. I sit her up and gently slip off her panties. She reaches down and pulls my pants open. My dick is hard, throbbing and glistening; her pussy is flush, open and wet. I stand there for a couple of seconds letting her imagine what's to come. Her breathing is heavy and hot as I lean forward so she can wrap one arm around my neck. I slip my arms under her legs then lift and spread them. She takes a deep breath as I lower her onto my dick and tenses up as she feels my head penetrate her opening.

"Relax. Breathe. You gonna be fine."

She lets out a low moan as I pull her to me and plunge my dick the rest of the way into her body then wraps her legs around my hips and her pussy tightens around me. I drop to my knees and gently lay her down on my jacket. She looks up at me glassy-eyed and excited, not knowing what to expect next. I run my hand through her hair, kiss her deeply and start pumping her tight wet pussy hard. Elizabeth cries out "AYEE", simultaneously moaning and sucking fast. With her arms around my neck, she digs her nails into my back with nearly every down stroke. I position her knees up and open her legs wider, lift myself, look down her body, and see blood smears on her thighs and tinted pubic hair. Her gaze drops and she smiles, knowing I'm pleased with her. I quicken my stroke as she is taking it easier now then another minute and I feel my dick explode inside her, our bodies shaking and quaking from the pleasure. After I pull out, a pink river of semen and blood flows from her and onto the floor.

"There's a mop in the back room," she says.

"We don't need that," I have no idea if the guys are finished in the back, so I open a roll of paper towels and hand her a pack of baby wipes. "Good thing you have a store."

"Hand me those Kotex over there," she points to the back shelf, "My sister told me that I might still bleed afterward."

"You told your sister about us?" I ask.

"No, she told me that a while ago."

We clean up and I unlock the door, it's almost 5:00 pm. I kiss her on the cheek and say, "you just passed biology."

After I had been led into the deli, Nicky and Sweet Jesus nonchalantly slipped into the alley and while Nicky opened the safe, Sweet Jesus taped up the back door window and tightened the screws in the lock, preparing the place to look like a break in.

Nicky opens the safe and his jaw drops, the floor is littered with stacks of money. "Hey, hey, get over here," he summons Sweet Jesus.

"Quiet man, Elizabeth will hear you."

"Are you kidding?" Nicky says, "MoJo is fucking that bitch crazy. She wouldn't hear us if we decided to blow this thing up. Give me the bags Deli Man is loaded with cash."

Sweet Jesus opens a garbage bag quietly while taking notice of Elizabeth's moaning and groaning coming from the store, then, he sees the money. "Holy shit!"

They stuff the money into the first plastic bag, blow air into it then drop it in a second bag and blow air into that one as well. It will keep the money floating through the sewer. Dino had opened the hydrant as we went to work.

The pair of thieves tug on the fishing line three times, and almost instantly get three tugs back from Frank. They attach the bag and drop it down the sewer. Nicky punches the glass in the door. It folds around his fist then they lock the safe and take off. Seconds later, a skyrocket goes off, letting them know that the money has been retrieved.

Nicky, Sweet Jesus, and Dino wait for me in the Raven. Nicky orders four vodkas when I get there. "What kept you?"

"Had to clean up," I tell him in an emotionless flat tone, "What about you? What have you been doing?"

"I've been cleaning house too." We clink glasses and he adds, "Here is to a clean sweep."

We drink and wait outside for the Deli Man's return. We don't have to wait long, as his car pulls up before we can get our second drink down.

He goes into the store and a few minutes later a police car shows up to shut off the fire hydrant. He points at us as he animatedly objects about the water rushing up to his door. The police unenthusiastically take his complaint then get in their car and leave. He stands in the door and eyes us angrily. We know how this works, the police can't do anything because he didn't see who opened the pump. He finally returns inside and takes Elizabeth's place behind the counter. We figure he is not going into the back until it is time to lock up. We are wrong.

About half an hour later, when we are on our third round, we see Deli Man pulling Elizabeth to his car by her arm. He shoves her into the front seat and quickly gets behind the wheel. He peels straight through the intersection, nearly hitting an oncoming car. The other driver slams on the breaks and lays on the horn.

"Time to go," I announce and down my drink. We head for the stash house as the sun sinks before us. "So, how much did we score?"

"Don't know, but it is big."

"Speaking of scoring, I heard you nailed Elizabeth," Dino probes.

"Yeah, I did, but keep that quiet," I warn him.

We arrive at the stash house in silence. The rest of the gang is waiting to open the bag.

After it is all stacked on the table and counted, we have 500 grand.

Nicky is elated. "Between this and the Kohl's job, we made nearly a million dollars in one week. I got 350 for the jewelry," he informs us. "I kicked ten percent up to my dad, but we still got 320 to split."

"You do know that 30 is not ten percent of 350," Frank tells him.

"Yeah, but it makes the math easier," Nicky says.

"Really," Frank says with amazement.

"320 split 8 ways is 40 thousand apiece," Nicky explains. "But we won't have to split this cash with him, as long as we keep our mouths shut about it. It's all ours, so that's another 62 grand apiece."

"But we didn't do anything," Maria points out.

Nicky answers her, "We are a crew. We are in this together. We share the risk. We share the rewards."

"That's cool," she replies, like it didn't really matter. "So, how risky was it? Were you able to keep Elizabeth occupied?"

"The noise from the fire hydrant drowned out all sounds. Besides, she was only interested in passing her finals next week," I try to put her suspicions to rest.

"What subject did you school her in this time?" asks Sweet Jesus.

"Biology."

He chuckles.

"What's your problem?" I'm thinking of decking him.

"Biology is probably your best subject."

I'm about to go off on Sweet Jesus when Nicky intervenes, warning us not to flash any cash around, that we have to keep low key for some time. I nod in agreement and Nicky divides the take from the Kohl's job.

I tell the group that I have to go home for a while. My mom has been getting on my case for running in the streets all day and night, her words not mine.

Again, Maria doesn't seem to care.

I tell her I'll be back at the Raven around nine and then we will go downtown to celebrate.

Nicky stashes the cash and joins me outside. "That little rat bastard," He is referring to Sweet Jesus.

"Fuck him," I say, "You said Deli Man was small potatoes but five large is major action. Watch your back, he already has you in his sights."

I go to my backyard lab first. I take a small magnet from the top shelf, carefully lift the center brick in the floor a fraction of an inch, and slip the magnet down the side. When I hear a click, I lift the brick carefully and turn the handle under it then back up a step, remove two more bricks an arm's distance apart, and reveal two more handles. I turn those inward and lift the three by three- foot brick door up and tilt it backwards. There are two powerful pipe bombs wired to the door, and in the hole, a steel box. I lay my share of the money in the box, minus a thousand dollars for tonight. I carefully lower the door, turn the two outer handles back, locking the door again, and replace the bricks. I turn the center handle, arming the trigger, and place one end of the brick in the slot; its weight being the key to the trigger mechanism. I very carefully remove the magnet, which unlocks the firing relay and gently set the brick in place. My money is safe. I go into the house and greet my mom.

CHAPTER 3
Family Business

I skip dinner, telling my mom, "Maria and I are going to do the city tonight."

She asks, "What are you celebrating?

"Nothing much; the end of the school year, the beginning of summer, Friday... Take your pick," I give her a big hug and press a hundred in twenties into her hand.

She objects, saying I may need it for tonight, but finally accepts it when I tell her I've been saving my pay for a couple of weeks. She thinks I work evenings making deliveries in the city. I give her a hundred or so every week, can't give her too much or she will become suspicious. Mostly, I simply slip money into her pocketbook after she gets paid. That way, she doesn't realize the money is there. She has worked so hard to keep me off the streets, especially after my brother died; well, was murdered.

Of course, her wish didn't happen, I was already an Original Sinner like my brother, so when he was killed by the 149 Gangsters—named for the street they lived in, not the number of gang members—I went after them with a vengeance unrivalled in Heaven or Hell. I may have been only twelve at the time, but like everybody else in the South Bronx, I had also been gang banging all my life. I was a battle-hardened warrior, looked like one, and acted like one. So much so, that my Mom took the money she got from my dad's death benefit and moved us to the nice private houses and tree-lined blocks of the North Bronx.

She would often tell me, "I won't lose another son to these streets."

It is nicer than living in an apartment but it really doesn't matter where you stay in New York, there are gangs on every street. I don't want her to know that I'm back in a gang; true, there is less fighting, but it's still a gang. She sees Nicky and the rest as a nice bunch of boys and girls, has no idea what we are up to, and I am going to keep it that way.

I leave, heading for the Raven to meet Maria, as promised. When I turn the corner I notice a tall man in a suit standing in the shadows of the trees, his face dimly lit when he drags on his cigarette. After you have been in as many bad situations as I have, you recognize another in an instant. I am walking into one right now and there is nothing I can do about it. I slip my hand into my right jacket pocket and ready my 007 switchblade. As I walk past him, he calls my name. I don't stop or twitch, just keep walking like I didn't hear him.

"Hey, Morris Johnson," he calls out a little louder, then a big fat man gets out of a black caddie just in front of me. He is at least six feet tall, well over three hundred pounds, and blocking the sidewalk. This is a bad situation all right.

"You got the wrong guy," I say as I turn to the man in the suit. 'A real Guido' I think, his shoes so polished they shine in the dark. He's right behind me, blows smoke in my face, and pulls my right hand from my pocket.

"No, you're the right guy," he puts my knife in his pocket; "Mr. Delitanni would like to talk to you."

"OK," I agree, "Tell him I'll be at the Raven."

"A real fucking comedian," the fat Italian tells him, "Get in the fucking car." He can barely get the words out he's breathing so hard and it takes all of his strength to get that bulky body out of the car.

That's when I notice it's the Deli Man's caddie. I think I can get around Fats and outrun him all day, but Mr. Shiny Shoes is too close and he has my 007. At this moment, I don't think I can get my dagger out from my back either. Yep, this is a real bad situation. I get in the car.

As we drive down the street, I notice Nicky standing outside the Raven. Having witnessed the whole thing go down, I don't know if that will help me, but at least he's aware of what is happening and won't be caught off guard.

Nicky runs into the Raven, whispers into Frank's ear, jumps over the bar, and then jumps back with a .38 in hand. Frank bolts from the club with Nicky close on his heels.

Maria throws one hand onto his chest. "What's going on?"

"Not now," he tries to push past her, but she stands her ground. "Look, some guys just grabbed MoJo in Deli Man's car. We've got to go after them." She turns towards the door, but Nicky grabs her arm. "Not you."

Maria starts to argue but can't get a word out.

"You need to stay here," Nicky looks at all of them, "Nobody leaves or gets in until I get back."

He jumps into Frank's GTO and tells him to head for the highway.

Benny kicks everyone out, except the five kids he is protecting, and locks the Raven's door.

The GTO roars up the highway, hitting ninety in minutes. They dodge cars on the Bronx River Parkway and fly past the police station without slowing down. Nicky is searching hard for the black caddie as they pass the park, but a few minutes later they are approaching Yonkers, and must face the fact that the caddie is gone.

The pair returns to the Raven and Nicky tells the others, "MoJo is on his own. We don't know where the Deli Man lives, or if they even took him there. Everyone go home and stay there. I'm going to see if my father knows anything about the Deli Man. I'll be discreet."

"Are you more worried about giving your father a cut, or trying to find your friend?" Maria chastises him, on the verge of tears.

"Don't worry," Nicky tries to reassure her and the others, "MoJo is tough. He won't talk."

"Again," she slams him, "Only worried about your money."

"Not at all," he admonishes her, "Remember this, all of you. You will only stay alive if you don't talk. Frank, I'll come get you if I hear something."

"We will be at the stash house," Frank says and the girls nod in agreement. "I'll be able to look after the girls if we stay together."

I'm squeezed between Fats and Mr. Shiny Shoes in the back seat of the caddie. Cadillac is a big car but Fats takes up more than half the back seat. There are two men in front, the driver is one of the bagmen who has been delivering money to the deli. I don't recognize the passenger, just an average looking Italian. We are heading north through the neighborhood and they don't seem particularly worried about being followed. I assume we are going to Deli Man's house, which could be a good thing, as I don't think they will kill me in someone's house, although, if his house is like mine, you can fire a shotgun in the basement and nobody will know. After a fifteen-minute ride, we pull into a driveway, where I'm hustled out of the caddie and through the back door of the house. I notice there are quite a few people hanging out on this warm Friday night, a good situation for me. The back door opens to the kitchen, where Deli Man awaits me.

I eye the layout, a set of kitchen knives on the counter, pots and pans hanging over the sink, and nothing else of use. Mr. Shiny Shoes reaches into my pockets, pulls out my cash wad, and holds it up.

Deli Man drags out a chair from the table and turns it around, "Sit down."

"I'll stand, thank you."

Mr. Shiny Shoes grabs the back of my neck and forces me down into the chair. He hands Deli Man the wad of crisp new bills and Deli Man fans through them.

"A lot of money for a boy your age," he tells me.

The Deli Man's cash is made up of used bills, so my new notes mean nothing to him. "I've got a really good paper route."

"You're so smart. You think I'm a joke, don't you?"

"What are you talking about?" I fake anger, "what the hell do you want, Deli Man?"

"That's Delitanni. Mr. Delitanni," he yells. "You show me some respect." He twitches with anger and impatience.

I duck to the left to avoid a right cross from Mr. Shiny Shoes. He lands a light fist on my cheek. I rub it softly, "Your boy hits like a girl. But seriously, why am I here, Mr. Deli Man?"

Shiny Shoes raises his fist, but Deli Man puts his hand out and stops him. "What do you know about my store being robbed today?"

"Your store was robbed?" I ask in disbelief. "And of course it has to be the black guy who ripped off the cash register," I say pissed off, while weaving in misinformation to throw them off. "Fuck you. I'm outta here, you racist bastard."

As I stand up, Mr. Shiny Shoes clocks me in the jaw, much harder. I bounce off Fats standing on my left and hit the floor. My head spins and as I lie on the floor, I know it's not time to go for the knives yet. But it soon may be if I can't talk my way out of this. I roll over, get to my knees, and purposely spit a load of blood and my tooth onto the floor.

Fats grabs the collar of my jacket and lifts me off the floor.

I sit back down, "I don't know nothing about a robbery."

"He's lying," Mr. Shiny Shoes says.

"So you get him to tell the truth," Deli Man commands.

I catch another shot in the eye, which I partially block, but not enough. Fats pulls me from the chair and holds my arms behind me. Mr. Shiny Shoes goes to work on my ribs and stomach. After a dozen punches, Fats lets go and I drop to the floor again. I'm face down, dry heaving.

I hear Elizabeth and her mother yelling in the passage outside the kitchen, in a mix of English and Italian. I make it back to the chair and hear Elizabeth scream, "He doesn't know anything about his money. He never went near the back."

I take the gamble, "Look, I only go into the store to help your daughter with her work because she asked me. I never stole anything. I even told her to put the beers we drank on my mother's bill because I didn't want her to get in trouble."

The four men start laughing but are quickly silenced by a look from Deli Man.

Elizabeth and her mother continue arguing, I hear her say something in Italian that ends with 'amore'.

"Quiet," her mother commands, "Your father will hear you."

"I don't care, I love him. He loves me too."

Deli Man storms out the kitchen so this is my chance. I can tell the two men behind me are not muscle, that's Mr. Shiny Shoes and Fats' job, but they are probably armed. Slowly, I start to reach around my back for my dagger. I can stab Mr. Shiny Shoes and possibly grab his gun from his left shoulder holster, as I had noticed that he is right handed. I'll shoot the other two first, Fats is too slow to get to me or the gun. Mr. Shiny Shoes is standing to my right, one foot on the chair, counting my money. The others are preoccupied with what is going on outside the kitchen.

Deli Man intercepts his daughter halfway between the kitchen and the living room, grabs a fistful of blonde hair and slaps her hard across the face. Elizabeth's head hits the wall, and a trickle of blood flows from her nose. His wife clutches his arm and stops him from delivering a second blow. He drags Elizabeth to the living room, his wife still hanging from his arm. He throws Elizabeth to the floor roughly and orders. "Check her!"

Mrs. Delitanni drops to her knees even as Elizabeth tries to scurry away from her. "Hold her still."

He grabs her arms and pins her down. Elizabeth kicks frantically, but her mother reaches up her skirt, as she is still wearing her uniform, and rips her panties off. She throws them and the blood stained Kotex across the room, shoves two fingers up her daughter, and pokes around for a few seconds. She pulls them out and repeatedly slaps Elizabeth's face with the slimy hand while yelling, "mignotta. Mignotta."

Before I can draw my knife, Deli Man lunges through the door and at me in a blind rage. He is throwing wild punches at me but I block them with ease. A minute later, energy spent and breathing hard, he grabs Mr. Shiny Shoes' arm for support, "Morire quel Niggero!"

I know exactly what he said. "Kill that Nigger."

It pays to know that one phrase in any language, as it has saved my life more than once. To know when it's time to fight or run, but unfortunately, I can do neither in this instance. Deli Man, Mr. Shiny Shoes, and Fats are all too close for me to pull out my dagger. If I do, I'll have to dispatch Mr. Shiny Shoes first, but Fats will probably kill me. Or perhaps even Deli Man, he's enraged enough right now. I don't think he's armed but I can't take the chance.

Mr. Shiny Shoes pulls a .22 from his leg holster.

"What are you doing? Not here, you idiot. Take him somewhere, and before you do it, cut off his fucking balls. Then bring them to me, I'm going to feed them to that stupid bitch."

Fats grabs my arm, leads me to the door, and as we are leaving, Deli Man tells them to also find my friend. Before I'm shoved back into the car I can hear whipping and screaming coming from the house. As we pull away, I notice the crowd has grown. No longer just people enjoying the evening, but the curious trying to catch a glimpse of who caused the fight.

We drive down Pelham Parkway, not too fast, stopping at all the red lights, the driver being careful not to get pulled over by the cops. I realize we are heading towards the Bronx dump, so there isn't much time for fancy plans. I have to do something before we get there, because once we reach the landfill, I'll have a bullet in the head and nobody will ever find my body. Hell, I'll be a skeleton before the sun comes up, thanks to the rats. If there is any flesh left, then it's the gulls' turn. The road turns into one deserted lane. It is now or never.

There is no way I can get to my dagger, or the shives strapped to my legs. Then I remember the .22 on Mr. Shiny Shoes' leg. With the right moves I may be able to get it and take out all four of them. But it is tight in here, and I don't mean space-wise. There is far too much tension and they are focused on the job at hand. To make a move, I have to get them off their guard, out of killer mode, so they don't see me as a threat. I've got to get them talking.

"It's true, we are in love. And you heard her, I don't know everything she said," I tell Mr. Shiny Shoes, "But I did understand when she said she loves me."

"How touching, Romeo," he answers sarcastically.

"I never hurt her. And I didn't know her father would go crazy."

"Well, he did! Now shut the fuck up, nigger," yells the passenger as he spins around and draws his gun.

"Whoa," yells Fats as the gun swings past his face.

"Hey, put that thing away," orders Mr. Shiny Shoes, "We are not messing up Mr. Delitanni's car."

"Then shut him up," passenger says, "She's my godchild." He holstered his gun.

I continue, "If you let me go, I'll leave the city for good, disappear. Mr. Delitanni will never know."

"Oh, so now he's Mr. Delitanni," says Mr. Shiny Shoes. "I'll make a deal with you. Tell me where the cash is and I'll shoot you right here."

He pokes me hard behind the ear and jaw, causing me to twitch.

"Don't like that, do you? But it will be quick and painless, and we'll dump your body in the street, so your family can give you a nice funeral. It's a horrible thing to let your mom and dad wonder what happened to you. Where you are, when you are coming back..."

"I already told you," I try to work up a cry but can't, "I don't know about any money, I was only there for Lizzie. You guys were young once, you know what it's like to be in love with a beautiful girl."

"I said shut him up," passenger shrieks.

"The money, tell me about the money."

"Look, you dumb, Dego," I yell angrily, "I don't know about any money."

Mr Shiny Shoes takes offense and elbows me hard in the gut.

I start to heave, on purpose, and throw up on his shoes. And just as I imagined he would, he jerks his leg up and out of the way, exposing his leg iron. I make my move. I grab his gun, flip onto my back on the floor of the car, fire a shot up at his head, and miss. The bullet bounces off the roof, ricochets off the window next to Fats, and finally lodges itself in his leg.

The men start yelling, "Get him. Shoot him."

Mr. Shiny Shoes lunges for his gun in its shoulder holster but I fire a second shot. This one hits him in the chin and the back of his head explodes, spraying brains and blood against the rear windshield. Blood splatters in my face. His gun goes off with a deafening boom, the bullet following an identical path to my first shot, it too strikes Fats. I realize the car is bulletproof and laugh at the thought of Fats being so big that he has his own gravity, drawing the stray bullets to himself.

Mr. Shiny Shoes is dead, Fats is struggling to draw his gun, and two bloodstains are spreading on his leg and gut. I see passenger's arm swing over the seat with his 9mm in hand and quickly, fire another shot up. As expected, it bounces off the roof and into the front seat. Passenger's arm jerks back, firing a bullet into the rear windshield. It bounces back towards the front and returns to passenger. All I can hear is ringing. I figure the seats are not bulletproof and fire a single shot through the back of the driver. The car speeds up and swings wildly from side to side.

The next second, everyone is thrown against the roof, except for Fats, as he is firmly lodged in his seat. I land on Mr. Shiny Shoes then back on the floor. Mr. Shiny Shoes slams into Fats and the driver is pinned by passenger's twisted body. We are tumbling like clothes in a dryer and another flash brightens up the interior of the darkened vehicle. Finally, we stop.

Fats is upside down, wedged in his seat, blood running up his neck from his shoulder. Mr. Shiny Shoes, deceased, is lying across him. I'm on top of him looking into the hole in his skull. Passenger is twisted like a pretzel, stuffed between the dashboard and windshield, dead. The driver is hanging, trapped in place by the steering wheel, his neck broken, the side of his face smashed in, blood flowing from his back and chest, also dead.

"I guess it's just you and me," I say to Fats. I'm not sure if he can hear me, because I can't hear anything, except ringing, as if I have stuck my fingers in both my ears.

I dig into Mr. Shiny Shoes' pockets for my blade and cash. I pull out two wads, mine is twenties, and his is in hundreds, fifties, and twenties, "That greedy bastard. Had all this cash and tried to pocket mine too. That's just wrong," I tell Fats.

Mr. Shiny Shoes is wearing a gold pinkie ring with a diamond bull's head. I feel the cut under my eye then twist and wrench the ring from his finger, and slip it onto my middle finger; spoils to the victor.

Fats is breathing slow, hard, and has stopped trying to get his gun.

I tell him not to worry, I won't leave him like this and place the .22 against his temple.

He jerks his head back a couple of times. At first, I think he is resisting, but then it becomes clear from the look in his eyes that he is motioning me to place the gun behind his ear. I do so and in a flash, Fats joins his friends.

I breathe in their life energy then exhale their souls into the night. I do not want to carry those spirits around for the rest of my life.

I push hard against the door. It takes a while but I finally get it open enough to squeeze through. I kick the door shut, go to the front and check the .22 revolver in the headlights. One shot left. I walk back to the road and look up. The moon is overhead, proclaiming midnight. I kind of wish I had not wrecked the car. I have a long walk ahead of me.

It's about 2:00 a.m. when I finally reach Deli Man's house. The block is deserted, the house is dark, and eerily still. I enter through the unlocked kitchen door, go down the hallway into the living room, upstairs, and into the bathroom on the right. I quietly close the door and pull the light string hanging in front of the mirror. I squint, as the sudden onslaught of light is too much to bear, but as my eyes adjust, I see my face. Bruised, battered, and blood stained. No doubt, it's not just my blood, but also the four mobsters'.

I rest the .22 on the sink, didn't notice until now that I've been carrying it at my side the whole time. I grab a small towel off the rail, wet it, and wipe my face. I wet it once more with the hot water and wipe my neck, and chest. I wet the towel one last time and use it to pick up the gun. I swing my hand in a small tight circle, wrapping the gun in the towel.

I kill the light in the bathroom then wait for my sight to adjust to the shadows. The master bedroom is across from the bathroom, I reach out and slowly turn the handle. I carefully open the door, step inside and creep up to the bedside. Mrs. Deli Man is sleeping on her side facing me, her short blonde hair flowing down her face. I brush it back. She looks like her daughter, only a little harder. I walk over to the other side of the bed. Deli Man is lying on his back, his lips slightly parted, breathing lightly. I raise the towel dripping water onto his face and into his mouth. His hand absently wipes away the liquid as he slowly comes to consciousness.

His eyes widen as he realizes who is standing over him and instantly grasps the implication of the red wet towel menacingly pointing down at his face; he lets out a slight sigh. I inch the towel over his right eye. Smoke rises from his face and blood spurts out onto the pillow. I drop the towel beside the bed, leave the bedroom, and quietly close the door.

A low whimper down the hall reaches my ears. It's the first sound I hear since leaving the caddie. I follow it to Elizabeth's bedroom door and gently push it open. She is curled up in the middle of the bed, a sliver of moonlight illuminating ominous tell-tale red stripes on the sheets. I peel the sheet back softly and she sobs a little louder as she stretches out on her stomach. Her white nightgown is stained red and I notice the welts starting at her ankles and running up her legs. A great sadness builds inside me, so deep that my own pain, the one that had been burning in my side disappears. Tears flow down my face and drip onto her wounds, I know I am to blame for what she went through.

I kiss and lick the blood from each cut and graze as I work my way up her body and onto her bed then lift the gown over her head. She slowly rolls over beneath me, and I see she is just as battered on this side. Every inch of her body is slashed, black, and blue. Her face is swollen, lips cut, and eyes nearly shut beneath the bruises. I hold myself up with my left hand and stroke her beaten face with the other.

Elizabeth shudders and shakes from the pain and emotion. "You shouldn't be here. My father will shoot you," she sobs.

"Your father knows that I am bulletproof," I whisper and kiss her softly on the lips. "I'm so sorry. I had no idea he would do this to his own daughter."

"I wanted you," Elizabeth declares then runs her fingers over my face, studying my bruises and swellings. "Did you really come there for me, or were you just there for the money?"

"I am here now," I say, "And there is no money here."

Elizabeth unbuckles my pants, I strip off my clothes, and slowly slide my dick into her. I turn her on her side, and then roll her on top of me. I hold her up by the hips and slowly gyrate and roll my dick inside her. I feel her pussy throbbing on my dick and we painfully and gently hump until day breaks. I feel her orgasm and know that she also felt mine. I lower her body onto mine and wrap her in my arms and legs. This time, it was much different for both of us.

As I leave, I tell her, "Remember, I was never here."

"MoJo, are you awake?" Nicky asks. Then he rattles the door of his cell and calls out again, "Hey MoJo, wake up, man!"

"Yeah, I'm awake. What time is it? How long have we been in here?"

"It's late Saturday night," Nicky says, "You been out all day, I thought you had died or something."

"Gee, thanks for your concern," I reply. I get off the hard metal bench and try to stretch my stiff and aching body. "I guess I was a little more tired and banged up than I could stand. I needed some sleep. Nails, did they question you?"

"No one asked me a God damn thing," he is pissed. "But you missed a lot of the action that was going on downstairs."

Nicky then recounts what transpired when Fitzpatrick and Mancotti –Batman and Robin as we call them because Fitzpatrick is a foot and a half taller than his partner–reported that Deli Man had committed suicide.

The captain hit the roof. "So, the wife comes home this morning after taking her girls to their uncle's house and finds him dead, gun in his hand. Are you really buying this?"

"That's her story," Mancotti tells the captain, "Do you think she's lying, that she killed her husband?"

"It did cross my mind, for starters. I have been in this job for twenty-two years, know how many suicides I have seen where the guy shoots HIMSELF in the face? NONE. Not a single case. So yes, I think the wife killed her husband, as I have seen dozens of cases where it was the spouse. Then... I got this bit of interesting news a while ago. Four heavy hitters, rap sheets that could paper the walls of my office, found shot dead in our suicide friend's car. But wait, it gets better, Mr. Delitanni's car is bulletproof. How rough is the salami sandwich business that the guy needs to ride around in a bulletproof caddie? Don't answer that.

"Also, consider this, at least two of the guys were killed by a .22 bullet in the head, or maybe all four were hit by .22s, still waiting for the coroner's report. It looks like they turned the inside of that car into the motherfucking OK Corral. And now for the kicker, Mr. Delitanni commits suicide with the last bullet in a .22 revolver. Know what this does look like? The start of a mob war. I don't know on who else's payroll you two are on, but the NYPD is paying you good money, so you'd better get your asses out there and find out WHO, WHAT, and WHY, and shut it down PRONTO. Am I making myself clear? There is NOT going to be a war on the streets of my precinct. You two sorry excuses for detectives get out there and do your jobs, or I will make sure you are cashing pension checks at the commissary in Sing Sing."

"Sounded like a real wild night," Nicky tells me.

"Like all Fridays," I reply, "Just Cowboys and Indians." Then sit back down on the bench.

So, if Mrs. Delitanni is going with suicide, and got Elizabeth and her sister out of the picture, she won't be talking again, which is good, as they won't give me up to the police. Although, I do wonder if she told Batman and Robin about our little robbery business and they are planning some retribution. I will have to run it by Nails when we get out of here.

Early Sunday morning we are taken to separate interrogation rooms. Batman and Robin take turns throwing threats around and try to get us to roll over on each other, which is simply a stupid game of cat and mouse, as they can't really question us without a lawyer being present, so even if we did slip and say something it would not be admissible in court. But we hold to the number two rule, 'Never admit to anything'.

Later, they come in and announce that Nicky pinned the killing on me, that I'm not one of them, that he is going to leave me hanging... I'm sure they are feeding Nails the same bullshit, I'm not Italian, I'll turn him in to save myself, that Blacks can't be trusted. What is exceedingly interesting is that no one mentions the five-hundred grand. After a couple of hours of complete garbage, they cut us loose.

"Hungry?" I ask Nicky.

"I could eat a horse," He replies.

We go to the diner by the train station, as it opens early every morning, even Sundays. A lot of transit police are in there, either coming off a shift or starting one. You can tell which is which by the orders they put in, steak and eggs are starting, steak and fries are ending theirs. We get some curious looks from the cops as we sit in a booth in the back eating our steak and eggs.

I ask Nails if they pressed him about his bruises. He told them he got them from a rough two-hand touch football game. I laugh, having given them the same crap story. I tell Nicky Batman and Robin returned all my money, the thousand I originally had and the thirty I took off Mike the Butcher, Mr. Shiny Shoes. I discovered Mr. Shiny Shoes was also known as Mike the Butcher because he had been one by trade, and as a mob hit man, got rid of his victims by cutting them up in a butcher's shop.

Nicky is also concerned that they didn't mention the robbery, because they must have been watching the store, which explains why they picked us up. They let us go only because the captain wants the quintuple homicide solved quickly, as nothing adds up. He must figure they believe we are in deep, and to just cut us loose means that we are in trouble.

Nicky tells me to go underground for a while, "you knocked off a couple of made men. That is never good and they will try to kill you. They are just hoping that we'll lead them to the cash first. I didn't want to but I'm going to have to tell my father about the job, since we are going to need his help to get you clean."

"Don't worry, I can disappear. No one will find me," I say with confidence.

Nicky nods in agreement.

He thinks I'm going to the South Bronx, and I let him believe it, but that is exactly the first place where the mob will look. I have other places to hide out, people Nicky knows nothing about. I tell him, "There is one thing you must do."

"Name it and you got it."

"Protect Maria. If anything happens to her—"

"You're not threatening me, are you?" he cuts me off, his face turning dead cold.

I have the same cold dead stare in my eyes. "It's not a threat. Just don't let anything happen to her. You know how I feel. You know how she is, so watch out, as they will try to use her to get to me."

"Don't worry brother, I know how this game is played, and exactly what's at stake. Just one question. Why didn't you leave after you did the Deli Man?"

"You fuck a girl once and she gives you her body. Fuck her again and you are in her heart. The third time and you'll have her soul."

"Are you going back for her soul?"

"No need to, she never told her mother I was there. Her mother probably thinks I'm dead and someone else killed her husband over the money. I'll talk to you in a couple of days." I give the waitress a twenty for a ten-dollar meal and we leave.

The inquisitive looks follow us out the door.

I didn't want to tell Nicky that I merely stayed the night because I felt bad for Liz. She took a terrible beating and I was only there for the money.

Nicky heads back home. I head for the train station.

Frank and Bonnie are arguing with Maria when Nicky arrives at the stash house after school.

Maria starts on him too, "You know where Morris is, don't you? He's hurt bad, I can feel it. I was up all night; the spirits won't stop talking me."

"OK, you have had enough bennies for a while," Nicky tells her. "And you need to stop with the witchy stuff too. You are starting to freak me out. I told you I was with MoJo, and he is fine. He took a couple of licks but he is OK."

"Then why won't he come home?" she demands. "If everything is all right, where is he?"

"Women," he replies exasperatedly. "Got to make sure no one is after him first. Give me a couple of days, and he'll be back."

"No," Maria orders the group, "we are going to the South Bronx. Morris told me where I can get help if I need it. And I am going there now."

"I told you that's a bad idea," Frank says. "You don't know anybody down there. You don't even know if he is there."

"Listen to the guys, honey," Bonnie consoles her, "You could be putting yourself and Morris in danger."

"He's already in danger. The spirits told me so," Maria states with certainty, "I am going to the pool hall either with you or on my own."

"Morris told me to protect you," Nicky says.

"I guess you're the one going with me then," Maria tells him.

"Yeah, I'm going with you. And when we find MoJo, I'm going to kick his ass for making me look after his wacko girlfriend."

"Then it's the four of us," Frank confirms.

"OK, Bonnie, you drive. Frank, you're riding shotgun." Nicky takes a sawed-off shotgun from under the sofa and hands it to him. He grabs a .38, puts it in his back waist, and a .22 in his jacket's pocket.

"What's with all the guns?" asks Maria.

"Did you ever listen when MoJo talks about where he lived?" Nicky asks her. "It ain't Disney World. Four white kids going down there looking for him are going to need some fire power."

Nicky instructs Bonnie to circle the block before double-parking in front of the pool hall and pick out an escape route if needed later.

"Frank, stay sharp, and keep a lookout for my signal," Nicky says as he and Maria exist the GTO.

"What's the signal?" asks Frank.

"People dying," answers Nicky.

The storefront pool hall isn't much bigger than the Raven's. There are two pool tables to the left. A couple of men are playing eight ball. Three card tables at the back have a dozen players around them. There is a full-length bar behind the card tables with an old gray haired leather skinned man tending it. A huge black man sits in front of the bar under a sign, which announces, "No gambling."

Nicky notices all the money on the tables and figures the sign is more decoration than a rule. He tells Maria, as he motions toward the man in the chair, "Ask him, he looks like he never leaves this place."

"Excuse me," Maria says softly, "do you know Charlie?"

"No." He replies, but barely looks her way.

"Morris Johnson told me I should come here and find Charlie if I was in trouble," Maria says with more confidence in her voice.

"Don't know no Morris either," the huge bouncer looks over the pair. "Hey, take your kid sister to the free clinic and forget about this Charlie guy."

"What?"

"He thinks you're pregnant," Nicky tells her and notices that all eyes are on them now. Two of the pool players had moved to the door. Nicky shifts the .22 pistol in his pocket.

"Hey, paisano, why don't you relax? Before you shoot yourself in the foot. What do you got there, a .22? You can't take all of us, you know." The big man leans forward, as if he is about to get up.

"I don't need to take care of everyone," Nicky stares him down. "I just need to clear the door, and my friends in the car will do the rest."

The two guys at the door casually return to their pool game but keep a wary eye on them.

Maria steps in front of Nicky, "I'm not knocked up. Morris said I could get some help here if I needed it." She looks around the room for some recognition.

A scraggily man with a rotten teeth smile steps forward from the far corner of the room, "I'm Charlie and I'll take you to Morris, but just you, Little Caesar waits here."

"OK."

"No way," Nicky objects immediately, "she goes nowhere without me."

"Are you serious, Smokey?" A tall woman with blonde streaks in her hair gets up from a card game.

Nicky can tell she is old enough to be their mother, but doesn't look it, standing there in a low cut short black dress.

"Is your life worth so little to you?" She tells rotten tooth man.

He retreats at once to his place on the wall.

Nicky can't take his eyes off the unknown woman, as she comes over to them.

She looks them over and asks Maria, "Are you in trouble princess?"

"Well, no, but ..."

"Then why are you here?" She answers before Maria can say anything else. "You think Angel needs your help? Let me tell you something, princess. He may be a jacket and tie Catholic schoolboy uptown but down here, among his people, he is respected and feared as a warlord and killer. And only a fool would follow a rattlesnake down a rat hole."

"That's the MoJo I know," Nicky agrees, "A psycho-killer."

"Princess, if Angel went to Hell today, the Devil will be praying for God's help. Go home and come back when you do need real help."

As she returns to her card game, they see three hearts tattooed on her arm with the name 'Charlie' across them. They hear Smokey telling the others he wasn't going to do anything to her as they leave. This was definitely the right place, but they were not going to get anything out of the people here, as Nicky already knew.

Nicolas Rocci sits at a corner table sipping red wine in the Raven. He is waiting for his son to return from the South Bronx. Benny, Salvatore, a dark and scarred Italian, and Nicolas are swapping stories of the old days. Benny is telling the men that Nails has put together a crew that rivals theirs. Plans are bold and daring.

Nicolas nods, he has already seen an example with the Kohl's heist, and he is quite certain the Deli heist was their doing too. Ripping off a money drop is a high risk, high reward job, and when done right you can walk away clean, but they did not walk away completely clean. They left doubt. Were they involved in the robbery, or did the actual robbers take advantage of their involvement with Elizabeth? Unlike in a court of law, doubt on the streets leads to death.

Nicky sees his father's Lincoln parked in front of the Raven and tells Bonnie to turn the corner before they reach the club. He gets out and tells them to go home. He walks up to the driver, "what kind of mood is he in, Pauley?"

"Not bad," the muscular driver tells him, "Go on in, you're OK."

Nicky approaches his father and Nicolas gets up and throws an arm around him. Salvatore is next. He grabs him by the back of the neck and shakes him up. Benny brings another glass and pours him wine. They all joke about the

Deli Man and his men being taken down by a kid. No names are mentioned but they all know who they are talking about. It's his father's way of getting to the facts of the weekend heist.

They finish the bottle of wine and Nicolas Rocci tells his son, "Let's take a ride."

Nicolas, Salvatore, and Nicky get in the Lincoln. Nicky and his father sit in the back, the other man in the front passenger seat, and without saying where they are going, the car pulls out. They stop on a remote street not far from the Raven, all four get out, and Nicolas Rocci opens the trunk, revealing a man bound and gagged inside. Nicky recognizes him as one of the bagmen from the deli. Pauley pulls up next to the Lincoln in a beat up old Ford. They transfer the bagman to the Ford and tape his hands to the wheel.

The car revs loudly, due to a brick pressing on the accelerator.

Nicolas rips the strip from the man's mouth and holds a small tape recorder up to him. "How much money have you been moving?"

"I don't know. I never look in the envelope."

"Come on, Rocko," Nicolas slaps his face, "You have been a bag-man for twenty years. You can tell how much money you're carrying from the size of the envelope down to the dollar. One more time, how much money?"

"Sometimes, twenty g's, sometimes more," the man answers in a way that suggests he is pleading for mercy.

"OK. That's good," Nicolas reassures him, "Who gave you the envelopes?"

"No one, Mister..."

Nicolas left hooks him in the mouth, knocking out his front teeth. An evil glare replaces the smile on his face, the calm voice is also gone, and a tone like a quiet yell takes over. "You know how this is played. Who gave you the envelope?"

"No one, I pick up the envelope from a mailbox. I don't see or talk to anyone." Fear rises in Rocko's voice.

"Who told you where the envelope would be?" asks Nicolas. "Answer wrong and you get to test your driving skills."

"Mr. Delitanni."

"Sorry, wrong answer," Nicolas shouts as he slaps the shift into drive and swings away from the car. The Ford fishtails away with a loud screech of burning rubber and a smelly cloud of smoke. They watch as the car's taillights grow bright red and weave wildly down the street.

It's obvious to Nicky the car has no breaks.

"When giving the driving test," his father tells him, "It is best to crash the car right away, before it can pick up speed." On cue, Nicolas is interrupted by a loud bang and the sound of shattering glass and twisting metal blocks away. "Now, if you ever pull a job in my territory without my approval," he grabs Nicky by the throat, "That is advice you better remember."

Nicky stands outside of Maria's apartment throwing pennies at her window. Eventually, she sticks her head out, "Do you know what time it is? What do you want?"

"It's 2:15," Nicky calls out to be heard, but not to wake her mother. "Come down."

"Is it Morris? Is he OK?" Her voice rises along with her excitement.

"Just get dressed and come down here."

A few minutes later, she leaves the building in a white dress, sweater, and sneakers, and Nicky quickly notices that not much else underneath.

She continues her questioning, but he tells her to just follow him. They walk a zigzag route through the neighborhood, cutting past a few alleyways and doubling back down some streets. Maria can tell they are making sure no one is following them. At about 3:00 a.m. they reach Noble Park a few blocks from her house.

"Where is he?"

"He said to wait for him by the swings," Nicky tells her, "I'll stay here and keep a lookout."

Maria approaches the swings while looking everywhere, but the ball field and playground are deserted. She sits down and starts pushing herself slowly back and forth, planning to wait all night if she has to.

I had planned to scold her for going to the pool hall and worked up a litany of reasons why it was a foolish and dangerous undertaking, but I forget it all as I watch her on the swing; I step out of the darkness of the playground bathroom, "Who are you waiting for, pretty Lady?"

"My boyfriend," she replies in a little girl voice. "Mind if I keep you company?" I ask.

"I don't know about that, he's kind of a jealous jerk," Maria's pitch rises uncontrollably. "How could you leave me without a word? I didn't know if you were hurt, how bad, where you were, or anything."

I quickly grab her up off the swing and wrap my arms around her. I squeeze her tight against my body and hold on until I feel the tension drain from hers. "I'm sorry, but I couldn't take the chance that someone was already scoping you out. I told Nails to tell you I was OK. Didn't he tell you?"

"Yours and Nicky's idea of OK is if you're barely breathing." Maria turns my face towards the street light and gently touches the bruise under my still swollen black eye. "You see, you're not OK. And I am sure you got a lot of other bruises under that sweatshirt."

"I'm a hundred times better than the other guys," I joke, "I am still breathing." I sit on the swing and she sits on my lap. I put my arms around her waist and rest my head on the back of her shoulder, her soft hair nestled around my un-bruised cheek.

"This is not funny. They could have killed you."

"They tried, but I'm bulletproof," I'm doing my best to put her at ease. "I know you're mad because I missed our Friday date. I promise I will take you out real soon."

"I forgot all about that," she says. "Elizabeth wasn't in school today. The girls at school said Deli Man killed her and her Black boyfriend. Others said they heard she ran off with you because you got her pregnant. And someone else said you slaughtered the whole family and the cops killed you this afternoon in a shootout."

"Wow, where do you girls dig up these stories?" I laugh. "As for Elizabeth, I don't know what happened to her, other than what I heard while I was in jail. Her mother took her out to the Island to stay with family. I guess she thinks whoever killed Deli Man could come back to silence her."

It is quiet, only the sound of crickets audible in the darkness. I start swinging us back and forth slowly. There is no breeze, so the air is still warm and slightly clammy. I can tell there is still a lot more on her mind.

She finally asks, "You're not going to kill her?"

"Who?"

"Elizabeth, you're not going to silence her?"

"No," I answer sternly. "Why would you think that?"

"That woman, Charlie, said you are a killer." Her tone holds a lot more accusations than her words do.

"Her name isn't Charlie," I say. All the things I wanted to tell her came back in a flash. "Why did you go down there? I told you to only go there if you were in trouble. And are you crazy? You were going to go with someone you don't know. Alone."

"He said he was Charlie. I thought those people were your friends, you know, from your old gang." Her voice starts to quiver; she is frightened of my anger.

"Charlie is dead," I state bluntly. "Has been for a couple of years. And not everybody in Fort Apache is my friend. In fact, I have more enemies there than friends."

"That woman, whoever she was, said you are a killer. Is it true? How many people have you killed?"

"Five more, no, six since I last saw you." I can't see her face, but I know this is upsetting her. "It's a really rough neighborhood and sometimes, it is kill or be killed. That's why I don't want you to go down there. Besides, I'm not hiding there. If you are hiding out, it is insane to go where people know you, making it easier to be found. So, go where nobody knows you, that way, no one can drop a dime on you."

"Take me with you," she pleads.

"You know I can't. I wish I could, but a black guy and a white chick draw attention no matter where they go," I explain, "and that is exactly the opposite of hiding out." Another few minutes of silence go by then I say, "It is really nice out here. I like this time the most, it is so peaceful."

Maria hops off the swing and turns around to face me. She grabs the chains, stops the swing then says boldly, "I'm not wearing any underwear."

I take a closer look at her and can see she is definitely not wearing a bra.

She lifts her dress and runs her middle finger up her slit. "What do you think about that?"

"I certainly like what I see."

"Yeah? Then you'll love what I do next." She shoves her finger up her pussy then runs it over my lips and sticks it into my mouth.

I take it in willingly and she starts pulling at my black sweatpants. "Are you sure you want to do this?"

"What's the matter, a big bad killer like yourself, afraid of a defenceless little girl?"

"Afraid of you?" I reply. "Of course I am."

"Let's get those pants off," she commands. "I promise I won't hurt you." She steps up on the swing and lowers herself down onto my dick.

It happens so fast I'm only semi-erect. But her pussy is so wet, I slide right in and my dick stiffens quickly. She sucks in a deep breath as I penetrate her and releases a long low sigh. We begin rocking the swing slowly at first then we pull hard on the chains, driving it back and forth and my cock deeper into her tightening vagina. I can feel her pulsating pussy keeping time to the swing's motion and my dick throbbing in rhythm with her. I feel as if it could go on forever. I want it to. I need it to.

She suddenly lets go of the chains, wraps her arms around my neck, and her legs lock around my hips as she starts to convulse. Her body jerks wildly and I grab her to keep us from tumbling out of the swing. My dick reacts to her squeezing pussy and I too go into spasms, which force me to my feet by the power of our orgasms. Maria is wrapped so tightly and firmly on my dick we can scarcely breathe.

"Oh God," she finally lets out and I bend my knees to let her stand. Bloody semen runs down our legs as we slowly separate. She kisses me hard on the lips and I slip my tongue into her.

She tells me, "Now, while you are on the run out there, you know what you have waiting for you here."

I give her my shirt to wipe herself off before we join Nicky, who is pretending to be asleep on the hood of a car. I start to toss the shirt in the trash but Maria takes it, and holds it to her breast.

"You're kidding. You are not going to keep that?"

"What do you think?"

"Girls!"

We walk to Maria's place and I sit with her on the steps; Nicky is lying on his back on another car.

As the sun rises, I kiss her once more, "You'd better go upstairs before your mother wakes up."

"When will you be back?" Tears fill her eyes.

"Soon, Nails' dad is working on it now. Don't worry."

Nicolas Rocci is sitting at the kitchen table sipping coffee when Nicky gets home. He calls his son into the kitchen and looks him over. Nicolas is neither pleased nor displeased with what he sees. "Shower and get dressed, we are going to church."

"Do we have time for breakfast?" Nicky gives his mother a kiss on the cheek, reaches into the frying pan, and pulls out a sausage.

She slaps his hand but doesn't stop him from popping the hot link into his mouth. "Go get ready," she tells him, "your plate will be waiting for you."

Nicky returns to the kitchen in a black suit, lavender shirt and thin black silk tie. He sits down to a plate of sausages, home fries, and eggs, and gobbles it all down as if he hasn't seen food in days.

"Slow down, you're going to choke," warns his mother. "You have time; your father is getting dressed."

Nicolas returns just as Nicky is finishing his second helping. Dressed in a dark blue suit and white shirt, he tells his son. "Get up and take your jacket off," he then proceeds to place a .25 Beretta sling on him and adjusts his tie. "Try not to shoot yourself," he jokes and slaps Nicky on the cheek.

His wife adjusts his tie in turn and kisses him on the cheek. "Look at my two handsome men. Finally working together, this is a great day."

"Did you shine your shoes?" asks Nicolas.

"Of course I did." Nicky replies.

"Doesn't look it," his father says, "You can shine them up in the car."

They walk outside and meet Salvatore and Pauley waiting by the Lincoln. It is gleaming from a fresh washing and polishing.

Salvatore opens Nicky's jacket, "Cute."

The four of them ride out to Long Island in relative silence.

As they pull onto the mansion grounds, Nicolas warns his son, "You say nothing, hear me? Not a single word."

Nicky nods.

There are six other cars lined up outside the mansion, Lincolns and Cadillacs, with their drivers standing guard. Pauley takes up his position by the car while the others join the meeting.

Nicky recognizes Joseph Banoa and his two men, but no one else. Banoa is a husky six-foot man with thick black hair. Unlike his father, who although at a mere five foot five still possesses his physique, he is also greying and looks much older than forty-two.

Only when an Old Man walks into the room does Nicky realize that he is at the Godfather's house. This is clearly a meeting at the highest level and no doubt pertaining to the deli robbery. Nicky has no idea what his father planned, but he's sure he's about to find out.

The Old Man finds his place at the head of the table, Banoa and his men sit to his left, and the Roccis on the right. The rest fill in on either sides–extra muscle so things don't get out of hand. Whatever happens, the Old Man will decide the outcome.

He began, "We are here to determine if Joseph Banoa has been dealing fairly with Nicolas Rocci. Nick, state your grievance."

"First of all, thank you for hearing me," Nicolas acknowledges the rest of the group. "Banoa made a deal to pay ten percent to move his packages through my territory. He paid ten g's for weeks, however, I have learned that he has been moving five-hundred g's and shorting me forty a week."

"That's a lie," Joe Banoa shouts.

Nicolas pulls out a mini recorder, slams it on the table, presses play, and lets everyone listen to the previous night's confession. When the tape ends, he continues, "Your man was very loyal, putting the blame on Delitanni, a dead man. If you like, I could ask your other bagmen if they can confirm his account of events. But it does not matter, your man was moving five times the amount you paid for, so you owe me."

"Is this true?" asks the Old Man, "How could you not know?"

"Delitanni must have been running some side action," Joe says sheepishly. "I will look into it."

"Yes, do that," orders the Old Man, "But it seems that Nick is not the only one short here. Understand? What do you figure the damages to be, Nick?"

"I calculate it to be six-forty grand."

The Old Man sits quietly for a moment, pondering his decision. He has to make Joe pay but he also doesn't want there to be bad blood between the two. If Joe really was unaware of Delitanni's actions, the stiff penalty will sting harshly. Finally, he speaks, "I believe Delitanni may have been operating outside of normal channels. However, Joe, it is still your responsibility to keep this sort of thing from happening. If not for this robbery, who knows how much more revenue we would have lost? Therefore, you will pay Nicolas Rocci five large. And of course, you will make restitution to me at the normal rate. A week should be sufficient time, yes?"

"Yes. But about the robbery," Joe glares at Nicky, "I believe there may have been some inside information given to the thieves."

"What inside information?" Nicolas challenges, "You paid me to allow you to move your money in my territory, not to guard it. Maybe you should have put someone other than a... young girl guarding it. And while we are on that subject, I believe the matter between Delitanni and the black kid was personal in nature, and it is resolved."

"Not at all," Banoa objects, "He killed five made men. He must at least pay for that."

"The other four were in the employ of Delitanni," the Old Man states, "So their deaths are on his hands. I have it from a good source that this was a family matter, and even though it ended badly for Delitanni, the matter is over. I think we are done here. I thank you gentlemen for your time."

With that, everyone got up to leave, except for Nicolas and his son, whom the old man asked to remain behind.

He says, "I hear good things about you, young man. The jewelry store heist, planned and executed by you and your crew to perfection, a good job indeed." The Old Man pours a sherry for them and toasts Nicky's future.

CHAPTER 4
Junior Mafia

Fr. Robinson stands at the main door to Cardinal Hayes' High School. He is checking the student body's hair length and proper school attire. There are two weeks left of school and he is still busting balls. I turn up the walkway to the door and I can tell he is impatient to lay into me. The other guys slow to let me pass, either they don't want to fail inspection or they can't wait to see me get busted. I am sure everyone is aware that I have been absent for the past two days, so when I reach the door I will be pulled into the Dean of Discipline's office.

I keep a steady gait as I approach, "Morning Father."

"Good morning indeed, Mr. Johnson," he replies and turns to follow me in.

He doesn't have to say anything else, I immediately turn left into his office, and give Doris, his secretary, a big smile as I march past her desk and into the inner sanctum. He slams the door shut with a resounding boom and snatches the sunglasses from my face as he passes to take his seat behind the desk.

Fr. Robinson is a huge six-foot man, black and grey crew cut, very dark, like an original African. He has an accent that is impossible to place, not quite foreign, but also not like any from America that I have ever heard. He takes off his collar and loosens his top button. A lot of times when a priest does that it is the sign they are about to bring the Wrath of God down on you.

He sits down at his desk, "Where have you been? It is Wednesday, no call, not even from your girlfriend pretending to be your mother. And you look like you've been to Hell, but only one man has ever returned from there, so that can't be it."

"No, not Hell, that's a three-day trip as I understand it," I answer. "But finals have started and I believe I'm exempt. I do have a damn near perfect average in all my classes. So, if I am exempt from the test I don't really have to show up, do I?"

"That is true," he says, "But unlike you, your mother called here Monday and Tuesday." Fr. Robinson pauses for a long moment. "She was worried because you weren't home all weekend either. She wanted to know if you had at least come to school. Have you spoken to your mother yet, son?"

"Yes Father." I remain rigidly at attention, not about to enlighten him as to where I've been. I told my mom I was with some of my old friends, downtown, since I had time off from school, and explained the bruises as football injuries, from playing tackle without equipment on the cement sidewalk.

She did not buy it.

"I have been the Dean of Discipline at Hayes for five years, and a teacher here for a dozen before that. I have seen a lot of young men come through those doors. Some have gone on to be doctors, lawyers, even a senator," he pulls a folder from the file drawer in his desk. "Others wound up needing lawyers. I have given you a certain amount of leeway, let you bend the rules a bit. Such as days with your girlfriend, I know you can afford the time off, and I hope she can too."

"She's a straight A's student like me," I state a bit too protectively. I don't like anybody talking about Maria, making innuendoes, and she is a good student.

"That is very good. But remember, I do not afford you this consideration because you are black," he's flipping through my record. "About a quarter of the student body is black, and another quarter or so Spanish. Almost from the first day you started attending this school you have shown a special quality, one that certain men possess, and it allows them to go on to achieve great accomplishments, and it is not just the smarts. No. You have a drive and determination to make your way in this world. To do something special, to be someone special, however...”

'Here it comes,' I muse, and a smile, ever so slight, takes hold of my stern and emotionless demeanor. I am thinking that it's going to be the sex talk, because sex is sin. It leads to death, death of the body, death of the soul. I heard it before.

“Mr. Johnson, you have reached the crossroads, come to a defining moment in your life, and you can go on to be that doctor, lawyer, great leader. It is all right there in front of you. Or you can make the foolish choice, squander what God has blessed you with, and wind up ten years from now, twenty, if you live that long, wondering what might have been. We are here to help you, but ultimately the choice is yours.”

I wait for a couple of minutes, not sure if there is more to come, like detention. Priests like to do that, give you the big inspiring speech, and then slap you with a couple of days in detention to think about it. Still, this is not what I was expecting, I don't know what kind of speech this was. Maybe the black eye made him more concerned for my life than my love life. After I figure he is done, I ask to make sure, “is that it? Can I go?”

“Yes. But before you go to the auditorium for study hall, I assume you are not taking the finals,” he starts to give me instructions.

“Oh no,” I correct him, “I am taking the math and science finals. I have a bet to win.”

Fr. Robinson laughs, “Of course you do. But first, let the nurse look at your eye and other injuries. You wouldn't want them to hinder your performance.”

I get home early, around 1:00pm, grab a beer from the basement and go upstairs to my bedroom.

I nearly heave the beer at Maria sitting on my bed. "What the hell, are you crazy?"

"Surprise!" She hops off the bed and throws her arms around my neck, "I knew you would go to school today, as you would rather die than lose a bet. Did you ace the tests?"

"They haven't been scored yet," I forgot I told her about the bet I made with the rest of the class, that I would finish before everyone else and ace the tests. The pot is worth $700.00 a test and she is right, I am not going to lose out, even with a contract out on me.

"Really," Maria says with a measure of disbelief in my modesty. "It was trig and chemistry; you would have aced the test while people were trying to kill you."

I do not know how Maria knew that I would come home after the test but here she is. I contacted Nails this morning and found out the men watching my house were gone. I had also checked on my mom for a couple of nights, and seen a car parked a few houses away. I figure they are hit men because there were four. Cops go out in twos. How she knew it was safe for me to come home is a mystery, but if I ask, she'll give me some story about saints and spirits or something equally crazy like that, telling her to come wait for me here.

She starts undoing my tie and kissing my neck.

"If I had remembered about your tests earlier than today, I wouldn't have done what I did in the park the other night," she tells me as she pulls my shirt off and drops it on the floor. "I would have rather waited to give you a real welcome home."

I unbutton her blouse and slide it half off her shoulders then run my hands over them and down her back. I begin kissing her softly up and down her neck and across her back. She flinches when I bite her around the bra strap and pull one side off with my teeth. "Do you regret the park?"

"No," she lifts my head and looks me straight in the eye, "Not at all. I was just thinking how I'm going to rock your world."

"The world rocked pretty good that night too," I unhook the bra and peel off her top. I work one hand inside the side of her skirt, the other around the back and loosen the zipper just enough to slip it off her hips.

"You Catholic school boys spend your time betting who can take a test the fastest." She steps out of her skirt and climbs on the bed on all fours, "Do you know what Catholic school girls spend their time talking about? Who can do their Catholic boyfriend the best. That's the bet I intend to win."

I climb on the bed behind her, she leans back against me, and stops me from taking off her panties, "leave your underwear on." She rises up onto her knees and rubs her body up and down mine then takes my hands and places them on her breasts, rotating them slowly around her areolas. "Sssss. Yessss," she moans. I let her take control, she knows what she wants, and I want to give it to her the way she wants it.

She turns around, pushes me down on my back and pulls off my wet underwear, which has a line of semen stretching towards her. "Bad boy," she scolds me and without warning slaps her hand down on my dick. My head slams back against the pillow from the momentary flash of pain. I hear her giggle. This girl is crazy. I open my eyes, and see her pulling down her panties. She has a wicked grin on her face and those eyes blaze like a cold fire. I am pinned down by blue marble fingertips gripping at my chest and her wide-open wet vagina slides up and down my dick. "Does that make it feel better, my Baby?"

I reach up and grab her by one tit and her hip, "It feels great."

She spreads her legs wider and drives her hips down harder. I can feel a river flowing from between her legs. I suck in a hard breath through my teeth and thrust my pelvis up into her gap. She coos with delight and quickens her writhing. "Oh, ride me, baby."

Her long black hair drapes down, licking my face as she rocks back and forth. Her eyes close as she reaches her own world of pleasure and her face takes on the glow of an angel, ecstasy reshaping the contours of her lips. Her strokes milk me of my semen and at the same time turn me to polished steel. Both my hands grip her tender tight ass. I hear, "put it in me, Baby. Give it to me now."

My fingernails dig into her cheeks and I guide her forward then back on my dick. We are so wet I slide right in, but she is still very tight and hisses and wiggles like a snake. She drops onto my body and bites down on my shoulder. I wrap her in my arms, one up her back to her shoulder, the other across her ass and hip, and take over thrusting with all my might into her willing body. I pull her knees forward to position her pussy for full penetration. Her tiny body bounces up each time I slam my dick into her with a sweet squishy sound followed by a low dreamlike moan in my ear.

"Now, I am going to rock your world," I whisper as I lift her head and sweep her hair back so she can see the devilish grin on my face. I pull out of her and roll her over, where she lies limp like a ragdoll. I turn her onto her stomach, lift her waist up to meet my hip, and love that she has surrendered control of her body to me. I run my hand between her legs and up her slit. It comes back soaked and sticky. I then rub my dick's head back and forth on her slit, listening to her cry out with pleasure. I finally rear back and drive forward as hard as I can and bury my hard-on as deep as I can in her body. She screams out a mixture of pain and pleasure as I feel her trying to crawl away. I lock my hands around her hips and pump furiously. In seconds, it is all over, as I expel all my energy and cum into her throbbing pussy.

The sun is setting against my bedroom window and there is a warm orange glow drifting through the cigarette whorls to the sound of 'Whole Lotta Love' coming from my stereo. I hear the front door open, then the heavy and tired footsteps of my mother climbing the stairs.

She knocks once then pushes the door open. Her weary and disgusted look washes over me as she stands in the doorway in her white nurse uniform. "Morris, I asked you not to smoke in the house," she scolds me. "Hello Maria."

"Hello, Mrs. Johnson," Maria says sitting up in bed, peeling off the covers to reveal that she is fully clothed.

"Is it time for me to meet your mother?" She asks with motherly concern.

"You don't have to," Maria answers, not understanding the implication, "But you can if you want to. I thought you might come home hungry so I made spaghetti and meatballs."

"Thank you, dear. Morris, she is a nice girl, don't ruin her life," she warns me.

"Gee Mom, thanks," I reply.

"He's not ruining my life," Maria defends me.

"Dear, you have no idea what you two are getting into," she starts the lecture.

I knew a sex talk was coming sometime today, and here it is.

"Sure it's all fun and games now. But what is it going to be like in a couple of months when you are up all night with a crying baby?" She picks up my baby picture from the dresser. "This one cried all the time and twice as long at night. And let me tell you about the kicking."

"Oh God, help me."

"Shush, I want to hear this," Maria wiggles up and puts her arms around my neck.

My Mom sat on the corner of the bed, "he kicked like the devil. I used to tell his Dad, 'I think he's fighting the

Devil in there'. And after he was born, I told his father the Devil won. I tell you, you don't want to have his baby."

"Yes I do," Maria blurts out. She immediately falls back on the bed and pulls the covers over her face, embarrassed.

"Morris, take her home." Mom gets up and leaves the room.

With the Deli Man's affair behind us, we return to our daily routine. During the week we move products; jelly beans for the white boys and weed for the blacks, in and around the neighborhood parks. We work in groups of fours, a moneyman to take payments, a runner to get the products and make the drop–never give anyone anything is the rule of the game, let the customer pick it up from a park bench or behind a car. A bagman sits and watches the stash, and last, a lookout to warn us if the police are making a move. We work two-hour shifts and switch up grouping in different parks and school playgrounds. On the weekends, we work at Orchard Beach, just north of the handball courts.

With the weather being as hot as it is, the beach is already crowded. The girls like working there because obviously, they spend the day sitting on blankets watching the stash. At the beach, we rearrange the team, a moneyman, two runners, and two lookouts. We take turns at each position; the girls do not come off their spot.

By Saturday afternoon, we have turned a nice profit, a couple of grand at least. We join the girls on the blankets and prepare to close up shop. This is the risky part of the day; picking up the beach bag with the drugs is an invitation for the cops to make a bust. First, Nicky and Frank take the money to the cars then one comes back to get whoever is carrying the drugs. We stagger our departure so as to cover the carrier. If it looks like the cops are about to move in, we signal him to drop the bag and keep walking. It is always one of us guys handling the money and drugs. Money can get you killed and drugs get you busted, we will never let the girls take those kinds of risks.

This day, things are not going as planned. Joey and Michael Banoa stand in front of us on the beach.

"You can leave your things where they are, we will take care of them; consider it a down payment on the money you owe us," Joey says, his hand wrapped in a beach towel. Michael has his hand wrapped too.

"Very funny," Nicky says and steps up to Joey. The towel is pressed against his chest. "If you want it, you're gonna have to pull the trigger. I guarantee you won't get a second shot off."

"I only need one, Mike only needs one, and the rest of my boys only need one shot apiece," Joey motions for Nicky to turn around. Nicky doesn't flinch. "Hey nigger, tell him, like this, nobody will hear a thing."

I can feel the eyes on the back of my head.

Frank puts a hand on Nicky's arms, "Let them have it."

"This ain't over," Nicky seethes.

"Damn right. You cost my family a mil, this ain't over by a long shot." Michael picks up the drugs bag and another guy comes from behind us for the money.

I pull the bag from Nicky's hand and pass it over. Before he can step away, I grab his arm and toggle my hand back and forth flashing the diamond bull's head ring. I nod at him and smile. He pulls away and scurries quickly from the beach.

When we get back to the stash house, Sweet Jesus goes straight to the hall closet and pulls out a box of handguns, "We got to go after them. We got to strike back hard."

"Not a good idea," I tell him. I pull my .38 revolver from its holster, dump the bullets out and toss the gun into the box.

"You were armed," he says in amazement, "And you did nothing!"

"I just picked up the moniker Bulletproof; I don't think I want to put it to the test again so soon."

Frank and Nicky laugh and unload their guns.

Nicky says, "They had the drop on us and MoJo is right; we can't go rushing over there half-cocked and get our cocks shot off. They will be expecting us to retaliate. We need to check them out, find out where they are the weakest, and hit them there."

"Wow, I never thought you would be the voice of reason," Maria tells him.

"Well, they hit us for what, three, five grand? We hit them for five hundred, and another five hundred in... let's call it penalty fees. I can afford to be magnanimous, but I won't be for long."

"You guys can stay here and plot your revenge, but without Morris. You, Mr. Johnson, owe me a night out and it is time to pay up." Maria grabs my arm and Betty's hand and leads us out the door.

She is not allowed to have a steady boyfriend until she graduates, and she thinks that having Betty around fools her mother into thinking I am dating Betty. I have told her a hundred times; you can't fool a mother. They know.

Nicky starts planning their next move when Sweet Jesus interrupts, "I can't believe you guys did nothing today, especially Morris. He's supposed to be this tough guy, big gang banger, warlord... He took the money from you and handed it over to them."

"Let me tell you something about MoJo," Nicky thumps him in the chest with his two fingers, really pissed off. "I knew the first time I saw him, three years ago, that he was not only tough but damn smart. Frank, Dino, and I were hanging out at the schoolyard after school when he and two of his friends showed up to play basketball."

Frank and Dino nod in agreement.

"The three boys were taking shots when Patrick O'Donahue and a couple of his Irish pals grabbed the ball. He told Morris and his friends they were on his court and had to move. Morris took the ball over to the next court, O'Donahue followed.

"Hey, you niggers, deaf or just dumb?" he sneered, "We don't want you niggers hanging on our rims like a bunch of apes dunking and bending them. Take that shit back to the fucking ghetto where you belong."

"I could tell Morris and his friends were ready to throw down, but after looking around the schoolyard and seeing nothing but white faces, they took their ball and left.

"Two days later, Friday afternoon, Morris returned with about ten guys. He goes up to O'Donahue and tells him he needs his court. Before O'Donahue can get a word out, these big blacks dudes start to fill the schoolyard. They are arriving on bikes, in cars, like an army sixty or stronger. Everybody exits the schoolyard quickly, but none faster than O'Donahue.

"Frank and Dino got up to leave and I told them to sit their asses back down.

"Morris sits on the ground by one of the gates; has a cigar box and is collecting money, one of his guys is taking down names. Soon, the guys break out into three on three games. The games go on all afternoon and into the evening; finally, I give Morris a 'what's up' nod as the three of us leave.

"The next day, Morris is waiting by the schoolyard gate. I'm on the school steps a few feet away. Patrick O'Donahue and his friends arrive at the gate and stop dead in their tracks at the sight of Morris.

"O'Donahue says low and sheepishly, 'Want to shoot some hoops?'

"I'm not your enemy," Morris announces boldly, "But I am not your mother fucking friend either. You call me a nigga again and I'll cut your punk ass tongue out of your head and shove it up your ass." Then he pulls out his dagger with lightning speed and stabs the ball in O'Donahue's hands. O'Donahue ran from the school, not even waiting for his friends.

"Nice knife," I tell him. "That little bitch is Patrick O'Donahue, we call him OD, because he's going to die early from the booze and drugs."

"Fuck with me and he'll die real soon. You Italiano?"

"Yeah, so, how many of those guys were here for a fight yesterday?"

"Enough. The rest were here just for the basketball tournament I set up. What are you, like Junior Mafia?"

"What?"

"You know, your dad or big brother is in the mob, so you think you're a tough guy too, just waiting to join the family business."

"Yeah, I like that, Junior Mafia, that's me." Nicky smiles contentedly.

"That wasn't a compliment."

"You know all those guys from where you came from?"

"Hell no, some were from the South Bronx, my old stomping grounds, but the others are from all over; North Bronx, Harlem, who knows where. I put up flyers announcing a winner takes all tournament, minus the house cut, and they just showed up. You know how niggas love basketball."

"I wonder what would have happened if say, someone fired off a shot."

"You would have gotten your crazy white ass blown away. Most, if not all of those guys were probably strapped. Basketball tournaments don't always end well."

"Do you arrange a lot of these tournaments?"

"No, not at all. I have however put together my share of... you can call them parties. But I do know how to raise an army when I need one."

"We spent the rest of the day in the schoolyard drinking beer, smoking, and shooting the breeze. Morris never had a problem at school or the neighborhood after that day, and later, I introduced him to Frank and Dino and the four of us became the good friends we are today."

Maria gives her mother a big kiss on the cheek then she and Betty head straight for her bedroom, ignoring Carl's attempt to ask about their day at the beach. I am standing in the living room doorway when her mother asks if I want to eat. Maria yells from behind the closed door that I don't. I swear she has sixth sense ears.

I whisper, "What you got?"

"I just put some lasagna in the icebox," she whispers back, "I can heat it up in a jiffy."

"No need to I'll take it like it is," I say.

Mrs. Marino touches my cheek then grabs my hand and pulls me to the kitchen, "This will only take a minute." She studies the ring on my finger and asks, "When did you become Italian?"

"I'm a little of everything," I say jokingly.

"That's interesting," she puts a large square of lasagna in the pan. "And when did you become a butcher?"

"About the same time I became Italian." I sit down at the table and wait for the food.

"Where are you off to now?"

"I don't know," I answer honestly, "Wherever the girls want to go. The movies I guess."

She sets the plate before me, sits down, and waits for my reaction. I take a big forkful then another, and nod in approval. She is an older version of Maria, same blue eyes and all, just perhaps a few inches taller, but is always saying that Maria will outgrow her. Maria says she looks like Sophia Loren, and at times, she does. Maria is obsessed with Sophia Loren, has pictures all over her bedroom like other girls have teen idols. I am just finishing the plate of food when Maria appears in the doorway in a short black dress that stops halfway to her knees. The top is a lacy low v-cut showing plenty of cleavage.

Sophia says to me, "I don't think you are going to the movies. I hope you have dancing shoes."

"Wow," is all I can say.

We say our goodbyes and leave.

Carl says, "I don't know how that girl puts up with him." "What? He's a nice boy," Sophia replies.

"Maybe so, but the way he looked at Maria..." he tells her, "If I was his girlfriend, what's her name, Betty. I'd be pissed."

Sophia laughs, "You think Betty is his girlfriend?"

"She's BLACK. Don't know what kind of black," he states and scratches his head, "but she is BLACK."

"First of all, you're an idiot," she scoffs, "and secondly, Betty is only here so my daughter can pretend to respect my wishes. This is OK, because a woman knows you can't hold back the river; a man builds a damn and floods his home."

"Oh yeah, watch me." He storms out the door and races down the stairs, shouting, "Wait a minute. Wait right there."

Sophia sticks her head out the window as he reaches the street.

We stop.

Maria has a disgusted look as he grabs her by the arm and says, "You're not going anywhere with this..."

I cut his words from his mouth as I slice open his chin. He steps back, just in time to avoid having his throat slashed. I pursue in quick steps pinning him against the wall.

He is a hundred pounds heavier and a few inches taller than me, but my 007 against his throat makes up the difference. "You don't put a hand on her or you will lose those fat little fingers. Got it?"

His eyes tear up as fear immobilizes him.

I take a step back and he remains motionless then I flip my knife closed and return it to my pocket as quickly and effortlessly as I pulled it out.

Carl runs back into the building and up the stairs.

Sophia is waiting for him at the door.

"I'm calling the cops," he yells. "That boy tried to kill me."

"I will kill you if you put your hands on my daughter again." She slams the door in his face.

Maria reluctantly enters my house clutching onto Betty, as if she is entering a house of horrors. This is the first time she is back since blurting out that she wanted to have my baby and is deathly afraid my mother is waiting to cut her head off or something sinister like that. They sit quietly in the living room while I run up to my bedroom to change and put on my dancing shoe as her mother suggested.

I knock on my mother's door and hear a weary, "Come in."

She is sitting in her chair by the window, so she obviously saw us come in.

"Maria and Betty are downstairs, are you going to come and say hello?"

"I don't think so," she answers, "She doesn't look too happy to be here."

"She is a little frightened. It would mean a lot if you said something to her, you know, let her know you're not mad."

I return to the girls waiting in the living room and Betty remarks that I look decent for a change, having done away with the leather jacket and jeans. They are almost whispering their comments like we are in church. I hear the horn blow from the cab outside.

I call out, "Mom, we are leaving."

"Wait a minute," she calls back and descends the stairs.

Maria stops, unable or unwilling to take another step towards the door. I take her hand as my mother enters the living room.

"You look lovely, dear."

"Thank you," Maria replies. Her mouth hangs open but no words follow.

"Betty, are you and Dino joining them?"

"Huh, me and Dino," Betty is surprised, didn't think my mother knew about them.

I laugh, mothers know everything.

"No. I have to go home; we have family in town."

"Too bad," Mom says, "I was hoping you would keep these two out of trouble. The last time Morris took her out, he didn't come home for three days. And when he did return, he looked like he had been in a dog fight."

"I told you, Mom," I protest angrily, "It had nothing to do with Maria. I didn't even get to see her that night."

"Well, just the same, don't be taking her to any of those parties you think I don't know about," she scolds.

I can feel the look on Maria face, an inquisitive accusation. I guess my mother is a little angry with Maria and is showing it by slamming me.

The horn blows again, thankfully.

"We got to go, Mom."

"Don't worry, we are going dancing," Maria says and kisses her, "Somewhere nice in the city."

The three of us climb into the cab and Maria immediately asks what parties my mother was referring to. I am not going to explain a gang banging to her, although, I am sure she knows what one is. I tell her my mom was just giving her a hard time then quickly change the subject, and start giving the driver turn by turn instructions to Betty's house. It takes a couple of minutes to get there, but it is enough time to change the mood. I give the driver the address of the Black Cat Club in Soho and we are off.

We make out the entire way, and don't realize we have reached our destination until the driver clears his throat. "Are you sure this is where you want to go? I don't see a nightclub around here."

"Yeah, this is the place," I assure him, "It's not marked."

I pay the fare as we get out, Maria looks around at the dark and deserted streets; I take her hand and lead her towards an alley.

"We're not going down there…"

"Don't worry, the door is in the back. It is a really nice club; you will like it."

We walk a few feet into the alley and a wino rises up out of the darkness, "Nice legs sweetheart, you got a quarter?"

"Ahh," she shrieks.

I ball up a dollar and toss it to him, "Here's a buck, stop looking up her dress."

He fumbles with the catch, "Oh no, it's OK, I don't see so good. I got the cataracts. Thank you Mister. Thank you."

We get to the black steel door, where a sign hangs above it, a red-eyed black cat with its back raised in a hump. I press the bell, a loud buzzer goes off, and I push the heavy steel door open. We enter a black light lit hallway covered in neon graffiti. At the other end, there is yet another steel door, painted red, with the same black cat on. The door opens and jazz blast out just as we reach the end.

"Well, goddamn Morris Johnson. And this must be the young lady you can't stop talking about. You are a beauty, dear. Robert Douglas." The two-hundred-and-fifty-pound line backer throws an arm around me and nearly breaks my neck.

The room is huge and the dance floor in front of the band sways to the sax player. Looks like all the tables are taken too, and, the two bars, which run the length of the room on either side, are elbow to elbow.

"No worries," Robert says as he catches my eye. "I reserved you a table off the side of the bandstand, not too close to the speaker, and very secluded. But in a dress like that, I'm sure you want to be seen. Morris, my man!"

We zigzag our way to the candlelit table behind Robert, who parts the crowd like Moses at the Red Sea. A bottle of champagne sits in an ice bucket with two glasses buried upside down to their stems. No sooner than Robert leaves after another neck-breaking hug, and Maria is leading me to the dance floor.

She throws her arms around my neck and starts swaying slowly to the music. "This place is perfect."

School is out for the summer. Girls are frantically talking about boyfriends, beaches, and bikinis. Maria lights up a Newport and takes a hard drag, nothing anyone can do about it now, she thinks. Five of her girlfriends sneak a puff, nervously looking around for Mother Superior.

One of her girlfriends says, "Uh oh."

"Put it out. Put it out quick," another girl cautions excitedly.

"No, it's not that," the first girl replies, "It's Joey Banoa. He's coming this way."

Maria has her back to him and does not turn around, hoping he won't see her and keep walking. She figures he's here to pick up his own sister, so if he doesn't see her he won't stop to talk. She is having a good day and doesn't want to put up with his crap, especially after the beach incident.

One girl calls out, "Hi, Joey!"

"Jesus Christ! What did you do that for?" Maria starts to walk away from the group.

"Maria, wait," Joey calls out to her and runs past the group of five. He gets in front of her and holds up his hand. "I just wanted to say that you and your girlfriends were in no danger the other day. I told my guys nobody better hit any of you girls."

Maria huffs, "you think I'm scared of you or your boys?" Her lips curl into a snarl like a dog about to bite. "You are lucky we were there. If we weren't, Morris and Nicky would have lit you fools up. They held back because they didn't want us caught in the crossfire. If we weren't there you'd be dead right now, Pizza Face."

"We will see about that," Joey rubs at his acne.

Maria knows how to get to him.

"And you should watch who you hang around with, no self- respecting Italian boy is gonna want what some nigger had."

"Well now, that's the thing," Maria places her hands on her hips and gives them a slow grind. "I don't need a boy; I got a real hard man."

"Yeah, I know how niggers are," he says, glaring at her jealously, "They'll stick their dicks in anything. Go ask Elizabeth Delitanni. Oh wait, I hear her father killed her rather than let her be with some nigger."

"Vaffanculo," she hisses, "he can be fucking every woman in the world, and I'll still want his dick inside me. But I'd never let you touch me. And if you were the last man on Earth, I would rather fuck a dog."

"Maybe I should teach him a lesson about what a nigger can do and what he can't."

"If you got a problem with my boyfriend, you can tell him to his face. Here he comes. I'd like to hear what he has to say now that you don't have a gun at his back."

Joey Banoa hurries off, not even looking around to check if Maria is telling the truth.

The girls come over and the one who called him hugs her. They had heard most of what Maria said, so they immediately start pressing her for details on losing her virginity. They all light up cigarettes, as Maria begin telling them about the past two weeks.

Joey Banoa, his brother Mike, and three other gang members are riding around the Rocci neighborhood on the hunt for Nicky's friends. They park on the corner at the end of the block from the Raven and watch Morris enter the club and leave with Maria.

Joey pulls out a pint of Jack Daniels, takes a sip, and passes it to his brother, "Have a drink little brother, we will be here a while."

"Who are we looking for?" the fifteen-year old asks, as he throws back a shot and then passes the bottle to the back.

"The Mick, the Spic, or the Greek, it doesn't matter to me," Joey tells them. "We are going to teach Nicky and his gang of faggots a lesson. Let them know who they are messing with. Hey, pass the whiskey, ya bunch of fags." He takes another drink and sees Sweet Jesus heading their way. "Look alive fags, we won't have to wait after all."

Arturo jumps out the back seat with a baseball bat, rushes Sweet Jesus, and knocks him to the ground by jabbing him in the stomach with the bat. The other boys surround Sweet Jesus and begin stomping on him.

Sweet Jesus rolls back and forth, trying to protect his head and face.

Joey grabs the bat from Arturo and says, "Let me show you how you kill a cockroach." He cracks him in the back, then the ribs, and takes a swing at Sweet Jesus' head.

Mike grabs his brother's arm in mid-swing, causing the bat to hit the ground before striking the fallen boy in the face. "Are you crazy, man? We don't want to kill him," he yells at his older brother.

"Speak for yourself," Joey tells him. "But all right, I think Nicky Rocci will get the message. Let's go." He hands the bloody bat to his brother and kicks the unconscious Sweet Jesus one more time.

The boys get back in the car and drive off, leaving Sweet Jesus lying on the sidewalk in a bloody heap.

Nicky and Frank are the last to arrive at the hospital. A couple of police officers are outside the room talking to Sweet Jesus' parents. Nicky and Frank are stopped by the cops and briefly questioned, who, naturally, say they don't know why anyone would beat up their friend. It's the same story they got from the rest of his friends.

"If you know anyone who would do this to my boy, you would tell them, wouldn't you?" Mrs. Ramirez pleads.

"If we knew anything, we wouldn't hesitate to tell the police," Nicky says sincerely. "How is he?"

"He may lose his eye," his father announces. The anger in his voice and distrusting look lets Nicky knows he's not buying their story.

Nicky rushes into the room. Sweet Jesus lies heavily sedated, his head and half his face bandaged, the unnatural sound of a breathing apparatus all one hears. The gang surrounds the bed. Maria sits in a chair holding his hand, Betty sobs softly on Dino's shoulder, and Bonnie, taking Frank's hand, begins to say something, but Frank pulls her to him and stifles her in his arms. There we stay, motionless and speechless, until a nurse announces that visiting time is over. We walk out in silence and the Ramirezes return to their son's bedside to wait the night.

Everyone is physically and emotionally drained.

I make a single declaration, "Time for war."

"We are going to strike back," Nicky says, "But not like you think. We can't afford a war."

"We declared war the day we walked into the deli with the intention of robbing it."

"Maybe so, but we can't afford a shootout with the Banana Brothers. I have a better idea," Nicky announces. "I know where they store their whiskey. We are going to hit their granny's house, as they have about $100,000.00 in stolen liquor."

"So, your idea to make them stop coming after us for their five-hundred grand is to steal another hundred?" I chastise him. "That is so stupid. They are going to put a bullet in your head, in all our heads. We have to strike hard and fast."

"And that is exactly what they are waiting for, which makes it the wrong move," Nicky declares, "We don't have the firepower to take on the Banoa family and they know it. This is a business, so when they realize we are ten times better at it and it costs them more than they can recuperate, they will back down."

We argue it out the rest of the night, but in the end, the rest of the gang agrees with Nicky. Everyone except Maria, she doesn't agree with either of us, but there is no third option. It is either kill them or rob them.

Frank and I wait in the truck a block away from Banoa's grandmother's house. Nicky, dressed in black sweats, waits in the yard behind the bushes. When the guard on duty helps the old lady upstairs for the night, Nicky climbs through the back porch window, moves into the kitchen, and switches the wine bottle. He has followed the guard for days to get an angle on the robbery and knows that after the old lady is in bed, the guard watches Johnny Carson and drinks a glass or two of wine. He waits patiently in the bushes until the guard's head drops.

Nicky climbs through the window again, cautiously approaches the man, lifts his limp arm, and drops it into his lap. He slaps the guard hard across the face and the man hardly utters a sound. Nicky takes a walky-talky out of his pocket, "Bring the truck."

Frank backs the truck up the driveway. I hop out the back. Nicky is at the basement door, "this place is loaded."

We wheel out one hand truck after another of liquor cases from the basement and load them into the truck. We hurry, but are not too worried about being caught, as the neighbors are used to midnight deliveries. And in this neighborhood, no one calls the cops to Banoa's mother's house. We clean out the basement in less than thirty minutes.

Before he leaves the house, Nicky switches the wine bottle again, rinses the glass, halfway fills it with regular wine, places it on the table besides the guard, and slaps him hard again. "That's for Sweet Jesus."

"If you really want to get payback," I say, "Shoot him in the head."

"A good thief doesn't leave any evidence," he tells us.

CHAPTER 5
Night Of The Raven

Frank drives the truck to Poe Park, where we meet two Irish guys.

"What's with the truck, Morris?" asks the tall redhead.

"A present for you and your gang," I inform him.

"Wouldn't be a shit-load of liquor that went missing from Banoa's house the other night?"

"I don't know anything about any liquor," I confess, "But I hear the truck is worth a little something. It's yours."

"You know we are not joining your war," Patrick tells me.

"Take the truck and it's your war too," I say.

"What do you want us to do with it?" Patrick's brother asks.

"Sell it. I hear the Banoas are in need." I toss him the keys and walk away. We get across the park and meet up with Nicky. He is waiting in Frank's GTO.

"When can we expect payment?" he asks.

"I didn't charge them," I tell him.

"What? You gave them $100,000.00 in booze for free." He is about to have a stroke.

"Not for free," I say, "We need an army. We are buying one."

"They didn't seem like they are willing to join us," Frank comments.

"Once the Banana Brothers find out that Patrick and his boys have their liquor they will be with us. Like it or not."

Patrick takes the wheel and drives off. Shaun is visibly upset with his big brother. Finally, Patrick asks, "What's your problem?"

"You are joining up with Bulletproof Johnson and Nicky Nails. Those two crooks are crazy buggers."

"Morris isn't the type that asks you to join anything," he tells his brother, "He offers you the opportunity to stay alive."

"For how long?" Shaun questions.

The soft low wailing of a baby invades Sophia dream and her eyes focus on the red LED display on the nightstand. The clock boldly announces 3:00 a.m. Sophia tries to ignore it. "The witching hour," she hears her thoughts proclaim. Again, whimpering fills the darkness. It snaps her to attention. "Must be an alley cat," she tries to convince herself. She turns over in the empty bed, determined to go back to sleep, but as she does so she catches a glimpse of Maria standing in the living room. Iridescent in the moonlight, statue-like, she's staring into blackness.

Sophia approaches her daughter cautiously, fearing it's bad luck to awaken a sleepwalker. "Maria, are you all right? Can you hear me, baby?"

"He's crying Mommy, but I don't know where he is." Her words come from far away.

"Who's crying?"

"My baby is crying and there is so much blood. Why is there so much blood?" Maria is standing knee deep in blood. It is warm, thick and dark, flowing around her legs, and it is rising.

"Wake up, Maria," Sophia whispers softly in her ear. "Wake up, honey, you are dreaming." She brushes the hair away from her daughter's face, whose eyes are dark, emotionless, and lifeless. She hugs her daughter tightly and strokes her hair again, "It's OK now. You can wake up. Everything is OK."

"I am awake," Maria states. "I thought I was the only one who could hear him, but you hear him too. Then, why can't I see him? Where is he, Mommy?"

"Shhh," Sophia leads Maria back to her own large bed. "Come lie with me. It's just a dream, everything will be all right." She lays her daughter down gently and pulls the covers over both of them. Even in darkness, she can see Maria's eyes are open wide and that she is barely drawing breath. Sophia spends the rest of the night watching over her baby.

I get to the stash house early in the morning, the girls are there of course, Nicky and Dino too. "I guess we are just waiting on Frank to head to the hospital?"

"Go ahead. Tell him," commands Betty.

"No, it was just a silly dream," Maria protests.

"You can tell me," I comfort her.

"It wasn't a silly dream," Betty retorts, "I had the same dream. Well, almost the same dream."

"It was nothing. I don't remember much," Maria tells me. "I was standing in a river... a river of blood and it was rising. That's it, I don't remember much else."

"Maria," accuses Betty.

"That's it! Oh yeah, it was pitch black, and I couldn't see a thing, or move either."

"That is not it!" Betty is frantic. "I had the same dream, standing in absolute darkness in a river of blood. Only, I know it wasn't a dream, I was awake, but I couldn't move."

"It's OK," I reassure them. I give Maria a tight hug then place both my hands on her shoulders and look her straight in the eyes, "You are upset about what happened to Sweet Jesus. We all are, but we will get through it together. Everything is going to be fine."

"It wasn't a dream, I tell you. It was a premonition," warns Betty.

"Here we go," Nicky throws up his hands. "The Voodoo Queen and the Good Witch of the East are at it again."

You need to take heed," Maria jumps on Nicky's case.

"OK, let's not turn on each other, it is not going to help," I can see things are about to get ugly. "From now on nobody travels alone. And everybody carries; we will give you girls .22's."

"A lot of good that will do," Bonnie says, "we don't know how to shoot."

"It's not that hard," Nicky tells her, "Just point and pull the trigger. You don't have to be a marksman; the guy will probably be a foot in front of you."

"We will head downtown later," I tell them, "There is a place where we can get some target practice in. It's down by the East River; we'll go shoot river rats. I practice there all the time, it will be fun."

"Not for the rats," Maria says.

Frank shows up an hour later and we head out for the hospital.

I grab Nicky's arm and hold him back a second. "I don't like this whole river of blood thing," I confess. "We need to send the girls someplace safe."

"I knew she would get to you. That this whole voodoo, witchy, spirit crap would mess up your head. And I warned you not to mess with her, that she would put a spell on you. One look and you got all hot in the crotch. Now look at you, you've gone soft on me." Nicky starts laughing, "I'm messing with you. We will get them out of town; send them to Atlantic City or something."

"Atlantic City! Yeah, that's a great choice, no mobsters down there."

"They will be safer there than toting .22s."

I tell Nicky I have no intention of giving the girls guns, I was merely trying to calm them. It's going to be up to the three of us; him, Frank, and me to guard them. I ask him straight up if he ever killed anyone.

His reply is that it is bad for business; he did shoot someone in the knee once. According to him, it is better to limp a little when making payments than not being able to pay at all.

He asks me the same question, if before the four men in the Deli Man's car, I had been a real killer. I answer yes, and like him, I don't take it lightly either. I tell him when you kill someone you carry that soul around with you and in return you give up a little of yours. But when necessary, I will not hesitate.

Before we get into the cars, Betty and Bonnie grab Maria by the arm and pull her aside. "Why didn't you tell him?" Betty demands.

"I did tell him," Maria snaps back.

"Not about the baby crying," replies Bonnie, "You left that little detail out."

"It was just a dream. It doesn't mean anything," Maria tries to convince her friends. "And I don't want to put any ideas in his head. Let's just wait and see. Please."

"You know this is more than just a dream and you shouldn't play around with something like this," cautions Betty.

When we get to the hospital, there is good news. Sweet Jesus is awake and talking. Not to the police though, he tells them he can't remember that day at all, as if the day never happened.

Nicky asks him if he had a banana or two for breakfast that day.

He replies, "I had a whole bunch."

"Know what would be nice?" Nicky says, "If we take a little vacation in Atlantic City. My uncle, or cousin, has a huge summer rental on the beach. Frank, Dino, and the girls can go down and get the place in order, as I don't think anybody's been there in two years. Me and MoJo will wrap thing up here and join youse guys. And when Sweet Jesus here gets out, he can recuperate on the beach."

The girls get all excited about going away for the summer to Atlantic City. They start planning on how much fun it will be to pass days at the beach and nights in the casinos. Then they start working on cover stories to tell their parents, knowing they can't leave without a good reason, and spending the summer in a house with their boyfriends is definitely not a good reason.

"We will tell them we are going down there to set up for my wedding," Bonnie says brightly, "Just us girls. Your mother will never object to that, Maria. And I'm sure we can convince your mother too, Betty."

"My mother, sure," Betty nods, "My Dad, I'm not so sure."

"Don't worry, we just have to get it past your mother, and she'll convince your dad. I'll tell her we are having the wedding at my aunt's house on the beach. She insisted that we come down there."

"But... what about the Fourth of July next week?" Maria sighs. "We are going to miss all the fireworks."

"Not on your life," I tell her, "We will bring the fireworks down there. Set them off on the beach. I am working on another rocket, even better than last year's."

"It is probably better that we set it off on the beach," Nicky nudges me. "Last year, you blew up Mr. Paterson's Buick."

"Huh, a slight miscalculation in thrust caused the stabilizer to break off at liftoff, making the rocket fly horizontally," I laugh, "good thing Mr. Paterson lives two blocks away, so I didn't have to explain it was my rocket that smashed through his windshield and exploded. But all in all, it was one of the best displays of the night."

That night, Maria's dreams are wild and chaotic and keep pulling her back to the river of blood. She is drowning in it, a sharp burning pain in her gut, and an unearthly scream throws her out of bed. She lies on the floor, afraid to move, afraid the demons in the dark will find her and drag her back into the nightmares. The thick salty taste of blood in her mouth makes her spit repeatedly and uncontrollably on the floor. Slowly, she draws her knees to her stomach and clasps her hands together.

She kneels on the floor with her forehead pressed hard onto her hands and begins to pray, "Hail Mary, full of grace. Our Lord is with thee. Blessed art thou among women, and blessed is the fruit of thy womb, Jesus. Holy Mary, Mother of God, pray for us sinners, now and at the hour of our death." She repeats it again a little louder. And again, louder still. Over and over, louder each time, tears burning her eyes. Then brilliant white light tear away the darkness. She is burning up with fever, her nightgown soaked with sweat, and her face as red as a beet.

Sophia grabs her up in her arms.

"They won't answer me, Mother. The spirits won't come. I'm afraid. They will take my baby. I am going to die."

"No, no, it is just bad dreams. You will be OK. God will protect you. The spirits will intervene for you."

Dino arrives at my house just before seven. I hear my mother getting ready to leave for work and tell him to go ahead and wake me. He doesn't need to; I haven't been to sleep yet. I stared at the ceiling all night thinking about Maria and her dream. She doesn't know about the river of blood, none of them do.

When Dino gets to my door, he is surprised to see me dressed and ready to go. We walk quickly and in silence. Bonnie and Betty had sent him, but they didn't tell him why. They didn't have to either, I know it's Maria, and she is freaking out.

When I get to the house, it is quiet, like a funeral is in progress. Maria won't come down and the girls won't let me go up. The rest of the guys get there later that morning. None of us can get the girls to come out. Eventually, Bonnie comes downstairs and asks us to wait a few minutes, then disappears for hours. I hear Maria tell them to send us away, that she is OK now. But her voice is not her own, it sounds like she is in a trance.

"You think they are tripping?" Nicky asks us honestly.

"You know they don't do drugs unless they are with us," I answer, "Especially not Maria. She barely does any when she's with me. No, they are spooked."

It is midnight when they enter the living room. Maria's eyes are red, as are the others', they have all been crying.

I take her in my arms and brush back her hair. It's wet like she just got out the shower, but I know that is not the case. We stand there looking into each other's eyes, feeling our thoughts, joining our souls. No words need to be spoken, I know what needs to be done. I take her by the hand and lead her into the garden. The others follow. We stand in front of the fountain; the three aged angels are supposed to be pouring water onto the earth. The fountain is faded, run down, hasn't worked in decades. We stand before the angels in the moonlight.

"Maria, before the ever-present Lord, and our friends, I promise to love you, honor, protect you, and cherish you as my wife now and forever."

"Morris Johnson, I am proud to take you as my husband. I swear to God, and to all, my love for you will never end. I am proud and honored to be your wife. And I will make you happy."

"Mazel Tov," Nicky adds sarcastically, "So, who is going to tell whose parent first? Because this I got to see."

"We probably don't have to tell my mother," Maria says, "She already knows."

"I think it's time for our mothers to meet," I tell her and rub her belly.

"Oh," Nicky blurts out.

Nicky arrives at the shed just as I finish resetting the trap on my stash. He sees the rocket in the corner and takes a look. It is only the shell, no nose cone or rocket engines yet, just a two- foot tall cylinder with fins. He remarks on how light it is, and I tell him that all rocket bodies are, that it's the payload and engines that add the weight. I lock up the shed and we start towards the train station, we are heading downtown to buy a wedding ring.

Nicky wants to know if I told my mother. I have not. I tell him that I'll break the news in church this Sunday; she will also get to meet Sophia, and not be able to kill me. At least not at that moment, she won't.

"Do you really think your mom won't freak out?" Nicky asks. "She is going to freak out," I admit, "But it will be a quiet freak out. She'll be all right in the long run, she likes Maria. It's me she's gonna want to kill."

"So, this whole river of blood thing," Nicky ponders, "It's just about her missing her period and being knocked up?"

"No. That's another matter altogether," I inform him. "We still have to get the girls out of town. Are we going to be able to use your cousin's place?"

"Oh yeah," he laughs, "But we are going to have to get our own key."

"What the hell does that mean?"

"Well, it's like this." Nicky tells me the story of his Cousin Peter and his gambling ring. His cousin had a Jersey State Trooper on the hook for a couple of thousand. Nothing really big, just as an insurance policy, a get out of jail free card he could trade in when needed.

"Let me guess," I venture, "The cop got tired of losing and rolled over on him."

"Oh no," Nicky objects, "Him and the trooper went way back, friends since high school. Besides, he would let him win a little, lose a little, kept him on the line, fished him real good. His wife, on the other hand, was not in on the arrangement. She found out about the gambling debt and went ballistic. She turned the whole bunch in. So, her husband and Cousin Pete were sent to the can. The good news is that we've got the place for two to five years, no worries."

We cross into Manhattan on the number five train on our way to the diamond district. We sit across from each other, and Nicky is trying to convince me to save my money and go on a heist. I'm laughing at such a crazy idea; this guy really hates to buy anything.

"I do have to get her something really nice. You know my girl knows her jewelry. So we are going to see my friend in the district."

"How do you know what he sells you ain't stolen?"

"As long as I ain't stealing it, it's clean."

"I'm just saying. I know a guy in the diamond district. We go in, bam, bam, bam," he snaps his finger with each bam, "We walk out with a nice piece and you have money for a honeymoon. A month or two in the islands, Jamaica for example, you and Maria kicking back on the beach, smoking Ganja."

"She's pregnant," I remind him, "And I'm not putting a hot rock on my wife's finger. And is it really a honeymoon if you have to leave town?"

"What? It's an insurance deal. We break a couple of cases; take some odds and ends, he gives you a nice wedding gift for your troubles."

"Nails, you're just itching for action," I tell him, "And I got some for you. Are you ready to pop your cherry?"

The subway cars are mostly empty in the middle of the afternoon and ours emptied out at 125th Street. I notice four Puerto Ricans eyeing us from the forward car; two of them jump off and run to the car behind us at 86th Street. I don't know if Nicky caught it, but I think it's safe to bet they are going to try mug us. I tell Nicky to get ready, I will take the two on my left and he gets the two on his left. For some reason, no one expects you to make a move to your left, but it does make perfect sense, you can pull your gun without interference. Like clockwork, the four approach us from each end of the car.

"Hey, don't I know you, white boy?"

Nicky doesn't answer.

"I know you don't want to know us," I say to the first guy on my left.

"Hey, Miguel, we got a couple of bad ass defondados. Give us what you got."

In an instant I shove my pistol in his waistband and push him into his friend, pinning them against the door. Nicky spins from his seat and pulls a move tripping one of the other would- be robbers into his seat with his gun in the guy's mouth. He motions for his friend to take a seat. The thing about getting the drop on someone, especially when there are more of them than there are of you, is to place your gun where they can't get out of the way and where they really don't want to get shot. And nobody wants to get their head blown off, whether it's the big one or the little one.

"So, you are trying to rob us, miracon. What do you think, they look like stick up boys to you, Ricky?"

"No. No. This is no robbery. He just looked like the guy that was messing with my sister last night," the guy who is about to become dickless explains.

"I don't believe that," Nicky says, pushing the gun upward in the guy's mouth and tilting his head uncomfortably against the wall. "Look at him. If he had a sister, she'd be as ugly as sin; she would have to pay guys to fuck her. These puñetas are muggers."

"No. No. It was a mistake. You are not the guys we thought you were."

Then, the train rounded the curve coming into the station, producing a long loud screech.

"Now," I yell. I don't know if Nicky can hear me, but he would hear the gunshot. I fire down the guy's pants and step back to take aim at his partner's face. Nicky's gun goes off in the first guy's mouth, throwing his head back against the window and clearing the gun from his smoking mouth. My second shot slams the guy's head onto the glass in the door and it spider-webs with a big red spot as he drops to the floor. Nicky swings his gun to the left and nails the guy between the eyes. I place a second shot in the back of Dickless' head.

The train pulls into the station and we return the guns into our jacket pockets, but keep our fingers on the triggers and move quickly from car to car towards the back. We don't run, but we do want to be at least three cars back at the station's exit when the doors open. As soon as they do, we hit the turnstiles and bolt up the stairs. We have to go up two levels to reach the street. I do not notice anybody at the front of the platform, so we should get out of the subway without any problems. I hear the train pulling out as we are making our way up the second set of steps. We hit the street and keep walking east.

"Now you are a killer," I congratulate Nicky.

"Nothing to it," he replies, "Just point and pull the trigger."

"Damn, I'm gonna have to ditch this gun. And I was just getting used to it."

"No big deal," he says, "We sell it to the Micks. They are too stupid to ask where it came from, and we got plenty more. I guess we are taking a cab from here."

Joey Banoa and two others walk into the Raven. He looks the place over and sees a pair of old Italians playing cards. He points to the first pool table by the door, "Rack'em up. I'll break." He walks over to the bar, "what do ya got?"

Benny looks him over hard, studying his face. "I know you! You're Banoa's boy, Joey Jr. Your old man and I go way back. I can tell you some stories..."

"Besides the memories, what do you have to drink?" Joey asks slowly and deliberately.

"I got vodka, rum, and gin. Straight up, soda, or juice?" "Three gins on the rocks," he orders, "and it better not be no cheap shit."

Benny lines up three small plastic cups on the bar, drops a pair of ice cubes in each, and holds up a bottle of Tanqueray, "Your father and I used to put this stuff away by the gallon. How is he these days?"

"Not so talkative," Joey grabs the drinks and turns away.

"Nine dollars, please."

"Start a tab," Joey says without looking back, "I might be here a while."

As I turn the corner, I see Nicky standing by the same tree where Mike the Butcher was waiting for me weeks ago. I give him a what's up sign and he tells me that Batman and Robin are down the block, staking out the Raven. Nicky has been here for the half-hour I ran home, but they haven't yet made a move. It troubles him because they know it's his father's place, so they can't be planning to raid it.

"Are you strapped?" He asks.

"Not the same piece from earlier," I answer, "But I have a snub nose .38."

"Yeah, me too. I switched out my other hardware for a nine," he says.

We consider slipping in the alley and ditching the guns, but decide to wait it out.

"Tell me, why did you buy an engagement ring and a wedding ring? You already said your I Do's."

"Because they come as a set, you dope," I am a little upset he would ask that. "You don't break up a set. And you can't expect me not to give her an engagement ring. That's just wrong."

"When are you going to give them to her?"

"Tonight," I tell him and motion with my hand towards the Raven. "I'm sure she told her mother by now, so she might as well start wearing them."

We light up a couple of cigarettes and wait for the cops to leave, which apparently is not going to be anytime soon, as we are on our third cigarette when we see Dino, Betty, Frank, and Maria arrive. We expect to see Batman and Robin roll up to the club, instead, they simply continue watching, but what they are watching has us confused. Nicky says they may be waiting for us. We agree to give it another five minutes, then, we will ditch the guns and go see what they want.

"Well, look who it is," announces Joey, "My old friend, Maria, the Slut."

"Hey, Junior, your dad wouldn't want you to be starting any trouble in here," warns Benny.

"Yeah, well, there are a lot of things my daddy wouldn't do that I would," he says and notices Benny shifting nervously behind the bar. He moves behind Maria and grabs her arm. Frank steps forward and Joey pulls out his gun. "Lock the door!"

One of the two boys who were shooting pool quickly goes to flip the dead bolt.

Joey looks at the pair and sighs, "This would be the time to pull out those guns, boys." He motions everybody to the back of the club.

The two card playing old men don't move.

Maria pulls away from him, "What is your fucking problem?"

"Oh, talking about fucking, I thought about what you said last time. I was going to bring my dog, Rex, but even he wouldn't do some nigger's cunt."

His friends start laughing.

Frank gently moves Dino aside, while also slowly slipping his hand behind his back to be ready to draw. He is just waiting for Maria to give him a clear shot.

"If you are so desperate for some pussy, Pizza Face," she moves her face to within inches of his. "Why don't you do like everybody else, and go fuck your mother!"

Everyone in the club breaks out into peals of laughter, including the two old men playing cards. She laughs the hardest. Then, there is a roar of thunder and Maria stumbles back, away from Joey.

"Shoot them," he yells.

The crackling of gunfire fills the room.

Frank pulls his gun, but is instantly driven back by flying bullets.

In seconds, the place is quiet. One of the boys reloads, lifts one of the old men's heads off the card table, and lets it drop back down again.

Benny is inching his way towards Frank's gun when the boy fires one shot, into the back of his head. Without delay, he turns his attention to the other three on the floor and fires a shot into Dino's and then Frank's forehead. He grabs the third member of the gang, "You want to do the black bitch?"

But the third boy is in shock, unable to answer, unable to move. The second boy fires into Betty's temple then tucks the gun into his belt and pulls a ski mask out of his jacket pocket. He slaps his partner on the shoulder, "put on your mask." As he opens the door and starts to leave, he hears a faint moan. He looks over at Joey and then at Maria lying on the floor. She is breathing heavily, pumping out blood from her stomach. "What are you doing man? Finish her and let's get out of here."

Joey stands over Maria with his gun pointed at her face, staring into the blue eyes that are starting to grow dark. His hands shake violently as he tries to aim, "This is all your fault."

"Vaffanculo!"

Nicky and I hear the faint pops of fireworks going off somewhere in the night.

We are about to ditch the guns when light from the Raven's open door draws our attention. Two bright flashes and bangs jolt us into action. Nicky runs down the sidewalk and I take to the street. Two black-headed figures run from the Raven then Joey walks out and holds his middle finger high over his head. A car pulls up and the three hop in. I am running as fast as I can but not getting any closer while firing shots at the trio. I can see muzzle flashes from Nicky's gun. The Ford Fury screams out ahead of us and races down the street, but it is not chasing Banoa's car, it turns at the corner and speeds off into the night.

I rip the door open, nearly taking it off its hinges and my eyes immediately find Maria lying in a pool of blood. Her white dress has three large red circles, two spreading across her chest and one from her stomach. I fall to my knees and gently lift her head onto my lap. She is barely breathing; her eyes fight to focus on my face. I brush back her hair then reach into my pocket and pull out the little box. I open it, she smiles, and I slip the rings onto her finger as darkness overtakes her. I am pulled down and kiss her, but I too continue to fall into the shadows.

CHAPTER 6
Blood For Blood

Lieutenant Mancotti gets on the radio and calls in, "Dispatch, this is car Zero-Three-Two-Two, Detective Mancotti with a possible DUI. Run this plate for priors, X-ray Echo Charlie Four Five Six."

The dispatcher replies, "Detective, why are you doing a traffic stop? Do you want a patrol car to back you up?"

He gives the dispatcher an angry retort, "My partner and I have a quarter of a century combined behind our badges, what the fuck is some rookie blue-balls going to do that we haven't done a thousand times over? This asshole just turned east on Pelham Parkway and swerved across two lanes ahead of us. I'm going to light him up and see what his problem is. Can I please get that plate information, if that is OK with you?" Before he releases the mike button, Mancotti flips on the lights and siren, and head towards Banoa's house.

The dispatcher radios back after a couple of minutes, "The car is registered to a Joseph A. Banoa. No priors or outstanding warrants."

"Thank you, dispatch," Mancotti replies in a calm, almost apologetic tone, "The asshole dropped a cigarette in his lap. I issued him a warning. Car Zero-Three-Two-Two out."

The radio hums with a request for all cars in the vicinity of Taylor Avenue to respond to multiple shots fired at the Raven Social Club.

Fitzpatrick and Mancotti take a quick look around for Joey's car before knocking on Joseph Banoa's door. Impatiently, Mancotti bangs on the door a second time. A light comes on in the foyer then on the front porch, Mrs. Banoa opens the door.

"Is your husband in?" Mancotti asks.

"Yes, come in," she says and swings the door wider. The two officers are no strangers to the Banoa's household, but the urgency of their actions fills her with dread. She knows they are there because of her son, but she keeps her fears to herself. They have barely passed the foyer when Joe comes out of the basement.

"We need to talk," Mancotti tells him.

Joe extends an arm towards the basement and the three disappear from his wife's sight.

"We don't have a lot of time; every cop in the precinct is heading to the Raven. Your boy decided to go Al Capone in the place."

"Are you sure?" Joe doesn't want to believe what he's hearing.

"He and his friends looked like they were up to something, so we tagged along," Mancotti explains, "just to make sure if they got in too deep we were there to pull them out, but we had no idea... We were sitting outside the club when the shooting occurred, so we still have no idea what damage they caused. I called in a phantom traffic stop to give that little stunod an alibi."

Big Phil stands up and makes his presence known.

Joe motions for him to sit back down at the bar. "Well, then he is in the clear."

"Maybe with the force, but he walked out of the club unmasked and flipped Nicky Rocci and Morris Johnson the bird."

"Did they see him?"

"Damn right they saw me," boasts Joey as he walks through the basement door.

Michael follows his brother in but lingers around the door. Joey strolls over to the bar and pours himself a drink.

His father can tell he already had a couple.

"It was great! We dropped four of Nicky's friends and a couple of old guys too."

"What the fuck? Did you take your brother with you?" Joe is hot. His fist clenches and his eyes roll about the room. He marches over to his son and slaps the glass from his hand then takes the bottle of scotch and smashes it at his feet. "What the hell are you thinking? I told you to leave this alone. That it is my business, and I would take care of it."

"I was thinking it was about time someone in this family shows some balls and sends Nicky and his nigger a message they understand."

"Oh, you wanted to send a message," Joe leaps halfway across the bar and comes back with a pistol. He digs it into his son's temple, "this is how you send someone a message. You put two in their heads, not their friends'. Did you take your brother with you?"

Big Phil has one hand on Joe's shoulder, the right one; ready to spin him away if he pulls the trigger, while the two detectives are trying to find a spot that won't put them in the line of fire.

"Of course not," Joey answers. He is not afraid or is simply too hopped up to know how serious his father is. "Michael is not ready for the real action. But don't worry about Nicky and his friend—"

"You should be worried about his friend," Mancotti interrupts, "He went up against five of your guys a couple of weeks ago, two of them professional killers. They're dead now, and he's wearing the pro's ring as a souvenir."

"We did some digging into Morris Johnson's past after that night," Fitzpatrick informs them. "His brother was killed by a rival gang some years ago. He didn't take it well, and the gang was completely wiped out in one bloody battle after another."

"I don't know what you think you did tonight," Mancotti tells Joey Banoa, "but what you did do was throw open the Gates of Hell and invite the Devil to fuck you in the ass! And I am sure he's going to take you up on it."

"Who went with him?" Joe asks the two cops. The gun is now resting on the bar.

"That I don't know," Mancotti answers quickly. "They were already in the car when I saw Joey. But at least they were smart enough to wear masks when they left the club. We have got to go; my captain is going to want to know where we were when all hell broke loose."

The two cops leave through the basement's back door and Mancotti tells his partner that he has no intention of sending the two other boys to their graves. If Joe Banoa wants their names, he is going to have to get them from his son.

Michael slips out a moment later. He has seen his father like this before and knows Joey's crew needs to be warned, or they are all toast.

Joe grabs his son by the face and holds him in a vicelike grip. "You know, back in the old days when the prince did something wrong, not even the king could beat him. Because he was royalty, the prince had a whipping boy who took his beating for him. It seems we have a similar problem here. I could never beat the information out of you, but I still need to know who was in on this job with you. So, Big Phil, he's all yours." Joe leaves the basement.

"Good thing you're drunk," Phil whispers in Joey's ear then picks the lanky teenager by the collar and slams him to the floor. He continues kicking him in the stomach, sides, and back. It takes a huge effort for Big Phil to get down on his knees. Dragging Joey up by the shirt collar again, he punches him in the face and knocks him out.

Nicky looks around the Raven, the pools of blood swirling around his friends' heads make him give up hope. Seeing

Frank's gun, he picks it up and sniffs the barrel. 'Damn,' he thinks, 'didn't even get off a shot.' He turns to his friend holding his girlfriend to his chest.

The sounds of police sirens are getting closer.

"MoJo, give me your gun." After receiving no acknowledgement, he reaches down and takes the gun from my side.

Nicky walks out just before the first cop car came to a screeching halt in front of the Raven. A crowd is gathering out front and Nicky blends in as the police charge in. He crosses the street to the deli, where Salvatore is watching the action from a safe distance.

"Here," he pulls the guns from under his shirt, "We need to bury these."

"What went on over there?" asks Salvatore as he sticks the guns in his pockets.

"Joey Banana killed my friends, Benny, and some other guys."

More police arrive and pour into the club. They try to separate Maria from me, but I won't let them. A paramedic asks to let him try save her, but I tell him it's too late. He places a hand to her neck and I slap it away.

"Please Sir, let me try revive her. I can bring her back even if it has been a couple of minutes."

I lay Maria down and let the paramedic put an air bag over her face and start pumping, while another cuts her dress down the front and places two large paddles on her chest. I hear a third man pronounce my friends N.S.L. (No Sign of Life). It's not long before the two working on Maria do the same with her.

Everything is disjointed. Time, sounds, and sights are all happening around me, but I am not part of anything. The cops are asking me continuous questions, like where was I when the shooting started, did I see the shooters, how many, why would anyone do this?

I respond to each the same, "I don't know."

More cops enter, they take pictures, and ask more questions, but finally, they cover Maria with a white plastic sheet. It is early in the morning when they begin to move her and my friends to the awaiting coroner's vehicles.

Our families are huddled together; Betty's father is pushing reporters away. I hear the loud miserable wailing of my friends' mothers, and notice how Sophia's lament is cut short as she faints and falls into my mother's arms when Maria's petite body is wheeled out. The cops are trying to hustle me into a squad car, but I pull away and head for my mother. That's when I see Batman and Robin and make a break for them.

Nicky catches me in the middle of the street. "Not now, not here. Our families don't know what happened," he says, "And we don't need to tell them this way."

Mr. Bonaparte, Betty's dad, asks me, "Why you not tell the cops what you know?"

"They already know," I tell him.

Batman and Robin are being grilled by their captain. "What the fuck did I tell you? I said I didn't want a mob war in my precinct."

"So, this is a mob hit?" Queries a nearby reporter. "Were the kids the target, or was it the other men in the club?"

"You want a trip to the morgue too?" asks the captain. "Don't print that, this looks like a robbery that went bad. That is the official statement. That is what you better print."

A uniformed cop grabs the reporter by the arm and takes him away.

The captain returns his attention to the two detectives. "This ends tonight. I don't care what you do, but you'd better bring someone in on charges. The

Commissioner and the Mayor are on my ass, have been ripping me a new one for hours. And now, they are talking about bringing in the Feds. I'll be damned if I take orders from the FBI in my own house. Now, get out of my sight, I don't want to see you two unless you have a perp in cuffs."

Michael arrives at the pizza shop, fifteen of Joey's crew are gathered in the back booths.

Nine guys and five girls are listening intently to Chris Caralucci telling them about the hit that just went down at the Raven. "They were all laid out on the floor, twisting and moaning in pain," he says with glee, "then, I topped them off. One in each of their heads, I'm telling you, after tonight, I'm a made man."

"On the contrary, you're a dead man," Michael tells him from a couple of feet away. Two of the girls slide over to make room for him in their booth. He declines.

"Joey said if we went with him to settle the score your father would surely give us our bones," Chris counters. "We did our part, at least I did. I don't think this little effe shot anybody tonight."

"Yeah, well, so maybe my father won't have him iced, but I wouldn't count on it. Right now he is kicking the shit out of Joey to give up your names."

All are taken aback, and Teresa adds quickly that she hopes he's all right. The other girls nod in agreement.

"You're kidding me, right? He'll be lucky if my father only beats him half to death. Youse guys, this is no joke and I don't think he will stop halfway. You need to get out of town, now. And don't come back unless I let you know it's safe. Understand?"

The two boys nod and take off.

Michael warns the rest to tell no one that he tipped them off then says he needs to get back home before his father realizes he is gone. He leaves the pizza shop gang wondering how bad off Joey is and if they will see each other again. Slowly, all get up and decide to go home. They start dispersing. It is no longer safe to be seen together.

Sophia stirs from a fitful sleep at 3 a.m., drawn to Maria's bedroom, but stops just outside the door when she sees Morris sitting on the floor in the moonlight, except there is no moon in the window. She goes limp, slumps down, and feels a warm breeze lift her hair and her spirit. Sophia laughs and cries.

She wakes again at daybreak, and realizes that she is still at her daughter's door, as is Morris on the floor. She approaches quietly, kneels behind him and wraps her arms around his neck. He is stiff and cold. She leaves him alone.

He spends the next two days in the room in a trance.

All funeral days start the same, not in a great mood, and so it is with the one for the four teenage victims of the Raven's shooting. The friends will be buried together, thanks to an anonymous donor. Reporters camp out at the local church waiting for the spectacle to begin. Even for New York, the shooting is big news, especially since the Daily News headline the morning after proclaimed, 'Mob Mows Down Four Teens In The Bronx.'

Dressed in a plain black dress, veiled hat, and court shoes, Sophia rings Alice Johnson's bell early in the morning. "May I come in?" She asks when the door opens.

"Of course," Alice takes a quick look around. Cops, reporters, and unknown others have been lurking around since the shooting. "I am so sorry for your loss. Maria is like a daughter to me and I still can't believe..." Neither can she finish her statement.

"She loves you too. Is so in love with your son, and that's why I am here," she says from behind the security of dark glasses. They sit on the sofa, hands clinched for mutual strength. "Morris has been at my house with Maria for the past three days. I'm afraid what is going to happen to him when she is gone."

"She is a great girl, like an antidote lifted him out right of the darkness after his brother's death," Alice informs her, "Now, he will return to that darkness. Only, it will be so much worse this time. I can't begin to imagine what he will do to those responsible."

"Yes, I can feel the evil pulling at his soul, and I wish there was something I could do, some way to save him, because he is a good boy. I have something else to tell you." Sophia is not sure how to break the news, "the kids got married. Well, she was going to have his baby and they made their vows before God and their friends. They were going to tell you, before... Morris is..." Sophia can't continue.

My mother and Sophia are sitting in the living room in their black dresses when I walk in; I can see they have been crying, but who hasn't. My mother calls to me, but I rush upstairs, as I am still wearing the same bloody clothes from the shooting and do not want them to see me, they might break down all over again. She tells me Sophia wants us to ride with her to the church. I agree from halfway up the stairs.

I spent the last seventy-two hours with Maria, but now, I feel her slipping away. And right here in my room, she is even more of a memory. Her scent is evaporating, her laughter floating, her voice a whisper, I am fighting to hold on, straining my eyes to see her fading from my bed.

"It's OK, this will be. Our child will find her way to you. Peace now."

But there is anything but peace in me. I scream but nothing comes out. I am ice cold and yet, I sweat rivers. My eyes burn like the desert sun and the wind-driven sand strips away my flesh in fiery agony. My life is gone. All that I was is no more. All I am is what they left me with, death.

The limo ride to the church is short. Everything is close by, so it is only a few blocks away. Both my mothers sit back, facing forward, and facing me. I can feel their eyes penetrating my soul from behind those dark glasses. I feel their sorrow, which they are trying to fill me up with. To replace the emptiness that sits before them, but I resist. I want to shut my eyes behind my black glasses, but they will not obey. They have not closed in days and they are not going to now.

The scene outside is crazy. Cops are pushing reporters and gawkers away from the car. I hear them yelling to get back behind the barricades. Other men, feds no doubt, are taking pictures of every vehicle lining the street and every person entering the church. I get out the car and hold out my hand, my mother takes it first, and then I help Sophia.

She gets weak knees for a moment when someone says, "That's Maria's mother with Bulletproof Johnson." But she quickly recovers her step as I squeeze her hand, passing my strength and power to her.

Two obvious Italians greet them at the door and escort them inside. I walk around to the side of the church and down the path that leads to the little graveyard in the back. "Nails, Sweet Jesus," I greet my two friends. "You look like a pirate." Sweet Jesus has a black patch over his left eye and leans heavily on a cane and Nicky for support.

"Told you," Nicky confirms. "You owe me five dollars. Nothing like a funeral to bring out the Guidos. The only thing they like more than a wedding is a good funeral."

"Are these your father's men?"

"No, they're from the whole Mafia family," Nicky spreads out his hands in a sweeping wide arc. "Except one," he adds in an acid tone. "Most of them are here for show, you know, trying to pretend they know someone. Or hoping to be noticed by somebody with real clout. The real guys, the made men, they'll be at the graveside."

I feel someone patting my afro and quickly turn, reaching for the hand. It's Bonnie, she had signalled to the other two not to tell me she was here.

"Sorry," she laughs, "Maria told me to do that. She always said your fro was like a black cotton ball. I couldn't resist."

She throws her arms around me and hugs me tight. I hug her back. She feels changed, thinner, gaunt in fact; this week has been hell on her. She hugs Nicky and then gently squeezes Sweet Jesus. "I saw your mom and Mrs. Marino come in, and we are almost ready to start. Nicky, do you know what you are going to say?"

"I'll come up with something," he answers, "You know me, I'm eloquent."

"You are going to give the eulogy?" I shake my head sadly.

"Yes, but first, a little something to take the edge off," Nicky offers a flask from his suit pocket.

"A drink, now," I protest.

"Not just a drink," he informs us, "A bit of wine with a tiny microdot. A little acid to help us send our friends off right."

"Oh, what the hell," Bonnie says and takes a gulp. We follow her lead.

"When are they arriving?" I ask her, as she seems to be in charge.

"They got here early this morning," she tells me. "I've been here all night, setting things up with the priest and nuns."

We all take another round, and then go inside.

The caskets are aligned white, black, white, black in front of the altar. White for the girls and black for the guys and although the lids are closed, you know who is in each by their size. Maria's mother, my mother, me, Bonnie, and her parents, are in the front row on the right side. The Bonapartes and Salakises are on the left. Nicky slides into the row behind us with his parents, and brother Sal. The rest of the church is filled with friends from their schools, and other family members, and of course the news people up in the balcony. The choir begins to sing and I start to zone out, wishing the acid would kick in already.

My brother Charlie is lying on the metal table. His clothes hang in the garment bag, his shoes beneath them. I kiss his forehead and tell him. "Tell Mom I'm sorry I can't be there today, but you know what I got to do." I slip out of the funeral home just before the mortician arrives to dress him then go to the roof of the leader of the 149 Gangsters and watch the sun rise without joy.

The gang gathers on the stoop, bragging about killing my brother. They feel safe, invincible, because they believe all his friends are at his funeral. They are correct, all his friends are at the church, but I'm not his friend. Today, I am his avenger. I have the perfect weapon, a brick, something common in the neighborhood. I have been sitting on the roof since dawn scratching AOD 12:12 into the brick with my dagger and after hours at it, the letters and numbers are deeply etched into the weapon. Something everyone will recognize as vengeance from above. The very thing Jose used to take my brother's life will now be the instrument of justice.

Jose killed him over his girlfriend. He and his gang ambushed Charlie at a gangbang after he learned his girl had gone there to meet with Charlie. During the fight, Jose grabbed a brick and bashed in his head. Four blows to the back of his head ended my brother's life. Now, one blow will end Jose's. The perfect weapon, silent, and it doesn't pick up fingerprints.

Jose stops and rolls a joint in front of the building.

I watch as he takes his last toke then release the brick from my hand and watch it fall straight and soundlessly down five stories. It grazes the left side of his head with a loud crack, like breaking old dry timber. It shatters his shoulder and collarbone too, but he did not feel it, the shards of his broken skull shredded his brain.

His gang splits up, three run up the stairs, four of them dash through the alley to the back fire escape. The way to win a fight when you are outnumbered is advance planning. You need a way in, a plan of action, but most importantly, an exit route. I wait by the roof door for the three coming up the stairs. I hear one guy slip and fall, then his friends.

Someone asks, "What is this stuff on the steps?"

That's my cue. I lock the roof door and run down to the fourth floor. The three guys are wiping the greasy film on the walls and holding onto the banister for support.

"It's napalm, assholes," I yell down to them.

"Napalm, what the hell is that?"

"It's all the rage in Nam. But this is my own concoction, Vaseline and kerosene. Burn in Hell, cocksuckers." I throw a lit bottle of the stuff down and a roar of heat blows past me. I expect to hear screaming but the fire sucked the air right from their bodies. When they inhale the hot gas it sears their throats, making screaming impossible. They twist and roll back down the steps to the landing, winding up in a flaming heap.

I hear the others banging on the roof door. It's solid steel, so no matter how hard they pull and push, they will not get through. I knock on apartment door 4A and an old lady answers.

"Fire. Fire. Fire," I yell. Then I run to her window and down the fire escape at the front of the building. I step over Jose's body sprawled out on the sidewalk and walk away. Four down and a bunch more to go.

Nicky takes the lectern with a big silly grin on his face. The acid has definitely kicked in for him. I wonder how long he was in the graveyard, and how much acid-laced wine he drank before we arrived.

Others are wondering too, whispers echo around the church, "Is he high?"

"Disgraceful."

"This isn't Church Day," blurts out Sal in a voice that silences everyone. "Monday work... Tuesday work... Thursday work... Friday... payday... ice cream... Saturday, we go to the park and ride swings... Sunday, Church Day. Monday, Tuesday, Thursday, Friday, Saturday, we go to the park, not church."

I turn back to face him, "This is a special Saturday. We are going to watch your brother make a fool of himself, then we go to the park."

"Papa says not to call people fools. It is not nice."

"Oh no, I'm not calling Nicky a fool," I correct myself, "I mean he is going to make us laugh." I give Sal a pound and a back of the hand to the back of the hand slap and he settles down. His face is gray. Everyone is gray. The entire world has gone gray, just as if the colors were washed away from my eyes. I'm thinking, 'Please don't let Nicky go too far off the wall.'

"I hear youse guys talking," Nicky begins his eulogy, "Why am I smiling? How can I be happy today? Am I stoned? All good questions, but nothing to do with what is going on here. I have been sitting there thinking about all the good fun, what the hell, crazy times I had with my brothers and sisters. Am I happy? Fuck, yeah..." He is tripping his balls off. Some of the guys in the back laugh. "We had some amazing times and I wouldn't trade them, or forget them. We called Betty our Voodoo Queen, partly for her Creole accent, but mostly because she always knew when we were heading for trouble and then led us the other way. We loved her for it, even though she was a huge pain in the ass. Mr. and Mrs. Bonaparte, she was loved. And Dino loved her more than life itself, he worshipped her."

I can't see Mr. Bonaparte's face across the aisle, but I figure it's twisting and twitching right about now.

Nicky keeps right on talking, "That boy took more bullets than anyone else that night. He had already given her his heart and that night they would have to kill him before they could hurt her. That's true love. That's the love we all had for her, any one of us would be glad to trade places with him. But Mr. and Mrs. Salakis, he definitely would not let us. Dino is perris, a hero, and one I am proud to call my brother."

"Hey, I'm his brother," objects Sal, "When is he going to say something about me."

"Basta!" Nicolas scolds his twenty-four-year-old son. "I told you we don't bring him," he tells his wife angrily, "After this you take him home."

"No. To the park, it's Saturday, we go to swing in the park."

"Yes." His mother reassures him.

"Maria... Maria..." Nicky pauses for a long time. He looks at me; I can feel the rage growing inside him, in all of us. "She was a witch, without a doubt. Every guy that took one look fell insanely in love with her, even me. I couldn't resist her. She drove me crazy, but I was glad to have her around. But she gave her heart to one guy, Morris Johnson. He has what we all wish for, what we would kill and die for, he has her eternal love." Nicky pauses again. A long agonizing time passes by, then the smile slowly returns to his face. "Frank and I go way back. Back to Sister Margret and the third grade final. I wasn't ready for the test, hell, I was never ready for a test. Frank was in the fourth grade. He was in charge of running the mimeograph in the office. He told me not to worry, 'there will be no test tomorrow.' That with the last bottle of ink already in the machine a little slit in the hose would fix that problem. Well, it seems that the ink was fed under pressure and as the pages came out blank, a pool of ink was spreading around Sister Margret's white shoes." He pauses again, the smile gone again as images run amok in his head. "Frank is a true friend, who would do anything for me. And I swear I will do everything it takes to get the guy who did this. This is not over. This is not goodbye. This is I will see you later, my brothers and sisters, and what times we will have again."

Bonnie is crying hysterically. I take her by the arm and lead her out to the graveyard. I hold her even as I fight back images and thoughts of deeds done and those yet to come. Acid was a bad idea.

Nicky and Sweet Jesus come to get us after the service ends. We get into a limo for the ride to the cemetery. I hand each of them a piece of paper with a name and address on it. "After we leave here y'all need to go meet these people," I tell them, "these are hideouts. They will protect you, but don't trust them, trust no one but us four."

"I don't understand," questions Sweet Jesus, "Who are they protecting us from, and why can't we trust them?"

"Nicky and I made Joey as one of the shooters, in fact, the leader. Make no mistake the Banoas are coming after us, and they will come after you to get to us. The people I have set you up with may turn on you if pressured but for a short while it will do. Sweet Jesus, I've got some Colombian connections, so we are moving into the cocaine business. We are going to need a new source of revenue as I am sure the Banoas are going to target Nicky's family businesses."

"You set me up with Colombians. Those guys are crazy cutthroat killers," protests Sweet Jesus.

"Yes they are," I agree, "but they have an army, and before this is done we may need one. Besides, you speak Spanish, you'll know when the throat cutting is about to start. Don't show any weakness. You look like a pirate, act like one also and you will be fine."

"Hey, it's good that you are looking out for these two, but I got a place to lay low," Nicky says. "In fact, me and you are supposed to go to Atlantic City, remember?"

"I wouldn't trust that place," I tell him. "Joe Banoa knows your family pretty well, he may know about your cousin's house too. He doesn't know about my connections in Philly, so you will be safer there. Tell your dad you are going to A.C. and keep on going until you hit Philly. And don't worry about me, I have places to hide out. What about you, Bonnie? Any concerns?"

"No. I guess I can hang out with Patrick O'Shea and his gang, as long as it is not for too long." We are pulling into the cemetery gates when she asks, "Why do we have to go so soon, and what about our families?"

"They will be OK. It's me and Nicky they are after now, doing anything to your families won't help them get to us," I assure her. "Tomorrow is the Fourth of July, I promised Maria fireworks."

We are kept waiting in the car while the gravesite is prepared. A perfect time to light up a joint and smooth out the effects of the acid we took earlier. I notice one of the limos keeps driving up the hill to another funeral gathering. I nudge Nicky and nod my head in that direction. We watch what looks like a payoff being made. He shrugs his shoulders to my silent question. Our limo jerks forward and we watch as the car that passed us makes the long winding trip back to the possession. The other black limo remains on the hill.

Naturally, the feds are buzzing around, snapping pictures of the real made men and their cars. Finally, we are all set up and sitting at the graves. The priest goes into another long dreary sermon and I tune him out. The last thing I want to hear is how God loves us. How great it will be for them in Heaven, how we will all be together again, and as happy as children on Christmas morning. I feel like stabbing him in the eye.

Nicolas Rocci hands his son a card, he opens it, takes a look inside and passes it to me.

"What's this?"

"Take a look," Nicky says, "It's your favorite person at his best."

I look at it. It's Joey, his face is black and blue, swollen and battered. One eye is closed and the other is gashed. His nose is obviously broken and probably the jaw too. I hand the picture back to Nicolas, "Is he still breathing?"

"Yes, of course he is."

"Then this means nothing."

Everyone starts passing by the coffins and placing their flowers on them. Tears follow. My eyes are locked on the black limo on the hill. Everyone has passed, everyone except for me. I struggle to stand, touch the coffins one by one, and I stop at Maria's. I pull my dagger from my inside jacket pocket, take the blade in my right hand, and slowly, deliberately, squeeze tight; tighter and tighter until the blood starts to flow. The blood drips from the tip of the blade onto the coffin. I slap my bloody fist to my chest, and then slap the bloody dagger on her coffin.

"Ah cazzio," yells Nicolas and smacks Nicky on the back of his head. "Go get him, goddamnit!"

Nicky rushes to me and reaches for the knife on the coffin.

"Leave it," commands Sophia. "It is his prized possession. He gives it with his heart, as he gave his heart. I want it buried with her, as Morris wishes."

"Blood for blood," I vow.

Sophia takes my bloody hand and wraps it in her handkerchief. She pulls me close and buries my head in her breast to hide my tears.

CHAPTER 7
Rocket Red Glare

My mother arrives home a few minutes after me from the gravesite and is surprise to see James Harris standing in the living room. She is also shocked to see all the boxes stacked up in the room. James was Charlie's best friend, like a big brother to me, and an Original Sinner, in fact, The Original Sinner.

"My God, James, I haven't seen you in years," exclaims my mom. "Not since you left for Vietnam. How are your mother and father these days?"

"They are good, Mrs. Johnson," he replies politely, "They moved back to South Carolina a few years ago."

"Morris, what is this about? What's with all the boxes? Where are you going?" she asks.

"I'm not going anywhere, Mom," I answer. "I packed some of your things. Actually, I had Jimmy do it while we were at the funeral. You have to pack your own clothes and stuff." I fight back tears, trying to sound in charge so she won't fight me. "You know what's going on, it's not safe anymore."

"We can go to the police..."

"That's not going to help! I've already lost Maria... I won't let anything happen to you." I can't help myself and finally break down in tears. "The only way they can hurt me now is by hurting you. I refuse to lose you too."

James is standing at attention, looking straight ahead into empty space. He is no longer the warlord I knew as a kid; he has become a soldier. He was gone when Charlie was killed and I know that had he been around things might have turned out differently. Now, I am entrusting him with my mother's life, the only person who can keep her safe. After some more objections from her, he convinces her that it is the best course. He knows I will not leave, nor will I let this rest, knows me well enough to know I have murder on my mind. They both know. We all know.

My mother takes time to stitch my hand. When she is done, she hugs me, "I remember when you were eight. And James, you and Charles brought him in, bleeding like crazy, with a long gash in his arm. Remember that?"

We both say yes.

"The three of you lying through your teeth, swearing he slipped and fell on a barbed wire fence. Like I wouldn't know a knife wound when I see one. The next day, you and Charles came home all bruises and smiles. I heard what you told Morris, 'we are your big brothers, and no one hurts you and not answer to us.' So," she gets to her feet. "Don't y'all worry about me; you take care of each other."

My mother leaves with James and a small carrying bag, just enough for a day. But late that night, a small van pulls into the driveway and I load the boxes. No one knows my mother left, and no one will know where she has gone.

Nicky walks through the door and strips off his clothes as he does.

Nicolas is right behind him and he's not happy. "You need to get your friend under control. I may be able to work out something with Joe Banoa, but not with him acting like a madman."

"How is he supposed to act, Dad? He just buried his pregnant girlfriend," Nicky explodes. "And what kind of deal are you going to work out? Do you think Joe Banana is going to turn over his son? You think he knocks him around a little and all's well that ends well? I don't think so."

"You don't know what you think you know," Nicolas tells his son. "This thing is not like you see on the TV. Joseph Banoa and I used to be partners. Back then, we didn't have it so good. That's when your mother was pregnant with Salvatore. Joseph knew I needed cash, a big score. He set up an armored car heist. Everything was arranged, the guards were paid off, it was supposed to be a cakewalk."

Nicky says, "This does not sound like a story with a happy ever after ending."

Nicolas and his brother Salvatore see the armored car after it leaves from its last pickup at a department store in the Bronx. They follow it for three blocks to the cut-off point. Joe Banoa runs the red light in a big wreaker, a tow truck for trucks, and broadsides the armored car. It careens out of controls, flips on its side and comes to rest in the middle of the intersection.

Salvatore pulls their car alongside the back of the vehicle and Nicolas climbs on the hood, then the roof, and finally up onto the side of the armored car. He has a gallon bleach bottle in his hand and empties the contents into the gun portal. It's a mixture of gasoline and water, with just enough gasoline to make it smell dangerous.

Salvatore pulls the car away, points it up the block then hops out and opens the trunk. He stands, waiting for the armored truck doors to open when a shotgun barrel pokes out the gun port and before he can move, a blast nearly cuts him in half. Seeing his brother fold into the trunk, Nicolas pulls his gun out, sticks it in the gun port, and fires into the cabin. The door drops open with a loud metallic clang and the shotgun toting guard scramble out. Before he can turn back to the truck, Nicolas fires a bullet into his head.

Nicolas jumps down from the truck, grabs two bags, drags them to the car, and tosses them in the trunk on top of his brother. He goes back for another pair, and then another, before jumping into the driver's seat and taking off.

"Joseph was long gone by this time, his part was simply to disable the vehicle and take off," Nicolas says, the pain of his brother's death renewed in him, "We were to meet up later and divide the take, but I had some questions that needed answering. That guard in the back was not in on the plan, in fact, I don't think it was the right truck, and Joe knew it. He should have let the truck go by, but he didn't, and your uncle Sal paid the price."

"Then why is he still alive?" Nicky is even angrier now.

"He swore he didn't know, that it all happened too fast," Nicolas continues. "Unsurprisingly, bad blood grew between us very quickly. So one night, Joe Banana thought it would be better to end it and instructed his brother to wait for me when I was returning from a liquor run to take me out, but again, things did not go as he planned."

Lucille Rocci calls her husband for a ride from the doctor's office. She is nearing her due date, and having a difficult time making weekly doctor visits now. Ordinarily, Nicolas does not mix his private life with business, but bad winter weather put him way behind schedule. He picks up Lucille on his way upstate with a trunk load of liquor, makes his drops, and they have dinner at an Italian restaurant in Mount Vernon. He has a couple of glasses of wine as they wait for the storm to let up and after a couple of hours there are a few inches of snow on the ground and light flurries in the night sky.

Nicolas and Lucille are on Mt. Vernon Avenue heading for the highway when their car passes under the railroad track and a single shot shatters the windshield. The bullet lodges itself in Nicolas' shoulder. The car swings violently to the left, sending it into a spin on the icy road. It slams through the guardrail, bounces down the embankment, splashing into the freezing Bronx River, and comes to a stop half submerged in the extremely cold dark water.

"Somehow, and I don't know how, I managed to get your mother out of the car and onto the bank. But she wasn't breathing. It was a few minutes before I revived her,"

Nicolas says flatly. "Someone must have seen what happened and called the police, and we were lucky, Mt. Vernon Hospital was only a few blocks away. Your mother gave birth to Salvatore that night. Back in those days, we would never target a man's family, so Banoa was treading on dangerous territory. That night Joe and I made an agreement not to settle our differences with blood."

"So, what was the going rate for a weak-hearted wife," Nicky asks sarcastically, referring to his mother's arrhythmias, "and a retarded son?"

Nicolas answers his son's incriminations with a full power right cross to his jaw, sending the boy crashing through the living room coffee table. He takes a step towards his son lying on the splintered wooden debris.

His wife shouts, "Nicolas!"

He turns away, and storms out of the house.

Nicky is slow to get up, wiping the blood from his mouth on his sleeve.

"Why must you anger him so?" questions his mother.

"He is a joke," Nicky replies. "This family gets no respect because he commands none. We get the scraps the Banoas won't take and he thanks them for it. That's not me. I won't take it!"

Lucille takes a towel from the kitchen, puts ice in it, and presses it hard inside her son's mouth. "He only told you part of that story, because he thinks I don't know the rest. It's true they had a falling out over the job, but it wasn't just about your uncle getting killed. We were having money problems, my pregnancy wasn't going well and it was costing us a lot. Your father took six money bags from the armored car, but when he showed up for the meeting, he only had four. When the word got out about the missing money, Joe put a hit out on your dad." She removes the towel from his mouth and the blood starts to flow again. She places the towel back in his mouth and guides his hand to hold it. "But your father was right, back then they wouldn't have made a move against a man's family. Back then, people had honor. So, the price for a weak-hearted wife and retarded son was a brother's life." She pulls a gold and diamond ring she wore on a chain out of her blouse. "Joe gave this to your father at the hospital the night I gave birth to your brother. It's his brother's ring, the one who fired the shot."

Nicky took the ice pack out of his mouth, "Am I supposed to call him Uncle Joe now? This story should have ended with a bullet in Joe Banoa's head."

"One day you will learn how far is too far," his mother warns.

It's Sunday morning, the 4th of July, hot and humid, even at daybreak. I'm up, I am always up, sleep comes in bits and broken pieces of hellish dreams, when I dream. I sleep for a couple of minutes, maybe an hour, then it's like someone puts paddles on my chest and the shock throws me across the room. But it's OK, I'm getting a lot done. I taped the gas line to the stove last night, pulled up half the kitchen floor too. I am working on the living room floor now. I have my crowbar, hammer, drill and a cold quart.

The church bells start ringing, I sing along, "Bing... bong... bing... bing... bong... bing." It's a horrible rhythm, someone ought to tell them to have their bells tuned. There is a knock on the door. I slowly peel back the living room curtain with my shotgun. There is a man at the door, wearing a black shirt and black pants. It takes me a moment but then I realize it's Father Robinson. Good one, Mom. I put the shotgun in the closet and answer the door, "Fr. Robinson, what are you doing here?"

"Is you mother here?" he asks.

"She's, out..." I can't come up with anything, so I don't. Besides, we both know he's here to see me, and we both know my mother is not coming back.

"Is it OK if I come in and wait?" he asks.

"Sure," I step aside and let him in, "It's not really safe to be standing at the door for either of us these days."

"Yes, I heard about your friends. My condolences, especially for your girlfriend, I would have liked to have met her."

"Yeah, well, maybe you two will run into each other in Heaven one day," I tell him with a touch of bitterness. "You want a beer?"

"Um, not before church," Fr. Robinson looks around the room curiously and is particularly interested in the floorboards I removed and the holes I drilled in the joists. "What do you have going on here?"

"A little home improvement project, I'm fixing the creaks in the floor. Do you want to tell me what my mother told you?"

"With your friends dying the way they did, she thought you might need some spiritual guidance, although, I never considered you to be a staunch Catholic, at least not from your comments in religion class."

"I'm no atheists," I tell him. "After all that detention and writing chapters from the Bible, I believe in God. And I believe He is a bloodthirsty vengeful bastard. Let's forget about Abraham and go straight to Moses. Nine plagues and God hardened the Pharaoh's heart. The Bible's words, not mine, just so He can send the big tenth, the Angel of Death. However, blood on the Israelites' doors, and they are kept safe, while the firstborn of everything else in Egypt dies. 'And there arose such a wailing the likes of which was never heard before, and shall never be heard again.'" Fr. Robinson tries to say something, but I keep on getting louder,

"I guess that's something people will remember for all times. But it gets better, God not only takes vengeance on the Egyptians, He turns on His people too. They just got out of slavery, are left alone at the foot of some mountain for who knows how long, and yeah, they got a little crazy. Is that any reason to lead them around the desert for forty years on a trip that should have taken a month, maybe two? After all, the commandments they were breaking hadn't even been given to them yet." I take a long drink and half-expect Fr. Robinson to grab the opportunity to defend God's actions. He remains silent so I continue, "I know why He took forty years to bring them to the Promised Land. By that time everybody He freed from Egypt had died, except Moses, and he was flat out denied entry." I shook my head sadly.

"And what about the Land of Milk and Honey, one little fact God neglected to mention, it was occupied. So they have to march around the city carrying an Ark, the people inside must have been laughing their asses off, and then BAM. The walls fall down and in storm the Israelites and slaughter everybody. The first battle of battles that will go on for centuries, hell, they are still fighting today. If God wasn't bloodthirsty, He would have led them somewhere vacant, He had forty years."

Fr. Robinson loosens his collar, and I am almost sure he plans to deck me. "Maybe I will have that beer. And while you are getting it think about this, that was the Old Testament, I thought we taught you about the New Testament too. We taught you about Jesus, about Love, about the Last Supper and the Last Sacrificial Lamb."

I return from the kitchen with a quart bottle and a glass and set them on the coffee table in front of him.

Fr. Robinson picks up the quart, unscrews the top, and takes a big gulp. Then he takes another. "It sure is hot today."

"So much for church," I say.

"Wherever two or more gather in My Name, I Am with you," he quotes.

"Oh yes, whenever something so horrible, so unbelievable happens, whose name do people call out? Jesus Christ. Why is that? I'll tell you why, 'Because He so loved the world that He sent His only begotten Son.' To be beaten, tortured, and nailed to a cross before the world. And when Jesus rises from the dead to prove He is God, does He do it so everyone will see? No, no one sees it, only a few people know about it... and for centuries more, people will die because of it." I take another drink. "If He really wanted to prove He was God and put an end to all the bullshit, He would have raised Caesar from the dead. Now that would have gotten the Romans' attention."

"The Emperor wasn't dead," Father says with half a smile. He's enjoying my raving.

Perhaps he thinks I'll get my anger out and then I'll be a good little Catholic again. Is he ever wrong, I'm not just ranting and rattling on about shit, I know God wants blood! And so do I. "I'm sure something could have been arranged. He could have got one of the Emperor's friends to do him in, like He did Jesus. How messed up was that? One of His best friends gives Him the kiss of death. I'll bet it wasn't called that until after Judas. Then Judas paid for Jesus' blood with his own. And still no one will ever name their kid that again. Nope, 'Vengeance is mine, sayest the Lord' I'm just the collection agency."

Fr. Robinson finishes his beer; he has been taking steady hits as I have been talking. He is now ready to leave, "You're forgetting the last words our Lord spoke as one of us, 'forgive them Father for they know not what they do.'"

"They knew what they were doing, Father," I say sternly of Joey and his friends, "I can't forgive them."

Fr. Robinson stops at the door, "Tell your mother I will pray for her." Then he says, "per sanguinem crucis Christi virtutem abluas omnes iniquitates vestras, et egredietur amplius noli peccare."

"What is that?"

"I am giving you absolution," he tells me.

"Don't I have to commit the sin first?" I ask. "And don't I have to be sorry for having sinned?"

"Well, as you always argued, God knows what you are going to do. And some day I'm sure you are going to be sorry for having done it. When that day comes, know that you are forgiven."

I return to my work, pulling up floorboards, drilling a passage hole in the joist, and sealing up the floor again. Have to make sure the entire first floor is prepared before tonight.

As night falls, fireworks light up the city sky. Neighborhoods, especially those in the Bronx, go to great lengths to outdo each other. Especially in the Banoa and Rocci neighborhoods, where illegal fireworks are a major business, and this night, the Banoas' display will outdo the Rocci's hands down because the Roccis will not put on a display at all.

The Banoa fireworks have been going for an hour already when Nicky and I take to a roof three blocks south of the playground. Nicky ducks with each explosion then points out several times that we are too close to the height where skyrockets explode. I laugh and inform him that even on top of the five-story building we are a hundred feet or more below the rockets' detonations.

"What are we doing up here?" Nicky asks.

"I promised Maria a rocket shot tonight," I say, "I will not disappoint her."

"Oh, you finished the rockets in your shed. But why here, and what are you waiting for?"

I explain that the rocket is in a trashcan in the alley and I have the remote ignition to launch it from the roof. We are sitting in folding beach chairs with a cooler of ice, beers, and binoculars. I light up a joint and pass it to him, "We are waiting for the guests of honor to this little party."

"Who's coming up here? Who did you tell?"

"Not up here," I pick up a pair of binoculars and search the crowd in the playground, "down there."

He looks through the other binoculars, "That's the Banoas. You're waiting for Joey?"

"That's right. When I launch the rocket it will go up about a thousand feet, then it's going to come down in the park. If all goes right, it will explode about six to ten feet above the ground. The perfect kill zone."

We drink, smoke, and watch. About half an hour later, Nicky elbows me in the side. "That's him. That's him."

I study the lanky boy crossing the street to the park, and get a good look at his face, the tell-tale signs of a broken jaw and nose, it's him all right. I press the single red button on the radio control launcher and hold my breath. I did not tell Nicky that the rocket warhead is a quart of nitro, and although I left no air space in the jar, the sudden thrust of the rocket engine could be enough force to detonate it on or right after lift-off. Not good.

I further cushioned the soup with wads of paper. After talking with Fr. Robinson, I replaced the balls of ordinary blank loose-leaf paper with pages from my Bible. The book of Exodus to be exact and I suspect none will survive the fiery explosion to come, but if they do, I want everyone to know that the Angel of Death is back. I painted AOD 12:12 on the rocket's body, which I don't think will survive either. I told Nicky it was my tag when I avenged my brother's death. Exodus 12:12, 'For I will pass through the land of Egypt that night, and I will smite all the firstborn in the land of Egypt, both man and beast; and on all the gods of Egypt I will execute judgements: I am the Lord.'

He is not too happy about leaving incriminating evidence at the scene, but understands my need. He also tells me that I am crazier than the Mad Hatter. Besides, we both know when this thing happens the Banoas will know it's from us. We don't care about the police; this is a fight to the death with the Banoa family.

"What's up, Little Brother?" slurs Joey from his stiff jaw. "Dad got you running the show this year?"

"And what the hell is the matter with you?" Michael scolds him. "Pop told you to stay inside and to keep out of sight for your own good."

"What, am I six?" laughs Joey, or a cackle that will pass for a laugh. "There is nothing to worry about; I took care of the Roccis, once and for all. Look over there, isn't it lovely? The neighborhood is silent. Too busy crying over their dead."

"That's not how pop described Morris and Nicky. He said they had blood in their eyes, your blood."

A couple of Joey's boys come over and pat him on the back. All have been keeping out of sight, but this is the Fourth of July, everyone wants to be out for the show.

"Hey Pete, where's Chris and Nathan?" Joey asks.

"Lying low," Pete answers. "Mike said your dad was out to get us. You told him I only drove the getaway car, right? I had nothing to do with the hit."

"What are you talking about?" Joey struggles to convince him he was in charge. He throws a lit wad of newspaper into a trashcan and it starts a blaze that ignites the fireworks. Bottle rockets are the first to go off, screaming out of the flames and into the night. "We are all going to get our bones for this. We are stepping up."

Big Mike, the football player, grabs Pete by the neck and shakes him. "My old man made me go with him on a delivery, how I would have given my right arm to have been there." He throws his right hand up to meet Joey's in a high five salute.

The buzzing of a million mosquitoes fills the air and his hand never makes connection with Joey's. It is eaten away along with his wrist, forearm, and half his bicep.

Pete sees the bright flash and nothing else. His face is pulverized, turned to a bloody oozing mask, torn from the powerful grip of Big Mike, the football player, and is sent thirty feet away. Joey's heart stops beating, as it is unable to compete with the sledgehammer-like blow delivered to his chest. He is flat on his back, the very essence of life squeezed from his body.

The rocket tears into the night with a loud swoosh, its engine giving off a hot blast of air as it flies past us and quickly shrinks into the darkness. I can breathe again. A couple of scant seconds pass and the light from the rocket goes out. We can no longer track its path. I am counting, barely audibly, I reach five and there is a brilliant white and yellow fireball over the playground.

"Yes," I shout.

The fireball grows instantly into a large angry flaming cloud, consuming Joey, Michael, and friends. A second later, the thunder of the explosion rolls across the neighborhood, reaching us on the roof. It carries with it the sound of shattering glass windows and the wailing of bodies not caught in the primary fireball, but still in the blast zone.

The warhead, besides containing the quart of soup and scripture, was surrounded with shards of broken glass– The bottom of beer bottles broken into chunks the size of quarters or half dollars. I tell Nicky I didn't have time to get enough buckshot and I thought it would make the nose of the rocket too heavy, perhaps pulling it off course. The glass was lighter, easier to obtain, and made a fine shrapnel material.

Everyone within thirty to forty feet of the rocket is peppered by scorching flying glass. It rips into them, through them, dropping many where they stand. Most don't even know what has happened. The scene is chaotic. Those not injured run from the playground. Those not so lucky lie on the ground writhing in agony. Joey's hair, eyebrows, and scraggily beginnings of a beard have been burned away. His shirt and a large patch of his chest in it are scorched. He stumbles to his feet and trips over Big Mike's one-armed body, the football player, and crawls through the eerily silent playground. The smell of burnt flesh fills his nostrils, the ghostly images of bloody corpses walking and lying about him adding to the confusion.

"Let's get out of here," says Nicky in absolute panic.

"Relax," I scour the scene below, looking for one person in the mayhem. "No one is gonna come looking for us here and it will be hours before anyone knows what hit them. Light up another joint, pop another beer, let's enjoy this."

Our vantage point is perfect; we are three stories above all the private houses on the streets. I can see mothers and fathers gathering up their children and running like madmen for help. I can also see others kneeling, rocking, and crying over the bodies of those who died. I see Joey struggling to pick up Michael's body, whose chest is torn open, his back blown out.

"God damn it," I yell, "He is still alive."

I hop over the fence and sneak up behind Sal sitting by the chicken coops. I grab him around the neck, or at least I try, because the best I can do is get my arm around his broad chest and shoulder. He jumps to his feet in a panic, lifting me off mine like a rag doll. Sal is big and strong like an ox. He starts to cry.

"Ha, I got you Big Boy," I shout, "You're my prisoner."

Sal swings around looking for me.

I swing around too, still hanging from his back.

"Morris, I knew that was you."

"Then why are you crying, you big wussy? Wait 'til I tell Nicky."

"I wasn't crying. I wasn't." He sits back down on the crate in front of the coops. "Hey, you want to see me choke my chicken?" He shoves his hand down his pants and starts shaking it around. "You thought I meant one of them, fooled you, didn't I? Good trick, right? Shake!" He pulls his hand out and offers it to me.

"I don't think so," I decline. "Who taught you that? Let me guess, Nicky. He's inside?" I don't wait for an answer and go in through the sliding door.

Nicolas is letting him have it in both Italian and English. I start smiling because I can't understand him in either language; just know that he is as mad as hell about last night.

"I told you to keep that crazy fucker from doing anything stupid," he yells.

Nicky shakes his head, trying to warn me to leave before his father knows I am there. I ignore the warning, listen, and wait behind his father.

"What the hell was that last night? You two ruined any chance of me making a deal with Joe Banoa. You will never get a shot at Little Joey now."

"Mr. Rocci," I interrupt, "It wasn't Nicky's idea. I had this in the works since the night of the Raven. He couldn't have stopped me."

Startled by my voice, he turns and takes a step towards me then stops. Obviously, he noticed my right hand buried in my jacket pocket. "Of course, it was your plan, he's not smart enough to come up with an idiotic idea like that. But thanks to your attack, Joey is gone. His father, no doubt, got him out of town. I was trying to arrange a meeting where we could have gotten a proper shot at him."

"Well, I figured that if I saw him, I'd blow his ass up. A bomb may not be as precise as needed, but it sent a powerful message. I don't know how you do things here, but where I come from, you kill one of us and we kill all of you."

"That is not how we do things here," he retorts. "I run this family and we don't kill innocent bystanders. Eight dead, twenty or more injured, some of them women and children."

"I'm not in your family. And if they were so innocent, they wouldn't have been standing so close."

"You killed his son, Michael. What do you think Joe Banoa is going to do now?"

"The same thing he was going to do before," I state calmly, "he is going to try to kill Nicky and me. We saw Joey leaving the Raven after shooting my... our friends. He's not going to let us live, and he's not going to turn over his son. This is going to go on until one of us runs out of blood to shed."

The three of us stand there in silence and I can tell Nicolas Rocci knows I'm right. No matter what kind of deals they came up with, it would have been a double cross on both sides.

"I tried to take Joey out when he was most vulnerable, as I knew he would be last night. But next time, it will be more up close and personable. Anyway, I just stopped by to let you know that our friends are watching your house. But don't worry about Batman and Robin; I'll take care of them."

"We don't kill cops," Nicolas commands.

"You don't," I defy him. "But don't worry, I don't want them dead either; not yet." I leave through the front door.

Nicolas Rocci shakes his head, "One day, you are going to have to kill your friend."

"Yeah," Nicky agrees, "But not until he gets Joey Banana. I owe him that much."

I start walking down the street quickly, my head down, as if I am trying to hide my face. I am two houses away when the detects pull up beside me.

Fitzpatrick is driving and he shows me his revolver, "Get in!"

I open the back door and climb onto the seat, "What, you're not going to read me my rights?"

"Where we are taking you your rights aren't going to mean much," says Mancotti. "Mr. Banoa wants to see you, and then he is going to cut your balls off and shove them down your throat."

"You Italians and cutting off people's balls, what's with that?" I jest then wait for the car to pick up speed before I ask, "Want to play 'Killer poker'?"

"We don't have a deck of cards," Fitzpatrick quips.

"Oh, we don't need cards," I tell him, "You just have to know what beats what. A knife beats bare knuckles, a gun beats a knife, and it beats the hell out of me why you would let me in the car with this hand grenade." I hold it up, the pin out on my thumb. "Throw your weapons into the back! Carefully, and one at a time!"

Both toss their guns onto the seat next to me.

We are still driving down the street, just much slower. I tell Robin to wrap his arms around Fitzpatrick's chest and handcuff himself. When he's done, I instruct Batman to pull over and do the same.

"Don't worry boys, I don't want you dead," I assure them. "You are Banoa's bitches. What I do want are the names of the guys who were on the hit squad with Joey."

"We don't know who was with him," Mancotti confesses quickly, "They were wearing ski masks."

"When they came out, yes," I agree. "But not when they went in, as Benny would have cut them down at the door. That is the first and last lie you tell. But I expected you to at least try squirm your way out of this anyway, and would have been insulted if you didn't... This is how we are going to work this out, you know the show 'Ironside', where Perry Mason is in the wheelchair?"

"You mean Raymond Burr," answers Fitzpatrick.

"Yeah, him. So, if you two don't give me the names of the others, I'm going to shoot you in the spine. Then you two can star in your own version of 'Ironside.' One more time, the names."

"There was the kid Pete, he died yesterday in that bomb blast. Then there is Caralucci, Christopher Caralucci, and Nathan Napolitano. Those are the guys you want," says Mancotti.

"See how simple that was?" I tell them. "Now, slide out of the car. And when you see Joey Banoa, tell him that he and his friends are going to burn in Hell. Everyone who took part in the Raven's shooting is going to wish they were never born. I promise."

I climb over into the front seat as the two cops stand on the sidewalk hugging each other. A crowd quickly gathers several feet away and I wish at that moment that I had made them take off their pants before getting out. I had put the grenade back in my pocket after they were handcuffed together but now, I take it back out and hold it up, "mind if I borrow your car?"

They shake their heads and give an embarrassed, "No."

I drive off down the street and turn the corner then about a block away I pull the pin once more. This time, I drop the grenade on the floor, get out of the slow moving car, and duck into an alley as it continues rolling down the street. Moments later, there is a loud explosion, signalling the Batmobile's destruction. Batman and Robin are going to have a hard time explaining this to their captain.

They are taken back to the precinct by a patrol car responding to their car explosion.

The captain quickly disregards their account of events as bullshit as witnesses gave reports of seeing them driving the car and me sitting in the back seat. It's Fitzpatrick's personal car so the captain doesn't give a rat's ass for the loss, he only cares that they are operating outside the law, and the F.B.I. is in his office.

Officially, in his office, sit two older agents, whom he knows well, and if they were not F.B.I. he would consider friends, and a young man in his twenties, who he instantly dislikes.

The first older man begins, "I'm Agent Black from the Bureau. This is agent White and Agent Green."

One could think those were cover identities, or that they are yanking the detectives' chains, but no, those are their actual names.

Sam Black is a thin chiselled man of German descent in his late fifties, William White, whom most call Willie White, is of similar build and age, from Texas, with the drawl to prove it, and Tom Green is new to the Bureau, just out of Nam, and an explosives expert.

"Your Captain says you know all the animals in this zoo, and that's good because we are going to need someone to get us on the inside." Agent Black continues.

"The Captain thinks..."

"Save it, cowboy," Willie White cuts Mancotti off. "You two have been lying with dogs for so long you don't even bother to scratch at the fleas anymore. Now, there are two ways you can work this, you can help us with this investigation..." he emphasizes investigation, "And help us get someone inside the Banoa operation, or, and it's totally up to you, you can do twenty years with them in a federal pen. You need to decide now."

"What do you want to know?" Fitzpatrick asks.

"I was looking at the blast patterns from the Fourth's Bombing," Tom Green says and clicks on a slide projector, which displays an aerial view of the playground street. "See these streaks radiating out from the north end of the playground? I have seen these marking before. They are consistent with a missile or bomb dropped on the playground. See how the marks are longer going northeast, that means the device came in from the southwest and I would think it was some sort of rocket because it was travelling at high speed when it exploded. It probably detonated no higher than fifteen feet above the ground."

"You two have purposefully been leading your captain to believe this whole thing is a battle between Joseph Banoa and Nicolas Rocci, but this latest attack, and the shooting at the Raven Social Club leads us to believe it is hormone-fueled teenage rage," states Agent Black. "And while we would like to get this thing under control as quickly as possible, we are also looking for a real opportunity here to get a man inside, namely Agent Green. He is going to help the Banoas get Mr. Morris 'Bulletproof' Johnson and in return, they are going to help him advance his career with the Bureau. Once inside, he can help us unravel the Mob from the inside out."

Agent White adds, "Johnson is the carrot Joseph Banoa can't resist. The police department has been downplaying the explosion as a fireworks display gone wrong but Banoa knows this is an attack. He lost a son, and another was seriously injured, he wants revenge. If Agent Green delivers Johnson, Joseph Banoa will be indebted to him, and Agent Green will be on his good side."

"Wait a minute," Mancotti can't believe what he's hearing, "You want to turn this kid over to the Mob?"

"Isn't that what you were doing when he blew up your car and made asses of you in the street?" counters Agent White. "I don't know what Banoa is paying you, but we are after the big payoff. We are aware that you have been doing some checking, so you already know this kid is responsible for at least two dozen murders in the South Bronx in about four years' time. This guy is a major warlord, but the Banoas are only now finding that out, and that is why they are going to need and accept our help. We need to take Bulletproof Johnson out soon, before he gets any bigger, because he is already running several gangs by proxy. If his friend and he take out the Banoa family, they will be running the Bronx in a year or two."

"As you can see, the Bureau doesn't just investigate the Mafia, we examine all types of criminal gangs and activities," says Agent Black.

"Ok, but you have to let us make the approach," Mancotti tells them, "We do this our way, because if this is not done right, you will be fishing all three of us out of the East River with a bullet in our heads."

CHAPTER 8
Thick as Thieves

It is another scorching hot summer day. Temperatures hitting the nineties, and kids and adults alike are playing around the fire hydrant sprinklers. Mancotti walks into the pizza shop and orders a couple of large pies to go.

As the pizza man starts working on the dough, a man at the counter watches the mirrored wall behind the oven and asks, "Who's the mook riding with you?"

"He's a Fed. There are a lot of them around after what's been happening the last two weeks," he says to the mirror.

"Yeah, tell me about it. A man can't walk five feet without tripping over one of them."

"Well, he's not so bad," Mancotti keeps talking straight ahead. "He's just back from Nam, an explosives expert; hasn't got a handle on that thing on the fourth yet. Believes it was homemade. But says the car trouble we had was definitely government issued, so once we track down when and where, we will have a lead on who is helping our friend."

"That's your problem," Joe says angrily, "I have my own. My dog ran away, so I have people out looking for him in all his old shitholes. I'm sure they will find my lost dog soon."

"I would tell your people to be careful, a rabid dog's bite is worse than his bark. But if I can help you find your dog let us know," Mancotti offers, "Your police department is always glad to aid its citizens."

"There may be one thing," Joe says. "There are so many people around his doghouse, he might be afraid to come home. I can spot them from a mile away."

"I'll see what I can do and suggest it to the new guy."

Joe Banoa taps on the window and one of the three big brawny guys, who were blocking the view of him from the street, goes to start his car. He walks past Agent Green and glares at him with obvious contempt. The three men disappear into the black window caddie and speed away.

Agent Green joins Mancotti at the counter, "How did it go?" "The pizzas will be done in a minute, pay for them." Mancotti walks out.

Nightfall finds my suburban block clear of all stakeout units, Feds and police alike have given up waiting for me to return. I drive down the street, pass my house slowly, and do not stop. I don't see anyone, but I can feel the eyes on me. It is a little past midnight.

"I got a light in the kitchen, someone opened the fridge," crackles the walkie-talkie in the car. The car drives two blocks, turns the corner, stops in front of the house, and the four men check their watches. "3:00 a.m., you go through the basement, you take the back door, and I'll take the front," says the man in the front seat. "We pick the locks and go in quiet, make a clean sweep and kill the bastard on sight."

They head to their respective places, pick the locks in seconds, and check their watches again. At 3:05 the doors swing open and instantly Jimi Hendrix starts playing 'Voodoo Child' loudly.

The lead hit man radios the obvious, "It's an alarm, he knows we are here. Go, go, go." They rush in with guns drawn. The man in the basement sweeps the room with his flashlight. The room is empty. The second hit man checks the kitchen, opens the cabinet doors under the sink then moves down the hall to the living room. The closet is empty, so is the room. The leader had run up the stairs when he entered, then carefully opened the bathroom door. He checks the bathtub then backs out and closes the door. In the bedroom across the hall, he fires three shots into the bed and then another three into the closet door, the silencer reducing the sound to six soft thuds.

"You got him," the second man calls upstairs.

"No, just covering the bases," he replies, "Get up here, I'm taking the next bedroom."

'If I don't meet you no more in this world
then uh I'll meet ya on the next one
And don't be late Don't be late.'
Blares from the bedroom speakers.

The head hit man kicks open the door to the empty bedroom. "He's not here. Ricardo, you moron, the place is empty," he radios his spotter.

"I'm telling you someone opened the refrigerator door," responds Ricardo, "He's in there somewhere."

The second hit man points to the ladder that leads to the roof then climbs to the top, throws the door open to the side, and quickly swings his head and gun from side to side, no one camped up there either.

At the same time, the third hit man goes to the kitchen and opens the refrigerator. Its only content is a small black box with a mechanical arm attached to its side. He yells, "It's a trap! Get out, now!"

Jimi comes to an end, the decibel's meter arrow drops to zero, and an earth-shaking, ear-shattering blast replaces him. I had flooded the space between the basement ceiling and the floor with gas and set a trigger. I knew the constant tailing would lead to this predictable ambush.

Tom Green watches as the house splinters, followed by a roll of thunder half a mile away. The second hit man is launched flaming and screaming into the air so fast that he cannot hear himself as he rockets fifty feet skyward. The roof lifts about thirty feet, flips over then falls back into the blazing hole. The charred and smoldering second hit man drops into the open gates of hell. The car waiting in front of the house's windows blow in, as do all the windows of the surrounding houses. The car is thrown tumbling through the air across the street, killing the driver on impact.

Tom says to the detectives in the car with him, "Your guy really loves explosions."

Bonnie shows up at the gravesite exactly at midnight one month after the funeral. She has not heard from the others since then, but Morris' doings have been all over the papers. Although his name is never mentioned, and the events are labelled accidental or under investigation, she has no doubt it is all his doing.

Sweet Jesus is already there, looking about nervously then thankfully, he spots her coming up the path. He informs her right off that he is just as afraid of the dead as he is of the living, then, proceeds to tell her that Morris took equal vengeance on those who killed his brother and on those who did nothing to help him afterwards.

"They were your friends too. And didn't Joey take your eye? You should be in this whole-heartedly. Be a man," she commands.

About five minutes later Nicky joins them.

"You are late," Bonnie scolds him, "And where is Morris? He said to be here at midnight, but he's nowhere to be found."

"Actually, I've been here since six this evening," says Nicky, who is wearing the tan coveralls of the groundkeepers' crew. "I've been checking out the area, making sure no one else is around. As for Morris, haven't seen him since the fifth. He's been a very busy boy, but I'm sure he hasn't forgotten. In the limo after the funeral, he made it seem like this was the most important thing on his mind."

"It was the only thing on my mind," I say from the shadows of a mausoleum a few feet away. "You people are loud enough to wake the dead. I have been here all weekend; well, up there keeping an eye on things." I point in the direction of the high rises several blocks away overlooking the Saint John's Cemetery. I join them and exchange a hug with Bonnie.

"Nice flowers," she says, rearranging the white roses in the vases in front of the tombstones. "And fresh, who has been bringing them?"

"I made arrangements," I tell her, and recant.

It was early Friday morning after the Fourth of July bombing and the florist was putting together four long stemmed white rose bouquets.

Fitzpatrick and Mancotti enter the Ever Green Florist on Woodhaven Boulevard, Queens, approach the counter and flash their badges.

"Batman and Robin," the middle-aged florist greeted the pair of detectives, "He said you would be stopping by."

"Who said?" asked Fitzpatrick.

"Bulletproof Johnson," chuckled the greying man. He continued to work as he spoke, "said you would be here to ask about the flowers. Told me to tell you anything you wanted to know."

"Who picks up the flowers?" asked Mancotti.

"No one," he answered. "I put them on those kids' graves myself. Not my usual services, but for what he paid, they will get flowers for years to come. Paid in cash, in case you want to know."

"What happens if you don't make the deliveries?" questioned Fitzpatrick.

"He said and I quote, 'There will be bloodshed'. He sounded like he meant it."

"So, he threatened you," said Mancotti.

"Oh no, not my blood," the florist corrected him, "Whoever stops me from making the delivery. I think he, or someone he knows is watching, believe me, a person doesn't plunk down a chunk of cash like that and not have someone watching out for his interests. So, do I continue to make the delivery?"

"It is just the flowers, right?" Mancotti asked the florist as he finished the last bouquet.

"Right," confirmed the florist, "Oh, one other thing, he said if anyone else came around asking the same questions I should tell you. There was a couple of guys two days ago, looked like hoods, they also said to keep on making the delivery."

Straight after making arrangements with the florist I went over to the Forest Heights Apartments, a group of three high- rises overlooking the cemetery. I walked up the stairs, stopping at each floor to check the view. Every window from the eighth floor and upwards had a full view of Maria's grave and the rest of the cemetery. The best view coming from the eleventh floor. I sat on a park bench between the buildings in army fatigues and watched the tenants come and go. Most were elderly Jews, Italian, and Irish; but there were also young Black and Spanish families. It was a quiet place.

I watched the mailboxes, waiting for just the right person to retrieve the mail for an apartment on the eleventh floor from A to G. Mr. Hartman turned out to be the correct fit, elderly and alone.

I snuck into his apartment 11F and watched him for three days. I hid in the spare bedroom; no one called, no one visited, and from the aged photos around his apartment, I figured he had outlived all his relatives. On the third day, as Mr. Hartman stepped into his tub for his nightly bath, I crept into the bathroom behind him, grabbed him by the shoulders, and yanked him backward. He hit his head hard on the tiles and slipped down under the water. I held him there gently by his shoulders until no more air bubbles rose to the surface.

I bought a dozen twenty-pound bags of ice from several stores, none in Queens, poured the ice over Mr. Hartman then refilled the empty bags with water and put them in the freezer. I then set up four video recorders with six-hour tapes in each and attached a video camera to them. I set the timers to record at 6am, 12pm, 6pm, and 12am, and returned each night to review the tapes and keep Mr. Hartman on ice.

There were mobsters, who sat for hours in hearses parked at various sites around the graves but never unloaded a single casket. Police teams often swept the area posing as mourners paying their respects, same mourners but different graves each time. The feds were the best. Dressed as workers, they spent more time looking around and absolutely none tending to any funerals.

The mobsters gave up first, lasting only a week; maybe all the police presence scared them off. The police pulled their stakeout teams the following week, the lack of criminal activities probably making them go look elsewhere. The feds found it a waste of time by the end of July. I cleared the equipment out of the apartment after that and waited for my friends to show up.

In a day or two, Mr. Hartman's ice bath will melt, he will be found, and pronounced dead from a fall in the bath. An unfortunate but natural cause of death, rest in peace Mr. Hartman.

Bonnie gets up from Frank's grave; she had told him something that I couldn't hear, nor did I want to. She thanks me for the forethought and says she thinks they appreciate it. I have a shopping bag with me and I begin passing out quarts of Bud. I stand in front of Maria's grave, Bonnie is in front of Frank's, Sweet Jesus takes Betty's, and Nicky is by Dino's. I crack open the beer and tell them to follow my lead. I slowly pour the beer on the grave while saying,

> *"To our brothers down below.*
> *To drown the fire and quench the soul.*
> *One by one we die alone.*

Drop by drop our blood to the rivers flow.
As we follow our brothers on the journey home."
"So that's why you do that," Nicky says.

"That is horrible," Bonnie admonishes me. "You are saying that Frank is in Hell. You're saying you believe Maria has gone to Hell."

"We must all go through Hell to get into Heaven," I say sternly, "Either in this life or the next. Even Jesus descended into Hell for three days before rising and He died without sin; I figure I give them ten times that period to make the journey for their sins. This little ceremony is to help them on their way to Heaven. And every time you drink, add a few drops of blood to keep the river flowing."

We take time to pay our personal respects to each of our friends then get down to business in the nearby mausoleum. I give them a contact sheet and tell everyone to memorize it as quick as possible and then destroy it.

Three used car ads will be placed in three different newspapers, two will have a phone number to call and the third will provide the time and date to call. I tell them to not buy the papers, to simply check and make a mental note, and we'll give each other at least a two-day lead to make contact. Bonnie's is a 69 GTO, Sweet Jesus' a 65 Mustang, Nicky's a 70's Lincoln Mark III, and I have a 70 Buick Riviera.

We also lay out plans for finding Joey and his accomplices. Nicky's idea is to attack Banoa's businesses right out, especially the liquor and cigarette smuggling operation, as it is the most vulnerable. His reasoning is that if it costs them enough money his own people may eventually turn on him and his son. They are already pissed over the rocket attack and the ambush at my house.

Nicky says, "I can't believe you blew up your own house."

"It held too many memories," I tell them sadly.

"Your neighbors were quite mad," he informs me. "The houses on either side were badly damaged, but none injured. However, Old Joe firebombed two of my father's strip clubs; there weren't too many people inside at the time, so no one got hurt. He just wanted to close the clubs, fight fire with fire."

"Don't worry, I have a new business venture for you," I tell him. "You are going into the fertilizer business."

"I like the sound of that," he says, "Sounds devious."

"You do know fertilizer is made from shit," Sweet Jesus informs him.

"Well, this fertilizer is going to be the by-product of our cocaine smuggling business," I tell them. "Sweet Jesus, you have been hiding out with the Colombians, what is their biggest concern?"

"Getting it past customs," he says, "they lose about fifteen percent of product."

"Then you are going to help them drop that number to less than one half of one percent. I have a process to turn hielo into ice, slip it past customs, and convert it back to pure cocaine. And we are going to do all this under the guise of a fertilizer company. We are going from drug dealers to traffickers," I announce.

"That's great," Bonnie says somewhat annoyed. "But what does that have to do with getting Joey and his friends? Isn't that why we are in this tomb?"

"Yes, of course it is," I assure her, "But we are going to need money to do it. Lots of money, but Nicky's businesses are going to come under increasing fire. They are going to shut down some of his resources, so we need another source, one Joe Banoa doesn't know about. And one he won't have the balls to go after."

She realizes I am right, but I can see she still thinks I have lost sight of what's important. "The Fourth of July attack was a double-edged sword. I wanted to kill Joey, for sure, but if it failed to do so I wanted to make sure he was front and center in the FBI's investigation. That way he can't leave the country. He can hide but he is stuck here. Sweet

Jesus is going to Puerto Rico to handle this new business, as he is much too identifiable right now to be of use. There are two types of people who can get close to your enemies undetected, the old, because they are overlooked as a threat, and a beautiful woman, because everyone is looking at her for all the wrong reasons. Therefore, Bonnie, you are going to get us close to Joey's friends. One of them is bound to know where he and his cohorts are. Then, we will find them and kill them. OK?"

"OK," she agrees.

The eighteen-wheeler pulls into the loading bay behind the warehouse at the Hunts Point section. Hookers are working the streets along the warehouse district of the South Bronx, as always. It is just before dusk this mid-August day, the heat wave has broken for now, and the DJ on the truck's radio is praising the Lord for the relief. The driver sees the white van parked in its usual spot and waits for his contact to approach. After a few minutes of nothing, he gets mad and climbs out of the rig.

"These fucking wop bastards always with the cock-sucking whores." He bangs on the back of the van door hard and angry. No answer. He pounds on the door even harder, "Come on, put your fucking dicks in your pants and let's go. I got a fucking schedule to keep."

"Sorry brother," Sean says behind him, the click of his pistol announcing his intentions. "But you are going to be even later than you think."

Lance, a big black husky truck driver makes no attempt to turn around. He puts his hands up and asks, "Are you sure you want to do this? Do you even know who you are ripping off?"

"Of course," says Sean, "But don't worry, it's not you. We are just taking the shipment you are dropping off here, and then you are on your way as usual. You see, you are not being robbed, you're just changing bosses."

"You're kidding me, right?" he asks. "Joseph Banoa will kill me."

"Put your hands down," Sean tells him, "When Joe Banoa asks you what happened here, you are going to say nothing unusual. You met the guys, made your delivery, and went on your way. What happened after that you don't know. Right?"

Sean pulls the driver, who is twice his size, back from the van. He opens the doors and shows him three men bound and gagged inside. Sean fires the gun equipped with a silencer multiple times then closes the doors again. "Right?"

"Yeah, right, I don't know nothing."

"Good, and my guys are almost finished unloading the liquor. Get back in your rig and I'll be in touch with you next month with a new drop point," Sean commands the driver.

Lance hurries back to his truck, forgetting to ask how he will be contacted. A black van passes him and picks up Sean; another gets into the white van. Lance quickly checks the locks on his rig and hauls ass out of there. He knows he is caught in the middle of a mob war; he just hopes he is not the next casualty.

Bonnie reads the ads for a 69 GTO, 'cars' prices from $570 to $640', that stands for Freeland, Pennsylvania. The next listing says 'good condition, needs some work—$3460 firm,' and the last lists a phone number as 824-1620, which stands for August 24th at 4:20pm. That's Nicky and he wants her to call two days from now.

She knows the Irish made the hit on Banoa's liquor operation, a simple 'tax and sell' business. Banoa's strong arm legitimate businesses pay for ten cases of liquor but only receive nine from the delivery driver, the missing case is the tax. For them, it is better to write off one case as breakage on their taxes than to complain to the distributor and have another delivered with a flaming rag stuffed in a bottle.

The 'sell' part of the business comes in the form of a free case of liquor that Banoa sells to illegal bars and clubs like the Raven. The white van had been delivered the previous week to one of Banoa's clubs with cold corpses instead of hot liquor inside.

She calls the number at precisely 4:20pm. "Hello," she says nervously when the ringing stops on the other end.

"Yeah, it's me," Nicky says cheerfully after the few seconds of silence meant to torture her.

She can almost see the stupid grin on his face.

"You sound so scared, what do you expect to happen, for a hand to reach through the phone and grabs you?"

"Well, we never discussed passwords or anything," Bonnie tells him.

"OK, we'll take that up at the next board meeting," he says sarcastically. "Listen, catch a train to Scranton, PA, there is one leaving from Grand Central at 7:30 tonight. I'll meet you at the station," Nicky jabs her one more time, "I'll be wearing a white carnation, code words, 'The dove is in the nest.' And then you say..."

She hangs up on him, wondering what he has going on in Scranton, but figures she'll find out when she sees him. It's better than having him jerk her around for who knows how long.

When she gets to Scranton, Nicky is there to meet her, with two other men, but no carnation.

He tells her they are going to drive down to a place south of Allentown where a couple of Banoa men will be passing through with a shipment of cigarettes.

The cigarette business is straightforward, they buy cases in the South where the price is low and sell them up North where the price is high, and the price is always higher in New York due to the taxes, which they simply bypass. They also have their own tax stamp and it's hard to tell the difference.

Bonnie waits on the side of the road in a car with a flat tire. She has on a short skirt, low cut blouse, and a long blonde wig, just the sort of outfit that will stop a driver on a deserted stretch of road in the middle of nowhere, and yes, ridiculously high heels. As the truck approaches, she gets out of the vehicle, jumping and waving frantically.

The passenger in the semi-truck hammers the driver excitedly in the arm, "You see that stop... stop... stop the truck."

"You got to be kidding," the driver says downshifting. "I'm not stopping."

They pass her by and the guy riding shotgun yells out, "You need a man, Honey?"

Bonnie had stuffed the underside of her bra, making her tits appear even bigger; she hops, causing them to bounce. Hearing the truck let out a loud hiss as the air breaks engage, she runs the twenty yards to where it stopped. "Oh, thank you... Thank you... Thank you," she says with one hand on her heaving bosom, panting loudly, putting on a good fake show. "I have been stuck out here for hours and no one has been by. I got a flat on my way back from a party. Can you two gentlemen help change my tire?"

"Go change the lady's tire, prince Charming," orders the driver, "You want to climb up here in the cab? It's kind of chilly out there."

"OK," she agrees and tells the other man the trunk is open. He storms down the road to her car, "This is bullshit, it was my idea to stop. Now he's going to hit that pussy while I'm changing a fucking tire." He flips up the trunk and Nicky sticks a shotgun in his face.

"No one is hitting that pussy tonight," Nicky says, climbs out, and orders the man to get in.

"Nice rig, uh baby," the driver smiles.

"Oh yeah, it's got a bed and everything in the back," teases Bonnie.

"Want to check it out?"

"OK," she says giggling and climbs into the back. As she does, she pulls a .22 out of the stuffing of her bra.

Gaping at her ass in the short skirt, he slaps it and is already halfway in the back when she turns around and pushes the gun up his nose.

"Is that supposed to scare me?" laughs the driver.

"A little," she says, "But my friend over there is about to scare the shit out of you."

Nicky jabs him in his groin.

The driver looks over his shoulder, sees Nicky, and a 12 gauge aimed at his balls.

"Why don't you back it up, lover boy, while you can still call yourself a lover, or a boy?"

The two men who had come with them march the driver and his partner off into the woods with Nicky's shotgun and while Nicky is re-inflating the flat tire on the car, two shots ring out. Without another word, the two men get in the truck and drive off, Nicky and Bonnie drive away in the car. Later, both truck and car end up in a chop shop in Pittsburgh. Bonnie stays a few days with Nicky, they party a little then she returns to the Bronx.

After a couple more losses in September, an enraged Banoa strikes back against Nicolas Rocci, by arranging accidents at his construction sites. The first, a crane lifting a two-ton cement pourer's cable snaps. The bucket crashes through two cement slab floors crushing several workers below. The cable then whips through the air and with a lightning-like crack cuts the crane cab and its operator in half. Days later, at another site, rivets give way and the side of a parking garage slides into the street. Several perish and many more are injured in the traffic accident that the failure causes. But the worst retaliation comes when the explosives storage shed suddenly detonates in the middle of the day.

The blast rocks midtown Manhattan and brings the Rocci Construction Company to a complete halt while safety violations are investigated.

I'm not immune from Banoa's wrath either. He has his men roughing up, and by that, I mean killing, dealers, gang bangers, and anybody else he thinks might know where I am. Of course, I'm not hiding out in the South Bronx, in fact, I'm living a few blocks from him on Pelham Parkway. Now that fall is here and cold weather is coming in, he has begun a little vendetta and cut off heat to buildings in the South Bronx, threatened several landlords, and they are all buckling under, naturally.

Victoria, James' sister has made it known that she wants to see me.

She and I grew up together, so she is like a sister and knows all the places to visit that will get my attention. She makes the rounds in all the gangs' hangouts, basement parties, bars, and dope dens. No one would ever dream of harming her knowing who her brother is, and who I am. And after the 149 Gangsters' War no one in the South Bronx crossed me again, at least not outright.

Besides, she is a five-five femme fatale, known as the Blood Queen, after she cut a gang banger's dick off, who had the audacity to attack her girlfriend. She hung out with the O. S. as long as I had, and learnt to fight just I did.

She waits for me at the Black Cat one night, knowing I would eventually show up. "Have you forgotten about your friends completely?"

"Of course not," I tell her, "But it does take some time to hear what's going on in the streets."

"Bullshit," she fires back, "You care more about your ofay friends than your own people, and this war you got going is now affecting us. Because you wanted to go hopping in bed with Master's daughter, the mob is cutting off our heat. What are you going to do about it?"

She is mad, but not as much about the situation as with me for causing it, and I do believe she may have other reasons too, reasons that only a seventeen-year old girl understands.

"I'll get the landlords' names from your brother and convince them to buy the coal for the buildings, or else."

"Don't you involve James in this mess," she warns me. "He's a war hero now, not a hoodlum like you and your friends."

"Look who's calling the kettle black," I tell her. "You have not been living an angelic life either. There is no guy who wants to be on your bad side, including me, and that is why I'm here."

Early in the morning, I am at the office of Solomon and Sons Real Estate in midtown. I enter the elevator and press the fifth floor button. A six-two Irish-looking guy catches the door just before it closes and gets on.

"Third floor," he says in a thick Gaelic accent. I learnt later that he was known as the Irishman because of his accent and light brown hair.

I look him over good and press the button. The door closes and we head up. He stands behind me at the back of the elevator, and I know at once he is about to make a move, but I am also quietly trying to cock the pistol in my left coat pocket. The elevator stops on the second floor, James rushes in, and kicks the Irishman in the groin. I whip out my pistol and strike a blow to his ear with the butt. We continue to beat him until the door opens on the fifth floor again. I get out and head down the corridor to the landlord's office.

I enter the outer office, where a pretty young black secretary sits behind a desk.

"Is Mr. Solomon in?"

"Do you have an appointment?" she asks politely.

"No, but he is going to want to talk to me," I say, pull out my switchblade, and cut the phone line on her desk. There are three office doors, one on either side and one behind her. "Don't you go nowhere, as I'm going to need a witness in a couple of minutes."

I walk into the office behind her and plonk down in front of the desk. An old man sits across and is not surprised to see me. I notice that he has a hand on a revolver in his desk drawer.

"You are wasting your time; I can't help you."

"Maybe," I tell him, "but hear me out. Most likely, the Banoas have threatened to kill you if you continue supplying heat and you're thinking that's the worst that can happen. But you're in luck, I'm here to help you today. You seem to have a spot of cowardice on your lapel, so let me get it for you." I pull out a bottle and squirt a clear foul-smelling liquid on his beard and chest.

He repels back in the chair and pulls the gun from the drawer.

"Whoa there, you don't want to do that, that cleaning fluid is highly flammable. You might kill me, or you might not, but you will definitely set yourself on fire. It may not kill you, but I don't think you want to burn your face off either. Put the gun down."

He does so.

"Now, hear me out," I console him, "You are going to sell your buildings to the Neighborhood Redevelopment Association. You will be off the hook with the mob and I won't come back to cook your ass. Hey Sweetheart, I need you to come in now."

The pretty young secretary comes in with terror in her eyes, James walking behind her, and within minutes, they sign the deeds to three buildings in the South Bronx.

"When I leave, I suggest you do the same, the mob doesn't like it when you kill their hit men."

As we walk out of the office, I kick the chair out from under the Irishman and he drops a foot. He starts to jerk wildly as he strangles from the clothesline tied around his neck and looped over the fire sprinkler pipe in the ceiling then back down to his hands behind his back. We hear Solomon and his secretary emptying file cabinets.

The next day the coal trucks arrive. Other landlords hear about Solomon and decide that ordering coal for their buildings is the easiest option.

James and I are in the kitchen of his second floor apartment above a pool hall. He is going over the documents we signed. "Back dating these documents was a good idea," he says, "no way the police will tie us to the murder or extortion charges. But why won't you let me make you a partner in the NRA?"

"No, that's OK," I object quickly, "I am happy just overseeing the superintendents of the buildings. Besides, if my name is on any of this stuff, it will draw undesirables..."

As if on cue, Victoria bursts into the room, "What the hell did you do, Morris?"

"I got the heat on."

"Oh, the heat is on," she yells, "But there are also two thugs in the pool hall trashing the place, and they are looking for you and James. I warned you not to get my brother mixed-up in your bullshit."

"Don't worry," James says, checks his nine, and sticks it in his back. "I'll go down there and put an end to this."

"Don't be a fool," I reply, "They'll kill you on sight. I got this." I go to the living room window and raise it up. I can hear the commotion bellowing out of the pool hall. A crowd has gathered in the street and I suppose some of the people inside are trapped. Two three-hundred pound Italians emerge from the hall. "Man, how many of these guys does Joe Banana have lying around?" I ask myself.

"So, nobody knows Morris Johnson, huh?" One of the mobsters yells at the top of his lungs. "Nobody knows his buddy James Harris either. I guess that little firebug just disappears like smoke in the wind."

"You got to do something, Morris," Victoria tells me. "They plan to kill everyone in there."

I stop watching what is going on outside and pull a small suitcase from under the couch. I unzip it, while still trying to hear what is happening down below as I assemble the small crossbow from the suitcase. I snap the bow's arms in place and I am about to load a bolt into the slot when more shouting reaches us.

"We are going to burn this place to the ground if one of you doesn't tell us where to find that bastard right now!"

"You got to be kidding me," Victoria is in my face. "They are going to kill everyone and you are playing with a fucking bow and arrow!"

"Quiet! I have to time this just right or—"

"Or what? Just shoot the bastards," Victoria commands, "What is up with—"

I grab her by the waist, pull her to me, and kiss her hard on the lips, no tongue. She pulls away in disgust, I slip out the window, and lie down on the fire escape. The fat bastard closest to me holds up a Molotov cocktail and lights the rag.

"Last chance," says the first man, "OK, cook these niggers!"

I squeeze the trigger on the crossbow and zip, the bolt rips through the air noiselessly and buries itself down in the shoulder of the man holding the lit bottle of gasoline. It bores into his chest through the lungs; he cannot scream, or exhale, he can only sip in the smoky air in front of him, and hold onto the bottle.

"What are you waiting for? Throw it already!" The first fat bastard turns to his partner, unable to see the bolt protruding from the shoulder, or the blood running down his paralyzed arm and dripping from his elbow, he can only see the burning rag getting dangerously close to the bottle's opening in a very shaking hand.

It drops to the ground.

A fountain of flames shoots up from the shattered bottle and engulfs the pair. The first fat bastard dances around, swatting at the flames spreading up his body. The second, falls, face first onto the burning pavement, smothering the flames beneath his dead weight.

Jackson, the big three-hundred-pound bouncer for the hall, walks out and throws a bucket of water on the first fat bastard, extinguishing the flames. He says something but I can't hear what, because Victoria is over her shock and again yelling in my ear.

"What the hell did you do that for? You could have just shot them; you could have shot them both."

"Yeah," I agree, not as loud, and still sitting on the fire escape where I am safe from her. "But then they would just send two more. I don't think they are going to find two more willing to come down here to look for me or your brother now. And that is how legends are born."

"You are so full of shit and sick," she storms away into the dark bedroom.

James comes over to the window, "I always thought I'd come back home and you two would have been hooked up. What happened?'

"I don't know," I confess, "I've just always seen her as your sister. But I did keep her safe until your return. I guess everyone thought I had first dibs."

"I think she did too."

Sweet Jesus glances around the lounge at Kennedy Airport, where he is waiting for the early morning flight to Puerto Rico. Slipping into a chair, he closes his eyes for a second.

When he opens them again, he finds himself staring at two Agents, Black and White flashing their badges in his face. As he is escorted to a holding room, he recalls Morris pulling him aside the night in the tomb, warning him that the FBI or NYPD would try to flip him. Oddly, Morris also proposed letting it happen. Because the best way to find out what cops know is to supply them with information, because what they ask lets you know what they are investigating. Sweet Jesus is sure Morris spoke in confidence because Nicky is paranoid about cops.

They start on him, "Where are you going? Are you running from someone, or something?"

"I'm not running at all," Sweet Jesus tells them, "My parents want me to go help my uncle with his fishing boats."

"Did your parents also suggest you travel under the name Edward Teach?" asks Agent Black. When he doesn't get a reaction, he informs Sweet Jesus that Edward Teach was the real name of Blackbeard, the pirate. "Your friends call you the pirate now, don't they?"

"Am I in some kind of trouble?" asks Sweet Jesus.

"You tell me," Agent White continues. "There is no crime for travelling under an assumed name, unless..." He pauses for effect, "...you are leaving the country or attempting to elude prosecution. You wouldn't know anything about a man found swinging by a cleaning lady in midtown."

"No!"

"OK, how about some fat grease balls getting roasted on Morris' old block?"

"Sorry," Sweet Jesus shrugs.

"Do you know what happens to people who try to run out on Morris?" Agent Black queries, "Then let me tell you what happened to most of the Original Sinners."

After three years of fighting the 149 Gangsters, they finally decided to end the war.

The latest warlord of the Gangsters returns to their gang's apartment, and with his members in tow, he goes to the bar and pours a tall whiskey, "It is agreed," he announces, "we will not cross the Prospect Avenue/Southern Boulevard border and they will not venture into our territory. All hostilities are to end today. We have all bled enough over this Charlie Johnson affair, it's time to move on."

"The Sinners agree with you," one of the gang's member states. He is wearing chains, studs, and a set of brass knuckles. A Bowie knife is strapped to his leg and the tell-tale bulge of a gun in his pants' pocket is also evident, a seasoned member of the gang. A triangle of skulls on his denim jacket over his heart means he is an enforcer, sits on the gang council and is the reason he is at the meeting. "I'm not so sure about that little shit Angel. He wasn't at the meeting either."

"Fuck him! He's the OS' problem, and they better handle their business." He flops down in his chair at the head of the room, sighs, and his head drops back.

The main room is dimly lit by candles and a small lamp flickers on the bar. Other gang members enter the apartment and are quickly followed by the girls. They start to drink, smoke, and party. The warlord sits motionless upon his throne, eyes staring uncaring at his kingdom, his subjects parading and performing like clowns at the circus.

One of the girls comes over to him and rubs his head, "What's the matter, baby? Are you tired?"

His head slumps to one side.

Her feet slide beneath her. She looks down and sees a pool of blood surrounding the throne. Her scream is barely heard over the music, and goes unnoticed, but as she scrambles away, the Enforcer realizes something is wrong.

He shakes the warlord by the face then he and another gang banger pull the man by the arms from his throne.

As his body is dragged from the chair, foot long copper pipes are exposed and yanked out of the chair's back. Four of them ooze blood as they protrude from his lifeless body. They drop him face down on the blood-soaked carpet.

Enraged, the Enforcer kicks the chair over, and sees on the wall behind it, 'AOD 12:12' written in blood. He screams in anger, so loud that he drowns out the music.

I bolt from the darkness of the bedroom to the left of where the throne was moments ago. In a blinding fury, I leap onto the Enforcer's chest, toppling him to the floor. Dagger already in hand, I stab him on the side of his neck, give it a quick twist, and rip it out. Blood gushes out like water from a hose. I'm up, slashing the throat of the next Gangster on my path to the door next, I plunge my dagger into someone's chest, and then I'm out the door.

I jump down the flight of stairs, landing quietly on the balls of my feet, and using the walls to break and redirect me down the next flight. I'm not sure how many Gangsters are hanging outside, but I don't want them to hear me coming, but I'm already on the first floor running down the long hallway to the entrance before I hear the others on the stairs above. I catch them so totally by surprise it takes them a minute or two to react. Just as I had planned, but killing the Enforcer was an added bonus; now the 149 Gangsters are without leadership.

I hit the street and the bright sunlight hits back, blinding me. I can't immediately tell how many people are out here, so I turn east and tear up the block. I am half way down the second block when I hear their voices yelling 'Get him!' and 'Take a shot!' The popping sounds of gunfire don't bother me; I know well-enough to zigzag through the street as I head for the borderline.

Their shouts grow so faint that I glance over my shoulder and turn onto Southern Boulevard. I can't believe it; those bastards are two whole blocks behind me. I flip them the bird and start walking up the Boulevard, have to give them time to catch up.

There are about a dozen chasing me by the time I duck into the alley on Leggett Avenue, panting heavily as they close in.

'This ain't going to be much of a battle' I think, as I burst into the basement apartment. My entrance brings the ten Sinners inside to battle mode. They draw guns and knives, and seconds later, the Gangsters come flying through the door. As expected, they are in no shape to fight, so I help them out. As a Gangster falls, I take his place, slashing and stabbing at the Sinners. And of course, I slash and stab the Gangsters who are winning. In fact, I spin and hack my way through the room until all lay dead...

"No one survived that clash," says Agent Black. "The 149 Gangsters were wiped out. All but a handful of the Original Sinners were dead too. Only those who were lucky enough to be somewhere else that afternoon lived."

"I heard some BS story like that," Sweet Jesus tells them. "You know that crap is made up. No one is sure what happened or what ended the gang war."

"Do you want to see the police report?" Agent White asks. "Every single guy in that basement had their throat cut. Some while they were lying on the floor. Your friend slaughtered everyone in there. We know it was him, because there were witnesses who saw him lead those boys to their doom."

"Then why don't you arrest him?" asks Sweet Jesus.

"Because what people say and what they will testify to are two different things entirely," adds Agent Black.

"Can I go?" asks Sweet Jesus, "You are going to make me miss my flight."

"Sure, go," says Agent Black, "Just be careful who you are running with, or after. Hey, maybe I'll come down there one day. I'll look you and your uncle up."

"Yeah," Sweet Jesus agrees, "Maybe you can go out on a fishing trip or something. We will trade fish stories." Sweet Jesus leaves the room just in time to make his flight.

Bonnie gets another message, this time from me. I don't jerk her around on the phone; I set up a meeting for Friday night.

We are in a club in Brooklyn, and I tell her that I have a lead on one of Joey's friends, Big Mike's younger brother, the late football player, who died on the fourth. I want her to befriend him, lead him on, and he in turn should lead us to the rest of Joey's gang. She agrees and promises to contact Nicky and me before meeting that bunch. I assure her that I'll have something special for them.

Nicky also contacts me.

After the problems at the construction sites, his father has been leaning heavily on him to get this thing wrapped up. Then Nicky casually mentioned going after the number runners again and his father came down on him hard.

In Nicolas' words, "You got away with it once because you were young and foolish. Gambling money has many masters, if you touch it again, they will retire you."

We both know there are only two retirement plans for the mob, a box or the river.

He tells me he's working on a more direct approach to our problem, so I tell him to tell his father not to despair, the fertilizer business is about to kick off. I just have one more guy to get in line.

I meet with the Black Spades' Warlord —not exactly the best name a gang could pick, in fact, I tell him it's redundantly ridiculous. Perhaps that is not the best way to make friends either, but the Ace of Spades —an even worse moniker, but everyone just calls him Ace — and I go back a couple of years. He is not a fan, but we worked together dealing drugs for a while and I tell him I need his help. He blows me off, as I knew he would, so I warn him the mob will be back. I tell him that if he watches my back, I'll watch his. He tells me the best he will do is not turn me over to them. His gang is not that large, maybe twenty strong, so he believes he's too small to draw attention. Three days later, the boiler in his building blows up, quickly convincing him that we do have a common enemy.

I introduce him to Nicky and arrange for him and his gang to move into Co-Op City. With the guns we provide and the people he can recruit, he will easily quintuple his numbers in no time.

Recruiting gang members is mainly about intimidation and location, you simply force those in your neighborhood to join. Co-Op City is a huge vertical neighborhood, if Ace takes control of one or two buildings, he'll have a hundred or more Black Spades before Christmas. Then, he can exact his revenge on the 'White Devil' to his heart's content.

Nicky is naturally apprehensive about partnering with the Black Spades but I convince him that I need their building, one of those we got from Solomon. Besides, he is not going to be in charge for long. I tell Nicky, "the thing about being a warlord is picking good generals and knowing when to retire them."

Ace wastes no time in attacking Banoa's businesses and gangsters. They rob his bars, legal and illegal; shoot it out with his dealers, in general, raise hell on earth, and the best thing about the plan is that Joseph Banoa doesn't know we are behind it.

The word on the street is that the Rocci war has made him weak. He failed to get us, so now, others are moving in on his territories. His people are being forced into a smaller and tighter corner, making it easier to get to Joey's friends.

Little Henry, Big Mike's brother, is making runs for Joe Banoa. At fifteen, he is already making collections from loan sharks, pimps, and any other debt Joe orders him to take care of. Banoa has begun using younger blood because I killed several of his top men, Nicky took out a bunch too, and the Irish also cut down a good number. To add insult to injury, the Black Spades are targeting anybody who looks like a mobster. Little Henry was easy to recruit anyway, he wants revenge for his brother's death and truly believes that working for Joseph Banoa will give it to him.

Bonnie has started showing up at the Corner Sweet Shop every day at 3:30 in the afternoon, just after school lets out.

On this day, she is wearing jeans and a white blouse, insinuating she is still in school. She dyed her hair blonde and now wears it tied back in a ponytail, which makes her appear at least three years younger, just the right look for Little Henry, who comes into the candy store once a week to make a collection. Bonnie, usually sitting at the counter drinking a shake, pretends not to notice him, but every now and throws him a furtive glance then looks away just as he peeks her way. She is playing cat and mouse; poor guy has no idea she is a tiger.

At first, he made the pickups with two or three guys, but once she started talking to him, he also began coming into the candy store alone, making his boys wait outside. It took five weeks for her to finally get her claws into him, and like any cat, she let him run and then pounced on him again.

"You're way too young to be a made man," she tells him one afternoon.

"Well, I haven't made my bones yet," he confesses, "But soon. I have a crew and everything. The men are older than me and a couple of them are Joey's guys, but I'm the boss. I don't answer to anyone but Joe B."

"Really, you must know his sons then, Joey and Michael," she lets him run. "My sister knew them. I was real sad when his brother died."

"Not died," he corrects her, "Was murdered. My brother too, but make no mistake, we are going to get them."

"I heard Joey will pay big money for anyone who knows where the Rocci gang is," Bonnie toys with him. "I bet if you told them where to find them, you'd get your bones for sure."

"Of course! Why, do you know something?"

"Not me," she says excitedly, "My sister knows a girl who says she is seeing Nicky Rocci. I don't believe her; I think she's full of shit. But I can find out where he is and I'll tell you and your crew. You can roll up on them and blast them. Then my boyfriend will be a real Mafia Man."

"Yes! Yes, I like that," Little Henry says enthusiastically. "I'll tell my guys tonight, we can get together at the bar and make plans. I got something real nice for those fuckers." Little Henry opens his backpack and shows her a sawed-off shotgun with the envelopes of money.

"Nice," she says, "but don't tell anyone yet. You don't want someone going behind your back to Mr. B and getting what should be coming to you. I'll get the information and then we can go meet your crew together on Friday. So, how many in your crew?"

"Four."

When you fix your sights on one thing for too long, you can't see anything else. Little Henry can't see this girl is too old to be in school, can't see he has never seen her outside of the candy store, can't see the story she is telling him is too good to be true. Little Henry can only see what he wants, that he is going to get his revenge.

They arrive in high spirits at the bar Friday night. Bonnie has on a short fur jacket, open of course, showing off her clinging silk blouse. An extra tight skirt, also short, but not so short she would look like a hooker, her hair is wavy, draping her face.

Little Henry walks in but the bouncer places one hand on Bonnie's left breast, stopping her at the door. "I'll have to check you out," he grins.

"She's with me, Carl," says Little Henry.

"Mr. B's orders," responds the bouncer, "No one gets in without a search, Little Henry."

"Henry," he says, "Just Henry!"

"He's big where it counts," Bonnie says and opens her jacket completely, knocking the bouncer's hand from her breast. "Does it look like I'm carrying a weapon?"

"The purse too," demands the bouncer.

She opens the little black handbag; it is filled with makeup. The bouncer smiles and steps aside, letting them open the second door and step into a sea of smoke and jukebox music.

Little Henry locates his crew in a booth at the back of the bar.

They watch her as she crosses the room, a couple of rounds are already on the table.

"I'll get us some drinks. No milkshakes tonight."

"OK," Bonnie agrees, "I got to go fix my face. Where's the lady's room?"

"It's over there, but you look great."

Bonnie disappears.

Little Henry joins his crew with a pair of drinks, sliding into the booth next to the other four guys. "Well, what did I tell you?"

"She is something," says Roman, "and after she tucks you into bed, I'll show her what a real man can do, Little Henry."

Bonnie walks over to the table, carrying a shoulder bag slightly larger than the one she walked in with. They all slide over, squashing together so she can sit down, instead, she places the bag on the table and remains standing.

Roman eyes her greedily, "Little Henry says you know where Nicky Rocci and his friend are hiding. So, where is he, Dolly?" "Outside, just itching to come in," she says and shoves the table into their chests. All grab the table to push it away, but Bonnie pulls out what looks like a Bic lighter and opens the bag in front of them. Right away they recognize the row of shotgun shells pointed at them and lean back against the booth's leather backing. "I told them there was no need to come in because you are going to tell me everything I want to know." She pulls up a chair and sits down.

"I'm not telling you nothing, bitch," yells Roman, trying to draw attention to the booth.

The music drowns him out.

"Nice try," Bonnie says a little loud herself. "Let me tell you what you are looking at here. It's like a claymore mine, the latest thing in personnel killing devices. This one is homemade, not as pretty, but still effective. The trigger I'm holding will send an electric charge to the five shotgun shells when I release the button. Everybody on that side of the table, that's you five idiots, is going to catch a face full of buckshot, while I'm sitting here safe and sound. Hands on the table!" yells Bonnie.

Roman was slowly reaching for his gun, but quickly does as he is told.

Bonnie continues, "This is a dead man's switch, so if I take my finger off the button you are dead. Was I not clear? Also, you don't want to be shaking the table, there is a mercury switch detonator in the bag, too much movement and boom. Now, where are Joey Banoa, Chris Caralucci, and Nathan Napolitano? And don't lie to me; momma hates it when you lie."

"Nice try yourself," Roman calls her bluff. "You can't set that thing off in here. The bouncer, the bartender, and at least two other of Joe B's men are watching this place.

You will kill us, but they will kill you too. And I bet your death will be worse than ours.”

"Five shotgun shells going off at once are going to be loud as hell,” Bonnie tells him. “I’ll bet you five to one, everyone is going to panic and run for the door. But I’ll tell you what I’m going to do, I’ll go to the bar and get us another round while you think about the position you are in.” Bonnie slides the chair away from the table.

"Wait a minute. Wait,” yells Little Henry. “If she walks away from this table we are dead.”

"See, smarts, and that’s why he’s the boss,” says Bonnie.

"Who, him?” asks Roman. “He’s nothing but a glorified errand boy. Look, we don’t know where Joey is, no one does.”

"Tsk... Tsk... Little Henry, you lied to me. You boys got to give me something. You said you don’t know where Joey is, but that can also mean that you do have an idea where his two friends are hiding.”

"We don’t know where any of them are,” insists Roman. “They took off after the shooting and haven’t been seen since. Besides, if we did tell you, you would still kill us.” “No I wouldn’t, I have to verify the information first,” explains Bonnie. “If I discover you lied, then you will be talking to Nicky Nails and Bulletproof Johnson, and they are not as patient as I am. But if you really don’t know anything I guess I’ll just go back and tell them to find someone who does.”

"No, wait,” shouts the boy sitting between Little Henry and Roman.

Bonnie had been eyeing him since she sat down.

He is sweating like it is still a hot summer night, rather than October.

"Shut up...”

"No way, I am not dying for Chris Caralucci. He killed her friends, came around bragging about shooting them in the head and all. Fuck him! I'm not dying for that piece of shit. He's in Saddle Brook, Jersey, with his aunt and uncle."

"Where do they live?"

"How the fuck do I know? Look them up. He called me from there one night, wanted to know if it was safe to come back."

"You know what, I believe you," Bonnie tells him. "Thank you for your cooperation." She gets up to leave.

"What about this?" asks Roman.

"When I'm out of range with the detonator the little green light will stop flashing. Just dump the bag in the trash," Bonnie leaves the boys watching the green LED flashing rhythmically.

We pick her up outside the bar.

"We are going to Saddle Brook, New Jersey, the hideout of one Chris Caralucci."

"You think they told you the truth?" I ask.

As we pass the corner she says, "Sure." She deliberately lifts her finger from the button and hands me the detonator.

Seeing the green flashing light fade out, the guys let out a sigh of relief.

Blinding bright white light illuminates the booth. A loud boom overpowers the jukebox. Instantly, people in the bar are diving onto the floor or running blindly in all directions. Panic is slowly replaced by horror, as the five guys' heads are splattered across the back of the booth.

CHAPTER 9
Friends and Lovers

Carlos, the Colombian from Washington Heights, arrives in Puerto Rico a week after Sweet Jesus. He comes in on a commuter jet out of Boca Raton, Florida, carrying two black medium-size travel bags and two scary looking sidekicks.

Sweet Jesus is at the airport to meet him with two scary guys of his own. "Did you bring the stuff?" he asks as they drive away from the airport.

"One hundred kilos of the pure Colombian, right here," Carlos tells him while patting the bag on his lap.

"You didn't have any trouble with custom?"

"Never even checked my ID." Carlos smiles, "if only it was this easy going the other way."

"Don't worry, it will be after this process," Sweet Jesus tells them as the car winds up the mountainside.

"It better be."

"You know Bulletproof," says Sweet Jesus, "He's a fucking genius."

They continue on through the country far from San Juan then stop in a small town with a few houses, a couple of stores, and a rundown shabby factory. A man pulls back the rusted corrugated zinc door as the car approaches and they drive right in. The door is quickly pulled shut behind them.

"Pense que he visto agujeros mierda aqujeros de vuelta a casa," says Carlos.

Everyone laughs.

The factory is little more than a huge rusty tin shack. There is a boiler that looks like it came from an old train at the back of the room, which it did. A steel staircase leads to a catwalk above the boiler, various sized pipes run from the boiler around the area, and one set gets smaller as it approaches a rubber conveyor belt. The belt runs over copper tubing, which snakes horizontally back and forth from a huge compressor. The conveyor belt ends six feet up at a playground slide that drops over a large metal bin on wheels. There are several bins lined up and ready to go.

Smoke from the burning coal is thick in the confined space as the slowly turning ventilation fan in the ceiling is doing the bare minimum to clear the air. The few hanging lights cut through the haze but the brightest glow comes from underneath the train boiler.

"How's the temperature in the boiler?"

"Esta bien, Senor Ramirez," replies a sweaty and shirtless worker.

"Ok. Let's have it," commands Sweet Jesus.

"This shit better work," Carlos says and dumps the contents of the luggage on the table.

Another older man waiting on the bricks of cocaine begins sticking long straws into them then drops the straws into test tubes of clear liquid, which turns dark blue.

"What you think, I come all this way with shit in my pockets?"

"Like I said, Bulletproof is a genius, so we have to make sure we are starting with pure products to get the best results," states Sweet Jesus.

The workers cut open the bricks and carefully transfer them to stainless steel bowls, the bowls are carried to the top of the catwalk, and the cocaine is poured into the steaming hot liquid. When the last of the cocaine is in the boiler, it is closed and sealed, and then the shirtless men shovel more coal beneath the boiler.

Two hours go by and the train whistle blows.

The older man starts the compressor; it is noisy and even smokier than the coal fire heating the boiler. He starts the conveyor belt, "We will wait for it to get cold."

"Yes, of course," confirms Sweet Jesus.

Carlos, who has been coughing and spitting since entering the factory, says, "I hope this isn't going to take too much longer. I'm about to die here."

"No, not at all," replies the old man.

The pipes under the conveyor belt are a frosty white. He turns a valve on one of the pipes and starts the liquid spraying onto the belt. It instantly freezes to a thick layer of ice as it rises up. At the top, sheets of ice snap off, slide down, and fall into the awaiting bin. He turns the valve again and increases the amount of liquid spray, increasing the thickness of the ice sheet.

"Not too much, Julio," cautions Sweet Jesus, "We don't want it to be sticky."

"No Mr. Ramirez, I make it just thick enough."

When the first bin is full, it is rolled to the side and another takes its place.

Carlos picks up a piece with his bare hands, "Damn, this stuff is cold."

"Colder than ice," remarks Sweet Jesus. He takes the piece, places it in one of the stainless-steel bowls, breaks it into smaller pieces with a hammer, and drops a piece into one of the test tubes of clear liquid. Nothing happens. The liquid remains crystal clear. "Chemically, the cocaine is undetectable, even dogs won't be able to detect it."

"Maybe as ice," Carlos challenges him, "but what about as a liquid when the ice melts."

To satisfy his curiosity, Sweet Jesus melts the remaining pieces in the bowl with a blowtorch and pours a few drops into another test tube. Nothing happens. "Convinced?"

Carlos is and the workers begin packing the cocaine Ice and regular ice in drums of fish. They seal the drums and Carlos writes down the tag numbers of the seals. They load forty three-foot-tall drums of fish and ice onto a truck to transport back to the city. From there a ship will take them to New York City. Step one of the process is accomplished.

"We've got to get to Saddle Brook before eleven," I tell Nicky and Bonnie.

"Why?" asks Bonnie.

"We got to find Chris before he sees his five headless friends on the news tonight."

"You think killing them was a mistake?" she asks.

"Hell no, they had to die," I tell her, "They would have warned him otherwise."

We arrive in Saddle Brook and drive around until we find a phone booth with a phone book.

"What the hell?" Nicky says with venom, "Is this the Caralucci ancestral home? There are a dozen different listings here."

Bonnie rips the page from the book and looks it over, "They are all over town, too. You guys believe in luck, there is a Caralucci pizza on Market Street. How about if we drive over first and see if Chris works there?"

I tell her it sounds better than a dozen break-ins and murdering our way through the city, and luck is indeed with us, we see Chris through the shop window. We work on a plan to grab him because we need him alive. Bonnie figures that since he is a delivery boy, we can call in an order and they will send him. We had passed a house for sale a few blocks away, we call and give its address.

At first, they refuse, because it's closing time, which we had planned, as we don't want them to expect Chris to go back to work. Because we know he is not going to be returning.

"I just moved into the house and the gas hasn't been turned on yet," pleads Bonnie. "If he comes over there will be a twenty in it for him."

The owner agrees and sends Chris with two pizzas.

He arrives at the house; Bonnie opens the door, and lets him walk into the dark. "You don't have any lights either."

"Don't need them, I don't live here," Bonnie tells him and grabs the pizza boxes.

I throw the hardest right cross I can out of the darkness into the middle of his face. He slams into the wall and stumbles forward. Nicky takes the next shot to his face, sending him back to the wall. He starts to scream, so I catch him by the throat just under the chin and quieten him. As I hold him up, Nicky goes to work on his body. When he runs out of steam, I let Chris drop to his knees and begin kicking him in the ribs and stomach, then end by stomping on his back.

We take a break, eat the pizza then duct tape his hands behind his back, and his mouth shut. We get him up and walk him into the garage, put him in the trunk of our car, and tape his legs together. We clean up the blood and vomit in the hall, throw the rags in his trunk, then park his car in the garage before we leave for New York again.

"Won't the cops find his car when they come looking for him?" asks Bonnie.

"He probably won't be reported missing until tomorrow," I inform her. "They can't see the car from the outside, and if they do actually search the house, the trail ends there. And by this time tomorrow he'll be dead."

The sun is rising over the East River when we pull the car onto the rocky road leading to the water south of the Hunts Point Market. We pull Chris out of the trunk and cut his bonds. He is swollen, and black and blue, looking much worse in the daylight. He looks around, possibly thinking of making a run for it, but has no idea where he is. There is nothing around except crumbled red bricks and the river.

"Come with me," I command and start walking towards the water. Bonnie and Nicky are sitting on the hood of the Ford, huddled together for warmth on this cold morning.

Chris hesitates for a moment then limps behind me.

I stop at the break-wall to the river. "See those holes in the rocks along the river's edge?" I point to the large slabs of stone and concrete that run five feet down the embankment and into the water. "Do you know what caused those round holes?"

"No," answers Chris, his voice barely louder than a whisper.

"Speak up," I yell, "No one can hear you out here. You can make all the noise you want; no one is going to hear."

"No, I don't know." He is more defiant, louder. "You plan to kill me, so go ahead. But you will be killing the wrong person. I didn't kill your friends, Joey and Nathan killed them. I didn't even want to go, he forced me. And when the shooting started, I fired over their heads."

"Let me tell you where those holes come from," I continue like I didn't hear a word he said. "The river rats chew through the rocks to get out of the water as the tide rises. Rats' teeth are so sharp they can grind right through rock. There are thousands of them down there, I know, this is my home. Here, I am king, lord, and master. All the rats here, large and small, answer to me. Now, I'm going to ask you a couple of questions, and if you answer truthfully, we can be out of here before the tide rises. Because there are only two reasons the rats leave those holes, the rising tide, and the smell of blood."

I pull out my .38 revolver and shoot him in the leg. I love shooting people with it, it's loud and scary, and gets their attention. Chris sees the quick flash, but the boom overpowers his hearing. He feels the burn in his right thigh and goes down screaming in agony. He begins to beg, and I walk a few steps away from the edge then tell him not to lie there, as it won't take long for the rats to smell blood. He struggles to his feet and hops over, still trying to convince me he is innocent.

"Do you know how we found you?"

"No," pain gives strength to his voice.

"Your five friends," I tell him. "They told us how you bragged about killing ours, just before we blew their heads off. Now, the first question. Where is Joey Banoa?"

"I don't know," he cries, "We took off right after the shooting at the Raven. I heard nobody knows where his father sent him."

"That's unfortunate," I tell him, "Because that is the only way you get to walk away from here." I shoot him in his other leg, this time in the knee. I hear some squeaks coming from the river's edge. I look back and there are a couple that have already ventured onto the rocky terrain. I kneel beside Chris and turn his battered face towards the water. "That little trail of blood has got their attention. Soon, the rest will join them, are you sure you don't know where your friends are?"

Chris rolls around on the ground. I walk a foot or two to the side and the first five rats – small by comparison– charge him, going straight for the bloody wounds. The pain intensifies as their razor-like teeth rip into him. Chris kicks and smacks at them then manages to grab one of the slimy rodents, squeezes it, and throws it across the rocky landscape.

I shoot one of the others, scaring off the rest. "This is only going to get worse. The tide is rising and the blood is calling them."

"My hand to God, I don't know where Joey is," he holds his hand up.

"There is no God here," I yell at him and kick his hand away. "There is only me and the rats. Where are your friends?"

He is painfully dragging himself across the brick-strewn field following me back toward the car. "Everyone has gone into hiding since you started killing people, no one knows where anyone is anymore."

"That's not true, your little gang knew where I could find you, and in a minute or two, my friends will convince you to tell me where I can find yours."

More rats come, four times as many, bigger too, and instantly dig into any exposed flesh. There is squeaking, screaming, and swearing as Chris tries to fight back. He attempts to crush the slippery vermin under his weight, snap their necks, and frantically rips them off his body and throws them away. Each rat's bite, like a miniature razor cut, tears a tiny piece of flesh, which is instantly dragged away. One, the size of a small cat, rips a chunk from his ear and scurries along then is quickly replaced by a larger and hungrier one that bites Chris' thumb off. More and more come, scamper around me then attack Chris as he tries to cover up. A small one runs up his pants' leg, and he jumps to his feet punching at his groin, the two bullets in his legs seem to no longer affect him.

Nicky runs over, throws gasoline on Chris from a plastic bucket we brought along, and shoots a match from the book. It ignites in the air on its way to Chris' chest and lights on contact, sending him whirling like a top and crashing back to the ground. The rats scatter, running all the way back to the bluff.

Bonnie takes her time walking over with a fire extinguisher and sprays him down. Before we got here, they had asked what I needed a bucket and fire extinguisher for, and I told them they would be necessary to get Chris to talk.

Chris is covered in cuts, badly burned, I imagine missing a nut, and ready to talk, "Nathan! Nathan's sister is good friends with Joey's sister." He says breathing heavily through the pain. "Nathan might know where Joey is, either him or his sister."

"OK," I whisper in his whole ear, "I told you my friends would convince you to talk. Where can I find Nathan?"

"I don't know," cries Chris.

"Oh come on now, you little scumbag," I say frustrated, "Look at them. You don't want them to come back." The bluff is lined with rats, several rows deep. Nicky had poured the rest of the gasoline around us in a wide circle and lit it up. "We are out of gas and don't have that many bullets left. Think hard and fast, where is Nathan?"

"Upstate New York," Chris answers in a rush. "His uncle used to work at Sing Sing and you can see the prison from his house. He lives on Spring Street, in a big yellow house, the only yellow house in the neighborhood."

"Good. Very good," I say. "Now, only one more question. Where... the fuck... is Joey... Banana?"

"I don't know," he begins to cry again.

Nicky hops over the fire, as it's starting to burn down. "Let me talk to him," he tells me.

I leave them, join Bonnie on the hood of the Ford, and light up a joint.

Nicky gets down on one knee, "Hey paisan! You've been a real stand-up guy, you been beaten, burned, and bitten by rats. You have taken more for your friend Joey than I would have taken for these guys. But you got to help me help you." Nicky pauses and slaps him a couple of times to revive him. "Hang in there, buddy, we are almost done here. The girl, she's Irish, she don't need a reason to hate your wop ass, but you did kill her boyfriend, so she wants you to die in the worst way. And Bulletproof, he's a fucking nigger, who knows what he's thinking? You know, he has been filming this whole thing. Tell me where I can find Joey Banana, and I'll put a bullet in your head right now. We can end this thing, no more rats, no more pain. You know you're not leaving here alive, just give me the answer and this is all over."

"I don't know."

Nicky walks back to the car and the rats begin to close in again. He takes out his pistol and takes aim at Chris' head. "He doesn't know."

I lower his hand as the rats start gnawing on Chris again. He is screaming, but no longer as loud, whereas the rats are squeaking with delight. "He killed our friends, but Frank was her lover, Bonnie it is up to you."

"Is this the place you were going to take us to learn to shoot?" Bonnie asks me. "This is where you target practice on the rats?"

I nod.

Chris' screams get lower, less intense, and he is covered by rats from head to toe.

"Let the rats win this time."

We sit on the car smoking as the rats eat Chris clear to the bone and the biggest ones run off with the bones. Surprisingly, it doesn't take long at all. Then again, there are countless numbers of vermin.

Our fertilizer business takes off even as we are taking down Joseph Banoa's.

Lance receives a new drop point to deliver his shipment of liquor to; it will be done at night in a Brooklyn warehouse district. The long empty street is easy to cover and lessens the opportunity for an ambush. Wisely, Banoa has deployed over thirty men to cover a block of four warehouses. Most are in and around the loading docks, then some on the roofs, a few in armored trucks to transport the liquor, and all armed with Stoner 63 machine guns fresh from the battlefields of Vietnam.

Lance drives his rig towards the warehouses at the end of the dead-end street. "I don't like this," he says nervously.

"Just do what they tell you to do," says a voice from the trailer, "And I'll take care of the rest. Remember when you stop to climb into the bed compartment."

Two men climb up onto the steps on either side of the cab and peer in with machine guns trained on Lance. "Any trouble getting here, were you followed?"

"No," he replies to the man hanging on his door.

The man waves his arm, the gate slides to the right, Lance drives forward into the yard, and sees an armored truck pull across the driveway behind him. The man on his door tells him to stop about fifty feet down the driveway; they hop off the cab and head to the back.

"They blocked the driveway with an armored truck," he warns the man in the trailer.

Mad Dog Madison, an eight-year vet recently returned to the Original Sinners, tells Lance, "Now will be a good time to get under that blanket. It's about to get loud back here."

The two men open the trailer; it is stacked floor to ceiling with cases of liquor. They wave the forklift drivers over. Two other men open the back of another armored truck. Several cars idle at the loading docks. The first forklift swings in behind the semi about ten feet away.

Cases explode from the center, with quick flashes of lightning striking out from the trailer, tiny orange fireflies, and tracer rounds singing to a deadly drum-roll. The first forklift is driven backward and explodes from the M60 machine gun barrage. A shorter drum-roll rings out from the trailer and more tracers, armor piercing then ballistic rounds rock the armored truck blocking the driveway. A second barrage cuts it in half and blows it up.

The men, realizing an ambush is on, run from the truck but are cut down by relentless machinegun fire from the docks. Those on the roofs of two of the buildings open fire on Lance's rig. The bullets ping the trailer like hail before a tornado, loud and ominous, but are quickly absorbed into the Kevlar webbing and chainmail surrounding the inside walls. After a minute, the storm ceases.

"My turn." Mad Dog Madison pushes front on the lever to his left and slides forward on the track. His chair and M60 are mounted on a platform, which is in a half-inch thick steel ball; the bulletproof shell extends beyond the trailer and pivots and rotates as the gun moves. He sweeps the docks left and right with short precise burst, those eight years behind an M60 has perfected killing men and destroying vehicles. Then, he aims at the roofs, picking off those who have not fled. The AP rounds of the M60 slice through the bricks with ease, and the ballistic ones that follow do the same to the men behind the brick. A minute later and a thousand rounds fired, the warehouse loading docks are silent.

Mad Dog Madison pulls on the lever in his left hand and retracts the shell, then, unbuckling the seat belt, he climbs out the back of the steel ball. He bangs on the trailer wall behind the cab, "let's go."

Lance climbs behind the wheel, amazed at the carnage created in such a short time. Car fires burning, bodies blown apart, so mutilated they barely resemble human beings; this is war. He drives through the remnants of the armored truck in the driveway and down the long empty streets of the Brooklyn warehouse district.

It doesn't take long for the news to reach Joseph Banoa. His twenty plus years bootleg booze business is over. From now on, it belongs to Patrick and Shaun O'Leary, and the Bainbridge Boys, minus thirty-five percent for the spoils of war.

Carlos, Nicky, me, and an older Colombian gentleman with a neatly trimmed silver-gray haircut and beard wait in a

Brooklyn warehouse not far from where the Battle of Brooklyn took place. We are there for the shipment of fish from Puerto Rico. It has been two days since Carlos sealed the forty containers and sent them to the docks, which arrived this morning and are being delivered to the warehouse across the street. They have been under constant guard to ensure no one tampered with the containers. I insisted on that. One of their men and one of mine took the ship back to New York. It passed through custom and now it's time for step two, turning ice back into hielo.

"You checked the seals and they are good?" I ask Carlos.

"Yes, these are the containers we shipped out. And as instructed I didn't touch anything."

"Great, then we are waiting for just one more player to join our game of hide and seek," I tell them.

Two large black vans with the letters, "D.E.A." proudly displayed in white pull up in front of the warehouse across the street. Three black sedans block traffic on the street.

"What are the policia doing here?" exclaims Carlos.

"I invited them," I state calmly. "Indirectly, of course. A well-known informant let them know a hundred kilos of coke are being delivered to that warehouse ..."

Carlos pulls his pistol. Nicky draws his.

"Relax boys. Do you two think it is a good idea to start a shootout in here with the DEA across the street?" They holster their guns and I continue, "You are not paying for a delivery service, you are paying to get your cocaine past the DEA. So this is a live fire test. The DEA knows there is cocaine down there. Let's see if they can find it."

"And if they do?" asks Carlos.

"I'll pay you the hundred grand and we are done," I assure him. "But it is better to lose a hundred kilos now than a thousand later when some real rat snitch bastard blows the whistle. Besides, they will be there for hours and they will never find it."

The DEA goes through everything, using dogs, an x-ray machine, and chemical analysis of the fish and the ice, but come up empty. After three hours, they pack up and leave. I call the warehouse and have ten five gallon buckets of the ice brought over to us.

I explain the process of heating the ice to a very high temperature and pressure. Using the reversing catalysis, the cocaine will separate from the other chemicals and reform. We shoot the steam into a low-pressure chamber and watch the coke snow in the glass like a giant snow globe. Once we get several grams, I pull the tray out and the silent older gentleman begins testing it. Test tubes of clear liquid turn a deep ocean blue.

"This is the only true test," I tell them and snort a large amount up my nose. The freeze is instantaneous, knocking me back from the table. Carlos follows and then Nicky. Finally, the older gentleman abandons his test tubes for his nose. After a few more lines and some time to work through the intense high, we work out a price and schedule to move a thousand kilos a week at a thousand dollars a kilo.

When Carlos asks what we are going to do with all the fish, I inform him those are bottom feeders, not fit for eating, that their sole purpose is to be used as stock for fertilizer. That way, the FDA won't inspect the shipments either. And by the time the EPA examines the fertilizer, the cocaine is long gone. It's a lot of fish and a lot of fertilizer.

We truck the coolant to the building in the South Bronx, fill the boiler, and in three of the apartments we make it snow cocaine. As the business grows, and it grows astonishingly quickly, the NRA takes over more buildings in New York, Philadelphia, and Newark, and all become cocaine-processing plants. The Rocci Construction Company does all the renovations to the buildings, making sure the boiler systems look like real heating systems instead of the stills they really are, at least on paper, and naturally, no one but me knows what chemicals are used in the process.

Bonnie was extremely melancholic on the ride back from the river. I glance over at her in the passenger seat as she blindly stares out the window. Nicky is in the back seat watching the video and laughing aloud. He grabs my shoulder, "I don't know why you shot this stuff, but this is good. Too good, we will get the death penalty for it."

"Don't worry, it won't fall into the wrong hands," I assure him.

He turns off the camera and stashes it under Bonnie's seat before getting out at Hunts Point. He tells us he will meet us in Ossining tonight. "I have some arrangements I need to make for our guest."

I resume driving, taking Bonnie back to the Bainbridge Boys territory.

"I don't feel anything," she tells me bluntly. "I don't feel satisfied. I don't feel relieved. I don't even feel remorse. I simply don't feel. And the strange thing is this is how I've felt since Frank was killed. Why don't I feel anything?"

"I don't know," I reply honestly. "Were you expecting to feel differently? Did you think killing this guy would make you feel better?"

She stares out the window, unable to look at me. I am a monster, a soulless vermin worse than the rats that devoured her lover's killer. But I know what she is afraid of, she's afraid that if she looks me in the eye, she will see herself staring right back.

"Maybe, I don't know. I was hoping that something would change. Because if we kill all of them and nothing does... then what?"

I don't have an answer, but know exactly where she is coming from; she thought that getting revenge on Frank's killer would somehow lift her out of her malaise. I knew it wouldn't, because no killing I've ever done has helped me. We pull up in front of the building where she is living on 205th Street. I turn off the car and we sit there for a long time in silence.

"After my brother was killed, I went after the guy, and killed him even before my brother was laid to rest. Then trailed his guys for three years after that and got them all. It didn't matter, nothing could bring Charlie back, and revenge cannot replace what you lost."

"What got you to pass the emptiness?" she asks, finally looking me in the eyes.

"At first, nothing, then, I met Maria."

"What will it take to get over her loss?"

"Death," I confide in her.

She gets out the car and walks to her apartment building. She opens the black iron gates that secure the courtyard then looks back, but I am already gone.

I head upstate to find the only yellow house with a view of the prison. I want to get there before nightfall, before the news of Chris Caralucci's disappearance gets out.

The news of the mob war on the streets of New York has been mostly suppressed by the Mayor and police Commissioner. Only the most heinous or public crimes have made it into the press, like the Battle of Brooklyn, as the papers dubbed it. Nathan's five dead friends hasn't leaked out yet, but it's only a matter of time before it does. But even if it doesn't make the papers or TV news, it has already hit the streets. If I were Nathan and heard that my friends got their heads blown off, and now another had gone missing, I'd be gone like yesterday's weather.

I park the Ford a block over from the small three-bedroom yellow house on Spring Street. It's a cold night but I keep one window cracked open to keep the rest from fogging up. I am by the park, where I have a clear view of the kitchen window at the back of the house. I only need to sit here to see who is inside, as sooner or later everyone winds up in the kitchen.

About midnight Nicky pulls up behind me in a Lincoln. I join him and we take a couple of hits of blow.

"Is he in there?"

"Yeah, I saw him at dinner," I tell him. "Lights went out about an hour ago."

"How do you know it's him?" Nicky asks.

I pull out three pictures, one of Nathan by himself, one of him and his sister, and lastly the whole family.

I had gotten their pictures right after I learnt their names from Batman and Robin. I broke into Chris' house around four in the morning, the best time as people are fast asleep and do not hear you snooping around. No one in Chris' pictures was smiling, the old man was a drinker, the mother went to bed early, and his brothers and sister looked like they were dying to get out.

I had to get Nathan's family pictures during the day, as they had a dog. Not a dangerous one like a German Sheppard, just a poodle, but any burglar will tell you that a dog, any dog, is trouble. I had to go into the house when no one was home, which meant, during the day while his mom was shopping. A couple of doggy treats for Fifi and I was in and out without any trouble. He has a happy family.

"Tomorrow is Sunday," Nicky says, "Let's hope his aunt and uncle are good Catholics and go to church in the morning, and he's not."

"I don't think he's going to be able to tell us where Joey is either. It's starting to look like we are going to just drop this guy too and come up with another plan for tracking down Joey Banana."

"Way ahead of you," Nicky says and takes another hit then passes the little ceramic case and glass straw over while the cocaine works its way up his nose. "I have another plan that will work even if he doesn't know where Joey is, but we need him alive for it to succeed. I really like the rats, but this time we are going to be subtle."

I take two big hits; one in each nostril, the blow is freezing my brains. "OK by me, as long as we get Joey."

It is a bright and early morning when we watch Nathan's aunt and uncle drive off to church. I'm waiting in the Ford again and Nicky had parked on the corner to see who left the house. He pulls into the driveway and taps the horn once, the signal that Nathan is alone. I can't spot him in the house, just saw the other two in the kitchen before they left, so he must still be sleeping. I cross the backyard and go to the back door, Nicky takes the front. We both use slim metal jimmies to pop the locks. We go to the bedroom in the back, and tap Nathan on the shoulder.

He wakes up startled.

"Get dressed you are coming with us," commands Nicky.

Nathan gets in the passenger seat and I climb in the back. Nicky drives around the block and I get out.

"I'll be following you, so you be a good boy and do what Nicky Nails tells you and everything is going to be all right."

After we get back to the city, we stop at a park and I get back in the car with them. Nathan puts on a black ski mask with the eyes sown shut and lies down in the back of the Lincoln.

"Did he give you any trouble? Any begging for his life?"

"Never said a word," Nicky tells me.

"Hmm, the strong silent type," I quip.

We drive to the Village and take him into a three-story brownstone through an alley. We walk him to the top floor and into a room with the window bricked in. I take off the ski mask and push him down into a metal chair. Nicky takes a thick leather strap and tightens it around his chest then ties his feet and wrists to the chair with smaller belts. Nathan remains silent.

"You know why you're here," I say.

Finally, Nathan breaks his silence, "I didn't kill your friends. That was Joey and Christopher. I didn't even want to go with them, they forced me. I thought they were only going to rough youse guys up. You know, to get back his booze, but when Maria walked in everything changed. They had words and she insulted him, that's when he went over the edge and shot her. I didn't even fire my gun."

"Yeah we know all that," I tell him. "And we are well past the 'who did what to who' stage. You are here to help us get Joey Banana, and before you tell us you don't know where he is, I want you to watch this little film. I call it, 'The pitiful But Befitting End of a piece of Shit Rat Bastard Scumbag.'" I project the movie of Christopher Caralucci on the wall in front of him. Nathan tries to turn his head but I grab him by the ears from behind and dig my nails in, "watch, this is the good part."

After the movie ends I whisper in his ear, "Don't be a pitiful piece of shit rat bastard like your friends and help us find Joey."

"Fuck you," Nathan yells defiantly, "You can suck my dick, nigger!"

"You are going to regret saying that," I inform him.

Nicky walks up to him and gets right in his face. "I really thought you were going to be a smart little guinea prick about this. Well, now we are going to have to kill you and it won't be quick like your friend Chris. You see, you are the last of Joey's friends, so we are going to go real slow until you talk. We are going to play a little onesee-twosee. Bulletproof is going to cut off one of something that you have two of every time you give an answer we don't like."

I slide the flat side of a bowie knife down his cheek and dig the tip in.

"You have two thumbs, he'll cut off one. You have two eyes; see how you like having just one. You got two big balls; you are going to be leaning a little to the left. And don't think you are going to sit there and wait to die, because if we don't get what we need from you, we hear your kid sister is a real good friend of the family."

I hold the picture of him and her in her white confirmation dress in front of his face.

"Please, for the love of God," he yells and struggles against the bondage, "We don't know anything. You fucking bastards should know that by now. Nobody knows where Joey is hiding."

"Not the answer we are looking for," says Nicky.

"Don't think he heard me, probably has too many ears." I quickly rip the bowie knife down behind his right ear.

Nathan hears the slapping sound of flesh hitting the empty room floor. He feels burning pain on the back of his head and a warm flow of blood run down his neck.

"Let's try this again. How do we find Joey?" Nathan doesn't answer.

I hold the bloody knife in front of his face.

"Give me a minute. My sister told me a while ago that some girl went to see him..."

"I told you we should have grabbed the sister," I tell Nicky.

"We still can," Nicky agrees.

"Teresa," Nathan blurts out. "She went to see him. After the killings, he needed something to calm him, so he called her to bring his stash. He didn't want his father to know. When she got back my sister said she was pissed, because he is in Florida partying with hookers."

"There we go," says Nicky, "But Florida is a big state, so you need to narrow it down."

"I don't know. But Teresa will."

"Let's kill him now and go get Teresa," I say.

"No. I can get her to tell me," begs Nathan, "I just need a phone."

Nicky leaves for the phone and tells me not to injure him anymore.

I'm not sure if it's for show or if he can tell how I'm feeling. My mind is re-running the night of the Raven. I hear pop, and then pop... pop... pop... again... again... and again. The door opens and bang... bang. I'm thinking of cutting this guy's throat as soon as we get Joey's whereabouts.

Nicky returns with two phones, one he plugs into the jack in the room, the other has a long line trailing out the door. I hold the receiver to Nathan's face.

Before Nicky dials Teresa's number, he warns him, "One wrong word and Bulletproof will cut off your tongue. Yes?"

Nathan shakes his head and the phone starts ringing. "Hello Teresa, it's Nathan. Nathan Napolitano."

"Really, like how many Nathans do I know? What do you want?" She is not happy to hear from him.

"Joey called. He wants me to take down another stash of pills, but he hung up without giving me the address in Florida." Nathan sounds as conversational as a man with a gun to his head instead of a phone can sound.

"Oh yeah," Teresa's voice jumps a couple of decibels and several tones, "You can tell that no good whore humping son of a bitch he can suck my DICK!"

Nicky smirks and fights back laughing aloud.

Nathan is in a panic; afraid Teresa is about to hang up. He yells, "Look, you stupid little cunt, you can tell him yourself when you see him." He realizes what he said and very nicely continues, "Joey did say to bring you with me, and to tell you the girls that were there last time were just for the guards. His father has him like a prisoner down there and he wishes he was back here with you."

"Oh, that's so sweet of him," she says softly then Nicky hears her voice snap back to a harsher tone. "But if he wasn't fucking chasing after that nigger's little cunt in the first place he wouldn't be there, and our friends wouldn't be dying."

Nathan and Nicky give me a strange look.

Nathan says, "Yeah, I know. But I need the address so I can rent a car."

"Rent a car, I'm not driving to Miami. You'd better be getting us plane tickets," she tells him.

"Yes, you're right. Where are we going? What's the address?"

There is a long pause on the line. Nathan is getting very anxious. Teresa finally speaks up, "I don't remember the actual address..."

Nathan and Nicky let out an exasperated sigh.

"It's a big white house on the river. I mean it literally looks like the White House. Forty-seven or seventy-four Biscuit Avenue, or something like that. Don't worry I'll know it when I see it. When are you going to pick me up?"

"I'll call you when I get the plane tickets." Nicky and I hang up the phones.

"I did good, right?"

"There is no river or Biscuit Avenue in Miami," Nicky tells him. "But lucky for you I've been there. The stupid bitch is talking about Biscayne Boulevard on the inter-costal waterway."

"We are good, right?" Nathan says excitedly, like a man trying not to get killed. "I told you what you wanted to know."

"Yes you did," agrees Nicky. "I guess we need to take a road trip to check it out."

"OK," says Nathan.

"Not you, moron," Nicky chastises him, "Me and Morris." Nicky is not calling me Bulletproof so I guess we are not killing this wop. Too bad, I was looking forward to a simple throat cutting.

"You're staying right here until we get back. But don't worry, I got some friends who will take good care of you."

Two big black football player looking guys walk into the room. They are wearing leather pants and vest, no shirts. One of the men has a scar across his chest running from below his neck to his stomach. Looks like someone tried to gut him like a fish. The other had several tattoos and brands on his arms and neck. The tat on his neck is of a chain with a broken link, and between the broken links, the letters OTC are branded into the flesh. I don't know about Nathan but these guys scare the hell out of me.

"Did I hear you right, you said you like to suck a nigger's dick?" asks the guy who had the back alley open-heart surgery. Then he steps in front of Nathan, pulls his huge cock from his leather pants, and slaps Nathan in the face with it, as if it were a black jack. It makes a much louder sound than the baloney I threw on the floor when I pretended to cut Nathan's ear off.

He slaps Nathan's face again, then again in the other direction. Each time, Nathan's head jerks from one side to the other, and each time, Heart Attack's dick grows bigger and harder. "We are almost there, boy, then I'm gonna teach you how to suck a nigger's dick."

"Ah, time for us to go," says Nicky uncomfortably. "Remember, no scars... that would show, and I still have plans for him when we get back."

We hurry out of the room and down the hall, back down the three flights of stairs, and out into the alley, trying to get away from the place as fast as possible.

"Where did you find these guys?" I ask Nicky.

"Do you really want to know?" He asks me.

"Yeah, I want to make sure I don't walk down the same alley."

"This place comes highly recommended, and after a week or two here, Nathan will do anything we want him to do."

"What do you want him to do? Never mind, I don't want to know, but he might have been better off with the rats. By the way, I need to burn this tape before we leave, and have to take care of something else. You make the flight and other arrangements so long and I'll catch up with you tomorrow."

"OK, this will be like a little vacation. Hot babes, cool beaches, homicide, you'll see, it will be fun."

I go to Bonnie's apartment. It's empty. I know she wouldn't have had much in it anyway, as she doesn't want to leave anything that may identify her here, but this place is completely empty. I make my way to the Four Roses Bar, the Bainbridge Boys hangout. I walk into the place and the crowd parts before me like Moses at the Red Sea. I don't know if it is because I'm a black guy in an all-Irish bar, or if my reputation precedes me. But I'm pretty sure none of these people has seen me before, as I've kept all my dealing to Patrick. The least number of people who can tie you to a deed, the fewer people you have to kill later.

I walk into the back room without knocking and drop down on the sofa, "Where is she?"

Patrick is sitting in a recliner, his arm draped over the back. He sits up slowly and takes his hand from behind the chair. I'm sure it crossed his mind to shoot me then thought better of it. "I don't know, brother; she took off yesterday, a little after you dropped her off."

"I'm not in the habit of asking the same question twice," I say.

Patrick realizes this is not a friendly meeting. He is very careful to what and how he responds, "I've seen Bonnie shoot a guy in the face at point blank range and not even wipe the blood splatter off. But the girl I saw yesterday was different. I don't know what you did this weekend but she came back and was done with this life. When I dropped her off, she asked me not to say where. Actually, she said not to tell Nicky where."

I sat on the couch and patiently waited for my answer.

"I took her to Grand Central Station. She wouldn't let me go in with her."

"What time yesterday?" "3:50 pm."

"Thank you," I say and get up to leave.

"If you really care about her," Patrick says, offering friendly advice, "You will let her go."

"I do care about her," I confide in him, "I just need to talk to her though, then she can go where she needs to be. And no worries, Nicky won't go looking for her, I'll take care of that."

'Crazy fucking bugger,' Patrick thinks and settles back down in the recliner.

Bonnie is punctual to the point of being annoying, so if she arrived at Grand Central Station just before 4pm, her train left no later than 4:15. There were six trains that left between four and 4:15, three went north, two headed south, and one travelled west. After checking a map for all the places along each route, I knew there was only one place she had gone.

I gas up the Buick and head up the Hudson Valley; I have a six-hour drive upstate, way too much time to think. As I move north, the leaves change from a rainbow of green, yellow, orange, and red to none at all.

My mind keeps replaying the night of the Raven, the fireworks, the last two gun blasts, Maria's bloody body laid before me with two gunshot wounds in her chest. The way Joey Banana looked at her at the beach. Twilight turns to night and then the deep darkness of mountain roads. I reach my destination too late to enter. I climb into the back seat and ball up under the blanket for warmth. The frigid mountain air penetrates the car in minutes, and I have several hours to wait until dawn.

The morning sun does little to warm the car or me, I gulp the ice-cold beer from the six-pack and swish it around in my mouth. I spit it out and wait a second before downing the rest. I hope beer breath is better than morning breath. I pop the tab on the second and down it too, a good old liquid breakfast. I stare at the walls that run along the road; must be close to twelve feet tall, and behind them is a castle. Has to be some kind of fortress that has been converted into a convent.

I drive through the open gates and along the winding roads that seem to lead nowhere. Everything is covered in white snow, glistening ice, and huge icicles hang from the granite ledges around the buildings. I finally end up in a courtyard in front of a massive brown oak door; must be the main hall.

It takes a lot of talking to convince the Mother Superior to let me speak to Bonnie. I start by telling her that Bonnie's sister has been killed in a car crash. She doesn't believe that at all. I finally tell her the truth, that I have killed several people seeking revenge for our friends' deaths. Not surprisingly, Mother Superior knows nothing about it. I tell her I need to know why my wife was killed and only Bonnie has the answer. Mother Superior leaves me in her office and a few minutes later Bonnie walks in.

She is wearing a long plain white dress down to her feet and a light blue smock-looking thing over it. She has on one of those funny little nun caps that hides your hair, also light blue. "That's a good look for you," I try to joke.

"You didn't hurt Patrick, did you?"

"Of course not, he and I go way back. He knew I'd go looking for you and he told me what he knew. I'm guessing you knew that too, which is why you told him not to tell Nicky, but not me."

"I think you understand why I have to do this," Bonnie's eyes are filling up fast, "I couldn't go through with it if Nicky was here."

"I'll square things with Nicky," I comfort her. We sit in big cushiony chairs by the bay windows. All the snow, ice, and clean mountain air make the room bright. "I have to know just one thing. Did Joey have a thing for Maria?"

"You know," she says with a little smile, "All the boys had a thing for Maria, and the first time you saw her, you couldn't take your eyes off of her either. She just had that effect on guys. Joey too, he was chasing her since she was twelve."

"Why didn't she ever tell me this? Neither of you did," I am angry but keep my cool.

"She didn't want you to do something crazy," Bonnie confesses, "she was afraid you'd go after Joey and start a war with the Banoas. I guess she thought she could handle him, we both did, we never thought he was capable of what he did."

"Even after the dreams," I point out, "after the whole blood river thing with her and Betty."

"We didn't know what that meant. You never told us about that until the night in the cemetery. I know you were worried for our safety, but I thought you were overreacting. I now know it's my fault they are dead and we should have said something when they jumped Jesus." For once, she pronounces his name correctly.

"You are not to blame," I tell her. "Joey is to blame, and he will pay. I will make him suffer, cut his balls off and stick them up his ass before I kill him..."

"Killing Joey won't change anything. Killing Chris didn't change anything for me. And killing all those guys who killed your brother didn't change anything back then either." She is tearing up again. The guilt is crushing her.

When you join a convent, you start your life over, you take on a new name, you become a new person, or at least you try to. Bonnie is trying hard to do just that.

"Per sanguinem crucis Christi virtutem abluas omnes iniquitates vestras, et egredietur amplius noli peccare."

"What does that mean?" she asks me.

"I'm sure you will find out in here," I tell her. "It's something a priest thought I would need one day. I'm no priest but I'm somewhat close to God, and I think it will serve you better than it could ever do me. There is one more thing I need to tell you. Remember the night in the tomb I told you not to go back to the cemetery because it wouldn't be worth the risk."

"Yes."

"The reason it won't be worth any risk is that I had them moved," I tell her.

Bonnie's eyes become big, real big, "How could you do that?

Why would you do that? Their families..."

"Everybody's family knows," I try to calm her down. "And it was Sophia's idea. She refused to let Maria lie in a hole her killer dug for her. They all felt the same way, and she begged that I move them the day of the funeral. So after we met in August, I had them secretly transferred to another cemetery." I hand her the address.

"Are they together? What about the flowers?"

"I can afford plenty of flowers. You said they liked them, so yes, the flowers will be placed there every day too. There are eight graves, so when the time comes, we can all be together again."

Nicky and I exit the plane in Miami with a small carry-on bag each. We packed only essentials, shorts, tees, and a bathing suit, because as Nicky put it, we need to blend in.

We are however, a couple of months too soon for spring break so everyone getting off the plane is either old or business people on convention. We blend in like a man wearing one black shoe and one brown.

We hop into the back of a cab outside the terminal.

"Do you know where St. John the Devine is?" Nicky asks the cabbie, who nods. "Good, take us there."

"A church... not a hotel?" I ask.

"The flight delay put us behind." Nicky is trying to speak in TV code, "We are going to have to go straight to the funeral instead of Aunt Bea's house. I just hope we get there before they take Uncle Paladin to the cemetery, as I don't know where that is."

"I'm sorry for your loss," offers the cabbie, "I'll get you there in a hurry."

I catch on, Paladin from 'Have Gun—Will Travel,' we are going to pick up hardware.

Leaving our coats and bags in the cab, we tell him to wait. We enter the back of the church and find the funeral has already started, in fact well into the mass. The casket is open and there is a picture of an old white man on an easel behind it. It's a small church and it's half-filled with mourners of all ages. Obviously, a family gathering.

"Don't tell me the guns are where I think they are," I say with disgust.

"That's sick man! They are in the two large floral displays on either side of the altar," Nicky responds, "My father shipped them overnight. Nobody checks funeral flowers."

"Why not just ship the hardware to a hardware store like my guys do?" I complain.

"To each his own," replies Nicky. "Look, we've got to get to those guns now or we will have to follow this old guy all the way to the grave, and that will take all day. Hey, you ever been an altar boy?"

"No."

"I was when I was ten. Just do what I do," says Nicky, while handing me a white robe from the side room.

We start walking down the aisle and I notice the priest giving us an odd look, as if he's about to question our presence. Thankfully, he keeps going with mass as we approach the altar.

"They already have altar boys, Nicky."

"Just genuflect and go to the white lilies on the right, the bag is under the Styrofoam block. I'll get the bag on the left."

We grab the two black bags and turn back up the aisle. Everyone watches as we exit the church. The priest never lost his place or slowed pace with the sermon.

We climb back into the cab still wearing the white robes. "Go." I tell the cabbie.

After Nicky tells him what hotel to take us to, the cabbie says, "I'm dying to know what you had to get from your uncle that you couldn't wait for the reading of the will."

"Are you really dying to know?" I ask. "Uh... No, not really," responds the cabbie.

We give him a hundred-dollar tip and watch him drive away in a hurry. We cross the street, hail another cab, and go to the hotel we reserved down on South Beach. Nicky announces that his father has been quite helpful, now that we are making him lots of money in the fertilizer business. He sent two sawed off 12 gauge shotguns, two Browning Automatic Rifles, four 9mm pistols, and a thousand rounds of assorted ammo for each of us.

"How much are we kicking up to your father?" I ask as we assemble the guns.

"Fifteen percent on the coke and another ten, the family rate, on the money laundering," laughs Nicky.

"Plus, he gets all of the building remodelling and the proceeds from the fertilizer. We need to renegotiate our business terms with your dad," I tell him.

"My dad is a terrible negotiator," warns Nicky.

"Twenty-five percent, we're getting screwed. And no grenades, I asked for a dozen."

"He specifically told me to tell you, 'no grenades'," Nicky wags his finger at me. "He said if we couldn't get Joey with this stuff, to devise another plan. He doesn't want you blowing up half of Miami Beach to get one guy. But he did give us the name of a high-end cat house where we can start looking."

We rent a car under another alias and go to The Russian Dolls on the north end of South Beach. The place is packed but we manage to muscle a spot at the bar. Topless girls strut along the counter, step above drinks in their spiked heels, bend over to shake their tits in customers' faces, and take their money. I order two Stoli's straight up and slide a C note across the bar. Two of the girls can't wait to show their stuff to us. We have both worked at Nicolas Rocci's places, so we are no strangers to the scene, know how to get the girls' attention, and how to keep it.

One girl, with dark red hair does a deep squat over my drink and asks, "Want me to freshen that up for you?"

"I got something that needs your charms, honey."

"My name is Cherry Bomb and I can blow... your... mind."

"Private party then," I whisper in her ear, "Me and my friend, you and yours."

Nicky is working on a little blonde.

They lead us to a space in the back, push us down onto the leather couch that runs around the small area, and start sliding up and down the silver pole in the center of the room. They are just getting into their act when two other women pull back the curtain and stare at Nicky and me. The first two women don't know what to do, as they are holding each other with the pole between them, one thing is sure, they are scared. Cherry Bomb starts to walk but the tall blonde newcomer grabs her by one arm. She says something foreign, which I can only guess might be Russian, and the first two women leave.

"I'm Svetlana," states the tall blonde, "And I run this place. You two are not here looking for a good time, I think not. You are here looking for the Scared prince, I think."

"What the fuck are you talking about?" asks Nicky.

"You would be Nicky 'Nails' Rocci," replies Svetlana, "And this is Morris 'Bulletproof' Johnson." She walks over to me and holds out her hand, like she wants me to kiss it. She is dressed in a long white gown with a slit up one side all the way to her hip.

I take her hand and stand up.

"You two gentlemen must come with me now, before anyone else sees you. They have been waiting for you to arrive for months. And in the last few days, they have been checking the clubs twice or three times a night."

"Let's just say we are... Oh, what the fuck," Nicky gives up the pretence. "Who is looking for us?"

"The Scared Little prince, or at least those that are protecting him, we get the news down here too. Five Italian guys killed in a Bronx bar. Must have been his friends, and it scared him really badly. You are very lucky you came here first."

"What makes you think we came here first?" I ask.

"Because you are still alive, they plan to, how do you say, shoot on sight," interjects the other woman. She is also tall, but mainly because of the heels, with long braided auburn hair running down her back and also dressed in an evening gown, obviously, not a stripper either.

"Yana is right. We will take you where you can see what you came to see and be safe." Svetlana leads us out the back of the club.

Yana, Cherry Bomb aka Rozalina, and Izolda, the little blonde, come too and take us to a high rise not far from the hotel we were at.

Yana gives the other girls a quick knowing look and they lead Nicky into one of the bedrooms. She opens the double French doors to the master suite, "You like?"

"If this is a setup, I'll snap your neck before your men can kill me," I warn her. "I can do it just so; you won't die but you will be paralysed from the neck down. You'll still be a hooker; you just won't enjoy it."

"That is the best sweet talk you can come up with?" she laughs. "Rumour has it that you can talk a nun out of her habit, so I know you can do better than that. Try a little harder for the girl who saved your life, it was me who recognize you in the club."

"Oh yeah?" I'm interested but not at ease. "How did you recognize me?"

"I have seen many men go through the club. Some are business men wasting their company money, some are husbands cheating on their wives, and some are gangsters, like your friend Nicky, dangerous for sure, but you have the look of a killer, a viper, cold, silent, deadly to the touch, and always ready to strike."

"Then why save me?" I ask.

"Svetlana said you would be coming soon, and when you do, to get her. You have good reason for wanting the Scared Little Prince dead, and she has good reason to help you. Come over here, let me show something." Yana crosses the bedroom to the other set of French doors and opens them. She is waiting patiently.

I hear Nicky laugh and fooling around with the girls in the other room. I hope he's only letting them play with his other gun.

I walk over to Yana and she points across the water.

"Is that where Joey is hiding?"

"Yes. This is why you came, no?"

"I was hoping to get a little closer," I tell her and start out on the balcony but she grabs my arm.

"They are always watching," she warns and closes the doors. "Tomorrow I bring you some binoculars."

"A telescope will be better," I tell her, "and a sniper rifle."

"You and your friend can stay here for as long as you like," she offers, "The penthouse belongs to a friend. He's in Arabia, only visits for a week or two at a time, and always lets me know before he arrives." Yana runs her hand across my stomach and up my chest. "Are you pleased?"

"I'm reconsidering snapping your neck," I move her hand from under my shirt. "But I'm not as easily pleased as my friend, or fooled. So, let's see what tomorrow brings."

Warm wet smelly liquid runs down Nathan face into his nose and mouth. He spits and puts his hands up to block the stream of piss raining down on him from Heart Attack's dick.

"Wake the fuck up motherfucker, this ain't no bed and breakfast. This is a B and B, that's balls and butts to you. You are going to make me some money today, or you are going to regret the day your momma pushed you out of her cunt. I get five dollars for a hand job, ten for a blow. You do remember how to suck a dick without your teeth getting in the way, you little bitch?"

Nathan shakes his head. While on his knees, he keeps his eyes down to the floor, in the submissive position. Piss stings his eyes but he does not wipe it away, because if he moves, more punishment will come his way. So he keeps looking at the floor in front of him, waiting for more orders.

"Go wash your stink ass, and put on your uniform," commands Heart Attack. "No one wants a smelly little bitch like you. Don't even know why I waste my time, but if someone wants that skinny little skanky butt you'd better give it up, and that's twenty-five dollars for me. Hell, I might let you eat today if someone fucks that shithole. You got ten minutes, don't make me come up here and get you."

Nathan jumps off the urine soaked mattress on the floor and hurries to the bathroom. The shower water is ice cold and burns as he washes but he can't stop to think about it. He throws on his uniform over his wet skin, shaking from cold and hunger, but he can't stop to think about it. He has to hurry to get downstairs to the main room or the Brothers will deduct twenty dollars from his tally. He has to turn in a hundred dollars or he won't eat today, but he can't stop to think about it. Nathan wonders if Heart Attack will feed him if he does let someone fuck him, it has been nearly a week since Nails and Bulletproof kidnapped him, and he hasn't eaten yet. Hasn't made twenty- five dollars either. Maybe Off The Chain will feed him, he's always saying that he doesn't want him to die on them. But he can't stop to think about it, he can only hope.

The main area is an old dark bar. Velvet lined booths, where the velvet has given way to hardened crusty semen stains, surround the room. A few tables with a pair of chairs arranged haphazardly in the middle of the room and a slightly raised small faded wooden dance floor in front of the bar complete the dismal décor. The men, young and old come in from the mezzanine level and look over the pit, sizing up their prey.

The clientele ranges from the professional types: doctors, lawyers, and judges to the young and curious, to the strange and sadistic. Jose, a streetwise prossie, what the men in the club call the male prostitutes, has taken Nathan under his wing. He is about the same age as the nineteen-year old Nathan, but he has been on the streets longer than even he can remember and hustle is his only way of life now. He slides up next to Nathan, grabs his hand, and kisses him hard on the lips, ignoring Nathan as he tries to pull away.

"Stop resisting," Jose scolds him. Jose is wearing his signature pink scarf, which hides a nasty scar on his neck, a midriff blouse, and Capri pants, all in various shades of pink. "What did I tell you? Lick it like you love it, spread it like you want it. You need to eat sister, and handies and bjs are not going to get you fed in this place, not unless you're fond of the swallow."

Jose works on Nathan's outfit, straightening the skirt, adjusting his fake breasts and hair. The faux femmes are dressed like women for the customers who want to fool themselves they are not gay or are afraid or incapable of approaching the real deal. Mostly, though, they attract the sickos, who want to humiliate and degrade them. Usually, the faux femmes are full-blown transvestites who have chosen to dress as women in homosexual sex parlors.

Not Nathan. None of this was his choosing, but these were the only clothes the Brothers gave him to wear. Not being a real tranie and not knowing how to act like one, means his life is also real hell. Those who do approach him expecting him to act like a woman are quickly turned off and walk away when he doesn't. But worse, those who see the shame in his sunken eyes heap further abuse on him as easy as they jerk their load onto his face, an act that he does not get paid for.

"Here, eat this," Jose passes him half a sandwich while the Brothers' backs are turned. "How do they expect you to look pretty while you are wasting away? Now, today, I'm going to steer a nice young boy your way, a first timer. You smear the lube on your thighs like I showed you and clamp down on his dick. He'll think he's fucking you while all he's really getting is a Slippery Sam. That's better than taking it in the face, right?"

"I don't know why you're wasting your time on this piaso," says Miguel. "He's only a night or two away from the end of the rope."

"Fuck you, bitch," retorts Jose. "Don't pay him no mind. He's jealous because I used to suck his dick when I first got here. Now, he's sucking mine. I don't know who fucked you over, but we'll get you through this, trust me."

Nathan didn't notice it happening, but suddenly, the bar is full of men. They are making out in the booths, talking romantically at the tables, and grinding slowly on the dance floor.

Jose shoves him onto a boy his own age, then pushes them both onto the dance floor, saying, "Get to know my friend Nancy, she'll be easy with you."
They stumble around the dance floor until both stop trying and just stand there holding each other. The blonde boy is starry eyed and scared. Nathan is plain scared.

Jose finally escorts them to a room off the bar, where there is an actual bed with sheets and an adjoining bathroom.

So far, Nathan has only given the occasional hand-job in a dark corner. Some guys like to know others are watching as they get jerked off. Once, he gave a guy a blowjob. He also thought the guy was going to cut his throat when he choked and bit down on his member. This feels different, better, but he still doesn't think he can go through with it.

Jose gently pushes the two boys into the room then whispers in Nathan's ear, "You got to eat, mi amor."

"What, you think the Brothers are going to give you a medal because you got his cherry busted?" Miguel says as he sashays by with a middle-aged man in a business suit.

"Bitch, I will cut you," laughs Jose. But he is wondering how Nathan wound up here. Most of the people come here because they are tired of working the streets, just like him, or owe a pimp and are working off the debt, or are straight up slaves to the Brothers. And whereas slaves are beaten regularly and forced to work, Nathan isn't getting beaten. They are just not going to feed him, Jose guesses, until they absolutely have to. Yet, they don't treat him like the other sex slaves either. Nathan is somehow special.

CHAPTER 10
The Castle

Nathan and the young john stand before the bed and neither seems to know how to make the next move. Finally, the john speaks up, "Oh my God, you're a virgin too. I was so afraid I was going to do something wrong and look stupid."

"No stupider than I will," Nathan says.

"Let's just sit for a minute," the john says. Both sit on the edge of the bed, the john places an arm around Nathan's neck, and moves in for a kiss.

Nathan pulls away.

"Maybe we should just get on with it," the young john says. "Take off your clothes." He strips naked and climbs into the bed.

Nathan takes a handful of gel, rubs it on his ass and thighs then slides into bed next to the young john and turns his back to him. He rubs the remaining gel on the young john's cock promptly, which is already hard and throbbing. Tentatively, he places it between his cheeks just below his ass and guides it between his legs. His body stiffens instantly as the young john starts humping, his dick sliding along the slippery thighs. The young john goes at him fast and Nathan feels vomit rise in his throat, but his stomach is empty, he can only dry heave.

"What is your name, Nancy?" whispers the young john. "I mean your real name."

"Nancy," answers Nathan, "Just call me Nancy."

"OK, Nancy," he responds. "This feels great, but I want to make you feel good too." He shifts his hips down and rams his dick up and into Nathan's ass. With all the gel on his body, the steel cock slides right in, causing a wave of burning pain to ripple up Nathan's spine.

Nathan kicks and tries to pull away, but a steel-like grip surrounds his chest and hip. The pain finally reaches his head. His face burns, tears roll from his eyes, and he lets out a yell that the young john barely manages to stifle by pushing his face down into the pillow.

Simultaneously, he turns Nathan onto his stomach and lifts him by the hip. "Relax, and this will feel good."

Nathan feels new waves of pain in his ass with each thrust of the young john's cock, starting as fire in his back, spreading up his spine, and down his legs. He clinches his butt tight each time the cock retreats from his ass, only to have it rip his asshole open again as the young john's weight crushes him into the bed. He struggles and squirms beneath him but cannot stop the assault. Nathan bites into the pillow and grips the sheets with both fists, his eyes burning from tears and sweat running into them. The young john goes on and on, each time drawing farther back and driving harder and deeper into him until Nathan can fight no more. Then the young john lets out a loud hot throaty groan and his cock throbs and jerks spasmodically in Nathan's ass.

"Now that was a good first time, wouldn't you agree, Nancy?"

The young john gets out of bed and disappears into the bathroom, where Nathan can hear him cleaning himself. He can't open his eyes; he doesn't want to see that face. He can imagine the sick twisted smirk and he can't bear to look at it again. He can't move either, afraid of what might happen if he does, but he can visualize the blood and scum that is about to run out of his ass and down his legs and he does not want to see that either. His face stays buried in the sopping wet pillow. Then he hears the young john leave, closing the door behind him.

The young john, Jose's sailor friend from the Spanish Navy, grabs Jose by the back of the neck and kisses him long and hard. Then he pulls out a fold of cash and gives it to

Heart Attack, "Three hundred dollars, well worth it for a white tail doe."

After his friend leaves, Jose says, "That's how you flip a newbie, not by starving the poor dear. But the next time will be easier, and soon he will be an old pro."

"You stupid fucking queer," says Off The Chain, "Do you think we care if he becomes a fag? Do you think we are trying to get him to join your little booty sorority?"

Heart Attack hands Jose a hundred dollars. "I don't feed anybody who doesn't make me money. And don't get too attached to your little pal, because when his owners come back, I think they might kill him anyway. We are only here to babysit the little shit and make sure he stays pretty for the funeral."

Jose opens the door. Nathan is lying dead still on his stomach. Trickles of pink fluid run from his reddened asshole. "That wasn't too bad," he says softly from the doorway. "I got you some food, but let's get you cleaned up first."

"I ain't no fucking fag like you," Nathan says angrily and curls up into a ball. "You set me up you fucking cock sucking prick. Get the fuck out of here, just let me die."

"Sorry, but we both know that is not going to happen," Jose apologizes, "The Brothers won't let you die and I can't watch you get tortured either. The people who left you here will be back, so you have to be strong enough to fight when they do. Strong physically and strong mentally or they are going to kill you slowly and painfully, a little every day."

Jose moves to the bed and cradles Nathan in his arms.

Nathan goes back to crying from the pain, but mostly from the humiliation.

I spend all day staring at the white house across the water through the telescope, which is setup at the foot of the bed, far from the window and balcony, so the guards won't pick it up. I moved the nightstand next to it and chart the movements of the men in the house. I count how many are stationed at the back, which faces me, how many times they patrol the estate grounds, and try to get an estimate of how many there are altogether. As far as I can tell, there are between twelve and eighteen mercenaries in and around the house at all times. Not once have I seen Joey Banoa. "This is crap," I complain to Yana, who is lying on the bed.

"I tell you, you shouldn't have that telescope set up during the day. They might see you," she warns me again. "You have been watching that house day and night for a week, nothing is going to change. Come lie down." She pats the pillow. "You will not miss anything."

I climb onto the bed and lie flat on my back staring at the ceiling. "That son of a bitch never comes out. I never see him at the window. How do I even know he's in there?"

"He's there," she says, exhausted from repeating the same thing over and over. "I've seen him. I can bring you girls that have been with him..."

"Have you been with him? Have you fucked him?" I yell in her face.

"No," she says calmly. "I have not. I am not a whore, I am an escort, and I choose the men I want to be with. Mostly, I keep them company, like I keep you company, because I choose to."

"These men that you keep company," I counter, "Do they pay you?"

"Yes, quite a lot actually," she says proudly. Her eyes light up a sharp chestnut brown.

"And if you choose to, do you sleep with these men?"

"Some, but only if I like them and choose to," She emphasizes I and her soft pink lips curl into a triumphant smile.

"Then you are a whore," I state bluntly and watch with satisfaction as the color drains from her face, the radiance dimming in defeat. "A well paid one, but you are still just a nicely dressed hooker."

Her auburn hair seems redder, her eyes definitely more intense, and her lips became swollen and dark.

Anger shows in the colors of her face and she is on fire, again. "And what are you, Mr. Bulletproof Johnson? With all your numbers and times and guns, you are just a killer."

We brought the hardware up to the penthouse two days ago. We figured that if these women were planning to kill us it wouldn't be with our guns, as after a couple of days, they have had ample time to do so. Not that the extra armament will do us any good where Joey is concerned anyway, the only hope is if he goes crazy and storms the penthouse, which is not likely to happen.

"I know." I lie staring at the ceiling.

She is lying next to me, breathing hard.

There is laughter and shrieks wandering in from the other bedroom. At least Nicky is enjoying himself.

Yana gets up, pours two drinks and lights up a joint. She passes me the joint and a drink of Stoli on the rocks. "Look, I didn't... I didn't fuck that boy. I was there to supervise the girls. I didn't fuck anybody over there. And it is true, I am here because I choose to be. Not because Lania, Svetlana's pet name, is making me keep an eye on you two."

"OK," I say.

Yana is a good-looking woman, and I have no problem fucking a prostitute. When Nicky and I were making collections at his father's strip joints, we would often sample the girls while the men bagged up the cash. Sometimes, we got two girls apiece if the manager came up short, and we always had a turn with the newbie. I told them I was the pussy inspector. If I got a good fuck, they moved up quicker. I'd fast track them to the private rooms. It was all bullshit of course, Nicolas Rocci couldn't care less what Nicky or I thought about the girls. As long as the cash was flowing, he was happy.

I just can't get my mind off of killing Joey, and how it will not mean anything. He is already in a big white crypt waiting to die, but killing him will not be enough, merely a relief for him. I have to kill him and I have to find a way to make him suffer.

Yana and I sit on the bed and watch the sun go down then I return to the telescope, because I have nothing else to do. Yana drinks, smokes, and finally goes to sleep. Nicky is fucking whatever girls are coming over, all day and all night. We are in a crypt too. We are the dead chasing the dead, and one thing about the dead, they don't move.

At 2 a.m. I have had enough and walk into Nicky's room. One girl is straddling his face and sucking his dick, another is lying by his side, licking his balls. His fingers are buried deep inside her and working feverishly.

"What are we fucking doing here?"

Nicky slaps the girl on the ass, she climbs off his face, and starts to get up but he pushes her head back down on his dick. The two girls are looking up at me as they work on his cock. "I don't know about you, but I'm getting a double header and eating cherry pie."

"There haven't been any cherries in those pies in a long time," I tell him, "Sorry ladies, no offense intended."

They ignore me. Their glassy eyes telling me they are stoned.

"You're stoned, aren't you?"

"It's 2 a.m., of course I'm stoned. You should be too, and neck deep in Yana's pussy. What the fuck are you doing? Let go. Don't look a free pussy in the hole, just be glad it's there and fuck it." He slaps the other girl's ass and she climbs on his face.

I return to the bedroom and climb back in bed. Yana pulls me close and places my hand over her breast. I pull it away and she yanks it again and puts its back on her breast. She squirms in her sleep, squeezes her soft ass against my hard dick, and moans softly. She is deep asleep, the kind of sleep you get when you feel safe and don't have a worry in the world. The kind of sleep I used to have, but not anymore.

Mid-morning, I call out to Nicky, "Hey, get in here, we have a moment."

Nicky races in and I turn the telescope over to him. There are three SUVs rolling up the driveway, exiting the estate.

Nicky adjusts the sight, "I can see the driver and maybe someone in the passenger seat, but I can't tell who. I can't tell if there is anybody in the back seats either."

The SUVs turns onto the main road and at the corner split up. "You thinking what I'm thinking?" I ask him.

He looks at Yana sitting on the bed with a huge mirror and lines of coke laid out before her, "How much has he been sniffing today? A fucking ambush? You're kidding, right? Those are armored SUVs, we would need bazookas to stop them. And we don't know if Joey is in them, or how many other fucking armed bodyguards are with him, if he is even in there. No, I'm not thinking what you're thinking, because you're thinking suicide with no possibility for success."

"At least I'm trying to come up with a plan," I yell as he walks out the bedroom. "What are you doing? Burying your face in these girls' pussies! Hoping Joey dies from the clap before you do!"

Nicky stops at the door, "These girls are clean. They get checked once a month and Lania only sends her best. You should try one, hell, you are boring Yana to death over there." He turns to Yana who has just taken a big hit and is twitching from the effects. "I'm sorry but he was not always like this. He used to be fun. If I had known he was going to sit around and act like a limp prick for two weeks, I would have come alone."

"I guess the loss of his girlfriend and now being so close to getting the guy who killed her..."

"Oh no," interrupts Nicky angrily, "Don't make excuses for him. He was a lot more fun before, but something changed MoJo. I don't know why, but you are different now. I know that after Maria you only really enjoyed the murdering, but at least you did enjoy that." He pauses for a moment then says, "It's Nathan. That's it, isn't it! You're mad because I didn't let you kill that little shit. But I told you I have plans for him, so we need him for now. And this whole 'they kill one of ours and we kill all of theirs' philosophy isn't healthy. Talk to Yana, get your wick wet, you need to get a perspective on life." Then he leaves.

"He is right you know," says Yana, having recovered from the cocaine freeze. "I mean about the ambush. They are probably going out for supplies, or changing the guards, or something. Joey probably isn't in the cars. I don't want you to get yourself killed for nothing. Come get a hit."

I kneel down by the bed and snort one line through the rolled C note then take the second hit in the other nostril. All our supplies are sent to the hotel and the girls pick them up for us, as Svetlana and Yana still tell us that it is unsafe for us to be seen around Miami. Yana leaves me sitting on the floor enjoying the freeze.

She goes to Nicky, who is in the kitchen making drinks. "Your friend is hurting. Why don't you try to help him instead of spending all your time with the girls?"

"I thought that was what you were here for. I know you want something from him, so maybe if you get him out of this funk he will give it to you. Drink?"

"What is that, a screwdriver?"

"You would think so, but no, this is a vodka sunrise." Nicky returns to the bedroom with his drinks and leaves two on the counter for Yana to take.

She returns to the bedroom with the drinks and sees me back at the telescope. It's getting dark and I'm trying to count shadows on the windows. She slaps the telescope end up and the eyepiece falls away from my face.

"Hey, I'm trying to see how many people they left behind."

"Here, have a drink," she orders, "That doesn't matter anyway. There are only two of you, and they are professional soldiers. Besides, your friend doesn't seem to be interested in suicide missions. He is more interested in living." She climbs onto my lap and puts her arms around my neck. We drink over each other's shoulder. Yana runs her hand around my face and lifts my chin. "What is it? Why are you so obsessed with killing the boy? I know he killed your girlfriend, but you act like you want to jump from the balcony and land on him like a lion. Knowing the jump will kill you too. Why?"

"Before we came down here I found out that he was in love with her. I thought he killed her as part of an attack on us, but now I know he murdered her." Rage is building inside me. I do feel like jumping from the balcony over to the house. I think about taking a car and driving through the front door, jumping out and shooting my way through the house until I get to him. Then I will fire shotgun blast after shotgun blast into him until he disintegrates before my eyes. "Killing is one thing," I tell her, "I understand killing her as retribution for our robbing him. Hell, I've killed for less. I would still have killed him, of course..." Somehow, talking to her makes the rage subsides, or it might be the liquor and cocaine. "But he murdered her. He couldn't have her so he made sure no one else would. When you murder someone you love, there is no punishment that can do you justice. Killing him will not be enough."

"Don't worry, he will pay," Yana says and kisses me softly on the lips, "And you... you will be alive to enjoy it." She hops off my lap and walks to the bathroom. For the first time I notice she isn't wearing anything under her silk robe. She starts a bath running, comes back into the bedroom, kneels down and snorts more lines, and I follow suit. We finish the sunrises and I say I'm going to make more.

"Make a pitcher and bring it in here." She says from the bathroom door.

When I come back with the pitcher, Yana takes it from my hand and pulls my tee shirt over my head. "Go get in the tub," she commands, and I follow orders.

The water is hot, probably too hot, but I am too high to care. The tub is one of those walk-in types, huge, like a mini pool. I lie back and let the water cover me up to my face. I feel my body go limp, as if all my muscles have detached at once. Yana says something from the bedroom but the water in my ears garbles the sound. I open my eyes and see her standing there, minus the robe and the two drinks in her hand.

I start to get up but she says, "Relax. Slide forward I want to get in behind you."

I do and she slips her body down and around me.

She wrapped her golden tanned legs around my hips and over my black hairy legs, gently lays my head back on her soft full breasts and the water refills my ears. "Everything is going to be OK."

With the warmth of the water, the soft tenderness of her body, and the coke tranquilizing my mind, I finally relax and for the first time in months, I feel peaceful. For the first time in months, I actually feel something.

Nicky was wrong when he said I enjoy killing. I don't, not since Maria died. I used to like the feel of my knife sinking into some asshole, who crossed me, or that little jolt of energy that rushes through my body when the revolver flashes and kicks a slug into a fool who didn't think I'd shoot him. Since Maria died, I have felt none of that, it is like eating food after the first forkful has burnt your taste buds, and there is no more sensation.

Human touch has become nonexistence to me, I can neither feel the warmth of another body, nor that of my own.

I have built a shell around myself, and inside that shell is a vacuum where nothing exists, not even me. Yana has been putting a tiny crack in that shell. I don't know how she did it, or why she did it, but there is a sliver of light cutting through the darkness. I feel her rise up to take a drink and then swallow behind my head.

"Promise me you won't try and attack those soldiers," she begs and strokes my hair.

"What makes you think they are soldiers? They could be mobsters. I've gone up against a lot of mobsters lately and I did all right."

"I know soldiers when I see them and..."

"Don't worry, I'm not for the suicide attacks," I assure her, "And the point to fighting a war is not just to win, but to survive to enjoy the victory."

Yana emerges from the bedroom late in the morning, just in time to see Nicky and two girls getting ready to leave. "Where are you going? And where is Morris?"

Rozalina and Izolda freeze in their tracks.

Nicky turns around to face Yana, "I'm taking Cherry Bomb and Honey to the beach. Just because they suck like a couple of vampires, doesn't mean they have to look like them too. And I don't know where MoJo is, I thought he was in the bed with you."

"No, I just woke up and he's not in there. You shouldn't be going out either. Suppose you run into some guys on the lookout for you. What are you going to do then?"

Nicky steps back between the two girls, wraps his arms around theirs, and sticks his hands into their beach bags. He pulls out two nines, "We also have beaches in New York, you know. The girls will be fine with me. I may not have the reputation that Bulletproof carries, but I can take care of myself, and them."

"And you are not worried about your friend?"

"Again, I thought that was your job." Nicky starts walking to the door with the redhead and blonde, although now, they are a little reluctant to go. "Besides, he took the other two nines and his reputation is all they said it is. He was kind of pissed off last night, so I'd keep an eye on that house, because when MoJo gets pissed off, things have a tendency to explode. We will see you later or see you never."

Nicky enjoys the sights at the beach. There are lots of people his age, tourists of course, he can tell from all the different languages he hears. When girls go for a swim, he stays with the bags and guns. He uses one bag as a pillow, with his right hand inside on the nine. The other bag is beside him, the other nine also within reach. 'This is nice,' he thinks, 'maybe I should set up shop down here.' He closes his eyes for some needed sleep. Before he drifts off, he also thinks, 'I hope MoJo ain't doing something crazy, he'll blow all my plans to hell, if he makes a move on Joey.'

A sprinkle of cold water shocks him back into this world and he springs up to see the girls standing over him shaking water from their hair. He has one pistol drawn and is reaching for the second.

"I think you should cover up your gun," warns Rozalina.

"And your other one too," giggles Izolda pointing to his hard-on.

"You girls are going to get shot if you keep messing around."

"We are hungry," complains Izolda.

"And we want you to buy us stuff," adds Rozalina.

"Buy you stuff?" Nicky asks.

"Yes. We don't want to go back to the penthouse," Rozalina tells him. "This is our time off and all we do is get high and fuck. It is like we are working. We want to have fun."

"We want to go shopping," Izolda grabs Nicky by the hand and tries to pull him to his feet. "But we are hungry, so we want to eat first."

"OK, but I have to make a phone call first," agrees Nicky. "Then we eat and go shopping. Now I know why nobody takes vampires out in the daylight, they turn into shopaholics."

The phone rings and rings in the mezzanine office, then finally, Heart Attack picks it up, "Yeah, what? Who is this?"

"Who do you think it is, motherfucker? Is my package ready for pick up?"

"Oh, I'm sorry, I didn't know it was you," Heart Attack apologizes quickly. He looks over the pit, Nathan is talking with Jose and Miguel, and he is laughing. "Not quite. There has been a little delay. I think..."

"Fuck all that," Nicky yells into the phone. The two girls are playing with his black curly hair. "If you two can't do the job, I'll find someone who can handle it, understand? You turn up the heat, I want my fruitcake in two weeks. Got it?" Nicky slams the phone down. He turns to the two girls and asks politely, "How hard can it be to terrorize one boy?"

The girls don't understand the question.

Heart Attack calls Off The Chain into the office and tells him about the brief but angry phone call. "It's those fucking spic queens, OTC, they are making this place all nice and homey for Nancy. We got to break it up and put the fear of God back into that boy."

"Charlie," says Off The Chain. "Charlie will put more than the fear of God in him."

"Yeah, but first, a little back room action is what he needs. Some seriously sick slave shit will wipe the grin off his face. And let's give the spic queens a taste too, OTC. Let them know they need to stay out of Brothers' businesses."

"Yeah, we ain't running no coffee club here," agrees Off The Chain, "Heart Attack, you have lost your edge. It's time you crack the whip. Get these bitches back in line."

Off The Chain kicks in the unlocked door where Jose, Miguel, and Nathan are sitting on a dirty mattress smoking an opium pipe. The air is clouded with the sweet smell of opiates. Off The Chain looms over them like a giant in a fairy-tale, mean, nasty, and horrifying. He reaches down, grabs Miguel by his processed curly blonde hair, and drags him screaming from the room. The other two scurry to a corner, knocking over the water pipe, and huddle together, shaking in fear. Their dope-induced euphoria quickly descends into a hellish nightmare.

"That's right, fear me," thunders Heart Attack from somewhere down the dark hallway. "I am the beast with great hunger and power. I rule this realm, I will inflict pain and suffering on all who do not acknowledge my awesome and absolute authority."

A loud sharp crisp snap of a bullwhip splits the dark. Heart Attack's presence fills the doorway, an eight-foot black bullwhip writhing in his right hand, and its tip dancing at his feet. Without warning, it flies at them, unleashing an ear popping crack inches from their faces. Instinctively, they scamper to separate corners, crunch down on hands and knees, and faces on the floor in the submissive position. Each one secretly wishing Heart Attack came for the other one.

Heart Attack grabs Nathan by one ear, inflicting instant and irresistible pain as he drags him from the room. Jose is left crying, shaking, and rocking back and forth on his knees. He is praying feverishly that he's not taken next, but his prayers go unanswered as Off The Chain returns within seconds to pick him up from the floor in a one-arm chokehold and carries him off into the darkness.

Heart Attack shoves Nathan into a room on the third floor no bigger than a closet. His massive body takes up the remaining space in the dark, leaving Nathan mere inches to breathe.

"You think you are in some kind of princess paradise, Bitch," spits Heart Attack down on his head. "You think you and your girlfriends have found gay-topia, because you can suck a cock without chocking. Or because they taught you how to pick an old pudgy fast shooter that doesn't hurt your little booty hole, your ass is golden now. You think your days are going to be filled with fairy dust and dicks that shoot rainbow sparkles.

Don't you?"

"No sir," whispers Nathan, scared senseless. Heart Attack has him pressed so hard against the glass wall he thinks it will shatter in his face, but he dares not push back either. He barely manages to keep his eyes open, as he tries to maneuver his face into a somewhat comfortable position on the slick surface. A light comes on in the room beyond the glass. He recognizes the red brick wall in front of him, the sealed windows, even the metal chair where he was strapped to once; it is the same room he was first brought to not so long ago, only this time, Miguel is there. But Miguel is not in the chair, he is cowering by the brick wall, hunched down like a rat, trying not to be noticed when the lights go on.

Someone else is sitting on the chair, someone big, husky like the Brothers, but not Off The Chain. This man is white. He wears black leather with spikes and chains like the Brothers, and biker boots with shiny steel-tip toes. Nathan knows what he is here for, and he tries to close his eyes, but Heart Attack has a firm grip on his hair, pulling and twisting, forcing him to keep watching.

The man in the chair walks over to Miguel, who is chained to the wall by one ankle and lifts him to his feet with one hand beneath his chin. He turns back to the two-way mirror and blows a kiss to Nathan then as quick as lightning backslaps Miguel, sending him scraping along the wall, as far as the short length of chain will allow. The black leather man takes two slow steps over to Miguel and again lifts him to his feet by his chin. Blood flows liberally from Miguel's mouth, but he doesn't make a sound. The black leather man holds his right hand high above his head, the brass knuckles shining in the dim light and brings his fist fast and furious in a wide rounding arch up into Miguel's stomach, folding him in half around his huge hand. Blood and vomit shoot two feet across the floor from Miguel's mouth, accompanied with a loud yelp of pain.

"There it is," says Heart Attack, sadistically satisfied. "It's like popping your cherry, once you get that first cry of pain out, the begging and pleading can begin."

Nathan feels the hard dick against his back. This is about to go from bad to worse, and it is going to happen now. He can feel Heart Attack's hand stroking his dick, getting it harder and stiffer. Nathan stops breathing.

"Oh yeah, you know it's coming. You think because your friends said don't leave any scars you were here for a vacation. Well, this is a vacation in Hell, motherfucker!" yells Heart Attack as he rips Nathan's panties up and off with such force that Nathan rises a foot up the glass. Heart Attack pins him there with an elbow in his back and his dick in his ass. Nathan screams and pleads the same as Miguel does in the next room. With his eyes pinned on the fists and kicks tossing Miguel against the red splattered brick wall, his mind fixes on the throbbing, burning, and tearing pain in his blood-soaked ass.

Time stops when your mind and body can take no more abuse. You go limp and give into whatever is happening. Sights, sounds, nothing registers anymore. Miguel had gone limp several minutes ago and the black leather man gives him a couple of goodbye stomps on his ass. Nathan doesn't get that same escape. He saw, heard, and felt every moment of the assault on both sides of the glass.

He assumes his assault is finally ending when Heart Attack heaves, "Now Nancy... this is... no fucking... picnic... we are having here." But it is not to be. Heart Attack twists him around and sticks his massive dick in Nathan's mouth. "That's it, clean up your mess. And get ready for round two," he says, working Nathan's head back and forth like a doll.

The room on the other side of the closet lights up. It's a room where Jose is hanging from an overhead pipe by a brown leather strap buckled to his wrists. Off The Chain takes Heart Attack's place in the closet, where Nathan is crumpled into a tight ball on the floor of the confined one-foot space.

Off The Chain pulls him to his feet.

His legs shake so badly that his knees knock together, making a clicking sound.

"Don't you worry, Nancy," says Off The Chain, "I never take Heart Attack's seconds, as he fucks a nigga raw down to the bone. But the show is not over yet." He slams Nathan's face into the glass. "These little queers want to be your friends? See what happens to friends around here."

This time it is Heart Attack in the next room and he has a cat-o-nine tails in his hand. He rips Jose's clothes off, baring his young skinny body, as it sways before Nathan.

"Don't do this. Please, Heart Attack, you can't do this to me. I make you money. I'm your best cock sucker."

"So, what are you going to do, quit? Go back to sucking dicks in the alleys and getting paid by a screwdriver in the neck?" Heart Attack yanks the pink scarf from Jose's neck, exposing the long blackened scar on the side. "I don't think so. I think you are going to keep your pussy-ass out of my business." He steps back and draws the whip high. The steel balls at the end of each strand hang motionless for a second then take off towards Jose's chest.

He doesn't have time to shut his eyes as the balls crash into his body like buckshot. Blood burst forth and splashes across the mirror. His scream echoes in the room and bores into Nathan's head. Off The Chain slams his face back into the glass as he retreats from the crimson rain. Heart Attack rhythmically slashes the whip in a crisscross motion, spraying Jose's blood around the room. Jose's body twists and turns, spins and twirls as the strands of the whip wrap around him. Within minutes, Jose is covered in open gashes from head to toe and hangs limp like meat in a slaughterhouse.

Off The Chain reaches up to the ceiling and pulls a metal ring. He pushes on one end of the wall and it splits open like the ruptures in the young men's souls. He slides one wall to the left, letting the panels fold and collapse effortlessly. Then he does the same to the other wall and the two torture chambers and small spy-way becoming a single blood arena. Jose hangs on the left and Miguel is broken and lying on the right.

Off The Chain drags Nathan to the chair and slams his sore bloody ass into it. He tightens a belt across his chest and straps Nathan's weakly flailing hands down. He then takes a thin leather strap and forces his head back and mouth open. He spins the chair. It swivels to the side and tilts its way back, so far back that Nathan's head nearly touches the floor and his legs kick frantically in the air. The other two beaten men watch from behind swollen eyes.

"This is what you have befriended," thunders Heart Attack. "This is why you have gotten your asses beaten today. This to me, this bitch, is nothing more than a walking toilet. Worth nothing but shit!"

Off The Chain pulls down his pants, straddles Nathan's face, strains for a second then drops a rumbling load of hot loose diarrhea-like shit into his mouth. He shakes his ass and more falls on Nathan's face, sliding up his nose and burning his eyes. Off The Chain stands up laughing, takes his hand, wipes his ass, and wipes it off on Nathan's blouse and hairless chest. Then he loosens one strap on

Nathan's arm and walks towards the door, pulling up his pants and tightening his belt.

"You ladies clean up your mess before you leave here," orders Heart Attack.

Nathan loosens his belts, flips backward out of the chair, and onto the hard floor. He is choking, spitting, vomiting. He pulls his blouse off and frantically wipes his face, chest, and hands. Then he repeats it again with a clean spot of his blouse, trying to escape the stench. Finally, he hears Jose moan and crawls to him. He undoes the leather strap from one wrist and Jose drops to the floor. They limp painfully to Miguel and remove the pin from his shackle.

"Tienes las manos con el Diablo," Miguel murmurs.

"What did he say?" Nathan asks.

"He says you are cursed," replies Jose through the pain. "Literally, you hold hands with the Devil. What the hell did you do that people would want to treat you this bad?"

"I witnessed a killing," Nathan confesses.

"No. No." Shouts Miguel, he has barely enough strength to sit up, but he has energy to confront Nathan. "No, if you witness a murder they just kill you, and it's over. You didn't just witness a murder."

Nathan sobs, "I went along with the guys who killed those people in the Raven Social Club a couple of months ago. I didn't want to go, but they made me. I didn't kill anybody. I swear, I was just there."

"Mi amor," Jose says sympathetically, "You are fucked."

"Es veneno," Miguel tells Jose. Then repeats in English, "He is poison."

I arrive back at the penthouse late in the evening with two huge bags of mackerel fillets. "Who knows how to cook fish?" I ask as I walk through the door.

Rozalina runs and grabs the bag from me, "I love fish." "Of course you do," I say with a smile.

"Where have you been?" Yana meets me halfway through the living room. Her chestnut hair and eyes are back to the angry shade.

"I've been fishing," I say it like it should be obvious. Then I add jokingly, "I missed you too."

"Lania has been calling me all day," she scolds, "You two are causing a lot of trouble."

I turn to Nicky, "so, you flew the coop too. Where did you go?"

"The girls and I went to the beach and then I took them shopping."

He is proud of himself, but I can also tell by the look on his face that he has more to say. Or maybe Yana had been riding him hard while I was gone. Either way, I am sure he'll fill me in later.

"You spent money on the girls? Let me get out my diary. Dear diary, today, Nicky Nails paid for something he could have stolen. And it was for a girl."

Nicky holds up two fingers.

"No, wait, he's in love. He bought stuff for two ladies. Ain't that sweet." Yana tries to say something, but I cut her off and continue, "I, on the other hand, was out getting a closer look at the house across the water." I pull out photographs from my jacket pocket.

"Are you crazy?" Objects Yana. There is no stopping her this time. "If they had seen you, you could have gotten killed. What were you thinking? You promised last night..."

"First of all, I'm not that crazy." I interject. "There's a fishing charter that leaves every morning and goes right past the place. I took pictures, that's all."

We move to the kitchen and I lay out the pictures on the table. I have shots, mostly close-ups of both sides of the house. You can see the guards with their machine guns nestled neatly under their jackets. Several basement windows have red dots in them. Then there are many pictures of a five-five ebony beauty with jet-black hair falling around her face.

"Who is she?" Yana is three shades angrier.

"Somebody I met on the boat. I needed a cover so I could take pictures of the house without being obvious," I explain and move on to the red dots. "These look like laser sites or maybe an optical alarm system."

"She is also with you in front of the house," Yana pokes her finger in the face of the girl standing by the front gate.

"I took her to lunch and talked her into riding around to see the estates with me. A lot of the places along the waterway are famous tourist attractions. Again, I needed a cover to get close- ups of the house."

"Did you have to fuck her?"

"No. What? I just kept her around to take the pictures," I say.

Yana storms out the kitchen and a second later, we hear the bedroom door slam. She slammed it so hard I don't know how the glass stayed in it. The girls look awkwardly at me then go back to cooking.

"Bro, when it comes to women you are a terrible liar," Nicky says laughing. "Even I can tell she is a lot happier in these pictures than in the ones on the boat. She looks like she has been fucked silly."

"Well, you know me, anything to get the job done."

"Talking about the job, what d'ya think?"

"You mean about making a hit on the place? It's at least a hundred yards from the front gate to the house, and no cover. Maybe fifty yards or so from the water to the back of the house, and again, no cover. At least four pill boxes on each corner—"

"What are pill boxes?" asks Izolda.

"Machine gun nests," answers Nicky.

"Is that bad?"

"Terrible," I continue, "Worse than showing Yana pictures of the girl you just fucked. Steel curtains in these rooms on the top floor, I'm thinking maybe Joey's rooms, but probably more machine gun nests."

"Even if you could get into the house, they most likely have a safe room. You would never get to him," says Yana from the door.

I am hoping she didn't hear the comment about the girl in the picture, but she probably did. "What's a safe room?"

She takes us into the living room and presses a combination of buttons on the TV remote and the whole wall unit slides two feet to the right. There is a small room behind it about the size of a bathroom—a regular one—not like the ones in this place.

"Its walls, floor, and ceiling are solid steel. It has its own air supply, food, water and satellite phone. A person can stay in here for a month. You would have to destroy the building to get a person out of a safe room."

"I guess me and you both know there is no way to get to Joey in that house," I finally admit to Nicky. "So, like I asked you the other night, what the fuck are we still doing here?"

"Like I said before," Nicky says flatly, "We came down here to check out our source info. It proved to be valid. You knew the first day you saw the place it would take a small army, or a fucking airstrike to get to him. Do you have any friends shipping home a Cobra or something? I don't, but I do have a plan. Ladies, will you excuse us?"

Rozalina and Izolda return to the kitchen and the cooking. Yana goes back into the bedroom and closes the door, a lot gentler this time.

"OK, what is the plan this time?" I ask in a hush voice.

"Oh, it's no big secret," Nicky says, "I contacted our bakers in New York and our fruitcake is going to take a little more time to fully cook, so maybe another week or two. When he is done, we are going back home, and Little Joey Banana will come running back too."

"That's it?" I complain, "That's the plan? We go back empty- handed and wait for Joey to come rescue his friend Nathan? That's the stupidest fucking plan you have come up with yet. I think those hoes have fucked your brains out!"

"No, he won't go back to rescue Nathan," he corrects me. "Nathan is not even a major player in the gang, not yet. But he is the key to getting Joey out of that house and back to New York, where you will make him suffer, and then kill him. And don't give me any of that crap about him suffering over Maria's death. Yana told me what you said. You cut that bastard's balls off and mail them to his mother."

"Yana told you..."

"Yeah, yeah, yeah, she was going on about how heartbroken you are. That girl is in love with you, I don't know why, but she is."

I start to object, but Nicky isn't finish with me yet. Obviously, Yana gave him hell today and he is going to give it to me. She can be sweet, but she is also very bossy and demanding.

"A woman doesn't get that mad and jealous over another woman unless she plans to fuck you herself. Which brings us to why I kicked those crazy bitches out of here, you have got to find out what they are planning."

"What makes you think they are planning something?"

"They are hoes! Hoes are always planning something," insists Nicky. "I don't know what exactly, but when Lania and Yana saw you in the club that night, those two bitches creamed their panties. You are a killer, so to me, it is obvious they want you to kill somebody. They are trying to pay you in pussy, or at least make the down payment..."

"Wait a second," I stop him. "You are the one getting his brains fucked out every night. From day one they have been sending girls here to pull double duty."

"Yes," he agrees, "And if it was me they were after for my family connections, then you'd be the one drowning in pussy and I'd be with the classy chick. It's you they want, so they are keeping me busy while she works on you. So please, for the love of God, and for the sake of my dick, before these hoes fuck me into a comma, go play nice with Yana and find out who they want you to kill."

"You could just tell them you had enough," I offer him the simple solution.

"I'm Italiano," Nicky says, pouring on the accent, "You think youse black guys are the only ones proud of your dick? I'm not doing this for myself, I'm doing it for all Italian men."

"I'll tell the pope to make you a saint. Saint Nicolas the Dick, the patron saint of whores."

"I already had to fake an orgasm three times this week to get these Russian babes to stop. MoJo, you really don't know what you are passing up here."

We all have dinner together, the first time since we got here. Then we go to the living room and watch TV, smoke, snort, pop a couple of pills and drink. I tell everyone we need to have a cool out night, things got crazy before and before things get further out of hand we should just relax and enjoy ourselves. Everyone agrees, especially Nicky. So we all get really stoned.

I am lying on my back. Maria's hair tickles my stomach, making ripples run up to my chest. Her warm wet lips suck up hard and tight then slowly go down, getting me harder with each juicy stroke. I can feel myself building to climax, but I fight it back, have to make it last a little longer. I am sure I'm dreaming but I want to keep her with me a while longer. I reach down, hold the hand that is gently rubbing my chest then reach further, and run my fingers through her hair

I slowly stretch out my left arm and pick up the 9mm from the nightstand. My right hand pulls Yana's head up to see the gun pointed at her face. She tries to shake free but I hold her firm by the hair. My hard-on beneath her chin is gone, "You want something hard to suck on?"

She gives one last hard pull and I let go. She sits back on her knees and butt between my legs. Her back is straight and her eyes glassy, she is proud but ashamed, "You were humping me in your sleep. I thought you would like a little morning glory."

"Is that what you hoes call it?" I ask caustically.

"You know, when I first met you I felt sorry for you." Yana gets up, puts on her robe then she walks out the bedroom.

I laugh but that did feel good, she knows how to give good head. Nicky was right.

"What the fuck is wrong with your friend?" Yana yells at Nicky.

"I don't know but most people say he is a bit psychotic," Nicky replies and thinks, 'fucking MoJo, please play nice.'

Yana storms back into the bedroom and slam the door shut.

I'm still lying naked on the bed. We have been in bed naked before but there was no sex involved. She feels good to hold and I guess she feels safe with me. Maybe Nicky is right, maybe she is falling in love with me, although, I wouldn't know why, or perhaps the entire attitude and sexy parading around is part of the plan.

She eyes the gun on the nightstand. I had taken the bullets out just to be safe.

"I'm sorry, but I thought you cared about me," she says.

"Why would you think that?" I ask.

"If you didn't care how I felt, you wouldn't have lied to me last night about the girl in the pictures."

"That was just business," I tell her again. "I needed someone to help me get the pictures. I would have taken you, but you said you've been there, so I couldn't, and it might have blown my cover. This is just business."

"You know, you are not the first person to lose the one you love," she tells me. "I know men who have lost their wives... lovers, and I have given them comfort, not sex."

"Well, what you were doing was comforting," I tell her. Now, I start to play my game. Nicky wants to know what's up, I'll find out. "But it felt a lot like sex. I do feel something for you, or better yet, there is something about you."

"I did want to comfort you, and sex." Yana comes straight to the point. "We have not been honest with each other. You stay here not because I keep you a prisoner, but because you want to. What we feel for each other is a kindred spirit. You love your dead wife; you feel as if you died when she died. I too know what it is like to be dead. I am what is known to my people as dead soldier girl."

Every hooker has a story. A father who abused her, a mother who didn't want or love her, or a brother who was too lazy to work and put her on the streets. But Yana's story is one for the history books.

Hers and Svetlana's story started when they were sixteen, back in their village in Mother Russia. A general who controlled the region would raid the villages for pretty young girls for his men, and inevitably, it came to Svetlana's and Yana's time. They stopped the school bus and took the best-looking girls that were of age.

The general would hand over the girls to his soldiers, a prize for their loyalty or something, but often, afterwards, some of the less desirable girls would be sold on the black market. The prettier ones became part of his private collection of whores. He trained them to be pleasing, sophisticated socialite puppets. Then he used them to pay his way up the chain of command and success. Who says the Russians are not capitalist?

After two months with the soldiers, Svetlana, Yana, and two other girls from their village escaped and made their way back home. The first girl was shot dead on the path to her farm by her father. He never said a word to her, simply blew her away with a hunting rifle, like she was an animal.

Svetlana's father turned her away too. The people in the villages considered any girl taken by the general as dead to them. Yana was set to marry a young man; they were in love, but both their fathers told her that she was dead to them. The young man, who had seemingly loved her more than the air he breathed, told her the same.

With nowhere to go, Svetlana and Yana planned to return to the general, but the other girl could not bear to go back, and hanged herself outside the village. Her people did not even bury her, Svetlana and Yana did, and buried themselves along with their friend.

"That was ten years ago," Yana tells me, "The general is now KGB, or so he claims, and runs his prostitution ring from Brooklyn, New York."

"So, whose kid sister is coming of age, Lania's or yours?"

"Lania's," she tells me, wiping away tears of painful times. "Thankfully, my sister is only fourteen. Ivan the Terrible as he likes to be called..."

"Of course, he does," I interject, and she laughs.

"He now entices girls with promises of becoming models or movie stars," she continues, "He sent Lania's sister pictures, telling her that Lania was a famous model and movie star in America. She wrote to Lania, telling her she will be coming over soon. We doubt we will ever see her."

"Let me see if I got this straight," I confirm with her, "you want me to kill your KGB pimp?"

"And his two partners," she adds, "but he is the one who runs the business."

"You know, you two could have just told us this on the first night," I assure her. "And I apologize for the gun in your face. But if it will make you feel better you can go back to blowing me."

She is sitting on the bed and gives me a peculiar look. "I'm kidding, call Lania, we need to talk."

Jose and Miguel are in a heated argument when Nathan wakes up. The trio has been shooting up continuously since their brutal treatment in the back room. Nathan can't understand a word the two Latinos are saying but he knows they are arguing about him.

He is only partially correct, Miguel is planning to leave and wants Jose to go with him, to get as far away from the Brothers and Nathan as he can. What Nathan does understand is that they keep saying O.C., which means Organized Crime.

Seeing that Nathan is awake, Miguel limps over to him. "Hey, kid, I've been here a long time and I've never seen the Brothers act like this. I keep telling Jose, we, I mean him and me have to get out of here."

Miguel tells them that Heart Attack had been grabbed by the Mississippi Clan. They cut him open from neck to guts to let the crows eat out his heart, what is referred to as a Mississippi Mauling, but as he told the story, he never had a heart for the white man, and instead, a black eagle sprang from his chest and devoured the clan's men.

On the other hand, Off The Chain claims to be the only free black man in the world. Once a prisoner of the Texas Chain Gang, he broke free when he no longer held onto any humanity and used his chains to strangle the guards and is now free to do whatever pleases him.

"These two are the most evil men I have ever met, but you have made enemies in the Mafia, they will hunt you down no matter where you run or how long it takes. And if that was not bad enough, the enemy you have is a man we know as a man without a soul."

"I told him," Jose comes to his side, "We will all get out together. If we leave you here, you will die. I can't let that happen. I won't."

"It's all right," Nathan tells them, "Because Miguel is right, you can't help me. The Brothers will kill you if you try, and I can't leave, the guys who left me here will be back. I can't run... they will find me. They did before and they will again. You two go."

"I need the hospital first," Miguel tells them, "My ribs are broken and possibly my hip too, and no amount of dope is going to fix that. Jose, if you stay you will end up in the dumpster."

Miguel asks to leave and the Brothers let him go.

Jose is passed out when the Brothers come for Nathan. They see that Jose has been feeding him heroin.

"No matter, Charlie will be here soon," says Heart Attack, "And he's not too particular how his meat is served. We will put him in the shower, at least he'll be awake, and Charlie will do the rest."

The ice cold water stings like a thousand needle pricks without their juice but Nathan is slow to rouse from his stupor, then he is dragged from one room to another and dumped on the floor like a rag. He is vaguely aware of a presence in the room, but muddled voices and shadows are all he comprehends. He slowly registers a man sitting on the steel chair and knows he's back on the third floor. He is too tired to fight, too high to care anymore, willing to give whatever pleasure the man wants, and willing to accept whatever torture the man wishes to deliver.

The man stands over Nathan, all three hundred pounds of fat sweaty blubber. "So Nancy, this is what the

Brothers are trying to pass off as a toy these days. I'd rather snap your dope addicted neck than to play doctor with you. But the Brothers made me promise not to scar that pretty little face, and I guess that means not twisting your head around either."

Nathan pulls himself up by grabbing the man's pants' legs. He fumbles with the belt, his mouth slightly agape, saliva running from the corner of his mouth.

The man slaps Nathan across the face, back down to the hard cold tiles, "You wish it was going to be that easy. You don't understand what I'm saying do you?"

Nathan rolls over and kneels, turns his back to the man then pulls down his own pants, and buries his face on the floor. He just wants it to be over so he can get back to Jose and his needles of oblivion.

The man studies his rear end, which is red and swollen, "This is pitiful and I will talk to the Brothers about this."

Nathan feels the man's hand on his left cheek, his fat stubby fingers gripping and pulling at him. He prepares to be fucked, but even through the heroin haze he can tell this is not the man's dick he feels probing his sore rectum. These are hard and bony knuckles on his butt and before his mind can fully come to terms with what is about to happen, the man shoves his fat tightly balled fist into Nathan's asshole.

Nathan sprawls out on the cold hard floor like road-kill, too weak to scream and gasps for air as misery once again invades the emptiness of his soul. He exhales and loses his last shreds of self-respect and consciousness and vaguely hears, "Didn't plan on that now, did you, Nancy?"

Nathan wakes up back in the room alone. His ability to move, even slightly, is gone. Miguel is gone. Jose is gone. The signature pink scarf is stuck to the wall with a screwdriver, a sign he has gone to the dumpster. Everything and everyone is gone, except the pain.

I have abandoned the telescope for good. We take a ride to Ft. Lauderdale, the five of us, on a day trip to the beach. Nicky and I would have preferred Miami Beach, but Yana is still scared that we will be discovered. I tell her that together Nicky and I can take on an army, however, Yana and Nicky would rather we do not. I insist and Nicky agrees that we pack for an encounter, just in case. We have one cooler-bag filled with beer, wine, vodka and ice, and another filled with sawed off shotguns and nines, and of course, ice.

We spend the day in the sand and surf, chicks fighting on our shoulders, all the things one does to forget real life. It is late at night before we finish off the drinks and drive back down to Miami drunk.

Morning comes much too soon and with it, Svetlana. She wants to talk business, but Nicky and I need to smoke and coke up first. She gives us a look of disapproval, doubting we are the people, or more to the point, that I am the killer I am supposed to be.

Yana convinces her I am.

Lania tells Nicky the story of Ivan the Terrible and her sister. Although it has been a couple of days since I heard it, I didn't mention it or the hit to him. I want him to hear it for himself, and to see if their stories correlate. They do, right down to the father shooting his daughter, their friend's suicide, and them being basically run out of town. The two women related the same story. So we have two choices, either they have practiced it enough, or they have told the truth.

"I have a question," says Nicky. "Why didn't the villagers go to the general and shoot the bastard?"

"Oh, some did take action," she tells him, then poses her own question. "Have you ever seen what is left of a farmhouse after it's been hit by a mortar? There are body parts everywhere. You Americans have not seen war, you send your boys off to destroy other lands. War is just a TV show to you."

"Damn, I'm sorry. I was just wondering," Nicky apologizes.

"No, I am sorry," Lania says, "Telling you this brings back a lot of pain. Here is the deal I offer, you kill Ivan and his two partners for us, and we kill Joey Banoa for you."

Nicky laughs, "I'm sorry, Lania, but your girls just don't look like the assassin types. What are they going to do, fuck him to death? Actually, that would probably work."

"No," she says angrily, "He takes a lot of pills to stay high. My girls can get to him and replace a couple of his pills with some that contain a kind of silicate. It will eat away at his intestines, and after about three, he will bleed out and die from septic shock. No one will know what is killing him until it is too late. The effects are irreversible, so even if he ingests only one pill, it will take a little longer for him to die, but he will die."

"Here's a thought," Nicky says, "Why don't you just give your pimp the bleeding ass of death pills?"

"Because he knows about the silicate poisoning, and us, so we would have no chance to use it on him."

"I can't let you do that," I join in, "If they suspected Joey of being poisoned, your girls, all of you would be in danger."

"And what my psychotic friend is not saying is that he has an overwhelming desire to see Joey draw his last breath himself," Nicky adds, "But the bleeding ass of death is pretty sweet. Also, there is this other minor fact, the Mafia does not go after the Bratva, and nobody fucks with the Triad. In the meantime, I've contacted New York and our package is ready for pick up. So, I'm sorry, lady—"

"We'll do it," I interrupt. "But you don't go after Joey Banoa.

Because Nicky is right, I want to see him bleed out."

"Wait a minute, MoJo," protests Nicky, "My father won't OK this, and we will not get any help from my family, if you know what I mean."

"Come on, be real, most of the shit you do your father is not OK with. I think the ladies know perfectly well the Mafia wouldn't do the job, which is why they came to me. Three guys, maybe a dozen tops, we can take him out. He's small potatoes. And if it is true this guy is KGB, he may have equipment we can use to get Joey."

"That is bullshit," Nicky counters, "This girl got to you. Do you know what's worse than a thief with a conscious?"

"What?"

"A killer with a heart!" But Nicky knows my mind is made up, so he turns his attention back to Svetlana, "Well, fuck it, but it looks like you got yourself a hit man. But we are still going to need some help from you. We will need someone who speaks Russian if we are to find out when your sister is coming and shut him down before then."

"I speak Russian," offers Yana, "We all do."

"Not you, he knows you too well," I tell her, "Besides, I need you to stay here and watch the house. I'll give you a number to call when Joey leaves."

"How will I know when he leaves?"

"When he leaves, everybody leaves, call me then."

"I think you just retired from being a whore, I hope you have a good pension. I want Rozalina and Izolda," Nicky says, "Them I trust."

"OK," agrees Svetlana, "I'll put them on medical. Usually, that gives them a month away from the club. Yana is going to be a little trickier to work out. But for now, you have to pay for the time she spent here."

"What?" Nicky is outraged. "This deal is getting worse by the minute."

"You know, the other girls were here on their own time," explains Yana. "I don't have that luxury."

"Unfortunately true," Svetlana agrees, "We have to put something on the books or Ivan will become suspicious. He charges a grand a day for her, I need $30,000.00."

"A thousand dollars a day," Nicky yells, "Thirty thousand, and he didn't even fuck her. That's a fucking rip-off."

"Well, she did blow me once," I tell him, "Pay the woman."

Svetlana looks at Yana and she kind of shrugs in agreement.

"Me... pay her. Why me? It's your dick that got sucked," Nicky protests vigorously.

"You're the one who said, 'Find out what they want.' They want their boss dead and thirty grand. Now you know."

"Fuck you, Morris. For thirty grand, I hope she sucked your nuts out through your dick hole." Nicky finally gives in, "When this is done, we are going to have to renegotiate our arrangement."

I wonder if Svetlana realizes that she just traded the devil she knows for one that is a thousand times worse, but I suppose she will find out soon enough that prostitution is a nasty business, no matter who runs it.

We set the two girls up in Brooklyn. They will keep an eye on Ivan, and Izolda will become a client trying to catch her cheating husband. Ivan operates a so-called private investigation business. It is simply a front for his rackets, and as I suspected, he has many sophisticated bugs and communication devices. We plan not to stop Ivan from bringing in girls from Eastern Europe, but rather supplant his operations with our own.

Once the girls are in place, we head for the Village to pick up our package.

We go through the alley entrance to Tail Feathers and when we are in the mezzanine office, I glance down into the pit. The place is worse than I first imaged.

"Is he ready?" demands Nicky.

"Oh yes sir, he'll do anything you want not to end up back here," claims Heart Attack.

"I don't know," Nicky prods the men, "This place looks pretty tame. What do you think, MoJo?"

"Looks like a place I'd take my mama for Sunday brunch," I add, "After church."

"Don't let the looks fool you," says Off The Chain, "we gave the boy the extra special treatment. That's why it took a little longer. Have to let it sink in deep."

"Where is he?"

Off The Chain goes to the railing of the balcony and yells, "Nancy, get your pretty little ass up here."

A minute later Nathan walks into the office. His hair is dyed a freakish dirty blonde, he is wearing a scummy French maid outfit; complete with falsies, fishnet stockings, and high heels.

He says looking down at his feet, "Yes sirs, what is your pleasure?"

I just say, "Damn."

"Well done," Nicky comments and lifts up the skirt to see if he still has his balls. "Nancy, huh? I like that."

Nathan follows us down the hall, his eyes on the floor the entire time. Nicky throws the hood in his face, "Put it on." He does without a word. I push his head down and shove him into the back seat. He lies where he lands and I take a peek to see if he still has his balls. As we drive off, I hear the soft low sounds of sobs from under the hood.

"Relived to be out of there?" I say to him, "Don't be, you just awoke from one nightmare and into another."

We are driving through Queens when Nicky tells him, "Take the fucking bag off your head and sit up." He does and Nicky looks at him in the rear view mirror. "Jesus!

You're a fucking ugly bitch. Lucky for you we don't want to date you, or for that matter be seen with you."

We cross the Triborough Bridge back into the Bronx.

"What we do want you to do, is keep this beeper with you at all times, understand?"

He is looking down in his lap, "Yes sir."

The Brothers did a number on him all right, maybe too well.

I take over from here, "When that beeper goes off, you have five minutes to call back the number. Not ten minutes, not six minutes, five minutes to make the call. You will do whatever the voice on the other end tells you. If it tells you to jump off this bridge, you jump. If it tells you to shoot your mama, you pump that bitch full of lead. Understand?"

"Yes sir."

"Good girl. I don't care what you are doing. I don't care whose dick you are sucking. I don't care who is fucking you in the ass. If you don't make the call in five minutes, or you fail to do exactly what you are told, Nancy, we are going to take you right back to that little fun house you just left. You don't want us to do that, do you?"

"No sir," Nathan is fighting back crying aloud, but tears are streaming down his face.

We come to the corner of his block and Nicky stops the car. "Get the fuck out," he yells, "I don't want people to think I can't get better pussy than an ugly bitch like you."

Nathan jumps out the car and scurries down the first driveway he comes to. We watch as he runs into a shed at the back of the yard and hides inside.

I say to Nicky, "You think I was too hard on him? Ten dollars says he hangs himself before morning."

"I hope not, I paid a hundred to those fucking guys," he laughs and takes the bet. "I need to talk to Bonnie, she can help us with the Russian."

"Bonnie is no longer with us," I tell him.

"What? What happened? Who..." Nicky swerves wildly through traffic.

"Whoa, hold your horses," I say, "She is still alive. She just decided to quit the gang."

"What? When the hell did this happen?"

"Before we left for Florida," I tell him. "Right after the whole Chris and the rats' episode. I guess it just became too much for her. She said she couldn't go on with this life, so she joined a convent. She didn't tell you herself because she said she couldn't face you and still go through with it."

"She joined the Black Robe Army and couldn't tell me," Nicky is pissed, "But she could tell you, the guy who killed his whole fucking crew for quitting on him. You, she is not afraid of."

I try to explain it to him, "You've got it all wrong. She didn't come tell me she was leaving, I tracked her down, mainly to ask about Maria and Joey. I think she feels she can't face you because you two are so close, me, I'm still an outsider. And for the fucking record, I didn't kill my gang because they wanted to quit on me. I killed those bastards because they wanted to make peace with my enemies. Bonnie wants to make peace with herself. Nobody can hold that against her."

"I guess so," Nicky accepts my reasoning, "But you have to learn to communicate better. I nearly crashed the fucking car just now. Bonnie is no longer with us. What the fuck?"

"Yeah, sorry about that. So, what is this big fucking plan of yours to get Joey Banana back here? You going to set him up on a blind date with Nancy and hope he dies of a heart attack?" I joke.

"No, we are going to get Nancy on Joseph Banana's crew and he is going to set up Old Joe for a hit," explains Nicky. "We kill the father and the son has to come back to take over the business. Then we kill the son. Although, taking a look at Nancy now, it is going to take some doing to get him in with the Banoas. I think the Brothers may have gone a little too far.”

“Are you going to make the hit on Joe Banana?” I ask.

“No,” Nicky says with a twisted grin that has come to mean trouble. “This is the best part of the plan. Sal is going to be the hit man.”

“Your retarded brother Sal?” I say in total disbelief. “I think you are the retarded one in the family.”

“Sal can do it. And I’ll prove it to you.”

CHAPTER 11
A Black Cat Is Bad Luck

Nicky and I show up in his backyard early in the morning. Sal is tending the chicken and is both surprised and elated to see us. He bounces around hugging us like we are Santa Claus and this is Christmas morning. It takes Nicky several minutes to calm him down.

"I'll go wake papa, he will be so glad to see you," Sal starts to run off.

"Whoa, hold on there, cowboy," Nicky tells him, "First, we got some family business to take care of, secret family business. And what did I tell you about family business?"

"Nobody outside the family knows our business and secret family business only us brothers know, right?" replies Sal like he is repeating his alphabet. Then he looks worried and whispers to Nicky loudly, "What about Morris?"

"Morris is family. What did I tell you about Morris?"

"Oh yeah," Sal grins, "Morris is our brother from another mother. A BLACK mother, right?"

"That's right," I agree.

Nicky continues, "Tell Morris what we are going to do to Old Joe Banana."

"We are going to tell him, 'Go to hell' and bam, shoot him in the face."

"OK, so you trained your brother like a rabid dog," I'm not really pleased with Nicky, "but that doesn't mean..."

"Huh, hold on a minute and just watch," Nicky stops me and pulls out his .38 revolver, puts it in Sal's hand and says, "Shoot Morris in the face."

Sal's eyes widen like a child opening his favorite toy on Christmas morning. He is full of amazement and shock, "Nicky, Morris is your friend... I mean brother."

"Family business... Do it," shouts Nicky.

"It's OK Sal," I say calmly. Then right after uttering those words I think, 'I hope that fool, Nicky, took the bullets out.'

Sal points the gun in my face and pulls the trigger, click... click... click... click. Then he laughs, "You were just fooling me. You knew there are no bullets. Morris, Nicky knew there are no bullets." He is truly relived.

I am too. "OK, so he's got what it takes to be a trigger man," I agree with this part of his plan. "But I don't see how your brother is going to get close to Joe to shoot him."

"That's the best part of the plan," Nicky says, "No one touches Sal and everybody knows it. Everybody!"

Nicky tells the story of Sal and his push broom.

Sal worked at the construction sites with their father and spent the days sweeping the office trailer. One day while his father was out, they were out of push brooms on the site and some guy took Sal's. He also called him an idiot and pushed him. Not hard, didn't even knock him down. The other men in the office told the guy he had made the worst mistake of his life.

"The next day when everyone arrived at work, they found the guy in the office, bent over with the push broom rammed so far up his ass the other end was coming out his mouth." Nicky finishes the story.

"No fucking way," I say, "You guys are so full of shit."

"I swear to God. Sal and my father started work at another of his sites that day. And Sal got a new push broom."

"It's true Morris," Sal says, not really knowing what we are talking about, "I sweep up the office. Can't have any nails lying around."

"OK, let me see if I got this straight. Your master plan is to have your brother kill Joe Banoa, because you think no one will touch him. I think that after he shoots Banoa in the face, his men are not going to care about your father, and kill him. Never mind that, what do you think your father will do to us? If he skewered some schmuck for touching his broom, I don't even want to imagine what will happen to us when we get your brother killed!"

"That's why we got Nancy. He's going to let us know every move Joe makes, and when he is alone. By the way, he didn't hang himself, so you owe me ten. I gave him his first orders yesterday, to go hang out at the pizza shop."

"I don't think this guy even takes a shit alone, and he's probably got someone looking out for the Ty-D-Bol Man."

We finally go into the house and have breakfast with his family. We inform his father about our time in Florida, not all of it of course, and definitely not about the intended hit on Ivan. He asks us what our next plan is for getting Joey Banana, and Nicky tells him he is working on something but says nothing about Sal or Nancy. We spend the day in the basement drinking wine and talking business. Nicolas is very proud of his son's progress.

Cherry Bomb and Honey turn out to be really good assets when they are doing something other than giving blowjobs. They have surveillance running on Ivan and his second in command. Using Ivan's own equipment against him, they find out the next shipment of girls is to arrive at the beginning of the year and that Svetlana's sister, Akilina, will be among them. They also got us the equipment that we use to track Nancy, like the beeper, which doubles as a homing device.

The other bit of information, which is no revelation to me, is how greedy Ivan is. He is not only trafficking humans; he is also using the same human beings to traffic drugs in and out of the Soviet Union.

If greed is the first deadly sin of criminals, overconfidence has to be number two. Although I would like to handle the Russians myself, with a price of a million dollars on my head, Ivan is as likely to turn me over to Banoa as he is to make a deal worth millions. Not to be guilty of or fall victim to the second deadly sin, I send Mad Dog Madison to make a new drug deal with Ivan the Terrible. We paint a stupendous picture and offer to help him make a fortune in the cocaine trade by being first in the European market.

He jumps at the opportunity, and through the bugs, we quickly learn how the entire backbone of his operation functions. We also learn that he plans to do to us what we are doing to him, which is to learn about our operation and cut us out completely. His greed and overconfidence will lead to his death.

Nathan cowers in the back of the shed, desperately avoiding the slivers of light through the cracks in the wooden door that threaten to expose him. He yanks off the last vestiges of shame and degradation that he wore and crouches freezing and shaking exposed to the winter's cold. He waits until nightfall then waits some more until all the swirling voices fall silent. Next, he waits again until the moon shadows are stretched long and away from him. Finally, he makes his way across the backyards. Across frozen lawns and through dead vegetable patches with their spike-storks torturously sticking out of the ground, he creeps towards the house, his feet icy and bloody from the short trip.

He tries the back door that leads to the kitchen, it's locked. It has never been locked in his life. He sneaks around to the side door, while remaining in the shadows. It too is locked. He turns the doorknob and draws his naked body back. With a force that comes from anger and anguish, humiliation and hurt endured, he throws himself against the door. The flimsy bolt locks give way and the door flings open. Nathan stumbles in, home at last.

He quietly closes the door and goes upstairs. Both parents and sister are all fast asleep, none heard a thing. Nathan locks the bathroom door and climbs into the empty tub. Then he turns the water on slow and a steady stream of heat begins to fill the vessel. The water gets progressively hotter as it rises, hot enough to remove the bone chilling cold from his body. Hot enough to scald his flesh as he sits motionless in the rising tide, but not hot enough to burn out the memories that play non- stop in his head like a horror movie. He knows there is no water hot enough to do that. He sits there the rest of the night, and into the morning, crying like a lost little girl.

Banging on the door and his father's angry yelling on the other side does not move him. He sits in the tub, now filled to overflowing with cold water, staring into emptiness. Suddenly, the beeper on the bathroom floor starts to hum and bounce around. Nathan grabs it, looks at the number on the little green screen, and Bulletproof's warning goes off in his head. He grabs a towel from the closet and races past his father to the kitchen phone.

His father yells as he rushes by, "Hey, when did you get here? And what do you think you were doing leaving your uncle's house without a word? And what in God's name did you do to your hair?"

The voice on the other end sounds strange, mechanical, but it orders him to go to the pizza shop, then, silence. He returns upstairs; everyone is up now, standing in the hall, staring. In his room, he gets dressed then leaves without saying a word. He has no idea what to say, almost as if he has forgotten how to talk, so he says nothing.

At the pizza shop, he is the same, his friends are happy to see him, the few who are left. They greet him, slap his back, but he jerks and twitches with each touch, barely saying a word. He finds a booth in the corner in the back and sits there, waiting for something to happen. Nothing does.

Every day after that he does the same, walks through the gauntlet of friends, sits in the back-corner booth and waits. He is also painfully aware that the last time he was here he had to flee for his life. He wonders if Mr. B knows he was part of the Raven's hit squad. He wonders if Nicky Nails has him sitting in the back-corner booth waiting for a bullet.

A week after he came back to the pizza shop, Teresa comes storming in and charges into his face, "You fucking little prick! You went without me, didn't you? Didn't you?"

Nathan doesn't know what she is talking about, merely regards at her with a blank expression.

"You went to go see him, didn't you? Probably laughing it up with your little whore girlfriends. You and Joey can go to hell!" Teresa storms out.

But the damage is done. On the other side of the pizza shop, in a booth in the back corner sits Joseph Banoa, his driver, and two of his men.

"That kid with the bleach blonde dye job, is that one of Joey's boys?" asks Joseph.

The three men look him over.

Nathan is about to explode then hears one of them say, "Yeah. Nathan something or other."

"Go bring him over," orders Joseph Banoa.

The man goes to get Nathan.

He is trembling as he approaches the booth.

"Relax! Marone," says Joe, "I'm not going to eat you. I just had a spaghetti dinner. You a friend of my boy? Where have you been? And what the fuck did you do to your hair? You look like a fucking queer; you know that?"

"I've been in California hanging out with the surfers," Nathan hears the words come out of his mouth but can't believe he's saying them. "I'm Nathan Napolitano, Mr. Banoa, and Joey can vouch for me. I took off when things got crazy."

"Smart guy," Joe says, "You need money? Need work?"

"Yes Sir, Mr. B!"

"Then you be here tomorrow when the place opens," Joe tells him. "And wash that faggot looking dye job out of your hair, it may be cool in California, but you're back in New York now. Tomorrow, you start driving for me."

"Mr. B, that's my job," says the husky old Italian, "How is he going to protect you if there's trouble?"

"If we run into any trouble, I'll be protecting him," Joe laughs, "Get him a clean .22. I've got other work for you."

Just like that, Nathan is back in the mob. 'Maybe this is what Nicky planned,' he thinks, then realizes. 'I guess he wants me to be his rat.'

If Joseph Banoa finds out where he has been, or what and who got him there, he's a dead man. If he doesn't turn rat for Nicky, he is worse than dead.

Before he leaves the next morning, Nathan gets another page. He calls the number. Another recorded message instructs him to report every place Banoa visits, what time he arrives, what time he leaves. Now it's certain, he is a rat. The worst thing you can be in the mob.

I send a message to Sweet Jesus; he is to send a shipment of liquid cocaine to Spain as industrial coolant. From there, it will be turned back into cocaine and shipped behind the Iron Curtain. On the return trip, Ivan's number two man will bring girls and opium. I also tell Sweet Jesus to alert the FBI, and to make sure number two's luggage is tagged with opium. I inform him that once we start the flow of cocaine into the Soviet Union, we will use Ivan's network of Bratva to keep it alive.

I finally meet with Ivan, top dog to top dog, to seal our partnership, even as his second in command is being busted at the airport. I pour a pile of pure Colombian on the glass tray in his PI office and we do line after line of blow. We are both good and high when I hear in my earpiece, "The target has arrived." I have my afro back so it completely covers my ear, making it easy to conceal the tiny earpiece.

I draw one more line in front of him then sneak a tiny vial of silicate behind the credit card I used to divide the cocaine. As expected, Ivan does not see the lethal additive being placed in front of him, as he is too busy watching Joseph Banoa's ex-driver attaching a silencer to his .45 revolver in the car outside. Ivan dives in one last time, snorting the deadly mixture up his nose and deep into his lungs.

What would have taken days to kill him had he ingested it, goes to work immediately, ripping apart the pathway to and the tiny air sacs called alveoli. Each breath he takes causes more damage, robbing him of oxygen and forcing him to breathe harder and agonizingly deeper. Minutes after snorting the last line, Ivan collapses onto the desk, blood flowing from his nose and mouth. Ivan the Terrible dies a terrible and painful death by drowning in his own hell.

Mad Dog Madison comes in just after Ivan has expired. He grabs him unceremoniously, hoists the skinny Russian mobster onto one shoulder, takes him outside, and dumps his body next to Joseph Banoa's ex-driver, whom he shot in the head seconds ago while he was waiting for me to exit the PI's office. Greed and overconfidence, the two deadly sins of the criminal, will always come back to get you.

While Mad Dog drives my recently departed ex-partner as well as Banoa's ex-driver to the Badlands south of Hunts Point Market, I go to meet Akilina and the other young immigrant girls to impart the bad news. I tell them there is a mix-up with their work permits and they will not be starting modelling careers as planned, instead, for them to remain in America, they have to work as au pairs. I inform Akilina, through Rozalina as my Russian is non-existent, that I have a special placing for her with a wealthy family that lives on Long Island. The man's niece is about to have a baby, and I want her to keep a watchful eye over her.

Nicky and I fly back to Miami and let Svetlana know that Akilina now works for me. As I promised, her sister will never be a whore.

We have Ivan's number three man running the business in Europe as our foreign liaison, a job he is happy to have considering the alternatives. Ivan's network of Russian Dollhouses in New York, Miami, and Los Angeles are now part of the Rocci family business and Rozalina, Izolda, and all the others who used to work for Ivan the Terrible now work for Nicky.

Nicky and two other men he brought along stay a couple of days to work out the transition of power. I convince Nicky to retire Lania also, unless he wants to be getting the bloody shits one day in the future. He readily agrees; better to have all new management as he puts it. I fly out the same day, without seeing Yana.

Akilina arrives at the vast Lucerella estate prepped for the job, having been told in advance that she will be interview by Mrs. Delitanni, Elizabeth, and the old man, Mr. Lucerella.

"Impress the old man and the job is yours," I tell her. To be sure, she knows how important it is for me that she gets the job. I tell her the story of the Russian Dollhouse, Svetlana and Yana, and of Ivan the Terrible's sudden departure from this world. Then I encourage, "The friends who came over with you, their quality of life depends on your success. You land this position and I stay in the au pair business, if not, I move on to another venture. And for your own safety, never ever mention or acknowledge that you have even heard my name. It would not be good for you."

I am sure Akilina will get the job, she is healthy-looking with shiny brass blonde hair, a younger version of Svetlana, and she draws men to her without much effort. The old man will find her irresistible and having no other women in the house except for Lucia, his sister, Elizabeth, and of course, the sixty-two-year-old cook, Akilina will become a Spring day in his Winter years.

Angelo Lucerella has over the years lost three sons and a wife to the family business. She, dying of a broken heart after her youngest boy, Giovanni, was gunned down on the streets of Brooklyn. Having no family left, except his sister and her two daughters, he awaits his niece's child with great anticipation.

Akilina is quick to realize that he is the only one who does because Lucia is full of venom for the yet to be born child. Often, her remarks give Akilina reason to believe that she wishes to smother the child as soon as it sees the light of day, or better yet, that the child will be stillborn.

As for Elizabeth, she speaks even more strangely of the child, as if it isn't even hers. She feels no attachment to the baby inside her and refers to herself in the third person. Saying things like, "I wonder if she will have her mother's eyes," Or "I hope she is beautiful like her mother."

From day one, Akilina thought Elizabeth was going through the baby crazies, which is what they call it in her country. She had seen her older sister and sisters-in-law go through them in the last month of their pregnancies. The babies became burdens and they resented them immensely, but Elizabeth is the worst she has ever seen, but after the preparation she had gotten from Morris, she had an idea why.

Within days of settling in, Akilina listens to Elizabeth's life story, one Akilina pretends to have never heard. She had come to the estate the day her father was killed, never left, and has resigned herself to the role of prisoner and never will. "This house is my prison for the awful thing I've done and this baby the penalty I must pay for trying to steal another woman's love."

Akilina and Elizabeth became friends fast, as they were practically the same age, and although raised worlds apart, shared similar likes and interests, but most importantly, Elizabeth now had someone to unburden her heart to.

The house is full of hard men, and Elizabeth's mother, who is harder than any man, is neither consolation nor comfort. There is, however, one man Elizabeth dislikes more than all the rest. His name is Tom Green. He is around a lot and watches her in a way as if to imply that he might want something. Neither has any ideas what that might be. Oddly, he doesn't seem to fit in, or even comes across like the other men.

When Elizabeth finally goes into labor, she suffers for twenty-four long hours. The baby does not come willingly or easily into this world, but Akilina, the doctor, and nurse make sure it does. At 11:23 p.m., much to her mother's dismay, Elizabeth gives birth to a baby girl, whom she immediately names, Maria. The only name she cried out during childbirth.

March 30th, 1972 Little Maria takes her first breath of air in this world, nine months to the moment her namesake drew her last, and when she opens her eyes for the first time, just as Elizabeth expected, they are crystal blue.

Almost automatically, Akilina finds herself the child's foster parent, as Elizabeth never holds the baby. She also never feeds her, changes her, nor comforts her when she cries. Akilina moves into the nursery and becomes the only caregiver.

Elizabeth is in the adjoining room and occasionally watches from the doorway as Akilina gives Maria her feedings. Sometimes, Akilina feels Elizabeth's desire for the child but she dare not cross the threshold. And when brought close to her, Elizabeth shies away, Akilina finally realizes that she has a real fear of her own baby.

Lucia Delitanni on the other hand, does not hide her displeasure or disappointment and moves her room to the farthest area in the mansion, a corner room on the north end, never once having laid eyes on the child. If it were not for the old man, this child would have been abandoned at birth. It is a fact that he had hoped for a boy but now that he has seen her, he is just as happy with a grandniece, despite her less than pure lineage that shows all too clearly in her face and complexion. Little Maria is a beautiful baby girl and Angelo loves her, only he and Akilina do.

On the first day Nathan starts driving for Mr. B he thinks it will be his last.

Joseph Banoa sees the beeper on his belt and asks, "What's that for, you're a doctor?"

"No," replies Nathan sheepishly, "I keep it for my mother, in case she needs me, she is not doing so well. It's her heart." Nathan isn't telling a complete lie. Living at the Tail Feathers taught him to lie on the spot, to know what a john wanted to hear and tell him so instantly. Even though the beeper isn't for his mother, it is common knowledge that she suffered a mild heart attack when he went missing and has not been feeling well since his return either. He never told his parents where he was. How could he? Simply told them the same lie about going to California. His father stopped asking, but his mother never accepted the story. He can tell by the way she looks at him and the way he can't look at her. Day by day her heart grows heavy, and he learnt the universal truth, that you cannot lie to your mother.

"Let me see that," demands Banoa.

Nathan hands over the beeper. What else can he do? Big G, Giuseppe, or Peppe as Mr. B calls his second in command takes the beeper and goes into a small electronic store on 42nd street. The three of them wait for his return, Nathan sweating bullets, hoping the beeper does not go off.

Big G returns and tosses it back to him, "It's clean. Just a beeper, no bugs or anything."

"It's a good thing, a boy should take care of his mother. OK, let's go," orders Mr. B.

Nathan drives to Brighton Beach and stays with the car, giving it a good wipe down while the trio go into the PI office of Ivan the Terrible. Nathan doesn't know who they came to meet or why, as it is made clear he is just to drive the car and not ask questions, but he does makes mental notes of everywhere they have been, as instructed by his other boss.

Two days later, Nathan gets another beep right after he drops Mr. B at home. When he calls the number, the recorded message advises him to pick up a new beeper at a store on Fordham Road. It is well after midnight and he knows the store will be closed, but he does as directed. Behind the gate, taped to the store window is a beeper exactly like the one he has on. As per orders, he smashes the old one and puts on the new one, figuring this one is bugged.

Nathan drives Mr. B around every day, and every night he calls the number on the beeper after he leaves him, always within five minutes, no matter what time he dropped him off or where, and reports in. He never speaks to a person, just that awful answering machine. A machine giving him instructions and another to report to, and never the same numbers, they aren't even in the same state sometimes.

The numbers are all over the place: New York, New Jersey, Pennsylvania. Sometimes, as close as the Bronx, and once, from his own house, just to fuck with him. They don't own an answering machine but one picked up and he left his report. They are as far away as California and Mexico, and he is quite sure it is to let him know that there is no escape. And there is no way to track down Nicky Nails either. After all, he doesn't have to go anywhere to retrieve the messages, Nicky can simply call the number at any time and get them from wherever.

Nathan drives Mr. B, Mr. G, and his other bodyguard back to the Brighton Beach location about a month later. Mr. G goes in and comes back out rather quickly again.

Mr. B goes into a rage.

Nathan learns that day that Ivan, the Russian, was supposed to deliver Morris Bulletproof Johnson last night to meet his death at the hands of Mr. B's ex-driver. Instead, the driver's job has become permanently his and Bulletproof Johnson's reputation has leapt into international status. He also realises that Bulletproof Johnson and Nicky Nails are going to come out of the dark one day soon to fuck this guy really good. Nathan hopes he will not be around when they do.

There is a condemned building on Macy Place. It is the only one left standing on the street and it has been bricked up like so many others in the South Bronx. But unlike other desolate and doomed edifices, no one breaks the walls to get inside this particular one. Other buildings are ransacked for their copper wiring and pipes, or are turned into shooting galleries by addicts, but this five-story beast standing alone on Macy Place has a reputation. It is said that if you put your ear to the bricks you can hear the thunderous voice of God, or the footsteps of the Devil inside, but whatever causes the noises that echo within no one wants to venture in to find out.

It is also rumored that the building rose up out of the ground one night as is from the pit of Hell, and is now the dwelling place of the Angel of Death. Other rumors have it that Bulletproof Johnson sealed the building and brought his dead girlfriend back to life inside. Now a true witch, her body cannot be exposed to light and he magically traverses the walls to be with her, make love to her, and she makes him immortal, invincible, insane. The kids in the neighborhood dare one another to touch the bricks that blockade the doorway. Some do, proving their bravery, but most people cross the street to avoid the building altogether, especially when the faint sound of thunder rumbles inside. The NYPD and the FBI have plans to storm the building, but hope they never have to.

The building on Macy Place is essentially a shooting range, or more accurately, a private training ground where I perfect my fighting skills. I have everything inside, from daggers, knives and swords to revolvers, pistols, machine guns, and high- powered rifles. I even practiced with grenades once, but in such an enclosed space, it is not the smartest thing I have done. I couldn't hear properly for weeks and had a monster headache. It is also where I bring people who need to be dealt with in a special way. I bring them in hooded and let them try fight their way out. No one makes it out. Therefore, it is primarily reserved for crooked dealers or those attempting to collect on my bounty who get top treatment.

The building is cold as a tomb in winter and hot like an oven in summer, but I persevered and have trained for months to take out Joey and his father, now I'm ready and getting impatient with Nicky and his plan.

Eventually, I tell him, "You already know every move he makes, just pick a place and time and let's ambush him. Hell, we can wait for him when he gets home, and gun him down on his doorstep."

"That's not the problem," says Nicky, "We have done too good a job destroying Banoa's businesses. If we kill him now, Joey has no worthwhile reason to come back. There isn't much to take over. I'm trying to wait for him to build back up his drugs and liquor trade."

"So now you want him back in business?"

"Yes, as it will all be ours when we kill them anyway. But your guys, the Black Spades, are making it hard for him to maintain his drug trade. Without that income his other businesses are struggling."

"I'll talk to Ace," I concur. "But then we make a move, I don't want to wait another year. At this rate we could have already picked off all the men in Miami one by one."

Nicky agrees that we should make our move by the end of the year.

I call a meeting with Ace and explain the dangers of greed and overconfidence. That being the only fish in the pond will one day get you caught. However, leaving other small fish around to attract the attention of the police means that you get to swim and eat longer.

His reaction to my suggestion, "Fuck the police. We will take them on too."

It is that statement that proves he has outgrown his position in my world.

Every dog in the team eventually tires of smelling the ass of the dog ahead of him and yearns to lead the team himself but he reluctantly does agree to pull his guys out of the valley and I immediately start looking for someone in his gang to replace him. With all the money to be made, the drug world is a very volatile place. Kingpins come and drug czars go, the only ones who last are those who are not too greedy and do not get overconfident.

Nicky contacts me late December, and we meet in the apartment of an elderly Italian lady across the street from the Bella Rosa. The old lady says something in Italian, which I interpret as a declaration that she doesn't want blacks in her house.

Nicky yells at her, "Shut up, Grandma."

"She's your grandmother?"

"Fuck no," says Nicky, "Just some old lady, but she does think I'm her grandson. I got you here to check out the bar with the black window. That's where it's going to take place. You were right, the Big Banana is never alone and this is where he meets with all his capos. He always has one around and at least one muscle, sometimes more. We can't hit him at home, as all the blocks around his house are guarded."

"I get it," I say with a murderous glee, "You want to clear the top shelf in one night."

"We don't need them all," Nicky continues, "But we do want to get him and three of the six. The other three are weak and will bow to our demands; they usually leave the meeting early anyway."

"I'm taking it that the black bulletproof glass doesn't bother you."

"Not with these it won't." Nicky hands me headgear that looks like a giant pair of goggles. "Put them on. It's the latest thing, called thermal night vision. With these, we can see through walls. Like Superman."

"Superman has x-ray vision, but I am liking these." I scan the black glass across the street and see pinkish blobs moving around inside. "It's going to be impossible to tell which one is Joe..."

"That's Sal's job. We are going to be outside the bar covering him."

"You're not still with that..."

"Look, Sal must be the hit man," he insists, "But we will take care of everyone else."

I figure there is an underlying reason he wants Sal to do this, so I let it go. I do however have a few concerns to voice, "Is that fat guy always in front of the door? Luckily, we can see through the glass, but do you know what it will take to shoot through it?"

"Yes he is," confirms Nicky, "And we have to drop him quietly right after Sal goes in. Then 20 gauge slugs at close range will take care of the glass."

"How close?" I ask.

"As close as you and I," he says, "Then we go to work with the nines."

I try one more time to change his mind about bringing Sal along, "You know, we can shoot the doorman, blast open the window and clean the place out with a few hand grenades. Same results, less risk."

"I knew you'd say that," Nicky knows me well, "But if we don't hit Banoa with the shotgun slugs, he might get to cover before the grenades go off. No, we need someone in his face, and Sal is the only one who can do that."

Nicky beeps Nathan to instruct him to pick up special spark plugs and to install them in the car without Banoa's knowledge. The spark plugs misfire when they heat up and Banoa orders Nathan to take the car to the shop for a check-up. Nathan has also been told to let the car cool down before taking it to the shop. Two or three times a week the car acts up, and each time the mechanic can find nothing wrong.

Nathan gets beeped the night before the Bella Rosa meeting, and is told to rev the engine hard before he picks up Banoa. He does as he is told, and the car nearly dies on the way to the Bella Rosa

"You take this car to the garage and tell that fat greasy fuck that I don't care if he has to take the whole damn engine apart, he better fix it or I will take him apart."

"Hello Mr. B, let me get the door for you," says fat man as he struggles to his feet.

"Jesus, Frankie, lose some fucking weight," yells Banoa and hammers on the door.

"Who..."

"What, are you fucking kidding me? Open the Goddamn door." Banoa shoves the door wide open when he hears the locks click. His two main capos and some muscle go in behind him. The doors are locked immediately.

"He is pissed," I tell Nicky, "Maybe we should come back when he's in a better mood."

Nicky laughs as we watch Nathan sputter down the street. Nicky, Sal, and I are in the old lady's apartment. Sal is in the kitchen, eating soup the old lady insisted on making. They are laughing away the hours as we watch for the other capos and their drivers to leave.

"They're having a good time," I tell Nicky.

"Yeah, she's senile and he's retarded. They probably understand each other just fine."

It's 1:00 a.m. when the lesser capos depart.

Nicky wakes Sal and gets him ready. He sticks on himself a fake scar running from his eye down his right cheek and a brown sharp trim beard that matches his freshly dyed hair. He slaps Sal in the face a couple of times to keep him awake, and then they leave through the alley and go down the block to the car.

"Old Joe is going to be sitting at the table. What are you going to do?" asks Nicky of his older brother.

"I am going to say, Nicky says, go to hell..." he pauses for a moment. "Then I shoot him in the face. BAM... BAM... BAM..."

"Your gun is right here by your butt. Remember, wait until he asks what you want. Then shoot him and drop the gun."

I am standing in the doorway of the building across the street just out of sight. My heart is pounding. This is the first time I am nervous about a job; I know we have no room for error. I see the car pull up and have to wait for the bar door to close before I can make my move.

Sal is at the door, "I have a message for Old Joe Banana."

"What the fuck did you call him?" Fat man asks. "Sal, you better not call him that, you hear. You call him Mr. B," he bangs on the door from his chair.

"What?" asks the inside guard through the peephole.

"Sal Rocci is here with a message for Mr. B," yells out the fat guard in the chair.

"Wait," the man at the door goes to the table. Banoa and three of his capos are playing cards. "It's Rocci's son, says he has a message for you."

"Which one?" asks Banoa, but also knows that Nicky would not be the one at the door.

"The retard," snickers the man.

"Like I said, which one?" They all laugh and Banoa nods his head. "This ought to be interesting."

The man opens the door and Sal walks in. "You checked him?" he asks the fat man seated outside.

"It's Sal," answers the fat man.

Sal is halfway across the bar when the door slams shut and I spin from the doorway and fire; one shot from a silenced nine right in the fat man's head. The bullet goes through his skull and thugs against the door.

"Fucking lose some weight, Frankie," says the man at the door and then hurries to catch up to Sal.

We stand at the window with the thermal goggles on, prepared to fire. Thankfully, the blobs are more defined at this distance, I can see arms, legs, and heads. I am trained on the man behind Sal, guessing he's the doorman. There is someone behind him a little further back, maybe behind the bar, it's hard to tell.

Nicky aims at the closest man to him at the table.

"Remember, when you see the flash, fire and pull off the goggles or you won't be able to see anything afterwards."

Sal is standing in front of the table. One of the capos is turned halfway around, laughing at him.

Joseph Banoa is across the table waiting. "What's the fucking message, you retard?"

Sal stands there a while, which feels like an eternity, and I'm getting really nervous.

I hear Nicky whisper, "Come on Sal, just like we practiced."

Sal blurts out, "Nicky says, in your face, Joe Banana!"

He laughs. "What?"

"Oh yeah," Sal says, pulls the .22 from his back, and fires three times.

The first shot hits Joseph Banoa in the forehead and knocks him out the chair. The hollow point bullet flattens out as it smashes through his skull. The lead slug roughly the size of a dime bounces off the back of his cranium carving another tunnel in his brain. It recoils two more times in Joseph Banoa's head, each time, digging through his memories, his ability to see, feel, and hear, finally removing his ability to breathe or his heart to beat.

The next two shots fly across the room.

The first flash of light and I squeeze the trigger, closing my eyes as I shoot. The 20 gauge pushes back against my shoulder, I let go, and it swings from my shoulder by the strap. I push the goggles back and they drop to the ground. I open my eyes and see a hole in the black glass the size of a softball, not what I was expecting. I fire two quick rounds at the man behind the bar from my silenced nine.

Nicky fires simultaneously with me and nails the man closest to him at the back. The shot pushes him into the table, toppling onto the man across from him. The shotgun swings from his shoulder, as he fires his nine at the man trying to get to his feet and draw. A couple of bullets drive him back and over his chair.

I have the best angle on the laughing man in front of Sal and shoot him down the side from his head to his torso. We realize Sal is locked inside the bar and blow out more of the window with the shotguns then smash the rest of the glass with the butts.

I have to tell Sal to get out of there. I guess it eluded Nicky to go over what he was supposed to do after shooting Banoa in the face.

We speed away from the bar, all excited. Sal is waving his gun around and yelling, "In your face, Joe Banana!"

"Hey, I told you to leave the gun," Nicky yells back at him.

"But it's my gun, Nicky. You gave it to me," Sal whines.

"It's no big deal, Nails. Just take it from him for now before he shoots me in the back of the head, and we crash."

Sal laughs.

"You won't be laughing when you're lying on the sidewalk bleeding to death," I tell him.

"I'm already bleeding," he says and sticks out his arm, "See."

Nicky pulls his shirt open and off. Blood is leaking out his forearm, but he is relived, "It's only a scratch. Probably got fragged by flying glass. He's fine. That's my big brother, taking care of business."

"Family business," replies Sal, "Super-secret family business. In your face, Joe Banana."

Nicolas Rocci isn't half as upset about the cut on Sal's arm, as he is furious that we took him along in the first place.

We are in the basement and Nicky and Sal are trying to tell their father what a good job he's done. Nicolas tells Sal he can never speak about tonight ever again and Sal agrees sadly. Then, not more than a minute later, he asks Sal, "So, what did you boys do tonight?"

Sal, all bright faced says cheerfully, "We shot Old Joe Banana in the face, bam, bam, bam."

"See why I am mad with you, Nicky?" his father says tenderly, "OK, you two take him to the farm tonight and stay there until I come for you. And Morris, how could you let him do this, I thought you were the smart one?"

I think about defending myself but keep quiet. If you run with the gang, you hang with the gang, law of the streets.

His mother hands me a bag of food, enough for a week or two, so I guess that means he's not coming up there to kill us. But it also means we are going to be there for a while. We leave the house and get back in the car, Nicky wants to drive.

I say to him, "I told you that was a bad plan."

"What? That went well, the old man is really proud of us. Couldn't you tell?"

We arrive at the farmhouse late in the morning, Sal jumps out of the car and runs to his aunt and uncle, who had watched us drive up the gravel road. They tell us their mother called hours ago, letting them know we were on our way. As it happens, this is the farm where we are turning fish into fertilizer.

Nicolas arrives two days later in a pickup truck with Sal's chicken coops in the back. When we finish unloading them, we leave Sal with his chickens and the others in the barn.

"You didn't have to go this far," Nicky tell his father with tears in his eyes, "He doesn't even remember the other night."

"I wish that was true," Nicolas says, his head hanging low, "That boy has a mind like a steel trap and doesn't forget anything. I can't risk him saying something to the wrong person and lose him forever. I know why it was important for you that he gets his revenge, but it's over now and he is happy here. Momma and I will come up and see him often, and you will too."

"Yes."

"Good, you boys get ready to go," he commands. All tenderness is gone from his voice, he's back to being a hard ass, "Now, you have got to end this thing you started."

Victoria answers the phone at her desk in the Neighborhood Redevelopment Association office.

The woman with a Russian accent asks, "Is Morris Johnson there?"

Victoria drops the phone on the desk, "It's for you."

"You know, Vicky," I say, picking up the receiver, "You need to work on your phone etiquette."

"Another friend of yours, I suppose," Yana says, "The house is empty."

"Thanks for the info. And as promised, you are free now, go live your life."

"You know where I am if you want..."

"If you want to start living again," I tell her, "You have to stop hanging around with the dead."

The phone goes silent for a long moment then Yana hears the dial tone kick in. She knows she will not see Morris again in this life but hopes that perhaps they will meet again in another one, one where they are both alive.

Nicky and I sit in the back of a limo high up on a hill overlooking Joseph Banoa's funeral.

"Looks like he is full of sorrow now," quips Nicky. "Burying your brother and now your father will do that to a guy."

"He could be sorrier," I say seriously, "And he still has his mother. But I can always take care of that right now." I reach for the high-power rifle between us.

Nicky puts his hand on the barrel. "You know that's not our way. We let him take care of his business then we take care of him later."

"You know it's no trouble, really, won't cost him anything extra either, I'll drop her right in the same hole."

"MoJo, you're a killer, not a murderer," Nicky reminds me. "The flowers are nice."

The following week, Nicky and his father drive out to Long Island. There is the usual line of cars parked in the driveway. Nathan is also there, wiping down the Lincoln, which is now running fine. The mechanic replaced the faulty spark plugs. His eyes hit the ground when Nicky steps from the car.

Nicky is startled as he walks past a parlour. Right there, he sees Elizabeth sitting in a chair, reading a children's book. A little toddler is at her feet, playing with her toys and her nanny. Although they have never met, he knows this is Svetlana's sister, looks like her too, just younger and with slightly darker hair. Neither woman notices as he passes, but the little girl eyes him curiously for a moment, and then goes back to banging blocks.

At the meeting, Joey and Nicky sit across each other, on either side of Angelo Lucerella. Down the table are the other bosses and their capos.

"You two have cost this family a lot trying to prove which bull has the biggest horns. We have lost millions, lost men, and prestige that cannot be replaced. This is the end. Joseph Banoa, you will take over your father's gambling, prostitution, and drug operations. But your family has lost key members, so I feel it is in the best interest that you work under the house of Rocci in the loan, labor, and all other businesses your father had. I also have to go to Florida to settle the business interests your father had there. I hope all this childishness is behind us."

Nicky, looking into the sheepish eyes of Joey Banana cannot hold his tongue, "If it was up to me, I'd put a bullet in his face right now. This little dago killed four of my friends, who on their worst day could outscore his entire crew."

Angelo grabs their hands, and the men around the table nervously snap to attention, ready for action. "This is not the playground here, understand me?"

"Yes sir," Nicky softens his tone, "I mean you no disrespect, I was just saying. This... his life is out of my hands. I promised Morris 'Bulletproof' Johnson that I would not touch him. He can kill Joey Banan... Joseph, himself. I am sure MoJo will hold me to that promise. Just to be clear, Joey, tell your mother not to put away her black dress."

A chorus of "heys" erupts from the table.

Angelo quiets them down, "Yes, this MoJo, Morris Johnson, an associate of yours. You need to get him under control."

"He's not so much an associate as a partner," says Nicky coyly. "We share some business interests, but I also have my own, and he has his." Nicky stands his ground and stares down Joey, who looks down and studies the tabletop.

"I would like to meet this MoJo," Angelo says with finality. "Sounds like a colorful fellow."

This time, it is the Rocci family that leaves first.

Nicolas is proud of his boy, that he did not back down, even if it was not the wisest move to make. Back in the car, Nicky confirms that it is Elizabeth he saw in the house. His father explains that she is Angelo's niece and Lucia Delitanni, his younger sister. That certainly clarifies many things for Nicky.

Nicky gives me the scoop on his meeting, "I got Joey back here but you are going to have to get him out of Long Island. I can't help you with that, you'll just have to talk to Mr. L about it. I saw Elizabeth."

"How did she look?" I ask.

"Sad, very sad, I told you not to fuck that girl," Nicky repeats himself for the millionth time on the subject. "I saw her little girl too, doesn't look like her with the black curly hair and all. Thank God she doesn't look like you either. Her mother is there too. Although I didn't see her, I think she's your real problem. You killed her husband and knocked up her daughter, all in one night, that bitch must want you dead real bad. But you already know that, don't you? I realized when I saw your Russian spy, really smart move."

He asks curiously when did I know where she was, and I tell him, the night we were both dragged into the jail cells and he told me she had gone to her uncle's house. I had been trying to keep tabs on her ever since, but it wasn't always easy. He finally understood why I agreed to take out Ivan the Terrible so quickly.

I confirm it. That I needed someone on the inside who had no ties to me or any of our dealings, someone who could be my eyes and ears, not just for Elizabeth, but also for my daughter, because they do need protecting, especially from Lucia, who is like a poison in the air, killing her daughter slowly and unobtrusively in plain sight. And that yes, she definitely wants me dead too. "After I take care of Joey, I'll deal with Mom."

"Keep this in mind, she is still Angelo's sister, so although she may be the one pointing the gun in your face, it is his finger on the trigger. You know full well there are only two ways out of a contract," Nicky reminds me, "You either die or you kill everybody who wants you dead."

"I think the only way out of this is to do both," I tell him. He agrees.

I'm speeding down Peconic Bay Boulevard way out on the Island.

A police cruiser flashes his lights and pulls me over. "Where are you going in such a hurry, BOY?"

"I have to be somewhere in an hour, Officer Roles," I read off his nametag.

"Is that right?" he asks looking over my '72 Buick Riviera. "Why, is this car stolen?"

"No. But lives depend on it," I take a needle and jab it into his forearm above the wrist.

He tries to jump back and reach for his gun, but I grab him by the shirt, pin him against the car, grab his hand, and force it down, keeping the .45 in its holster.

"Now, listen carefully, because this is very important." He continues to struggles, but after more than a year of workouts, I'm more than capable of keeping a firm hold on the situation. "You only have an hour and the more time you waste, the more likely you are to wind up in unbearable crippling pain."

He stops struggling but I do not loosen my grip. I continue, "I don't know you and you don't know me either, so I'm obviously not here for you. But these are the current facts, I injected you with a powerful neurotoxin, that in an hour will start destroying your spine and brain tissue. If you do not get the proper antidote before then the effects will be irreversible. Here's the thing about neurotoxins, there are so many that without knowing exactly which one I gave you and how much, no hospital will be able to help you. We clear so far?"

Officer Roles nods. His arm is already starting to burn inside.

"I didn't give you enough to kill you, as that would be too easy. I know, you could just shoot me and accept the fact that you will be dead soon as well. However, the dose I injected you with is merely sufficient for you to become paralyzed or severely crippled and cause constant agonizing pain. Imagine what you are feeling now a million times worse all over your body. And you won't even have the ability to put the gun in your mouth to pull the trigger."

Officer Roles' face starts to contort from the pain, so I release him, and he grabs his arm.

"Now, I'm going to forget about the BOY stuff because I need you to take me to see Mr. Angelo Lucerella. I know you are like his special private cop, so you can get me in. And don't worry, he doesn't know it yet but he definitely needs to talk to me before the hour is up, or all those little ones who are at his house are going to have a very bad day. So you see, not only will you be saving yourself from a lifetime of misery, you will also be saving all those kids. You're going to be a hero. Now, let's go, and we are taking your car, as we don't have that much time," I command.

Officer Roles waits with me in a large room with a long wooden table and about twenty chairs around it. Out of the bay doors, I can see dozens of children running around, mothers and their babies, and a three-foot-tall birthday cake modelled just like this house. I see Elizabeth, Akilina, and Little Maria at the head of the table behind the cake. Akilina is holding the baby on her lap.

In walks Angelo through the doors with Joey Banoa in tow, then Tom Green, and a half dozen other men.

Of the nine men in the room, I only know Joey.

Tom Green whispers into the old man's ear as he sits at the table. Two of the men begin closing the drapes to the bay doors.

"Leave them open," I say in haste.

Angelo waves his hand and the two men stop. Tom Green and Joey stand next to Angelo, Joey on the other side of the table from me. The other men take up positions around the room.

Officer Roles steps back, away from me.

"Looks like you went through a lot of trouble to come here today. What's on your mind?" Angelo asks.

"First, let me just say that when a man of your stature says he wants to meet you, you make it your business to meet him." Then continue, "Let's put our cards on the table, shall we?" I sit down and pull out a small cylindrical device that looks like a gas canister with a red button on top, which I am holding down. Joey steps back and the men around the room draw their weapons. Angelo and Tom smile at me.

"You don't need that," Angelo says, "You didn't go through all of this just to blow yourself up with Joey here. I know you have a better plan than that."

"Of course I do," I agree and smile back. "But I don't have a lot of time, right Officer Roles? He's my ride back. I gave him a little injection that in less than an hour from now will make his life pure hell. I have three points to make and then we can get down to business."

Angelo nods.

I resume, "The number one reason why people don't build castles anymore is that your enemies always know where to find you. The number two reason is, if someone is motivated enough, they will find a way in. And number three and probably the biggest reason people stopped building castles, is that what starts out as a fortress quickly becomes a death trap. The reason I'm holding this is not only that it will blow up and kill everyone in this room, but it is also a dead man's switch that will detonate a bomb outside that will kill a lot of those little kids. Now, let's talk business."

Akilina's attention is instantly drawn to the room off the garden with the big bay doors when Angelo and his men abruptly leave and go inside and sees the man who employed her as a spy.

I gave her a number to call and report back on her days off when she was away from the house and alone. Much like Nathan's, it's also an answering machine, but she is meticulous, and leaves detailed messages about Elizabeth, the baby, and conversations that they share, usually late at night when the others are asleep.

Akilina had quickly learnt that this was not a nice place and that despite how I had tried to candyfloss the place, these were not nice people either. This was a mob family and criminals are criminals no matter where in the world they live. She also learnt a whole lot more after Lucia heard about Joseph Banoa's assassination.

The woman is so enraged that I still live that she has made blatant threats to kill the demon spawn her daughter bore. On a shopping trip that Elizabeth, Little Maria, and she were on, Akilina considered calling and giving the code I had told her to use if they were in imminent danger. I told her to call and simply say, "Deli Man," and I would get them out. She refrained from making the call that day, and yet here I am, staring down Angelo and all his men.

"You're holding the bomb," Angelo says, "We are all listening."

Noticing Akilina's interest fixed on the garden room, Elizabeth glances there and sees Morris sitting at the table. Her spirits soar, imagining that he has come for her. In minutes, he will march through the big bay doors, sweep her and his baby up into his arms and carry them away like the hero in a dime romance novel. She takes the baby from Akilina and clutches Little Maria tightly to her breast for the first time. Anticipation is overwhelming her, lifting her body out of the chair, mere seconds from breaking free of this prison.

In contrast, Akilina sees the strange glare take over Lucia's countenance at seeing her daughter holding her own daughter and instinctively reaches out, holding Elizabeth in the chair by her leg. Thankfully, Lucia has her back to the doors and cannot see who has arrived at the house. Akilina feels an uncontrollable terror; if the woman becomes aware of Morris' presence, that he may very well have come for Elizabeth and his child, it is possible she will do something horrific to both of them.

"You think that this war of ours, Joey's and mine, is over money. Who robbed who and what not? I am here to tell you, that's not it at all. We are here because he wanted something that he could not get, Maria."

"That bitch," Joey yells.

"See, even the mere mention of her name gives him fits," I say. "Well, I'm here to let you know that it is not over. He killed my wife and unborn child. I'm no child killer but I will destroy anyone who stands in my way. It will never be over, not until he faces me in battle, and I take what is owed her. He took her life and I will take his. So, if you truly want this to end, you send him here." I slide a piece of a Bronx map from my pocket across the table, "It is a place where we settle differences with honor."

"Why not just shoot him now and get this over with?" Angelo offers. "Someone, give him a gun."

"Because that is not my way, and I'll give him the chance to defend what he has done. If he fights and wins, then this is over. If I win, then I hope you will consider this matter done. If he does not show, there will be other times, other parties, other deaths. So, tomorrow, at dawn. Oh, and here is something you might enjoy, this will be a gladiator's battle. Something from your heyday."

"You know you can't kill me now because they will kill you," Joey tries to sound tough, "You think I will come alone so you can get away with my death."

"Don't come alone," I warn him, "Bring at least two people, more if you like. You will need somebody to carry your body back to your mother. The rats around there will eat you alive."

I order the men to take a seat with their boss. A quick twist of the device and I set it on the table and back away. The red button detonator stays down but blinks rapidly. I explain that the device has a motion detector, which is now active, if anyone attempts to leave the table before I disarm the bombs it will explode.

I take one last look at my three girls, Elizabeth, Akilina, and Little Maria, whose crystal blue eyes reflect heaven's light. I register the desperation in the two young women's faces, then turn and leave.

Officer Roles complains of headaches and fever, I tell him he is running out of time, so I'll drive. I get back to my car and leave him in his. "You need to drive east on Peconic Bay Drive, when I get to the transmitter and disarm the bombs, I'll radio you where the antidote is located."

"The radio and antidote are not in your car?" he asks.

"Of course not," I say in disbelief, "If it was, you could have shot me dead, found the antidote and radio, and this whole episode would never have happened. That is the dumbest thing I ever heard. Drive!"

I drive down the road, heading back to the city then pull off the road a mile away and retrieve my suitcase. I flip the kill switch and the flashing red light on the radio panel stops. The blinking button on the device on Angelo's table stops and pops up.

I radio Officer Roles and tell him the antidote is at the County Dinner on Route 48. I know he knows where it is, he eats breakfast there every morning.

Angelo gets everybody to move inside the house, says there is a storm coming in from the ocean. His men take the presents to the gun range in the basement and inspect them for bombs.

After a few minutes, Tom Green announces that a claymore mine was discovered in the cake. "The way it was placed," he explains, "The only survivors within ten feet of that cake would have been Elizabeth, Akilina, and Little Maria, as they were sitting behind it."

Officer Roles speeds into the diner's parking lot with his siren screaming. He skids to a halt and races to the counter. He is feverish, his body aches, and his stomach is twisting into knots. "Where is it?" he yells at Karen, the waitress.

"Keep your shirt on, honey," Karen hands him an eight- ounce cup with a lid on it.

Officer Roles snatches the lid off and chugs the hot liquid down. He starts coughing from the burning sensation of the fluid and the full effects of the flu virus I injected him with. "What is this?"

"Chicken soup, just like you ordered," replies Karen looking at him oddly. "You don't look so good. I think the guy was right, he said you caught the flu."

"What guy?"

"The guy from dispatch. Said you radioed him and asked him to order you a cup of chicken soup. That you think you caught the flu bug."

Officer Roles will be spending the next two weeks in bed, sick but not paralyzed or dying.

Joey Banoa shows up in the Badlands at dawn as ordered, accompanied by three of Angelo's soldiers.

I am already there, with Nicky Nails and Sweet Jesus, who decided to fly in last night when I told him about the meeting at Angelo's house. I wish Bonnie was here too, but I didn't even try to contact her.

About two hundred other people from various street gangs and mob families are on hand to witness the beat down in the Bronx.

Two tables have been set up about a hundred feet apart with all kinds of weapons: clubs, knives, swords, and pistols of various calibres. Joey chooses a .45 and starts to walk away from the table.

"Is that all you are going to take?" asks one of the soldiers.

"Yes, I'm going to shoot that motherfucker in the head and get it over with."

"You might want to take a look at your opponent over there," he cautions him. "He is loading up with knives, two swords, body armor, everything on his table except a gun. I don't think he's planning on this being a duel."

"You are going to need a holster for that revolver, unless you want to stick it in your belt," says the man behind the table.

"What are the rules?" asks another one of the soldiers.

"Pretty simple, they stand side by side, with no weapons in their hands, and when told to begin, each will try his damndest to kill the other fucking guy. Haven't you guys watched any movies? The rules haven't changed in two thousand years."

"What happens if he runs out of bullets?"

"There are plenty bullets and he can grab any weapon from any table he wants during the fight. My advice? Put on body armor and a double holster if you are going with the guns."

I am just about done.

I have on a steel chest plate and legging, steel forearm covers, two swords, a Japanese Katana, and a sabre across my back, two belts of one-foot-long swords crisscrossing my chest, and a belt of daggers ranging in length from three to five- inches around my waist. I also have a pair of spiked fingerless black leather gloves on and carry a two-foot diameter round shield on my left arm. Finally, I pick up a six-foot African spear and start towards the battlefield.

"I have to admit; you look like one seriously crazy killing son of a bitch. Joey has a pair of .45s on, don't you think you should take at least one of these guns with you?" asks Nicky. "You know the old saying about bringing a knife to a gunfight."

"This is not a gunfight, it's a gladiator's bout, and I don't have a knife, I have a lot of knives. This is a death match. Joey Banana is the one who is not ready."

"Combatants, to your marks," yells the officiator.

Joey hurries to the six-foot flag staff in the middle of the rocky field.

I take my time, walking slowly, deliberately, letting him soak in the menacing metal I am wearing, giving him time to let the fear of the moment grip his soul. I check the crowd. I spot Ace and several of the Black Spades, Patrick and the Bainbridge Boys are here too. Many more from the South Bronx, Harlem, Lower East Side, Brooklyn, and several biker gangs have also shown up.

Joey shakes his hands at his sides nervously, like a gunslinger getting ready to draw. The officiator has his pistol at his side, just in case someone tries to start early. It has been known to happen.

I finally reach my spot on the other side of the flagstaff and stab my African warrior spear into the rocky soil. We are side by side, a foot separating us, facing the officiator.

The officiator asks Joey if he's ready.

Joey stammers, "I guess so, yes. Yes, I'm ready."

The officiator asks me, am I ready?

"READY TO KILL," I announce loud and clear.

"Then have at it," announces the officiator and steps back.

Joey looks at me and quickly reaches for his revolver. I pull a three-inch dagger with my left hand and stab it through the trigger guard, through the holster, and into Joey's right thigh. He yelps in pain and starts to back away. I grab the katana, stepping towards him, and slice him down the cheek. At first, no blood flows, just a burn that tells him he suffered another wound already. Then a trickle of blood begins to run from below his eye to his chin.

He hobbles a few quick steps in retreat even as I stand my ground then draws and fires with his left, the bullets fly past me and the people behind me duck and scatter. He has fired three of his six shots and now takes careful aim with shaky hands. The crowd flees to one side of me. He fires two more shots and I throw the shield in front of my face. Two sledgehammer-like blows rock the shield back and two deep dimples protrude towards my face. I reach back, grab the spear and throw it hard and fast before he can line up his last shot. The spear cuts through his left shoulder, dislodging the gun.

Joey pulls the dagger from his hip and draws the other .45, while running back towards the table. He fires a shot wildly behind him without looking and drops the gun in the process. He reaches the table limping slightly on the right and bleeding down his left arm.

I have abandoned the shield and stand within striking distant, my sabre extended to his eye. "You didn't think it would be that easy. You could not be so foolish."

He slides along the table, trying to get away from my razor-sharp blade and selects a new weapon.

"Choose wisely," I say.

He quickly reaches for a pistol and I come down just as quick, severing his right thumb.

"No," I tell him, "Not that one." My sabre is back in position, pointing at his nose.

He reaches back and clumsily picks up an English broad sword.

"Better," I say, "I would have gone for something lighter, missing a finger and all, but two-handed you should put up a good fight."

"Why are you doing this?" He asks. "Why not just kill me?"

"All these people came to see a good battle, not a quick bang bang, or a simple stabbing," I tell him stepping back. "I've waited a long time to hear you plead for mercy. To see you beg like a dog. To feel your bones crack beneath my boot. I am going to cut you to pieces and enjoy every drop of blood that falls."

Joey lunges forward, hacking downward with the sword, strikes the ground, and nearly trips over it. I slap him across the face and neck with the flat side of my sword. His face instantly reddens and swells. "Are you sure you don't want to try another sword? The Japanese are good and easy to handle."

He throws the broad sword down and walks back to the table.

His hand hovers above the pistol and I say, "Don't do it. This time I'll cut your fucking hand off."

He picks up a katana, like the one I first used on his face.

"Now you got the idea. Grab it with two hands and let's have at it."

The clash of metal fills the air. I step and move around easily, avoiding his attacks, and a quick jab here or light slash there keeps him from getting too aggressive. The year of training at the Macy Place building has honed my skills sharper than the blades that flash about our heads. I am careful not to stab too deep or into any spot where I would strike a major blood vessel. Joey, I believe, is trying to cut my head off.

After slashing his arms and legs, poking him in the chest and abdomen a couple of times, I grow bored of the swordplay. I block his next swing with my steel clad forearm, drop my sword, and punch him across the eye with the spikes.

He stumbles backwards to the ground, grabbing his face. Blood pours between his fingers and I kick his thumbless hand away. Four round holes dot his face, one above his eye, one piercing his lower eyelid, and two more in his cheek. I drop down with both knees on his chest and stomach, and the steel pad cracks ribs loud enough to hear. I punch him with a left and then a right, cutting and tearing at his face. I thump the half-inch spike into his chest and stomach, producing tiny pools of blood, and causing large volumes to splutter from his lips. I take one more full swing at the side of his jaw and hear it snap like a dry oak branch.

Gurgling blood and barely able to speak, I hear, "Please, please, no more."

"What's that you say?" I ask then stand up and jump down on his knee; it breaks like dry wood.

Joey screams in anguish, "No more, please God, no more."

"Oh no, you can't be finished yet," I kick him on the left side, the one without broken ribs. "There is still plenty of flesh left on your bones." I then kick him with all my might. It breaks those ribs and rolls him onto his stomach. "Yeah, look at all this fresh meat back here."

I pull out two five-inch daggers and plunge them in at an angle just below his rib cage on either side of his spine. He practically jumps to his feet, spins around, and falls back down onto his back. This causes the blades to tear out of his sides, delivering the two deepest wounds he has suffered so far. Blood gushes out of him faster now.

His mouth moves but his voice is so faint that I have to put my ear to his lips to hear, "Kill me now, I'm begging you to."

"That's it," I answer, "That is all three. Just one more thing, say you are sorry to Maria for murdering her and I'll send you on your way to Hell."

Joey mutters, "I'll be sure to fuck her good for you when I get there."

"Oh, my friend," I tell him, "I'm not sending you with that still attached." I grab a handful of his manhood and take the blade from my chest. His eyes are wide open as he reaches up weakly to grab my hand. I shake my arm and his hand drops away limply. I hack once, he screams, then again and blood sprays out of his pants, his dick and balls come off in my hand. His eyes roll back in his head, I pull his broken jaw down, shove his dick and balls into his mouth, and slap it shut.

I stand up, covered in blood up to my elbows. The shiny metal armor is streaked and smeared with crimson. I can hear him choking on his own flesh and walk away.

The crowd is standing in absolute silent shock.

I pick up the .45 lying on the ground, walk back, kneel down beside his head, and say, "After I'm done here, I'm going to pay your mother a visit too."

He weakly shakes his head from side to side.

I rise to my feet and blast away at his chest, three, four, maybe five times, until the gun clicks repeatedly.

The crowd starts to disperse to the rumbling of "damn" and "fucking crazy, man."

Nicky and Sweet Jesus run over, as I am disarming, "I told you this was no gunfight."

Nicky says, "And I told you cutting his balls off would make you feel better. What did you tell him before you killed him?"

"Just something for him to think about for all eternity. Sweet Jesus, I need you to tell your FBI friends to stake out the Black Cat if they want some interesting news."

"FBI? Who's been talking to the FBI?" Nicky asks nervously.

"Relax," I say, "I've been giving Sweet Jesus information to feed to the Feds. It keeps us in the loop."

"What loop? How come you don't tell me these things?" demands Nicky.

"Ever noticed how you don't take news well?" I tell him.

As we leave, we see the three mob soldiers bagging up Joey Banana's body, the officiator is collecting the weapons, and the rest of the crowd is gone.

All you can hear is the squeaks of the rats along the river.

Nicky is called back to Long Island. With the death of Joey Banoa, he is going to make capo and head up the rest of the Banoa's family interests under his father. Nicky has earned his bones.

"Only one minor detail," Angelo tells him, "Some of the other bosses are questioning where your loyalty really lies. You know what we need you to do."

Nicky agrees by saying, "I'll get it done."

He is then taken into the room and emerges a made man.

"You know he will never turn on his friend," criticizes Lucia.

"And you were never a good judge of men," says Angelo. "You married a man who was weak and who covered his weaknesses with cruelties. That dulls your judgment even more. His friend did all this for love, and now that the desire is fulfilled, he will drop his guard. Nicky Nails will do anything for power. He desires my job, and one day he will have it, but to get my job he has to first kill his friend. His desires have yet to be fulfilled."

Nicky returns to the Bronx and I ask him how everything went out on the Island.

"We are thick as thieves," he responds.

There is much to be done and little time to do it in. The killing of Joseph Banoa, the father, has put the mob war back on the front pages of the newspapers. Nothing sells papers like murder, but unfortunately, it also puts Nicky and I back on the police radar.

The papers dredge up all the old stories, the 'Execution of the Raven 4', this time focusing on the four teenagers gunned down one summer night, the 'Five Headless Horsemen,' now written as a foreshadow to the 'Mob Massacre at the Bella Rosa'. This is the stuff that sells. And now, the papers have two new names to headline, Nicky 'Nails' Rocci, the face of the new Mafia, and Morris 'Bulletproof' Johnson, mad dog killer or mob muscle man?

We figure the FBI threw our names out there to apply pressure for our capture, although, there is little to no evidence tying us to any crime. The most the police have on me is a weak case of destruction of property for blowing up Fitzpatrick's car. Oddly, a tape recorder found stuffed down in the back seat, carefully manipulated by me, naturally, proves I never threatened the cops and they gave me the car willingly. What caused the explosion is still unknown.

Nicky revels in the notoriety, I do not. Our sudden fame means that we have to stay hidden and it is giving our associates a case of the shakes. Being in business with someone under federal investigation, means you are under investigation too. The Feds are looking into the NRA, the fertilizer business, and of course, hunting for the hit men who took apart the Bella Rosa. Nicky and I have plans to wrap all that up for them neatly, and finally get Lucerella off my back for good.

"But first things first," I tell Nicky, "There are still a couple of people who took part in our friends' deaths who have not been given their due."

"I'm telling you, this kill one of ours and we kill all of yours, is a bad character flaw," Nicky says as we cruise 11th Avenue early in the morning.

The black caddy has blackened windows, making it impossible to see inside. The hookers are working the streets and we are working on a tip from one of Nicky's girls, and it is golden. We stop her at 11th Avenue, between 44th and 43rd Street. Nicky honks the horn once.

I start rolling the window down and call out, "Nancy!" Nathan is alongside the passenger's window before it reveals who has summoned him. As the window lowers and exposes my face, I stick my nine in his face, "Want something hard to suck on?"

He straightens up instantly. He is back to blonde hair, a yellow halter top, fake breasts, black skirt, fishnets, and high heels. His eyes widen even more when he sees Nicky behind the wheel.

"I haven't seen you for a couple of weeks," I say, "Looking good, shaved legs and everything. Does your mother know you're out here doing this? Get in the fucking car!"

"It's nice that you and your sister wear the same size, isn't it?" taunts Nicky as we pull away. "You haven't been answering your pages—"

"It hasn't gone off," Nathan quickly reaches in his bra and pulls out the pager. "See, there are no new numbers. Maybe it's broken or something. I thought with Mr. B gone..."

"Relax," I say, "Nails is only fucking with you. But we do need you to do one more job for us."

We drive back to the Bronx in silence. I know Nicky and I are both thinking the Brothers really did a number on this guy. We go down the rocky road to the Badlands.

Nicky stops the car and says, "Everybody out!'

Nathan's eyes are still as big as saucer. He knows where he is.

"Recognize this place from the film, don't you?" I ask. "Of course, you do," I answer for him.

Nathan is back to staring at his feet.

"Come with us," I tell him and we walk towards the river. His steps are unsteady in high heels.

"Watch your step. Don't trip on the bones of your friends." I pull out a small brown paper bag and hold it open in front of him. "Reach in there and get that," I command.

Nathan reluctantly reaches in and pulls out a .22. He holds it loose and nervously, not gripping the handle at all.

"You never shot a gun before, have you?" I ask.

"I told you I didn't shoot anybody," he starts to sob. "I never even fired the gun."

"Relax, I know that, but I'm talking about since then. You still never fired a gun, have you?"

"No." Nathan is still not making eye contact.

"Well, go ahead, load it up," I say, holding the small brown paper bag up to his face.

He sticks his hand in and retrieves a handful of bullets, but drops a few as he loads five into the revolver.

I grab his hand and give it a shake, the cylinder snaps into place. "Go ahead, pull the trigger. Take a shot."

"What?"

"What!" Nicky repeats Nathan's question immediately. I didn't tell him about this part of the plan.

I say, "Shoot something. Shoot anything. Shoot me. At this range you can't miss even with shaky hands."

"Morris, what the fuck are you doing?" Nicky is going for his gun, but I catch his hand.

Nathan is still looking down, the gun hanging, his hands trembling like they are about to fall off his arms.

I reach over and lift his hands, pointing the gun at the water. "Pull the trigger, Goddamn it!"

Bam. Nathan fires a shot into the river. His hands still tremble, but less violently now.

"That's it, see, that wasn't so bad."

The words burn through Nathan's head like hot lead from the gun and bring back a flood of bad memories. Tears well up in his eyes and stream freely down his face, all the shame, pain, and anguish has returned with those few words and the loss of control they bring. His hand drops to his side again.

"You know, I don't like guns either," I tell him, while placing my arm around his shoulder. "They make it too easy. It makes it too easy for a mouse to roar like a lion. But each time you pull the trigger it gets easier. Go ahead, take another shot. Hey, shoot Nicky, he put you in that fucking dress."

"Hey!"

Nathan raises the gun and fires obediently into the river. His head never lifts, simply does as he is told.

"Yeah," I tell him, "That's right. Nicky didn't put you in that dress, did he? You put it on the night you were told to get in that car and go with people you didn't want to be with. Did it ever occur to you to just say no? To say 'I'm nobody's bitch', of course not, and that's why I don't like guns. They turn little bitches into murderers. Go ahead, take another shot."

This time, Nathan fires without hesitation.

I hold the bag up in front of him and he drops the gun in. I crumple the bag up and stuff it in my pocket.

Nathan is wiping his eyes.

"Look at me!" I command.

His eyes finally make contact.

"Go the hell home and take off that fucking dress. You are going to call the number on the paper in this envelope and read what it says. Do not change a single word, understand?" I pause and hand him the envelope. "Then get the fuck out of town, and never come back. It's for your own good." We leave him standing by the river.

"Think he'll do it?" asks Nicky.

"He got in the car, didn't he?" I say. "I've got to go set things up for our friends."

"My dad is not going to like this," cautions Nicky.

"Sure he will, we are clearing Sal's name."

Nathan does as directed. The number he calls is answered by Mancotti.

He tells him that Morris 'Bulletproof' Johnson killed Joseph Banoa. He says that he opened the back door and let Morris in with the .22 revolver. That instead of leaving as instructed, he lingered and hid in the back of the bar and witnessed Morris shoot Mr. B in the head. That Ace of Spades and another Black Spades member lay down the cover fire from outside the bar. He ends by telling Mancotti that he then followed Morris home, where he saw him hide the gun in the tool shed.

"Sounds like a butt load of shit to me," says Fitzpatrick, "Why didn't he say something sooner? And why would Johnson keep the gun? This doesn't add up."

"Maybe not," Mancotti agrees, "But we have to check it out."

Mancotti looks around the garage and then moves to the tool shed. There is still a huge hole where the house used to be, but the garage and tool shed in the back are standing and undamaged. The tool shed is unlocked.

"For all we know he wants to frame someone else for the murder," Mancotti postulates. "Anyway, if we find the gun that killed Banoa, we can put that bastard away forever."

"If he lives that long," adds Fitzpatrick and steps on a loose brick on the floor. "Hey, I think we've got something here."

Fitzpatrick removes one of the bricks and notices a handle. Mancotti finds the other brick and handle. They turn them simultaneously and lift the hatch. The explosion destroys the shed, the garage, Fitzpatrick and Mancotti. Body parts, bricks, bent tin and splintered wood rain down across the adjoining backyards.

The .22 revolver with Nathan Napolitano's fingerprints all over it is recovered by the bomb-squad later that night from a steel safe in the hole. Undoubtedly, Nathan Napolitano is now the main suspect in the murder of his boss Joseph Banoa, as well as the two detectives Fitzpatrick and Mancotti.

I arrive at the Black Cat at 9:00 p.m. for dinner and drinks with Victoria. I asked her to meet me there to discuss an urgent matter concerning the NRA. We eat and drink wine in a subdued candlelight glow. She is dressed to kill, wearing a tight clinging dress that highlights every delicious curve, and her hair has wave upon wave of black curls draping her face and tumbling down around her neck. I feel she has the wrong impression or is trying way too hard to impress me. But I can't say that I am not dazzled.

"Why haven't we ever gotten together, Morris?" she asks.

"Are you kidding?" I tell her, "You're like my sister."

"I would have accepted that a couple of years ago, but not now, I see the way you are looking at me."

"I admit," I confess, glancing at her cleavage, "You have brought out the big guns. But I still remember you when you were eight."

"Eight? What happened when I was eight?" she asks.

"You came to my house and told me that your girlfriend, what was her name, oh yes, Suzie. You told me Suzie had just told you that boys had dicks and you demanded to see mine."

Victoria throws a strawberry at me, "No, shut up. That's how you see me? I couldn't ask my brother what a dick looked like, so who else was I going to ask?"

"Asked, more like ordered," I correct her. "You know; you were the first girl I ever showed Mr. Johnson to. But when I asked didn't you have one too, you said no, and proceeded to show me your vagina. And when I asked how you pee, you told me from the hole. I took a look, and when I poked my finger in—"

Victoria reaches across the table and slaps the word out of my mouth. Her hand moves quicker than an old western gunslinger. I am shocked and momentarily dazed. "That! That right there is why you don't have a boyfriend," I shriek.

"Because I slapped you..."

"You slapped me when I did it the first time too!"

"Well, it hurt," she says angrily, "I didn't know you were going to do that."

"OK," I say calming down, "So why did you slap me now?"

"Because I remembered how it hurt," she says.

"You on the other hand must have liked what you saw because you told Suzie and she came over the next day to see it," I inform her. "She also showed me her vagina, and we discovered together what actually went in that little hole."

"You fucked my girlfriend Suzie?" Victoria leaves her seat this time to slap my face.

"For about a month," I tell her, with my hands guarding against another attack. "Then she got tired of coming over and moved on to someone else, I guess. She also told me to never tell you. Anyway, that's how I see you, as the friend who got me laid. How is Suzie these days?"

"Three years ago her mother sent her down south to live with her aunt, and then came back with her baby cousin. Want me to give her your number?"

"No thanks," I decline the offer. It's time I tell Vicky why we are here, and hope she doesn't slap me again. "Anyway, I wanted to talk to you about the Neighborhood Redevelopment Association. You're in trouble with the FBI for using it as a front to traffic cocaine."

"What? I don't know anything about cocaine dealing..." Victoria says, looking like she is about to strike again.

I lean back from the table, she's as fast as a snake, "I know you don't but the Black Spades have been using some of the apartments they rent from the NRA to store and deliver drugs, and you approved all the apartments they are using. So, it kinda looks like you are in on the deals too."

"Morris Johnson, you low life dirty fucking worthless scumbag, you set me up, didn't you?"

"Well, I kinda needed someone's name on the papers, so it was either yours or your brother's." I try to soothe her temper, which is reaching breaking point, "And it is easier to clear your name, as you have no real gang ties. I told the guys that I was coming here to talk to you, to make sure you say the right thing to the cops if and when you are questioned, and we will move the operation elsewhere."

"I can't believe you. To think that I thought I was in love with you all this time," she starts to sob, "And you were using me to sell drugs."

"Ha ha, that was great," I reach across the table to kiss her but she pulls away and attempts to leave. I grab her around the waist and my hand slides across her ass. Man, she has grown up. "Wait, sit down. Please sit down and let me explain what we are really doing here," I whisper in her ear.

"You better tell me this is a late April Fool's prank," she says with tears in her eyes.

"Good God, you really do love me."

"Yes, you ass, I really do love you. I don't know why..."

"OK but forget about that for now. Do you see who just walked through the door? Over by the bar," I look quickly to the right and her eyes follow mine.

"Is that Ace from the Black Spades?"

"Yes, him and two of his lackeys are here to kill us," I tell her straight out then wait a moment for it to sink in.

"I was wrong, you are not trying to get me framed, you are trying to get me killed," Victoria is over being hurt and back to being mad.

"Not quite, I am clearing your name with the FBI and hoping you help me fake my death." I explain that the FBI has bugged the Black Cat and has been recording everything we said until Ace walked in. But that I also have a man behind the bar with a jamming device, which has just destroyed their ability to record anything else we say.

"You let them record that conversation about you sticking your finger up my pussy when I was eight?" Another slap came and I almost ducked it.

"You started that conversation, not me, I just wanted them to hear and record that you don't know anything about drugs." I inform her that they may in fact have agents in the restaurant, so we have to keep our voices down. I then tell her that Ace and his flunkies are under the false impression that we are drinking drugged wine, generously provided by Nicky, and that when we go upstairs to make love they will follow to kill us. I explain that as things stand no one will believe that I am dead without positive identification of my body, unless they think I died trying to protect her.

"I have a better idea," she says, "Why don't I take this steak knife and stab you in your black heart?"

"Because the idea is for me not to die," I reply. "And I am also trying to help your brother."

"Oh nigger, please," she hisses, "How are you going to help my brother?"

"He's going to run for office, maybe senator or congressman. He is a war hero but with a history of gangs and questionable friends, namely me, but if you die in a fight against drugs and gangsters, no one will dare question his background when he campaigns against them. The NRA is washed clean and so is he. He might even be president one day."

"President of what?" she asks sarcastically, "He knows about the drugs and my fake death here?"

"No," I caution, "He knows about the drugs, of course, he's OS, but he, like everyone else, has to believe that you and I die for real, at least for now, because everyone will be watching him for signs that this is a setup. In a couple of years, you can come back, as his cousin from down south or something. Although, I don't think he will buy into it completely. So, will you do it? For me, for James?"

"On one condition," she says seriously. "Take me with you. Wherever you are going to be dead for a while, or whatever your crazy ass is going to do next, I want to be there too. You are not dropping me in Woodintwannabether, Mississippi and forget about me. You got that?"

I grab the bottle from the table and take her hand, "Hold on to your hat, it is going to be a long crazy trip."

We walk up the backstairs to my apartment on the top floor of the building, go through the living room, then into the bedroom, and turn on the lights. She is instantly startled to see two naked bodies in my bed, a man on top of a woman. They groan, she screams, and runs back to the living room. I go after her.

"They are alive," she says, "No, I did not think you had two live bodies to fake our deaths. I can't do this, it's murder."

"Yes, it is," I agree, "But you are not murdering them, Ace is. Believe me, if they hadn't fucked up, they wouldn't be here. Two other people would but not them. He is a drug dealer who is ripping us off and hurting customers by cutting our product with arsenic to increase his profits."

"And the girl, what's her crime?"

"She is pulling reverse roofies. Drugging her clients so they think they had sex and charging them extra for the time it took. So, you see, nobody is innocent here."

Victoria paces back and forth in the living room, wrestling with her conscience.

"You say you want to go with me wherever my crazy ass goes next? Well then, first you have to go through the bedroom and then out a secret exit in the back. Don't worry about them, they are completely drugged up, won't even feel a thing."

She doesn't stop pacing.

I check my watch and know Ace and his two executioners are about to come through the door soon. I pull out my nine and point it straight up at the ceiling, "OK, I understand, this is too much for you. We'll go back downstairs and shoot our way out of this place, but—"

"No, I want to go with you. It's just... they surprised me, that's all. They won't feel it, right?"

"Not a thing," I tell her, "The coroner can tell if they are alive when they get shot and then burned."

"And burnt?"

"So they can't be identified accurately. Come on, I have to start the gas before Ace gets here. Just don't look at them."

We cross the bedroom to a closet, I open the trap door, and Victoria goes down the ladder. I turn off the lights, start the gas flow, descend the ladder, and lock the trap door above us. We cross the stockroom to the back, go down the backstairs, and out the alley at the other end of the block.

When the light goes out in the bedroom, a fourth member of the Black Spades enters the Black Cat, stands by the door, and gives Ace a nod. Ace and his accomplices go into the back stairwell, pull sawed-off shotguns out of their pants and quickly ascend the two flights. Ace has been here before, so he knows the layout. Taking a small crowbar, he quietly pries open the door. Noiselessly, they position themselves outside the bedroom door.

Ace peeks through the opening and sees his victims, motionless on the bed. "After we take care of Bulletproof, we hit his friend Nicky Nails," he whispers, "By morning I will be the new drug czar of the Bronx."

The three men swing the door open and fire into the bed. The flash from their guns ignites a sea of flames around them instantaneously. The fire races past them along the walls, ceiling, and floor, engulfing the entire apartment. They try to make their way back out, but the air is quickly depleted and the heat is intense. The windows explode from the tremendous pressure and flames shoot out into the night sky, making certain no one leaves the apartment.

Fire officials determine the apartment had been recently painted with napalm and the top floor had had rarefied air pumped in, a death trap for anyone with a gun.

In the ruins, they find swords, knives, an air pistol, and a crossbow, but except for the three shotguns of the hit men, no other guns. The police, FBI, and coroner determine that Morris 'Bulletproof' Johnson and his girlfriend Victoria

Harris died from gunshot wounds and the all-consuming fire. The three unidentified gunmen burned to death.

News of Morris 'Bulletproof' Johnson's, AOD 12:12, death skyrocket and light up the underworld like the Fourth of July, Christmas, and New Year's Eve all at once. Some are sad, others breathe a sigh of relief, but most have misgivings and keep an eye open over their shoulder.

News also reaches Long Island, in the form of a picture of a bull's head diamond ring on the body that was taken at the morgue.

Akilina refuses to believe the endless hearsay accounts and on her days off and shopping trips when alone, she still calls the number and leaves her reports.

Elizabeth, who, after her daughter's first birthday, has been happily awaiting Morris' return, collapses. She remains in bed with Little Maria, only allowing Akilina to feed and change her, then return her to her arms. She has been carrying the little girl everywhere since the party, mainly to spite her mother, but also to be ready when Morris returns for them, knowing in her heart that he will not forget his daughter, that he will come for his Maria.

She knows, because there is a brown bear, a gift she does not recall opening at the party, but which was in Maria's bed that night. The bear has a gold chain around its neck and a crystal pendant that Akilina says looks like a cross. Elizabeth on the other hand sees a dagger.

Elizabeth has taken to wearing the pendant under her clothes and has never shown it to anyone except Akilina– whom, after the party, confided in her that she was sent by Morris– and begged her to swear to never tell anyone about it. Because when she holds it up to the light just right, she can see the name Lizzie. But all that is over with Morris' death and Elizabeth finds herself spiraling down into the depths of depression.

As deep as Elizabeth sinks from seeing the picture of a bull's head ring, Lucia rises to equal heights and beyond. Finally, this boy, who took everything she had, this thief in the night who stole her husband's life, this defiler of her daughter, who ruined her chances of marrying her to power and riches, and instead left her with a demon, this boy, burnt here on earth, and now in Hell. Lucia could not be happier than she is this day. Let her daughter wallow in despair for this boy, she cannot wait to dance on his grave.

The news reaches California, where Svetlana and Yana have been making inroads into careers as movie stars. With the knowledge and money they accumulated, neither had trouble getting the roles and living the life they always dreamed of.

Svetlana doesn't believe it; Yana knows it's not true either. She feels it in her heart, the way a woman feels for a man who truly loves her. She has only known that feeling twice; once, for a boy who gave her up as dead, and now, for a man who set her free to live. Morris the killer is dead, but Morris, her lover, is now alive. He will come for her, all she has to do is wait.

Nicky 'Nails' Rocci, Sweet Jesus Ramirez, and Sister Catherine–Bonnie in the full black habit of a Sister of Charity– attend a private and closed casket funeral at the neighborhood church in the South Bronx, where Charlie Johnson was also memorialized. Nobody else cares to attend. Fr. Robinson performs the service, but no one speaks, at Morris' request. In a letter to the priest that arrived two days after they had spoken, Morris stated, 'Let my deeds speak for my life.' His body is laid to rest at the St. John's Cemetery in Queens, in the grave to the left of Maria Marino.

As Bonnie looks down at the beautiful white roses in the vases that protrude from the four headstones, she whispers, "Do you think he will ever come back?"

Nicky answers her, "He's gone from this life."

Victoria Harris' funeral on the other hand was a huge affair. The same church had been packed just two days previously to capacity, with mourners flowing out the doors. The woman who was the heart of the neighborhood and helped so many out of dilapidated apartments into bright clean and liveable housing was well loved.

The drug dealers who took her life outraged the community to such an extent that her brother James is eventually driven into the senate by the public outcry for her.

As soon as Morris is buried, Elizabeth continues sinking into a place so low that eventually, feeling utterly helpless and hopeless, she takes a handful of pills, plonks Little Maria in Akilina's bed, returns to hers, and hopes to close her eyes and never hurt this much again.

They rush her to hospital and after seeing that she is on the mend after having her stomach pumped, Akilina calls the number and says, "Deli Man."

Two hours later, Nicky shows up at the hospital.

He spends the night in Elizabeth's room and when she comes to, he tells her, "The answer is always 3 p.m. Pittsburgh."

As if by magic, Elizabeth loses her sadness and depression, starts referring to Little Maria as her daughter instead of his, and to herself as Momma.

Nicky starts coming around more often. Not just for the mob meetings, but also to see and check that Elizabeth, Little Maria, and Akilina are doing well. He isn't afraid of Lucia either, in fact, she has become afraid of him and hides whenever he is around. The girls don't understand why.

One morning, before her mother awakens, Maria takes the pendant from around her neck and toddles down the dark halls, the crystal in one hand and her brown bear,

Beary, in the other. She climbs into bed with Lucia and drops the crystal into Grandma's mouth as she snores loudly.

Lucia wakes up and yells, "Get out. Get out of here, you little witch."

The three-year old jumps from the bed and runs down the hall again, laughing and giggling then climbs back into her mother's bed, "I told you Grandma would be mad at us."

"What did you say? Are you bothering your Grandma again? Good girl." Elizabeth drifts back to sleep.

Next morning, Elizabeth is frantically searching for her pendant.

Akilina tosses the sheets back and forth.

Elizabeth asks Little Maria, "Did you take Momma's necklace again?"

"Yes," she answers innocently. "OK, where is it this time?"

"In Grandma's belly," laughs Maria with a crazy little laugh that comes out of nowhere.

Akilina laughs too, "Well, kiss that pendant goodbye."

"Mars," She has taken to calling Maria the odd nickname because of her peculiar laughter, as it is something truly out of this world. "Why did you do that, Momma loves that pendant, and now it's gone," Elizabeth says sadly.

"Beary told me to drop it in the dragon's mouth, and then she will roar no more," Little Maria says, swaying back and forth while holding the dirty beat-up bear by one arm. "Don't worry Momma, Beary says you will get a prettier one soon."

Lucia awakes with terrible stomach pains. She complains all day, but Elizabeth and Akilina smile and laugh behind her back, knowing the pendant is going to hurt like hell coming out. Had they known how badly, they might have felt safe laughing in her face.

The following day, Lucia cannot get out of bed, she has cramps, is feverish, and passing bloody stools. By the third morning, Angelo has her admitted to a hospital, where it is simply too late, and she dies from internal hemorrhaging.

Lucia's funeral is small, attended by Angelo, Elizabeth, Akilina, Little Maria, Nicky, and a host of mobsters, who simply feel obligated to show their respects. And not a mourner in the bunch.

Maggie, her older daughter doesn't even bother to attend.

Nicky tells them after the funeral, "The bloody shits, huh? What a way to go."

A week later, a package arrives for Elizabeth. It is a pendant like the one she had before, but bigger and a real diamond. The card simply reads, "Happy Birthday Sugar Tits." It is June 4th, her twenty-first birthday.

"See, Momma," Little Maria says whilst sitting on her lap playing with the pendant, "Beary said you would get a new one, and you did."

"Do you talk to Beary a lot?" asks Elizabeth suspiciously.

"No, only when everyone is sleeping. And sometimes he wakes me up to tell me a story," she says.

Elizabeth looks the toy over carefully, it is a talking bear but it doesn't tell stories, only a few phrases, and she is sure the batteries died a year ago, at least.

Bored with the necklace, Little Maria grabs the bear and runs off to play.

That night, Elizabeth lies awake staring at the brown bear tucked under the little girl's arm. "Morris," she whispers. Nothing. "Morris," she says a little louder. "Morris!"

Angelo is sitting in his chair in the living room when Little Maria runs in and climbs up onto his lap holding the brown bear by the arm. "Beary wants to tell you a secret, Uncle Anelo."

"You almost got it right that time, little princess. OK Beary, what is your story?" Angelo asks looking down at the bear in her arms.

"No Uncle Eggalo, you have to hold him up to your ear so only you can hear." Maria says curtly and holds the brown bear up to him, "It's a secret."

Angelo takes the bear in one hand and holds it close to his ear, "OK, like this? What are you hiding, Beary?"

"Time for you to go to hell," a voice from the past says.

A sharp needle jets out of the bear's chest and sinks into Angelo's neck. Then just as quickly and silently, the needle retracts into the bear's fur.

Angelo tries to call out but feels the fire in his head overtake his face muscles. Seconds later, he realizes he can't move his arms or legs.

Maria takes the bear and asks him, "What's the matter with Uncle Anggelo, Beary?"

"Nothing my little angel, time for Uncle Angelo to take a nap," the bear tells her.

"Goodnight Uncle Angelo," says Little Maria and runs from the room.

Angelo can't blink, his eyes are losing focus. She's a smart kid, got it right again. He feels his heartbeat slowing down. He feels death.

Elizabeth returns to the house after the funeral with Akilina, Little Maria, and Nicky.

She turns to Nicky almost immediately. "Why my uncle? Why did you do it? I can understand my mother, as she was a real bitch, even before I came to this prison, but my uncle was nice, and good to me. And he always treated you like family..."

"I didn't do this, Elizabeth," Nicky tells her quickly. "Not your mother, not your uncle, none of this was my doing. You say your uncle was good to you, yet he kept you and Little Maria here as bait, or perhaps as a shield. Either way, it wasn't because he loved you, but as a trap. At least he left you the house and everything that is not mob related."

"Then it is Morris," she says. "And he is coming back for us."

About The Author

 A native New Yorker, born and raised in the Bronx, James L Hill spent his adolescence years in Fort Apache, the South Bronx 41st precinct during the 60's, during a time when you needed to have a gang to go to the store. Raised on blues, soul, and rock and roll gave him the heart of a flower child. Educated by the turmoil of Vietnam, Civil Rights, and the Sexual Revolution produced a gladiator. Realizing the precariousness of life gave him an adventurous outlook and willingness to try anything once, and if it did not kill him, maybe twice.

12 years of Catholic education and a couple of years in college spread between wild drug induce euphoric years, which did not kill him, gave James an unique moral compass that swings in any direction it wants. A scientific mind and a spirit that believes nothing is impossible if you want it bad enough guides his writings. He enjoys traveling to new places and seeing what life has to offer.

James began writing short stories and poetry back in his early years. In his twenties moved on to novels. He worked in the financial industry and later got a degree in computer programming, his other love. James has a successful career as a software engineer designing, developing and maintaining systems for the government and the private sector. He has been programming for nearly forty years in various languages.

After years in the computer world he returned to his first love, unleashing the characters in his head. Still a hopeless insomniac, he feels free to pound out plots. James L Hill is a prolific storyteller writing crime stories, fantasies, and science fiction, with a slant on the dark side of life.

The next step on his journey naturally led to the business of publishing. He started RockHill Publishing LLC not only to produce his own work, but to give others access to the literary world. His computer background and experiences in word processing gives him insight into what it takes to publish good books.

The Killer series is an adult crime novel centered around the life of Bulletproof Morris 'Mojo' Johnson. *Killer With A Heart* introduces us to the young gangsters and mobsters in the conflicting worlds of Organized Crime.

Killer With Three Heads has the boys from the Bronx return as international criminals and more deadly than ever.

The Emerald Lady is a pirate/mermaid adventure/love story set in the Golden Age of Pirate and the first novel in the fantasy Gemstone Series.

Pegasus: A Journey To New Eden, his science fictions deal with the emotional effects of technology, and answers the question, "How do I feel about nuclear war?"

Head of The Family

Chapter 1

Time to Kill

The sign over the door of the two-story brick building on the corner reads, *Sons of Italy Social Club*. Or at least, that is what it said years ago before five of the letters fell off. But it has been there long enough that the missing letters, the O's and the I's, left their mark on the brick façade. The blackened glass windows look out to the east and north while double steel doors angled between them face the busy intersection. They swing open, letting in the bright morning sun; they are not locked. The *Sons of Italy Social Club* is never closed. The blinding daylight draws everyone's attention to the thigh-high black leather boots, red micro-mini skirt, and rabbit fur jacket that barely clothes a raven-haired ebony Queen. Five men and a barmaid squint to focus on her until the doors shut and the light gives way to a more normal view.

"Marone!" says the old man sitting at the card table facing the woman. The other two middle-aged men nearly snap their necks doing a double take. "You got the wrong place, honey," he continues, slicking back his gray and black dyed hair. "This is a private club. You want the bus depot down the block."

"I think I'm in the right place," she coos and saunters deeper into the room. "I'm here for Benny. It's his birthday and I'm here to make him a man."

A skinny pimply-faced boy standing at the pool table's voice cracks with uneasy arousal, "I'm Benny, but my birthday ain't until next week."

His pool partner, a slightly older boy, slaps him on the back of his head.

The woman stops at a table two feet from the boys, places her foot on the seat of the chair, so they can see right up the skirt, and reveals everything she has to offer. She kicks the chair and it slides across the floor to the pool table. Benny's friend hustles him to the chair and pushes him down onto it. The three card-playing men position their chairs for a better view and one of them calls out, "Red, put on some music."

The barmaid flips a switch and the club fills with Disco sounds, loud and pulsating. The woman starts swaying her hips and shaking her tits, which are now out of the rabbit fur and protruding from her red halter-top. She swings one leg high over Benny's head, giving all the men a preview of what's to come, while spinning around and thrusting her naked butt in his face. She slowly rubs her bare bottom down his chest and onto his lap. Benny already has a hard-on sticking up through his jeans and she is sure the other men have them too. Hands on her knees, she gyrates and bounces on his lap, rotating her cunt so close to his face he can smell her tangy juices and feel the heat that produces them.

The men are spellbound when she leaps up, spins around in the air, and lands on his lap again, wrapping her legs around him, and her ankles lock around the back legs of the chair. His face buried in her ample cleavage, he can feel his pants filling with cum. Ashamed, he tries to stop but his body is out of control, trapped by her overpowering essence. Everything is happening too fast.

The woman runs her hands through her long silky black hair, taking all eyes with them. She reaches down into the back of the rabbit fur jacket, as the men are glued to every move and watch intently as she pulls two .22 revolvers from her back. Hypnotized like rabbits in headlights, they don't even blink when she fires point-blank into the pool player's face. Then with the gun in her right hand, she sweeps across the card table, placing a slug in each man's forehead.

"Sorry Benny, this is as close as you get to being a man," she whispers in his ear before putting a bullet in it. Then pushing him to the floor, she quickly goes to the backroom door and kicks it in with a black thigh-high boot. With disco music blaring behind her and two .22s outstretched before her, she freezes in the inner office's doorway.

"Vicky! I knew it was you I heard getting the boys all worked up," says Nicky Nails with an easy smile. "Haven't seen you in ages. Did you leave any of my guys alive?"

"I told her to kill them all!"

"Goddamn it, MoJo! This is a day for surprises." Nicky's eyes beam at the sight of the man standing behind Vicky in the back office.

If you enjoyed reading this book, please leave
J L Hill a review and let him know.

Here are more titles by JL Hill:

 Killer With Three Heads

Here are more titles by James L Hill:

 Pegasus: A Journey To New Eden

 The Emerald Lady

RockHill Publishing LLC

There are some lessons that only time can teach, but
you do not learn talent, you only perfect it over time.

www.rockhillpublishing.com